ROSA'S ISLAND

Val Wood

CORGI BOOKS

TRANSWORLD PUBLISHERS
61-63 Uxbridge Road, London W5 5SA
A Random House Group Company
www.transworldbooks.co.uk

ROSA'S ISLAND
A CORGI BOOK : 9780552148467

First published in Great Britain
in 2001 by Bantam Press
an imprint of Transworld Publishers
Corgi edition published 2002

Addresses for Random House Group Ltd companies outside the UK
can be found at: www.randomhouse.co.uk

The Random House Group Ltd Reg. No. 954009

Penguin Random House is committed to a sustainable future for
our business, our readers and our planet. This book is made from
Forest Stewardship Council® certified paper.

MIX
Paper from
responsible sources
FSC® C018179

Typeset in 11/12pt New Baskerville by Kestrel Data, Exeter, Devon.

Printed and bound in Great Britain by Clays Ltd, St Ives plc

13

To the people, past and present,
of the real Sunk Island

ACKNOWLEDGEMENTS

My thanks to Catherine for reading the manuscript and to Peter and Ruth for their constant support and encouragement.

Books for general reading:
John Whitehead, *Sunk Island*. Highgate Publications (Beverley) Ltd, 1991
Meadley, *A Sunk Island Miscellany*
The Victoria History of the County of York East Riding, Volume V. Published for the University of London Institute of Historical Research by Oxford University Press, 1984
The Country Life Book of Nautical Terms

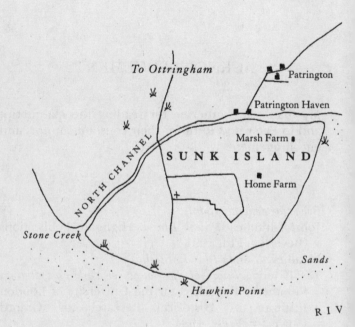

To Ottringham

Patrington

Patrington Haven

Marsh Farm

SUNK ISLAND

Home Farm

NORTH CHANNEL

Stone Creek

Sands

Hawkins Point

RIV

Author's reconstruction *c.*1833-40
Map by Catherine S. Wood BSc.(Hons)

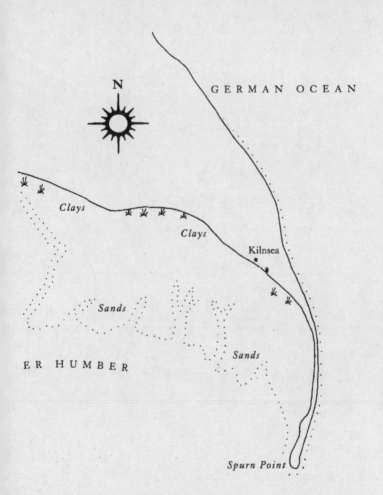

PROLOGUE

The river's waters eddied and broke over the bank of sunken sand, covering it with a watery blanket and then retreating. Again it came and drew away. And again. Over the years the sand-bank grew wider and higher and the constant rhythmic waves of the estuary surged and flowed and caressed its edges, flooding the greening centre only at high spring tides.

Sonke Sande, a bare and empty lonely isle risen from the deep Humber bed. A still land and silent save for the haunting cry of the wild geese who stretched their wings in flight above it.

'Tharlesmere. Frismerk. Ravenser Odd's come again.' The villagers who watched its mystical rising from the marshy mainland shore spoke in whispers of the lost lands of long ago, lands swept away by the swollen waters and their in-habitants drowned. Others shook their heads in disagreement and said that the sea had brought it, washing it down from the eroding cliffs of Holderness and into the estuary.

However it had come, this lonely, mist-shrouded land, there was one opinion on which they were in accord. It was river land and the river one day would claim it back.

CHAPTER ONE

'Now, lassie, tell us again what your ma said.' The Sunk Island farmer crouched down beside Rosa. 'Where did she say she was going? Was she going to Patrington market?'

Rosa shook her head, her thumb in her mouth, her dark eyes gazing into the farmer's blue ones. Why didn't they listen? She had already told them where her mother had gone. She was going to join her da. She took her wet thumb out of her mouth and wiped it on her pinafore. 'She's gone to Spurn to meet my da's ship.'

The farmer rose to his feet and pursed his lips. 'It don't look too good, Mrs Jennings,' he said to Rosa's grandmother. 'Why would she tek it into her head to go all that way?'

Mrs Jennings looked down at Rosa. 'She's been walking by 'river for 'last few weeks. Took bairn with her most times.'

'We'll organize a search on all of Crown land first, but if she has gone to Spurn we'll have to notify Kilnsea constable. They'll not want us tramping all over peninsula, road's too danger-ous. Besides,' he said bluntly, 'we've a lot o' work

13

on now 'weather's turned. We've more embanking to start as well as 'spring sowing.'

'We're talking about a woman's life.' Mrs Jennings's voice was sharp. 'She's been gone since
yesterday. Doesn't that mean owt to you?'

His face softened. 'Tha knows as well as me
that if Mary's tekken it into her head to go down
to Spurn, owt could have happened. She could
have tummelled into a ditch or dyke, watter's
deep after all 'rain we've had. Or got stuck on
'marsh.' He dropped his voice. 'We all know how
she's been for 'last few years. She's never been
right since yon foreigner left.

'But we'll keep looking,' he assured her as she
turned away. 'We've got men working on 'river
bank and on 'channel. They'll know if she's been
down there, they'll have seen her. There's no
hiding place on this land.'

'Aye,' she said wearily. 'I know. I know.'

'Will Ma bring my da back home?' Rosa asked
eagerly as they went back into the farmhouse.
'Will he come in a ship with golden sails like she
said? And will he have gold and silver like he
promised?'

'There'll be nowt like that, so don't be thinking
it.' Her grandmother was terse. 'Your ma filled
you up wi' fancy ideas and none of it was true.'

Rosa sat in a corner and considered. Her
mother had promised. She'd said that her da was
a Spanish prince and that one day he would
come back in a great ship with billowing sails,
and sail around the Spurn Point and into the
Humber. They would go aboard to meet him and
he would dress them in fine silks and jewels and

take them back with him to his own country: a country where it was always sunny and warm and the people sang and danced all day and the women wore flowers in their black hair.

'Spain's not windswept and isolated like it is here on Sunk Island,' her mother had whispered in Rosa's ear, 'where 'river is constantly beating at our door, and where we do nowt but work every day that God sends.'

It would seem then, Rosa silently reflected as she sat in her corner, that her mother might have gone without her. It was true, as her grandmother had said, that her mother had frequently taken her down to the Humber, where the water lapped at the marshland and where gangs of labourers were reclaiming the land which the river rejected.

Her mother would stand on the embankment holding Rosa fast by the hand if the tide was high, so that she wouldn't fall into the deep muddy river, shielding her eyes from the brightness of the water and staring down in the direction of the peninsula where the sailing ships rounding the narrow tongue of Spurn followed the pilot ships to avoid the hidden sandbanks, and came into the Humber.

'We'll see him pass, Rosa,' she used to mutter. 'Have no fear. He'll pass Sunk Island and send a signal to us.'

But he never came and Rosa grew cold and fretful and tugged on her mother's skirts so that they could go home to a warm hearth and the steaming broth that her grandmother always had on the fire.

Her father had gone away before she was born, but she had a picture of him in her head, painted by her mother in bright descriptive colours. 'He's so handsome, Rosa,' her mother would sigh. 'On our wedding day he wore a black suit and white shirt which showed his sun-browned skin, and his hair is black and sleek, just like yours, and he gave me this ring.' She held out her left hand. 'Spanish gold, it is, not base metal like 'fellows round here give their wives.'

And Rosa had listened to the stories for as long as she could remember, and believed that he would come.

It was nearly a week later that there came a hammering on the door of Marsh Farm and a message for her grandmother to go at once to the village of Kilnsea where the cottages huddled precariously between the river and the sea.

'Can you tek me?' Rosa heard her grandmother say to the caller. 'Mr Jennings is poorly, he can't go and I daren't drive 'trap down that lonely road, I'd be scared of tummelling into 'water.'

'Can I come, Gran?' Rosa asked eagerly, hoping that there was news of her father and his ship.

'No.' Her grandmother patted her cheek. 'It'll be late when I get back. Stay here and mind 'house and keep fire in and set table for supper and get whatever your grandfer needs.'

Her grandfather wanted for nothing and the fire blazed with dry driftwood and after she had set the table with a clean cloth and soup dishes, she sat on a stool by the fire and waited for her

16

grandmother to return with her mother and father.

'It's Mary, right enough.' The boatman came out of his cottage to greet Mrs Jennings, and led her towards his boat shed. 'I recognized her straight away even though she's been in 'water for a while. 'Constable's been and agreed wi' me that it was her. I'm sorry for thy loss,' he added, 'and for 'young bairn.'

Mrs Jennings looked down at the swollen waterlogged body of her daugher, lying in a coggy boat and respectfully covered in a white sheet. 'I've been expecting it for many a long year,' she said huskily. 'Poor lass is at peace now.'

The boatman nodded. 'Aye. Well, 'sea took her, but 'river fetched her back like it allus does. We'll bring her home for thee.'

CHAPTER TWO

'Sunk Island isn't really an island, you know, Gran.' Rosa skipped alongside her grandmother. 'So why is it called that?'

Rosa was now seven and had started school for the first time that day. Her teacher had pointed to a large map on the wall and told them that this was the island of Great Britain and was where they lived. It had sea all the way around it.

She had wanted to tell the teacher that she was wrong, that they lived on Sunk Island which had water around three parts of it; but she held her tongue for the mistress was very strict and would brook no disobedience, and Rosa was glad that she had, as the teacher then traced with her cane from the Spurn peninsula and along the river Humber and, pointing to a rounded smudge of land, said that that was Sunk Island.

Her grandmother seemed to be lost in thought. Her head lowered to watch where she was walking was covered by her black bonnet, which hid her face. Rosa shook her hand to attract her attention. 'So why is it called an island?'

'Because once it was,' she murmured. 'You'll learn about it at school afore long. Everybody does. I did when I was a bairn and it was still an island then. Ships came along North Channel then, and we had to get a boat to go to Patrington Market.'

'Where are we going?' Rosa asked. Her grandmother had collected her from school but they were not headed in the direction of home, but walking down a long track towards one of the other farmsteads.

'Home Farm. Visiting Mrs Drew!' Her grandmother was brief. 'Now hold your tongue. I'm trying to think!'

Two dogs prowling in the yard barked at them as they approached the farmhouse door but then wagged their tails and came to sniff at Rosa. 'Wait here,' she was told. 'I won't be long.'

Rosa climbed into an empty hay cart and sat down to wait. She wiggled her toes in her new boots which were too large and made her feet sore, but her grandmother had told her that she would grow into them. It was very tiring being at school and having to pay attention all day, she decided. She had looked out of the window of the old farmhouse, which was where the school was held, as they had no proper school on the island, and saw and heard a flock of wild ducks as they flew towards the marshy land of the estuary. She had craned her neck to watch their quacking flight and the teacher had seen her and brought her to the front of the class and asked what she was doing.

'Watching 'ducks, miss,' she answered truth-fully. 'They're flying to 'mud flats.'

'Watching 'ducks!' the mistress said sharply. 'Instead of doing what?'

Rosa couldn't remember what it was she should have been doing, so she was put in a corner with her face to the wall until she could remember. It was only by dint of listening to the teacher and the hesitant chanting of the other pupils that she remembered. They were learning their times tables. She'd put up her hand and was then allowed back to her desk.

It was a warm September day and Rosa was glad to be out of school and into the open air. She hated the closed-in feeling of the school-room and constantly had to tear her gaze away from the window, where across the vast fields she could see lines of scythes-men in their cotton shirts and cord breeches, moving rhythmically and in unison, their scythe blades flashing across the ripened corn.

'Hello, Rosa.' Matthew Drew gave her a bashful grin as he crossed the yard. 'What you doing here?'

She shrugged. 'Don't know. I came with my gran. She said I had to wait here.'

'I heard Ma telling our Maggie that Mrs Jennings'd be coming afore long.'

Rosa frowned. Matthew was ten and attended school with her, along with three of his five sisters, Nellie, Lydia and Delia. 'My gran says there's no secrets on Sunk Island!' she said.

There were few families living on Sunk Island and those who had made their homes in the

20

scattered farmhouses and cottages had mostly lived there for generations. With the exception of the wheelwright, the blacksmith, a shoemaker and cow keepers, they were all farmers, tending the rich fertile land as their fathers and grandfathers had done before them.

'I'm going fishing in a minute,' Matthew said. 'Do you want to come?'

Before Rosa could answer, the kitchen door opened, and Maggie, Matthew's eldest sister, called to her to come inside and for Matthew to change out of his school clothes and help Delia feed the hens.

'But I'm going fishing wi' some of 'other lads,' he complained. 'They're waiting on me!'

She indicated with her thumb for him to go inside, then said, 'When you've finished you can go, otherwise you'll be in bother with Ma.'

Rosa followed Maggie inside. Home Farm was a bigger farm estate than her grandfather's and the farmhouse was bigger too. She went first into the back kitchen where a fire burned in the wide fireplace. A crane and hooks were set into the fireback and a piece of beef sizzled and spat as it turned on a spit. In the wall next to the fire was a bread oven, and next to the back door beneath a window was a deep stone sink and a wooden hand pump. In the corner of the kitchen stood a wooden washtub and posher, and on the shelf above was a row of box and flat irons.

The twins, Lydia and Nellie, were sitting with Delia at a scrubbed wooden table in the middle kitchen. A bright fire was burning in the inglenook and a large kettle hanging over it emitted gentle puffs of steam. The sisters were dressed as Rosa was, in navy dresses with a white pinafore over them, and dark stockings and laced-up boots. They stared curiously at Rosa as she came in, but at a command from Maggie they got up from the table, opened the staircase door and ran up the narrow stairs to change out of their school clothes and put on their old ones. Maggie smiled at Rosa and led her through to the parlour where her grandmother was sitting with Mrs Drew.

'I expected a visit,' Mrs Drew remarked as she opened a cupboard door at the side of the fireplace. There was no fire burning in here but the grate was laid ready with sticks and logs. Mrs Drew wore a plain high-necked grey gown and a white apron, with a flat cotton cap secured by pins set upon her head. After a moment's hesitation, she took down an earthenware tea service with painted blue flowers from the shelf and laid it on the table, then sat down and poured the tea. 'I heard as you might be flitting.'

'Aye, well, word soon gets around in our community,' Mrs Jennings said, 'and I don't mind, as it saves me a deal of explanation if you know why I've come.'

Mrs Drew glanced towards Rosa, who hadn't been invited to sit down and still stood just inside the door. 'Who'll tek over 'tenancy?'

'Fowler, our foreman. He's a good young fellow, we couldn't have managed without him this last year. He asked if we'd put his name for'ard to Crown Agents if – when – Mr

22

Jennings—' She didn't finish what she was saying and pressed her mouth into a thin line.

'I do understand, Mrs Jennings.' Mrs Drew was sympathetic. 'It will be very hard for you.'

Mrs Jennings sighed. 'Aye, it is. A lifetime spent here. But we shan't move yet – not till, well, till Mr Jennings passes on. He wants to die here.'

'Of course he does,' murmured Mrs Drew. 'Of course he does.' She poured two cups of tea, and then got up and taking a small beaker from the cupboard filled it with milk and handed it to Rosa.

'Does Rosa know of 'change of circumstances, Mrs Jennings? That she'll be moving?'

Mrs Jennings sipped her tea and took a proffered slice of fruit cake, and as Rosa was offered a piece also, warned, 'Don't drop crumbs, Rosa! No, she doesn't, Mrs Drew. I wanted to get things settled first before I told her. You see, my cousin who I'll go to live with in Patrington is a single woman, never been married and had bairns.' She pursed her lips and continued. 'Never wanted any either, and though she's offered me a home wi' her, mainly I have to say because she needs somebody to look after her now that she's getting on in years, she's not keen on having our Rosa.'

She gave a sniff. 'She never saw eye to eye with my Mary and when she married 'foreigner, she vowed she would have nowt to do wi' her again. And she didn't. And she's never seen 'bairn either. Never once.'

'Why ever would you want to live with such a

dowly woman, Mrs Jennings?' Mrs Drew was astonished.

'Beggars can't be choosers, Mrs Drew. And by 'time we've sold up, there'll be no house and nowt much left for me to live on.'

'So . . .' Mrs Drew said slowly. 'The purpose of your visit to me?'

'I want to ask if you'll have Rosa to live here with you? Treat her as one of 'family.'

'But I've got a large family already, Mrs Jennings,' Mrs Drew demurred. 'Why, our Delia's same age as Rosa, I don't know if I could manage anybody else's bairn.'

'Reason I'm asking.' Mrs Jennings leant forward and Rosa heard her corsets creak. 'You and our Mary were expecting at 'same time; she said as how good you were towards her, when it was her first bairn and her husband going missing and all.'

Mrs Drew nodded. 'Aye, and it was my ninth, and eight of 'em still living, bless the Lord. She was a right bonny lass, was Mary.' A slight sad smile lightened her plain features. 'Such a great pity *he* never came back, though a lot of folk never expected him to.' She shook her head. 'He was a foreigner, he never would have settled here on Sunk Island.'

'But our Rosa is an islander,' again Mrs Jennings leaned towards Mrs Drew, and again Rosa heard the creak of whalebone. 'An islander like her ma and me, and her grandfer. It's said that one of Mr Jennings's great-grandfaythers worked for Colonel Gilby's grandson, William.' She sat back and folded her arms across her ample bosom. 'And you can't go back much further than that.'

Rosa had been only half listening but she pricked her ears on hearing the name Gilby. She had heard only today at school of Colonel Gilby, the founder of Sunk Island, who had been leased the land by King Charles the Second when it was little more than a sandbank. Colonel Gilby had built the first house which was still standing, and started the embankments which even today, the teacher had said, were still being raised to save more and more land from the Humber.

'This is a very special place.' The teacher had gazed down at them as she walked between their desks. 'Amongst the richest, most fertile land in England, and all of you,' her finger had pointed around the room at each of them in turn, 'should consider yourselves privileged to have been born here.'

Rosa had dared to put up her hand. The teacher had raised her eyebrows. 'I trust this is a worthwhile question, Rosa Carlos?' she'd said, 'and not a time-waster.'

'Miss,' she'd piped up. 'So who does 'land belong to now?'

'A good question and very topical,' the mistress answered, and Rosa had preened. 'It belongs to the King, King William the Fourth. God bless him.'

'God bless him,' the children had chorused.

'All land gained from the river or sea belongs to the King or his successors. Sunk Island has been in the hands of 'Lords of Holderness for many years, and they rented it out to the

25

farmers.' She had gazed at them all in turn. 'But from this year, this year of eighteen hundred and thirty-three, the land is to be leased direct to the farmers who live and work here, so that they may look after it themselves.'

'We'll have a deal of extra expense,' Mrs Drew's voice interrupted Rosa's meditating, 'now that 'Commissioners have leased directly to 'farmers. We've maintenance of banks to fund and Brick Road's been started already. We'll get some help from 'Crown I know, but there's a goodly amount to come out of our own pockets.'

Mrs Jennings nodded. 'I know all that, Mrs Drew. But bit o' money that's left after we've sold up 'farm will be Rosa's, either for her keep or to use if she should wed when she's of age.'

'Well, I'll have to speak to Mr Drew of course. Decision will be his.' She gazed at Rosa for a moment before saying, 'I wouldn't want 'child to go where she wasn't wanted. You'd want to see her of course, every so often?'

'Well, Mothering Sunday would be nice.' Mrs Jennings's eyes suddenly became moist. 'Seeing as I've lost my own daughter. But more than owt, I want to be sure that Rosa will be cared for if owt should happen to me, and that she'll stay here on Sunk Island where she belongs.'

'But you'll be here for a good few years yet, Mrs Jennings,' Mrs Drew assured her. 'You're hale and hearty for your years. You'll not be leaving this mortal coil for a long time!'

Mrs Jennings gave a deep sigh. 'God willing I won't.' She repeated, 'God willing.'

CHAPTER THREE

'And you say that Fowler wants 'tenancy of Marsh Farm.' Mr Drew was seated by the kitchen fire in his usual chair and addressed his wife as she brought up the subject of them taking the child Rosa.

'Eventually,' said Mrs Drew. 'Though 'day can't be far off. I hear that 'doctor is calling on Mr Jennings every morning.' She clasped her hands together and murmured a quick prayer. 'It would be our Christian duty to take her, Mr Drew. Mrs Jennings wants her to stay on Sunk Island where she belongs.'

'But at whose expense, Mrs Drew?' he said sombrely. 'Have you thought of that? Will 'health and strength of our own kindred suffer if we take on another mouth to feed?' He eyed her keenly and there was a bright spot of colour on each of his cheeks which often appeared if he became overwrought or anxious. 'The good Lord moves in mysterious ways. We must pray for guidance.'

She had expected this. She knew him to be parsimonious. 'Mrs Jennings says there will be a little money left after they have sold up, and Rosa is to have it.'

'Ah!' His small blue eyes glittered. 'Well, we must pray, Mrs Drew, and perhaps by 'morning we'll have the answer.'

Mrs Drew sat on by the fireside after her husband had gone upstairs to bed. She wanted to take the child, not only for her own sake but for her mother's.

She had always liked Mary Jennings. At seventeen she had been pretty and merry, always singing, always a word for everyone she saw, and Ellen Drew, already with six children and heavily pregnant with her seventh, watched her with a wistful admiration for her energy and enthusiasm for life, whilst she, not yet thirty, felt tired and old.

All the young men on Sunk Island were in love with Mary Jennings, but she would have none of them, she was waiting for someone special, she said, and would know him when he came. They all heard about him when he did come, for he swam across the channel from Patrington to Sunk Island, instead of waiting for a boat to take him across the narrow stretch of water. The men working on the embankment had watched him as he dived in fully clothed, and climbed out to ask them in a strong foreign accent what was this place that was cut off from the rest of the world.

Most of the labourers were Irish, and some of them had replied that it was the Devil's own country, for no-one else would want to live there, in the land that belonged below the waters of the Humber.

He had laughed and shaken himself dry like a dog, and set off walking across the vast treeless pastureland, where the first person he met was Mary. No-one knew what their first words were, they only knew that Mary had met her special person and was quite besotted by the handsome stranger. He appeared to feel the same way about her for they were often seen walking across the flat windswept landscape, where there were no hiding places, with their heads together and their arms entwined, and the older people tutted and said no good would come of it, and the younger ones, Ellen Drew included, gazed with envy at the romance of it.

Mary had brought him to the Drews' farm and whilst Mr Drew took him on a tour of the estate, Mary sat with Mrs Drew as she suckled the baby Matthew, and told her that they were to be married in the church on Sunk Island. The whole of the population turned out to watch Mary marry her foreign gentleman and wild were the rumours as to who he was. Some vowed that he was a gypsy, some that he was an escapee from the law, but others firmly believed what Mary had told them, that he was a prince, with a castle in Spain.

'Come along up, Mrs Drew.' She heard her husband's voice call from the top of the stairs and she sighed. She had hoped that he had gone to sleep and would permit her to do the same, but it was Saturday night and tomorrow morning he would go to church and pray for forgiveness for the weakness of the flesh. She was now over childbearing years, at least she hoped she was, as

29

Delia, their last child, was now seven years old; her flux had dried up and her husband no longer had the excuse for his excesses, that he was procreating as the Lord intended.

She climbed into the feather bed and closed her eyes as she lay beneath his panting body and hoped that the children in the next room couldn't hear his moaning and mutterings, asking God to forgive him for his wicked tendencies. She too prayed. I can put up with this, dear Lord, but please don't let me be caught with child, and she knew that she was being wicked. Her husband had told her so, so many times, when she had begged him not to make her pregnant yet again. She had given birth to Jim when she was nineteen, then Henry two years later, Maggie was born when Henry was two, then Flo when Maggie was one. She had a respite until the twins Nellie and Lydia three years later, then miscarried the following year.

'You have enough children, Mrs Drew,' the doctor had informed her. 'What need do you have for more? You must speak to your husband and advise him it will not be good for your health to have another child.'

She had told him, but he said that it was the Lord's doing, that the act of marriage was designed for the procreation of children and that they must not go against His teachings. He was a churchwarden and a lay preacher and he addressed assemblies, bringing into the text that the Lord's word was to be obeyed. And so she became pregnant with Matthew and nearly died.

He left her alone for a time after that, and

made more frequent visits into the town of Hull, when sometimes he would stay overnight. He would dress in his best grey coat and his stove-pipe hat and make the difficult journey from Sunk Island across the wide landscape of Holderness into the port of Hull. But when he returned he spent so much time on his knees praying to the Lord that his work was neglected, the embankment on which his men were supposed to be working was breached and he was called before the Lords of Holderness to explain himself. So she let him back into her bed, and Delia was conceived.

When she heard that Mary too was carrying a child, she wondered how it was that she could look so fresh and radiant. Even though Mary was overcome with grief at her husband's disappearance, when her dark-haired, dark-eyed child, Rosa, was born, the baby delighted everyone with her blithe and sunny presence, whilst her own pale-faced child, Delia, lay still, viewing everyone with sad grey eyes and petulant mouth.

'Have you thought any more about the Jennings child, Mr Drew?' she asked after supper the next evening.

'You mean 'Carlos child,' he remonstrated and she was surprised that he had remembered Rosa's proper name, for she was often referred to as the Jennings child. 'Yes, I've been to talk to Mrs Jennings today. Mr Jennings is in a poor way. He'll not be much longer on this earth but will be joining our Heavenly Father.'

Mrs Drew caught sight of a look between

Maggie and Henry and saw a warning raise of Maggie's eyebrows at Henry's impudent grin.

'The Lord be praised,' said Mrs Drew firmly. 'And save us sinners.'

'Amen,' said Maggie as she cleared the table, but Henry grinned again and went out of the room.

'So are we to take her? What decision shall we make?' she asked, whilst knowing that the decision wouldn't be hers.

'We are to take her under certain conditions,' Mr Drew replied. 'The money Mrs Jennings will have left can't be ascertained until 'effects have been sold up, but I have asked Mrs Jennings to speak to 'Crown agents on behalf of Mr Jennings who can't speak for himself, to put forward our name to take over 'lease of Marsh Farm.'

His bottom lip protruded defiantly as if he expected his wife to object, and Mrs Drew glanced at Maggie as she heard her draw in a sharp breath.

'But Jack Fowler wanted it! Mrs Jennings told me that he'd asked her to put his name forward!'

'Aye, so she said, but that was 'stipulation I made. If we're to have 'child, we want 'tenancy.'

'But we've more than enough land,' his wife demurred. 'Why would we want that small acreage?'

'It's prime land and near enough to 'river for further embanking. Our Jim is twenty-one, another couple o' years and he'll want his own farm. Marsh Farm will do very nicely.'

'Whatever will Mrs Jennings say to Fowler?' Mrs Drew glanced again at her daughter who had sat down on a chair near the wall and was clasping and unclasping her hands.

'That's up to her, though she doesn't have to tell him owt, she just has to speak to 'agents, and if we don't get it then we don't take 'bairn.'

He pulled himself up in the chair, he was only a short man and he expanded his chest like a turkey cock. 'The child's not our responsibility. Not our fault that her mother went off her head after he went away. We don't owe them owt.' He fired off these statements in rapid succession and his wife wondered at it.

'No,' she said slowly. 'Of course we don't.'

Maggie was on her knees blackleading the kitchen range when her mother came down the next morning. She muttered good morning.

'You're up early, Maggie,' her mother said, getting oats out of the cupboard to make porridge. 'Couldn't you sleep?'

Maggie shook her head. 'No,' she said miserably. 'I kept thinking of Jack Fowler and how disappointed he'll be if he doesn't get Marsh Farm.'

'Were you walking out?' her mother asked gently.

'Not exactly.' A faint blush came to Maggie's cheek. 'But we were heading that way. I've seen him once or twice. Accidentally, like.'

'I see.' Her mother stirred the porridge and added a pinch of salt. 'Don't let your da see you. Not yet. Not until things are settled about Marsh Farm, anyway.'

Maggie gave a short laugh. 'Well, he won't stop

on Sunk Island if he doesn't get it! He won't want to work for our Jim. They don't get on. So that'll be 'end of my chances.'

'What nonsense, girl.' Her mother turned to smile at her and was surprised to see the look of misery on her face. 'There's lots of young men that would fall over themselves for you.'

'Where?' Maggie demanded. 'Not on Sunk Island, there are not! And when do I get 'chance to go anywhere else? Fayther won't hear of me even going to 'village fairs without Jim or Henry go with me.'

Her mother nodded. Mr Drew was especially strict with Maggie and with Flo. The twins Nellie and Lydia had much more freedom, but then they were only just twelve and he didn't consider that they had yet joined the ranks and perils of womanhood.

'I'm sorry, my dear,' she said softly. 'But that's 'way that it is.'

Maggie picked up her brush and polishing cloth and got up from her knees. 'To my way of thinking,' she muttered, 'as I've observed with other families, firstborn daughter nearly allus stops at home and looks after 'parents in their old age, whilst other, younger daughters go off and get married and have families of their own.'

'I'm sure you're right, Maggie. My older sister stayed at home with our parents, but she wanted to do that. She allus said that she didn't want to swap a familiar hearth for an unknown one.' Ellen Drew looked wistful. 'She made 'right choice, I think. She was content.'

Maggie gazed at her mother for a moment, then said with a catch in her voice, 'Fayther would say it's in hands of 'good Lord. I just hope and pray, Ma, 'good Lord doesn't tek you first and leave me with me fayther.'

CHAPTER FOUR

Mr Jennings, Rosa's grandfather, lingered for another six months, and two months after his death, after consultation with the agents of the Crown, it was agreed that the tenancy of Marsh Farm should be given to Jim Drew and that Rosa should go to live with his family.

Jack Fowler packed his bag and prepared to move on. This spelt disaster to him, he said, happening when it did. 'I'll have to get casual work till Martinmas,' he told Mrs Jennings. 'Nobody'll tek me on contract until then. I'm that mad,' he said bitterly. 'This would have been a right good chance for me. Drews have plenty o' land without this, enough for all their sons to work.'

'Young men don't allus want to work for their fathers,' Mrs Jennings interrupted. 'Maybe Jim Drew wanted his own place. This is a good size to start up on your own.'

'But it won't be his own, will it?' Fowler said. 'He'll have to farm it as his fayther says. He won't brook any arguments, won't Mr Drew.'

'Well, I'm sorry, Jack. I'd have liked you to

36

have it, especially after all 'help you've given us over 'last couple o' years. But I had Rosa to think of. They wouldn't have taken her to live with them if I hadn't put his name forward.'

'I'm not blaming thee, Mrs Jennings,' he said and shouldered his pack. 'It's that scheming old hypocrite James Drew that I blame.'

'Why dost call him that?' she asked curiously.

'Just what I heard tell once, over in Kilnsea, afore I came to work on Sunk Island. I overheard some boatmen talking over their ale. They clammed up when they realized I was listening and said no more.' He gave a lopsided cynical grin. 'But I'd heard enough to know that that God-fearing law-abiding preacher isn't all he seems to be.'

'Be careful what you say, Jack Fowler,' Mrs Jennings warned. 'It doesn't do to blacken somebody's name. Not without proof.'

He walked to the door. 'I don't have that,' he said. 'And I wouldn't even bother to try and get it. I onny know what I heard. Anyway, I'm off. Sunk Island won't see me again.'

'No?' She lifted her eyebrows. 'No pretty girl to tempt you back?'

'No,' he replied. 'Not now. Maybe once, but not any more.'

Rosa had overheard the conversation outside the kitchen door and as soon as she heard the outer door open and Jack Fowler's voice calling goodbye, she came into the kitchen. 'When do we leave, Gran?' she asked. 'Will it be soon?'

Mrs Jennings nodded. 'Furniture's to be sold tomorrow, and we move out 'day after.'

'Don't you want to take it with you to Aunt Bella's house?'

Mrs Jennings gazed around at the furniture, the wooden table, the old oak chairs which had belonged to her parents, the pendulum clock ticking on the wall. 'There's no room at Bella's house; besides, she says that her furniture is better quality than mine.' She wrinkled her nose. 'But it's not. This is good solid furniture, hand-made by a craftsman, your great-grandfayther himself. Hers, why, you hardly dare sit on it in case it collapses.

'But I'll tek my linen, my second best, and I'll pack up 'good quality for Mrs Drew to give to you when you grow up. And my best china that's hardly been used since I was a young bride. It would have gone to your ma, to Mary,' she said softly. 'If she'd set up in her own home.' She gave a deep sigh. 'But of course she never had 'chance.'

Next day after school Rosa helped to empty drawers and cupboards and lined a deep pine chest with clean brown paper. This was to be packed with the belongings she was taking to the Drews' house. 'I'll put some of your ma's things in as well,' her grandmother said. 'Some of her little treasures that she kept from when she was a bairn like you; and her wedding ring,' she carefully put the plain gold ring in a small box, 'and a few trinkets and suchlike that maybe you'll tek a look at when you're grown. Just so's that she's not forgotten,' she added.

Rosa's memory of her mother was already fading. She remembered the walks down to the riverbank and her mother calling across the water whenever a ship's sail was seen, but of her face she could remember little. What she recalled most of all were the stories that her mother told as she tucked her up in bed, of her father, the Spanish prince, who would one day come for them.

Perhaps, she mused, as she lay in bed that night and gazed at the flickering dancing shadows, thrown up from the fire onto the white-washed walls. Perhaps he'll still come. He won't know that Ma is dead. She turned over onto her side, tucking her hand beneath her cheek. I wonder why he came here anyway? I'll ask the teacher on Monday if Sunk Island is very far from Spain.

The next morning the sale of effects began. It was early June and already hot, with a heat haze drifting over the sweet smelling hayfields which were almost ready for cutting, and a gentle breeze wafting in from the west. The farmers' wives of Sunk Island came to look and buy, for they wanted to help Mrs Jennings who had lived in the community all of her life. Other people had travelled over from Patrington and the villages of Keyingham and Ottringham on the Holderness mainland, when they heard that there was a sale of good farm furniture. Many were looking for bargains and some had come out of curiosity.

'It's a sad day for you, Mrs Jennings.' Mrs Drew stood in the yard with Maggie, who smiled at Rosa, though Rosa thought that she looked slightly low-spirited. The last time she had seen Maggie she was very cheerful.

'Life has a habit of changing,' Mrs Jennings replied. 'And we're not always consulted.'

'Would you like to come back with us today, Rosa?' Maggie bent to ask her. 'We've got a bed ready in 'room I share with Flo, just till you settle in. Then you can go in with Delia and 'twins later on if you want.'

Rosa glanced at her grandmother, who nodded. 'Aye,' she said. 'You can do, there'll not be much comfort here once everything's gone. Just me feather bed. I'm insisting on tekking that. Our Bella's beds are that hard and lumpy it'd be like doing penance every night. And me jug and bowl.' She lowered her voice. 'And 'chamber pot. I'm a bit particular about that sort o' thing.' She pursed her lips. 'I don't like thought of using anybody else's. Besides, mine's china wi' flowers on it.'

'Quite right,' agreed Mrs Drew, 'I should feel just 'same. Well, all right then. We'll take Rosa back with us and Jim can pick up her box later.' She moved off towards the house with Mrs Jennings. 'Jim said would I look to see if there was anything he might need. Perhaps 'table and chairs, though I expect he'll still live at home for a while.' She glanced over her shoulder to where Rosa was standing with Maggie. 'Who does Rosa favour, Mrs Jennings? In personality, I mean?'

She had been surprised at the reaction of Delia when she was told that Rosa was coming to live with them. 'I don't want her to come,' she'd said fretfully. 'She onny does what *she* wants!'

Matthew had interrupted her. 'I do,' he said. 'She's allus asking questions at school and 'lessons are better, 'cos 'teacher explains what she means.'

'And she gets into trouble,' Delia had griped. 'She's allus looking out of 'window to see what's going on. She has to stand in 'corner then,' she'd added with satisfaction. 'And she got 'cane one day.'

'Is she—?' Mrs Drew hesitated as she questioned Mrs Jennings. 'She's not wilful or disobedient, is she? Because I'm afraid that Mr Drew is very strict with his children. He gives 'girls the strap as well as 'lads if they misbehave.'

'She's never had 'strap, Mrs Drew, and nor did her ma! Never ever been need.' Mrs Jennings looked shocked. 'I've allus brought her up strict like, and though she's allus been a deep child, preoccupied you might say, she's never been wicked. Never!'

'That's all right then.' Mrs Drew patted her arm, for Mrs Jennings had a worried expression on her face. 'We won't worry about it. I know that Mary went a little strange towards 'end, but that wasn't surprising being left as she was, and with a bairn to bring up as well.'

'Aye,' Mrs Jennings responded with a sigh. 'For him to just disappear like that! I'll never understand it. He borrowed Mr Jennings's hoss to ride into Hull – said he had to meet a ship. 'Hoss came back on its own a week later but no sign of him. Our Mary was devastated.' She blinked her eyes. 'It's brought all 'memories back, Mrs Drew, selling up today. I'll be glad when it's all done.'

Mrs Drew patted her on her arm again and Mrs Jennings said with a catch in her voice, 'And you'll let Rosa come to see me, won't you, Mrs Drew? Mothering Sunday would be nice. And when 'bridge is made over 'channel she'll be able to come on her own; God willing I'll still be here by 'time it's finished!'

'There's no need to wait for Mothering Sunday,' Mrs Drew assured her and thought that when Jim was settled into Marsh Farm, Henry would be busier on their own farm, and Maggie could perhaps then be allowed to go off on her own. 'Our Maggie will bring her over,' she said. 'Perhaps once a month?'

But they were busy with haymaking during June and the women of the house and the children, too, worked long hours preparing food for the workers and taking it across to the big barn where they ate, and the itinerant workers slept. Even school was neglected and not all the pupils turned up for lessons, being needed at home and in the fields.

'I'll take Rosa to see her gran, shall I, Ma?' Maggie asked during the latter part of August. 'If we don't go soon, we shall be in 'middle of harvest and shan't be able to.'

'Yes,' her mother agreed. 'Go on Sunday after church and take Mrs Jennings a fruit cake. She'd like that.'

Rosa's spirits rose when she was told that she would be visiting her grandmother. She had had a good summer, she had enjoyed the company of Maggie and Flo, whose room she was still in, by choice, and she liked the twins, but not Delia who was spiteful and irritable and would sometimes pinch her as she passed her.

There were the two older brothers, Jim and Henry. Jim was quiet, inclined to be gloomy, and she sometimes wondered if he wanted her there, for she often found him gazing at her with a downcast expression on his thin face. But Henry had given her a sly wink on her first day after supper, when Mr Drew had placed her in front of him and lectured her on how to behave, and how she must always remember that the good Lord was constantly watching over them and noting everything they did.

She'd stood with her hands behind her back and her lips tightly clenched as he droned on, and it was then that Henry, standing out of sight of his father's gaze, had winked his eye and pulled a face and almost made her laugh.

Sunday morning was warm and fine and she had on her best dress and a new bonnet which Maggie had made for her out of an old flowered dress of her own. Her hair, which was thick and black, had been braided tightly into two plaits so that it wouldn't come undone, but even now as they knelt in church she could feel wisps of it straying and tickling her neck.

'Come on then,' Maggie said merrily. She seemed much more cheerful, as if the prospect of an outing pleased her, and they left the others to go home, whilst they set off towards Patrington.

'Can I come?' Matthew shouted after them. 'I won't be a bother!'

'No,' Rosa called back. 'Aunt Bella doesn't like childre'.'

'So why are you going?' he yelled. 'You're onny a bairn!'

She turned her back on him and gave a little skip. He was always following her around, offering to show her where there were birds' eggs and the best dykes for catching tiddlers, and she had decided that eventually she would allow him to show her. She might even ask her gran if he could come with her on a visit one day. But not yet. He would have to wait until she was ready.

'We'll go across 'channel,' Maggie said. 'Henry keeps a boat there, he won't mind if we use it.'

Then they heard a piercing whistle and on turning around they saw Henry waving to them and shouting for them to wait.

'Da said I had to go wi' you,' he said as he caught up with them. 'Sorry, Maggie, but you know how he is.'

Maggie muttered something incomprehensible and Rosa looked up at Henry. He was stockily built like his father but there the similarity ended. Henry had an open merry face and was quick to smile and to joke, whilst his father appeared totally humourless.

'Can we go in your boat?' Rosa asked him. 'Cos we're going to see my gran in Patrington.'

'Well, I don't know about that,' he said solemnly. 'It might cost you.'

'How much?' she enquired. 'I'd have to ask my gran for some money.'

'Well, I'll tell you what. Give us a kiss and we'll call it quits.' He grinned at her and Maggie gave him a shove.

'Don't tease her,' she said. 'She's onny a bairn.'

'Aye, and a bonny one. When she's grown into a beauty, as she will, I'll be able to say I was first to steal a kiss!'

Rosa lowered her lashes and looked at the ground beneath her feet. The track was muddy and squelched beneath her boots. If we have to walk round by Salthaugh Grange, she considered, we shan't get there for hours. 'All right then.' She proffered her cheek. 'But what about Maggie? Does she have to pay?'

He pulled a face. 'Well, I won't want a kiss from my sister, will I? I might get her to make me a bit o' cake or a few tarts or summat. She's a right good baker is our Maggie.'

'But not much good at owt else,' Maggie muttered. 'And not to be trusted to go out on my own, not even at seventeen. Wish I'd been born a lad!'

'What?' he objected. 'And be at Da's beck and call all hours of 'day? Can't do right for doing wrong! At least Ma's not a taskmaster like *him*. Our Jim'll be glad to get away I don't doubt.'

'Ssh.' Maggie looked down at Rosa. 'Little ears are flapping.'

'Anyway,' he said, and they were almost at the narrow channel which divided the island from Holderness. 'I'm not coming with you to Mrs Jennings. I'll come as far as 'marketplace and then meet you there after.' He grinned. 'I'll be in one of 'alehouses. You can come and find me.'

She gasped. 'I can't do that!' she said. 'You know I can't. If Fayther should hear – or Ma!'

They climbed into the little boat and Henry shoved off from the bank. Rosa felt a thrill as the

45

water swayed beneath her. She couldn't remember going off the island before and although this was only a narrow channel, she felt as if she was partaking in a great adventure.

'It's all right,' Henry was saying to Maggie. 'I'm onny joking. I'll look out for you from 'window. Can't have much anyway, Da would smell it on me breath, and besides I've to be sober for 'morning. I've to go wi' Da and Jim to look over Marsh Farm. Da reckons new accretion is sour and hasn't been worked proper. Old man Jennings left it fallow. Da wants to sow it wi' grass and clover to bring it right.'

'Well, Da knows about farming,' Maggie began, and Henry interrupted her. 'Aye, and about God and 'Devil. He's an expert on all o' them.'

Mrs Jennings's cousin's house was built of grey brick, not of mud and thatch like others which lay along the dusty lane. It was situated close by the stone-built St Patrick's church, called, because of its stately splendour, the Queen of Holderness. The church, an outstanding edifice with a magnificent spire, was a landmark from both the river and the long roads of the flat countryside for many miles. The village had a weekly market, and a Hiring Fair each Martinmas. Timber was brought into Patrington Haven, a mile out, but as Sunk Island's accretions built up towards the mainland, so the haven was gradually silting up and the merchants, fishermen and farmers were starting to take their trade to Stone Creek at the west end of Sunk Island.

46

Maggie knocked on the door of Miss Dingley's house. The brass knocker, shaped in a lion's head, gleamed, and as Rosa looked up at it she wondered if that was her grandmother's work, for she always said that she liked her brasses to be well polished.

A young girl in a white cap and apron answered and asked them in, when Maggie explained who they were. 'Mrs Jennings is out at 'minute,' she said. 'She's just slipped to 'butcher's but won't be long. Miss Dingley is at home,' she added. 'I'd best tell her that you're here.'

They waited a few minutes in the small hall and then were ushered through into the parlour where Mrs Jennings's cousin, Miss Dingley, was sitting in the window, with the blinds half drawn over the lace curtains to keep out the sun.

She sat upright in her chair, a dark wool shawl over the shoulders of a purple bombazine gown, and a lace cap on her grey head. 'I saw you coming,' she said without preamble. 'I thought, here are strangers to Patrington who don't know their way about. And then, when I saw 'child, I fathomed that it would be my cousin's kin.

'Come here,' she said to Rosa, 'and let me take a look at you.'

Rosa walked across to her chair and stood in front of her. Gazing solemnly at Miss Dingley, she gave her no smile as she thought that none would be expected, but simply bobbed her knee.

'What's your name?' Miss Dingley asked. 'It's something foreign, but I can't remember what.'

'Rosa,' she replied, and wondered at her name being called foreign, for she hadn't known that it was.

'Hmm! And how old are you?'

'Eight,' she said, and wished that her grandmother would hurry up from the butcher's. 'Will Gran be long?' she asked. 'Cos we have to meet Henry and get back.' Some instinct told her not to mention the alehouse, or was it perhaps the warning look on Maggie's face?

'And who is Henry?' Miss Dingley addressed Maggie with suspicion, and looked down her sharp nose at her.

'My brother, ma'am. He brought us over 'channel from Sunk Island.'

'And you are?' Miss Dingley continued to gaze at Maggie.

'Margaret Drew, ma'am.' Maggie bobbed her knee.

'And still living at home? Not in service?'

'No. There's plenty to do at home, Ma says, without me going off to do for other people.'

'Mmm,' Miss Dingley nodded. 'Your mother sounds like a sensible woman. How many of you are there?'

'Eleven, counting my parents and Rosa.'

'Eleven! Good heavens. Not so sensible after all! And will none of them leave home and give your mother some peace?'

'Flo wants to go into service. She's sixteen. Da wouldn't let her go before, he says there are too many perils waiting away from home. And 'twins, Nellie and Lydia, want to go if Da will let them, Delia's too young yet.'

'And your brother has taken Mr Jennings's farm?'

'Yes,' Maggie answered patiently. 'My eldest brother, Jim. Then there's Henry, he's 'middle one, and Matthew, he's eleven.'

Miss Dingley shuddered and put her hand to her brow. 'Eleven!' she said and Rosa wondered if it was Matthew being eleven, or the fact that there were eleven of them, which was putting Miss Dingley in such a dither.

'I thank the good Lord that I've been saved from all of that,' she murmured, and broke off as the front door slammed. 'That will be your grandmother, I expect,' she said to Rosa. 'No-one else slams 'door the way she does.'

'We're used to having 'door open at Gran's house,' Rosa told her. 'We never shut it except in winter. I expect it slipped out of her hand.'

'You're very forward, child.' Miss Dingley frowned. 'I didn't ask for your opinion, nor am I likely to.'

Rosa, chastened, looked at Maggie who gave a slight raise of her dark eyebrows and a warning glance, but they were saved from any more disparagement by Mrs Jennings entering the room. On seeing Rosa, she gave an exclamation of pleasure.

'Well, I never. My, how you've grown!' she said, and Miss Dingley humphed and muttered that it would be a bad day for them all when children stopped growing, for they would then have a nation of little people. But Mrs Jennings ignored her remarks and spoke kindly to Maggie and thanked her for bringing Rosa. She also asked

49

them to sit down and make themselves comfort-able, which her cousin hadn't done.

"Girl is just making some tea,' she said, settling herself onto a hard chair. 'I've reminded her to make sure 'kettle's boiling and that she puts 'leaves into 'pot, for I declare she forgets so often and all we get is hot water. And I made a cake onny yesterday and put it into 'tin. I must have known you were coming.'

She seemed remarkably cheerful, Rosa thought, in spite of having to put up with Miss Dingley, but then her grandmother continued, addressing her remarks to Maggie.

'You wouldn't believe what they sell for meat in that butcher's,' she said. 'I've come back wi' just two chops for supper cos there was nowt else worth buying.' She sighed. 'When I think of hams I've cured and hung in my larder, of mallard and widgeon I've roasted on 'spit over 'fire. And nobody made rabbit pie like I did. Mr Jennings allus said so!'

'I'll ask Henry to drop you a couple o' rabbits in next time he comes across, Mrs Jennings,' Maggie offered eagerly. 'We're just about over-run with them. We've allus got more than we need.'

'Why that's kind of you, Maggie. That'd be a real treat. Sunk Island rabbits taste better than any other.'

'I don't see how that's possible,' Miss Dingley intervened. 'A rabbit is a rabbit wherever it comes from!'

'They get well fed, Miss Dingley,' Maggie explained. 'Sunk Island crops are better than any

50

other in Holderness. It's a fact,' she added, seeing the look of utter disbelief on Miss Dingley's face. 'That's why they get a good price for corn.'

'And why 'farmers grow rich and can afford all those children!' the old lady said sharply. 'Well, that's enough of farming talk. You'd better see to that tea, Cousin, for I think 'girl has forgotten it again.'

'I'd get rid of her if it was left to me.' Mrs Jennings rose grumbling to her feet. 'She's useless. Can't cook, can't dust, doesn't know how to make a bed or a fire!'

'Well, if you think you can find somebody better,' Miss Dingley defied her, 'I'd like to see her. She was 'only one willing to come. Girls are not trained 'way they used to be,' she criticized. 'When I was a girl my mother taught me, same way as yours did. But those days are gone.'

Rosa began to fidget and wish that the tea and cake would come and then they could go back and find Henry. The visit wasn't turning out to be so exciting after all and she longed to go back to Sunk Island.

CHAPTER FIVE

Rosa's grandmother walked with them to the marketplace. 'You mustn't mind Aunt Bella too much,' she said to Rosa. 'She's not used to young people; and she was allus old even when she was young, if you know what I mean.' She turned to Maggie. 'She never had that lightness of spirit which most young lasses have. Never courted any lads as far as I know. But she's all right,' she added. 'I'm getting to know her and I'll soon have her round to my way of doing things.'

Maggie smiled. 'I'm sure that you will, Mrs Jennings. I was wondering,' she pondered. 'About that girl. Does she live in?'

Mrs Jennings shook her head. 'No. She won't,' she said. 'That's part of 'trouble, she lives here in Patrington and wants to go home at night, and 'young madam never gets here early enough in 'morning. Why, by 'time she gets here I've done 'fire grates, blackleaded 'range and cooked 'breakfast.'

'But there's room, is there?' Maggie asked. 'Room for a girl to live in?'

'Oh, aye,' replied Mrs Jennings. 'There's room

up in 'attic. It's small, enough room for a bed and a chest of drawers. And anybody coming would want to bring their own feather bed, just like I did,' she said. 'Why do you ask? Your ma wouldn't let you come?'

'No,' Maggie said. 'Not me. But our Flo wants to go into service and I was thinking that if Da thought she was going to somebody they knew, then he'd let her go. Oh,' she said, uncovering her basket. 'I nearly forgot. Here's a fruit cake for you. Our Flo made it.'

'My word!' Mrs Jennings was delighted. 'If onny she would come! I know she'd do things right and I'd make sure she was looked after. She wouldn't go out after dark or go meeting any lads.'

'I'll ask Ma then, shall I, Mrs Jennings? See what she thinks? She'd have to ask my fayther of course, but I can't think that he'd raise any objections.'

And Flo would be so pleased, she thought. Like Henry, Flo didn't get on with their father and was inclined to argue, whereas she and Jim simply put up with his idiosyncrasies.

'Shall I see you again soon, Rosa?' her grandmother asked, and patted her cheek. 'You get more and more like your ma.' She put her hand into her purse and took out two sixpences. 'Here,' she said. 'There's one each. One for Maggie for bringing you, and one for you to save up for summat special. I know there's nowt to buy on Sunk Island, but keep it for next time you come to Patrington.'

Rosa stood on tiptoe to give her grandmother

a kiss on her leathery cheek and felt a strange lump in her throat, as if she was going to cry. But she didn't want to cry for she wasn't sad or hurting, and was quite happy to be going back, looking forward to climbing into Henry's little boat and being rowed across the water.

Henry called to them from across the market-place. He had plainly been drinking for he swayed as he walked. 'Hello, Maggie,' he called. 'Hello, Rosa! Are you set for a trip across 'briny?'

'Henry!' Maggie was furious. 'What's Da going to say when he sees you?'

'Ah, dear old Da!' Henry hiccuped. 'He will say, Maggie—' He waved a finger in front of her nose and, startled, she backed away. 'He will say that I'm as drunk as a piper.' He took a deep breath. 'As drunk as a – wheelbarrow! That I'm plunging into 'depths of dizzy – phew – pation. That I'm doomed!'

'For heavens' sake, Henry!' Maggie grabbed him by his coat. 'Oh! We'll never get you home. You shouldn't have drunk so much!'

'Sorry, Maggie,' he prattled. 'I had more 'n I nintended – intended! I was going to meet this girl, you see, onny, she didn't come or couldn't come, and all 'time I was waiting and watching for her, I had another drink to help pass 'time. You know how it is!' he pleaded.

'I don't know how it is! How could I know?' She pulled on his coat and dragged him down the lane towards the haven. 'And what girl?'

He put his finger against the side of his nose and patted it. 'Never mind! *You* know how it

54

is, don't you, Rosa?' He turned to Rosa for sympathy, but she shook her head. She didn't really understand what was wrong with Henry, or why he was falling over his own feet, or why Maggie was so cross with him, and cross she was, for she was being quite brutal with him, pushing and slapping him as soon as they were out of sight of other people and heading for the channel.

'You're not fit to row,' Maggie stormed. 'You'll have us all in 'water. Get in 'damned boat,' she shouted at him. 'Get in, Rosa. I'll have to row back.'

'No!' Henry grabbed the oars from her. 'I can do it. It's my boat.' He pulled on an oar and the boat skimmed around in a half-circle. 'You see!' He pulled on the other one and the boat skimmed around back the way it had been. 'You just have to get 'hang of it, that's all.'

'We can't sit here all afternoon, going round in circles,' Maggie hissed at him. 'Now give me those oars!'

'Shan't!' He grinned and leaned away from her. She reached across towards him and gave him a shove. 'I'm warning you, Maggie,' he muttered. 'Don't go too far. I'm not drunk, just well oiled. Perfectly capable of getting home. Home!' he sang. 'Home is where my heart is! Home is where Da is!'

Maggie gave him another shove, and he leaned back, creased with inane laughter. He lifted up his legs in glee. 'Yah! Hah!'

'Stop it,' she cried. 'Stop it!'

He pressed against Rosa. 'Give us a kiss, Rosa.'

55

He breathed ale on her cheek. 'Nobody loves poor Henry.'

'You smell funny!' Rosa drew away. 'Sort of sour. Like when 'yeast is frothing.'

'Get off her,' Maggie demanded. 'Leave 'bairn alone. Now – will you give me those oars!'

'No,' he said defiantly. 'I won't. I'll row.'

Maggie seized an oar and pulled it from his grasp and with her other hand pushed him again. The boat tipped precariously and Rosa grabbed hold of the side to steady it. Henry put his arms up to defend himself and leant away from Maggie, but he leant too far, his legs swung up and he overbalanced, tipping backwards into the water.

'Oh you idiot, Henry,' Maggie shrieked. 'You peazan! No, don't! Don't! You'll have us in 'water as well,' she yelled as Henry, spluttering, grabbed hold of the side of the boat, rocking it perilously. 'Go to 'bank. Go on, climb up onto 'bank.'

People came running when they heard the commotion and saw someone in the water, but they started to laugh as Henry, his clothes dripping and his hair hanging like rats' tails over his face, climbed out onto the bank.

'Might have known it'd be you, Henry Drew,' someone shouted. 'I knew you'd tummel in sooner or later. That'll sober you up.'

'Yah!' Henry shook a fist in the fellow's direction and tried to squeeze the water out of his jacket and trousers. 'This is my Sunday jacket,' he groaned. 'This is your fault, Maggie Drew.'

'Not my fault,' she retaliated. 'You promised

you wouldn't have much to drink. What'll Ma say when she sees your clothes in such a state?'

'I'm nineteen years old, Maggie. I shouldn't have to worry about what my ma and da say.' Henry climbed into the boat, sat down and pulled on the oars, his ducking making him almost sober. 'If I was working on some other farm they wouldn't know what I was doing.'

'If you were working on another farm you wouldn't have had 'day off and you wouldn't have had any money to throw at 'innkeeper's apron,' she said sharply. 'You don't know when you're well off.'

Rosa sat looking from one to the other, not knowing what to make of the situation, then Henry caught her eye and gave her an impudent grin. 'Let that be a lesson to you, Rosa,' he said in a false whisper. 'Don't let 'demon drink get to you or you'll never hear 'end of it.'

He was shivering by the time they were almost home. The afternoon sun had gone down and a cool breeze had sprung up. 'I'm going to run,' he said when they were half a mile from Home Farm. 'I'll nip upstairs and change and see you at supper.'

Rosa waited for sparks to fly at supper time, but there were none. Maggie kept up a long conversation with her mother about Miss Dingley and her house and the problem of getting good servants, and Henry slipped into his seat at table unobserved by anyone but Rosa, who eyed him surreptitiously and wondered how he could eat such a hearty supper when he must surely have swallowed such a lot of water.

*   *   *

Mr Drew agreed that Flo could go to Miss Dingley, under the personal supervision of Mrs Jennings. The other girl was given notice and Flo went off to her first position at Martinmas, the time of a mass movement of labourers, servant girls and hired hands all over the country, who put themselves up for the best offer they could get for their services at the Hiring Fairs.

Many of the farm workers on Sunk Island were skilled men who were willing to stay on at the farms if the pay and conditions were right, and so they negotiated with the farmers, rather than stand in the marketplace and appeal for a new job. Some were regulars, married men with families who lived in tied cottages and had a loyalty to their employers. But there were others who wanted to move on and they packed their boxes, heaved them onto their shoulders and took a chance that the next place of work would have better pay, better food and a chance of promotion.

Rosa went with Mrs Drew to see Flo settled in at Miss Dingley's house, and once more Henry took them. This time there was no drinking in the inn, and he waited for them in the market-place where the hirings were.

'Henry!' His father called to him. Jim and Matthew were with him. Jim had his hands in his pocket and had a sullen look on his face, whilst Matthew kept darting off to look at what was happening. There was entertainment in the marketplace as well as the hirings: fiddlers were playing catchy tunes, and an acrobat was turning somersaults, whilst in many shop doorways there were singers telling of lost love, found love, dead mothers and similar heart-rending ballads, and holding out a cap or cotton bag to collect any offerings.

There were hawkers too, selling their wares, bags of cottons and fustians for the farmers' wives, sprigged muslin to tempt the young girls. There were stalls selling meat pies and sausages, fresh fish just caught from the sea, shrimps and eels from the river, and the stallholders called out to come and buy without delay; the women wore shawls over their shoulders to keep out the damp November air, and the men puffed on their clay pipes or chewed on wads of tobacco.

'We need six more labourers,' Henry's father said as he came across to him. 'Jim thinks we can manage with less, but we've further embanking to be done at Marsh Farm. With six men we could easily get another hundred acres.'

'We're growing too big,' Jim muttered. 'How we going to manage two farms? And besides, corn prices are falling.'

'By 'time the land's ready for sowing, Matthew will be old enough to work full time,' his father said sharply. 'And I'll worry about prices of crops like I've allus done! Now then, Henry. Go and see about them labourers. Pick willing men, I want nobody that's not ready for a hard day's work. Tell 'em they'll be employed on a weekly basis, all found. If they get drunk or don't turn up then they'll lose wages. Tell 'em there's to be no messing about. There's drains to be dug, banks and walls to be built.'

He turned to Jim as Henry moved away. 'Then we'll enlarge Marsh Farm house and make it fit to live in.'

'It's fine as it is,' Jim muttered. 'There's onny me going to live in it. I don't need a bigger place.'

'Pah!' his father mocked. 'We've got to plan ahead. You'll be looking out for a suitable young woman afore long. You'll be getting married and having bairns.' He stared his son in the eye. 'And if you don't, then one of 'other lads will.'

'How can you think on it?' Jim spoke in a low voice. 'I never wanted this land in 'first place. Suppose, just suppose—'

'Enough!' His father rebuked him. 'Not another word. You know what happened. It was 'Lord's work.'

''Devil's more likely,' Jim muttered.

'It's 'Devil speaking through you now.' His father took hold of Jim's coat collar and even though he was much shorter than his son and had to stretch up to reach him, he pressed his face close to his. 'Don't forget,' he whispered. 'The Lord giveth. The Lord taketh away.' He dropped his hands and gazed at Jim, whose face was flushed, and his eyes turned away from him. 'Now go,' he ordered. 'Choose two farm hands for Home Farm and make sure they're reliable with good references.'

Henry had been watching from a distance. He'd spotted some likely-looking men, strong and muscular, and was about to go towards them when he saw his father seize hold of Jim.

'What's up?' he asked as Jim slouched towards him with both hands in his breeches pockets. 'What's going on wi' Da?'

'Nowt,' Jim muttered. 'Nowt to do wi' you anyhow.'

'Nowt!' Henry's voice rose in anger. 'What do you mean, nowt? You're a grown man. How can you let him treat you like that, here in middle o' Patrington for everybody to see?'

Jim shrugged. 'They'll onny think I'm soft in 'head and Da is boss. Which I am – and he is.'

'I don't understand you,' Henry persisted. 'Why—?'

'Leave it,' Jim demanded. 'Just thank God you're not in my boots, that's all.'

CHAPTER SIX

It was a sunny morning in early May when Rosa decided that she wouldn't go to school that day. I'm nearly ten, she thought. I've learned things already. I don't have to go. Delia was walking in front as she usually did, Matthew behind her, dragging his school bag in the dust, and Rosa lagging in the rear.

The twins, Lydia and Nellie, had left home and were in service at the same house in Ottringham in Holderness. Flo was still with Miss Dingley and Mrs Jennings, and was described by Mrs Jennings as 'a treasure'. Maggie was still at home and, at twenty, had given up the thought of ever finding a husband, her former suitor, Jack Fowler, having left the district without even saying goodbye. Mr Drew still piously attributed everything to the will of God, be it drought or the breaking of the riverbanks; in the case of household disasters such as the breaking of eggs in the hen coop or the milk turning sour, this was considered to be Mrs Drew's inability to manage affairs efficiently. In his evening prayers he asked God to give strength to the young queen who now occupied the throne and to ask her to look kindly on the affairs of her Crown land.

'Come on, Rosa, we're going to be late,' Matthew called to her. 'I don't want to get a black mark, not now when I'll soon be leaving.'

Matthew's father had insisted that he stay on at school until he was thirteen, although he had been allowed to take time off for haymaking and harvesting. 'You need a good education,' he'd told Matthew. 'It's not enough that you know how to sow and reap. To be a farmer today you have to watch corn prices from abroad as well as 'home market. It's different from when I was just starting out.'

Matthew had been reluctant but there was no arguing with his father: what he said was law. Matthew didn't really mind school and he liked being with Rosa, although he had to be careful that the other lads didn't realize it or his life would have been unbearable. So he joined in with playing jokes on the girls, pulling ribbons out of their hair and knotting their pinafore strings, or putting spiders or frogs in their desks.

'Leave her,' Delia called. 'Let her be late if she's a mind to. Why should we care? She's nowt to do with us.'

'Don't be daft, Delia. And don't be so mean, either,' Matthew retaliated. 'Course she's to do with us, she lives with us.'

Delia tossed her head and walked on. 'She's nowt to do with me.' She looked over her shoulder. 'But we all know that you're sweet on her, Matthew Drew!'

Matthew started to race after her. 'I'll get you for that.' She began to run. He caught up with her and pulled on her thin brown plaits, forcing her head back. 'Why should I be sweet on her? She's onny a bairn, same as you.'

'Ow!' Delia kicked out at his shins and he jumped back but didn't let go. 'Cos you're allus hanging round her, tekking her across marshes and catching tiddlers and that.'

'You could come too if you liked,' he argued, 'but you're that dowly you never want to.'

'Phew, I've got better things to do than trail about wi' you,' she scoffed.

Rosa slowed down as the other two quarrelled and looked round for somewhere to hide. There were very few hedges, though many deep ditches which divided the fields, but nothing else, no buildings or walls, only Marsh Farm and that was too far off for her to run to and not be seen. She gazed across at her former home and meditated. It's Drews' land now and Jim Drew is living in our old house all on his own.

She'd looked through the window one day and seen the familiar kitchen which had been so cosy when she had lived there with her grandmother, but now was stacked with boxes of crockery and household ware which Jim Drew hadn't bothered to unpack. The fire grate which had always been blazing, with a kettle steaming over it, was full of cold grey ash and a few dead sticks. Jim came to his mother's house to eat and only went to the Marsh Farm house to sleep and wouldn't have his mother or Maggie come in to clean for him. He always looks miserable, Rosa thought, as she scrambled into a steep-sided ditch. Mrs Drew wishes he would find a wife.

She clung tightly to the side of the grassy banks, for the water was deep in the ditch and she knew that should she slip she could drown. She peered over the top. Matthew was looking round for her. Delia had run off towards school from where there was the sound of a handbell ringing. Matthew was scratching his head in puzzlement and she gave a little smile and wondered what excuse he would make for her. Delia, she was sure, would paint the worst possible, blackest picture. That Delia disliked her intensely was quite obvious, but Rosa cared not in the slightest for her opinion.

Cowslips were growing in scattered clumps along the banks and behind the ditch was a straggly hawthorn hedge, planted to give some protection from the prevailing winds in the flat landscape. It was also home to blackbirds, hedge sparrows, wrens and long-tailed tits, and Rosa could hear their complaints as her presence disturbed their habitat. As she crouched, trying to keep still, she heard the rustling of long-tailed field mice and saw a sleepy hedgehog shuffling out of a nest of leaves and straw. Wild violets and golden celandine grew in the hedge bottom, whilst above her the long stalks of cow parsley waved their creamy heads and exuded heavy perfume which tickled her nose and made her want to sneeze.

She saw Matthew give one last look round before going through the gate and across the yard; she waited a few minutes more before she scrambled out of the ditch and headed off in the opposite direction towards the marshland and the river, as she and her mother used to do when they were keeping a lookout for her father's ship.

There would be men working there, she knew, for there was constant work on the accretions as more and more land was claimed from the river, but they wouldn't bother about her, they probably wouldn't even see her, she thought, and if they do I'll just say I've got a day off school.

She took a deep breath. She valued solitude and this she had missed since living with the Drew family. There was never a time to be alone, always someone asking questions, talking, busy doing, and what she wanted more than anything was to feel the silence and isolation of the island wrap around her.

She gazed up into the vast infinite sky. It was so wide and boundless and made her feel so small. There were no hills or undulations to obscure the landscape, no trees against the skyline, only acres of rolling farmland and a wide canopy of drifting clouds floating against a backdrop of pale blue and meeting a slender finger of brown river, and beyond that the low grey line of Lincolnshire, at the horizon.

'Hah!' She gave a little laugh and started to run, then lifting her arms up, she gave a jump and somersaulted, her skirt, petticoat and pinafore flying over her head. Her plaits came undone and her long dark hair ran free.

She half ran and skipped down long tracks, sometimes cutting down the sides of cornfields or along the wide dykes, avoiding when possible the farm workers who were out in the fields. Some of them looked up as she passed and she gave them a cheery wave and most waved back, and she continued on her passage towards the river.

There were few houses on Sunk Island, and those which were there were old though substantially built. There was talk at the Drews' dinner table that more were to be built as the island accreted and more embanking was undertaken, and farmers, answerable now only to the Crown agents, were eager to come and work and live on the rich fertile land.

'Where's tha going, little lass?' A voice hailed her from across the fields. A man was standing by a bullock-drawn waggon, cupping his hand to his mouth as he called.

'Hawkins Point,' she called back.

'Don't tummel in,' he shouted. 'It's muddy, there's been some flooding down there.'

'I won't,' she called in answer, and, worried that he might come after her and fetch her back, she quickened her stride.

The sun was getting higher as she reached the marshy waterlogged area along the edge of the river, though the wind was blowing strongly and whipped her hair around her face. The tide was going out, flowing swiftly down deep runnels and narrow channels on its way back to the river, and she looked down at her feet to find the dry patches to walk on.

'Always watch your feet.' It was as if her mother's voice was speaking to her and a sudden vision of her face, which she had lost before, came back to her. 'I will, Ma,' she whispered. 'I'll be careful. And I'll find out where my da is so that you don't have to search any more.'

It was with this sudden clarity of vision that she knew that was why she was here.

As she watched where she put her feet so that she didn't sink, she trod on clumps of yellow kingcups and thrift. Grey sea lavender spread a carpet over the marsh and crane flies buzzed around it, and as she stepped carefully she took hold of the tall reeds and rushes to steady herself, to come at last to the lonely Hawkins Point.

There was nothing in the land behind her. No habitation, not a single person to be seen in the silent isolated landscape, no sound but the sigh of the river, the cry of the birds, the herring gulls and curlews overhead, the piping of the redshanks and plovers which were sifting out crustaceans from the mudflats. The wind soughed through the grass and rippled across the young green corn, for the reclaimed land was cultivated almost to the edge of the marshland.

She stopped and wrapped her arms around herself as she saw a grey heron standing motionless among the reeds, and she too waited without moving, until she saw it pounce and emerge with a struggling frog between its beak. It flew with its long legs trailing, along the river's edge towards a thick bank of reeds. She waited a moment and then another appeared, flying low in swooping graceful motion from the direction of the dykes, to join its mate.

With a satisfied sigh she found a dry patch of ground. The walk had made her hungry and she sat down to eat her dinner. Mrs Drew and Maggie were generous with food, there was always a good table at the Drews' house, and Maggie today had packed her dinner bag not only with bread and cold bacon, but with a hunk of cheese and a thick slice of fruit cake as well.

She gazed out at the river as she ate and although the land was empty, the river wasn't. The river was busy with craft making their way to or from the port of Hull.

How did Ma know which ship my da would be on? she wondered. There are so many. Some she recognized as coal barges, making their slow way upriver. Some were fishing smacks coming in fully laden with cod and haddock from the northern fishing grounds and others were merchant ships from all countries of the world.

From her position at Hawkins Point she saw a coggy boat pulling towards the narrow channel which once led to Patrington Haven, but which now petered out to an inlet, close to where they had crossed in Henry's boat. She noticed too, as she looked the other way to the west, a small cutter with its sails lowered going into Stone Creek where the farmers shipped off their grain.

'So what you doing, Rosa? Playing twag?'

She jumped, so engrossed in watching the river that she hadn't seen or heard any movement behind her. Henry was standing there with a grin on his face.

'Give us a bit o' cake,' he asked. 'I've not had me dinner yet.'

'Why haven't you? Didn't Maggie pack you up?' She broke the cake in half and handed him a piece.

He popped it in his mouth and chewed before answering. 'I was sent for,' he said. 'Word got back to Ma that you hadn't gone to school.'

'Delia!' she said petulantly. 'I knew she'd tell!'

He shook his head. 'Not Delia. Some fellow saw you and went to tell Ma. He was worried about you and said this is where you were heading.'

'I'm all right,' she said. 'I wouldn't have come to any harm.'

'That's what I said.' Henry stretched and yawned. 'But Ma and Maggie said I had to come and find you.' He looked down at her and grinned. 'They didn't want Da to find out you'd missed school.' He transferred his gaze beyond her and pointed at the progress of a Dutch merchantman as it sailed upriver. 'Look at that!'

Rosa gazed at the ship. 'What is it?' she asked huskily, for the sight of the vessel had made her feel strangely excited. She hadn't seen such a ship before.

'A Dutch fluyt. What a sight, and soon to be gone.'

'Why?' she whispered. 'Where's it going?'

'It's an old ship and soon everybody will be using steam power and it won't be needed.'

She barely listened to what he was saying but kept her eyes firmly on the ship. The sails on the three-masted vessel were set to catch the breeze as it moved gracefully along the river. Its decks were long and narrow and were piled with timber. 'My da is coming on a ship,' she murmured. 'Well, he was going to come, but he's taking a long time.'

Henry sat down beside her. 'He might not come,' he said slowly. 'Don't think on it ower much in case you're disappointed. It's been ten years since he went.'

'I'd like him to come.' She turned towards him as the fluyt drew away from them. 'I really would.' Her mouth trembled. 'Then I could tell him how my ma waited for him.'

'Aye,' he said softly. 'I know. But we don't allus get what we want. I'd like to have my own farm instead of working for Da. I could go off, I know, but Ma would be upset and I'd never earn enough to save up for a place of my own.'

'Jim's got our old place,' she murmured. 'But he doesn't like to live in it, does he!'

'No, he doesn't.' Henry drew his knees up to his chin and looked thoughtful. 'He doesn't like it one bit. Not 'farmhouse, I don't mean. He doesn't like 'land around it. He says it isn't good land.'

'My grandda had it,' Rosa began.

'Aye,' Henry interrupted her. 'But some of 'land got flooded and it wasn't properly drained and some of 'dykes got covered in. He never made a good living from it. I'd have it,' he brooded, 'if onny Da would let me. I'd work it properly if it was mine.'

They heard the sound of voices and laughter and looking back across the marshland, they saw a group of men coming their way. Rosa sighed. It seemed that her solitude was over.

'Hello there, Henry,' one of the men called across to him.

Henry stood up. 'Don't come across. You'll get

your boots wet. Come on, Rosa,' he said. 'Let's go, you'll have to come back another day. Onny tell me when you do and I'll mek an excuse for you.'

They slopped their way back across the marshland and Henry confronted the men. 'What's up, Danny?' he asked. 'Why aren't you at work? That long dyke's supposed to be finished this week.'

'Sure and it is finished,' said another man, 'or almost. But it's too nice a day to be spent up to your knees in water.' He smiled at Rosa. 'Or to be spent in school. Now wouldn't you agree with that, young lady?'

He crouched down besides her. 'Better to be catching butterflies and frogs than learning spellings?'

She smiled and nodded. He had a friendly face with blue eyes and crinkly grey hair, an older man than the others.

He looked up at Henry. 'You don't remember me, Henry. You were just a wee lad when I was last here.'

Henry shook his head. They had had many Irish working for them over the years and although he had employed this gang of men for the embankment, he hadn't known them. 'I don't think so.'

'Seamus Byrne.' The man rose to his feet. 'Ten years ago. My brother and I were here – er, working for your da. How is Mr Drew?' he added. 'In good health?'

On hearing that he was, he said, 'You must tell him I was asking about him. And is this one of your many sisters, Henry? I remember years ago, your ma had a fresh babby every time I came back.'

'I'm not his sister,' Rosa butted in. 'But I live with them. My ma's dead.'

'I'm sorry to hear that.' The man dropped his voice. 'She'll have gone to a better place, there's no doubt of that. So what's your name? Are you an island child? Or did somebody bring you to this godforsaken plot?'

'It's not godforsaken!' Rosa said boldly. 'We have our own church and it's a very special place, everybody who lives here says so!'

The man looked taken aback. 'Sure and I beg your pardon, I didn't mean to offend.' Then his eyes twinkled. 'It's just that my home is amongst the mountains of Ireland and here couldn't be more different.'

'Well, you could go back,' Rosa said calmly. 'If you don't like it here.'

He shook his head. 'Ah, child, if only it was so easy. There's no work in my mother country—'

'And a price on your head too, Seamus,' one of the other men laughed. 'Don't forget that!'

He dismissed the fellow's remark with a disparaging grimace. 'Take no notice of him, he's a witless youth. So what's your name?' he asked. 'So that I can remember it when I think of you, for undoubtedly I will. You're a lot like my own daughter was at your age. In fact,' he said, 'you could even have Irish blood to my way o' thinking?'

'No,' Rosa said. 'I haven't. My ma was from Sunk Island and my da was from Spain. I think he was a prince,' she added cautiously, hoping that he wouldn't laugh, as some did when she told them.

He didn't laugh but looked curiously at her. 'A Spanish prince! Now wouldn't you just know it? With those dark eyes and that lovely hair, why, your daddy couldn't be anything else.' He leant towards her again. 'And what did you say your name was, child?'

'It's Rosa,' she said. 'Rosa Maria Carlos.'

CHAPTER SEVEN

She was given a beating by Mr Drew for being absent from school. Delia told him. She made out that it was an accident, but she said in a loud clear voice at supper that Rosa had missed her favourite lesson at school that day, botany, and that they'd been outdoors collecting wild flowers.

She'd put her hand to her mouth in pretended dismay as Mr Drew demanded, 'Missed a lesson? How's that?'

There was silence around the table. Matthew glared at Delia, but she just pursed her mouth into a smirk and looked away.

'Mrs Drew?' her husband questioned.

Mrs Drew looked reproachfully at Delia, then at Mr Drew. 'Rosa missed school today. She didn't go in.'

'Why not?' He turned to Rosa. 'Were you sick?'

'No.' She was honest. 'It was too nice a day to be in school.' She remembered the Irishman and what he'd said. 'Better to be catching butterflies and frogs than doing spellings. I went down to 'river. I saw a heron. It caught a frog. And then I saw its mate.'

She saw Henry smile but his smile disappeared as his father bellowed at her. 'Go stand in 'corner, face to 'wall!'

'But – I haven't finished—'

'You have finished! There'll be no more supper for you, my lass. You'll stand there until we have all done and then I'll attend to you.'

'She's onny a bairn, Da!' Henry protested as Rosa got up from the table. 'Everybody plays twag at some time or other.'

'Not in my household they don't.' His father's face reddened at the confrontation. 'I'll not have disobedience, especially not from one who isn't my own, but who is my responsibility. Saw a heron,' he muttered. 'You can see a heron any day of 'week!'

When supper was finished and cleared away, Mr Drew called her to him. 'Get me that strap that's hanging behind 'door and then stand here.' He indicated a spot in front of him.

'Da!' Henry was still in the room. The others had left. Matthew and Delia had hung back but had been ordered out by their father. 'Leave her be. She doesn't deserve 'strap just for missing school!'

His father pointed a finger. 'Nothing to do wi' you. I make 'rules here. It's my Christian duty to punish for wrongdoing.'

'Christian duty! You mek it up as you go along!' Henry bellowed. 'And don't say it's nowt to do wi' me. I'm sick of being told to mind me own business.' His face was livid. 'I'm no more than a labourer here. Not allowed to mek decisions, not allowed to have a say in owt!'

He wrenched the strap from his father's hand and tossed it into the fire. Rosa stood back in dismay. Surely he was making it worse for her than it already was?

'Get out!' his father shouted. 'If you don't like 'way things are around here, you know what to do.' His normal measured voice had become coarse, his manner rough.

Henry turned and crashed out of the room, almost falling over Matthew who was standing outside the door.

'Is Da really going to give Rosa 'strap?' Matthew whispered but Henry didn't answer and rushed outside.

The tongues of flame were licking around the leather strap and Mr Drew took the poker and fished it out. He held it up, dangling it like a mottled snake in front of Rosa's eyes.

'Did you see 'way 'flames licked around it?' His eyes were penetrating. 'That's how it will be in hell for miserable sinners.'

'How do you know?' Rosa whispered.

'How do I know?' he railed. 'It's in 'bible. That's how I know! If we don't live a godly life and repent of our sins then we go to hell!'

Rosa thought again of the Irishman who had told her that her mother had gone to a better place. So how did *he* know? It was very confusing.

Mr Drew dropped the strap into the hearth. But if Rosa thought she had been let off she was mistaken, for he reached into the corner, behind the chimney piece and brought out a thin cane. 'I don't usually use this on 'girls,' he murmured, 'but as 'strap is temporarily out of use, I have no other option.'

Rosa put both hands across her mouth and spat on them, then rubbed them together. Matthew had shown her how to do that. He'd said it took the sting out of a beating. Only it didn't. Three times on each hand, which, she thought, was four too many just for missing school. Matthew had had one on each hand for forgetting to lock up the hens.

She flinched at each stroke but didn't cry. She clenched her teeth and decided that it had been worth it, if only to see the heron catch the frog.

'Now, girl,' he said when he had finished and Rosa stood shaking her stinging hands. 'Do you repent?'

'I don't know,' she said truthfully. 'I'm not sorry that I went.'

'Not sorry!' He was aghast. 'You go against my rules! Do you know what will happen to you if you don't go to school?'

'I will go to school,' she explained. 'It's just that sometimes I don't want to. Sometimes I want to do what *I* want and today I wanted to go to the river.'

James Drew sat down heavily. 'What manner of child have we taken on? Mrs Drew!' he called towards the kitchen. 'Mrs Drew. Come here at once!'

His wife came scurrying in, wiping her hands on a towel and looking anxious.

'We have taken a viper to our bosom, Mrs Drew.' He wiped his forehead with a handkerchief. 'This child is wilful. Did you know that when you decided that we should take her in?'

Mrs Drew looked startled. 'I – erm. No, I didn't.' She glanced at Rosa. 'Mrs Jennings said that she'd never given her 'strap.'

'Then more fool her. If she had, then we wouldn't have 'problem we undoubtedly have now.'

'Perhaps not, Mr Drew. Rosa took 'day off because 'weather was fine and – ' She hesitated. 'She probably didn't think that it was wrong.'

'Not think it wrong? What sort of household are you running, Mrs Drew, when you're failing in your teaching of these children? Especially one who isn't ours. We need to take especial care in 'upbringing of one who isn't family. And of foreign extraction to boot!'

He rubbed his sparse beard thoughtfully. 'That's it, isn't it? She has her father's blood in more quantity than her mother's. These foreigners don't work in 'same way as we do, they take time off whenever they feel like it. Just look at those Irish louts. First fine day and they down their spades and go off to spend their money at 'nearest inn.'

'There was an Irishman asking about you, Mr Drew.' Rosa crossed her arms across her chest and put her burning hands beneath her armpits. She never called Mr Drew anything but that, though she called Mrs Drew Aunt Ellen, as she had asked her to. 'He said he hadn't seen you for many a long year.'

'Who asked you to speak?' Mr Drew ranted.

79

'Speak when you're spoken to! What Irishman? There's dozens of 'em all over Sunk Island.'

'He was called Seamus. He was asking Henry—' She broke off as she saw Mr Drew's expression change from anger to unease.

'What? What was he asking Henry?'

'I don't know, just if you were in good health. He's been working on one of 'dykes with the rest of 'gang.'

Mr Drew got to his feet. 'Go on! Off you go.' He dismissed her and she breathed a sigh. Her lecture and punishment were over.

'I have to go out,' Mr Drew informed his wife abruptly. 'Where did Henry go?'

'Out? Now?'

'Why shouldn't I go out?' he said brusquely. 'It's not late and it's not dark. Where did Henry go?'

'I don't know.' She told a small white lie. She didn't know, but she could guess. She had seen Henry walking swiftly and determinedly down the track towards the channel. He was, she was sure, heading towards his boat and one of the inns of Patrington, out of his father's reach.

But his father mounted a cob and caught up with Henry as he was unfastening the rope of his coggy boat.

'Henry!' he bellowed. 'Wait. I want to ask you summat.'

'What?' Henry's voice was sullen. He had no wish to talk to his father.

'Who's this Irishman who's been asking about me?'

'I don't know,' Henry muttered. 'Never seen

him afore, although he reckons he's seen me. Seamus something or other. Said he used to work for you. Byrne!' he remembered. 'Seamus Byrne.'

His father took in a deep breath. 'Where's he working now?'

Henry shrugged. 'He was on one of 'dykes over near Hawkins Point.'

'Get rid of him,' Drew said sharply. 'Tell him we're cutting down on men. He's a trouble-maker,' he added, seeing Henry's astonished face. 'And we can do without them.'

'She's not afraid to speak 'truth,' Mrs Drew murmured to Maggie as they dried the supper dishes. 'She just speaks her mind, without think-ing of 'consequences.'

Maggie smiled. 'She's got courage, I'll say that for her. I expect when she's older she'll think afore she speaks.'

'I don't know if she will,' said her mother. 'She's honest and straightforward. She's not really wilful but if her mind is set on something then she'll just go ahead and do it.'

Rosa's mind was set on something else later in the summer. Haymaking was over and she was back in school, but she hadn't been to see her grandmother for weeks and she wanted to go, she wanted to ask her something.

'Matthew!' She met him in the yard one late afternoon as she returned from school. Matthew had finished school now. His father said he needn't go back any more after haymaking. 'I'm going to see my gran. Do you want to come?'

'Aye.' His face lit up. 'I'd like that. When?'

'Well, I asked Maggie and she said we couldn't go for another week or two. She's busy making jam and chutney. But I don't want to wait, so I thought on Sunday after dinner.'

Matthew's mouth dropped open. 'They'll not let you go on your own!'

'I shan't tell them,' she said. 'I'll not be missed. We'll have our dinner, and then your da always has a sleep in 'parlour, and your ma and Maggie will be busy in 'kitchen. They'll think I'm out playing somewhere.'

She gazed at him and blinked her long dark lashes. 'If you'd like to come we'll be back afore they notice.'

'I don't know.' He hesitated. 'I'll have some jobs to do first. And we'll both get 'strap if we're found out. Da says I'm not too big for 'strap.' At thirteen, Matthew was already taller than his father and Henry, and as tall as Jim, though not as thin.

'But that'll be too late,' she said. 'Can't you do them when we come back? We won't stay long. Gran allus gives me a sixpence,' she added as an incentive.

Matthew chewed on his lip. He'd often rowed Henry's boat. He'd like to go. 'All right. Onny don't let our Delia know, 'cos she's sure to tell.'

They left the house separately after Sunday dinner was over, Matthew heading for the barn and Rosa nonchalantly walking towards the pastureland. They met up when they were out of sight of the house and ran towards the channel.

It was hot, a heat haze shimmered over the

land and Matthew unfastened his shirt buttons and rolled up his sleeves. 'You'll have to fasten them again when you see my gran and Miss Dingley,' Rosa said. 'Miss Dingley is very proper and she doesn't like bairns.'

'Aye, I know, but I'm not a bairn. I'm a working lad now.'

Rosa looked up at him. It was true. He no longer looked like a schoolboy. 'So does your da give you a proper wage?'

'No.' He pulled a face. 'He says I've to work for my keep till I'm fifteen. Then he'll think about paying me.'

'He's a bit mean, your da, isn't he?' Rosa commented. 'If you went to 'Hirings you could get a job with a wage, even if it wasn't much.'

'I could,' he agreed. 'Henry said I should go while 'going was good; that I should get experience on another farm. He said he'd left it too late and wished he'd gone.'

'So why don't you?' she asked.

He turned deep blue eyes towards her and then looked away. 'I like it here on Sunk Island – and besides, one day 'farm will be ours, Jim's and Henry's and mine.'

'You might fall out over it,' she said. 'And you're 'youngest so you're last in line.'

He smiled. 'We won't. I heard Jim telling Henry he'd get shut of Marsh Farm as soon as he could. He can't stand 'place and would rent somewhere on 'mainland. Henry says he'd have it. Which means that I'd have Home Farm.'

She frowned. Henry had said that Jim didn't like Marsh Farm and she still didn't understand why. They were working on the land now, draining it and getting it ready for resowing. In a few years' time it would be good prime land.

'Why doesn't he like it?' she asked curiously.

'Don't know, he won't say.' He looked thoughtful. 'I know it sounds daft but, well, it seems as if he's scared of summat. He puts off going there.'

Henry's boat was tied to a stake at the side of the bank and Rosa climbed in whilst Matthew unfastened the rope. 'Can I row?' she asked. 'Will you show me how?'

He hesitated for a moment. 'All right.' He swapped places with her. 'Our Maggie knows how to row, I don't see why you shouldn't.'

She took the oars and dipped them into the water and paddled them gently, then as she felt the boat move forward she started to row, pulling hard on the oars across the short distance of the channel.

'Well,' said Matthew admiringly. 'I'd swear you've done it afore.'

'I haven't.' She shook her head, pleased with his praise. 'But I watched Henry and it seemed easy.'

'It is here on 'channel. There's no rough water. But it's different out on 'river. You'd have to know 'tides or you'd be carried off into deep water. Anyway,' he said. 'They'll be starting to build a bridge soon and we'll be able to walk across. We won't be an island any more.'

They were both silent then, and Rosa thought how sorry she would be. She knew that it was what the farmers and their wives wanted, but she liked living on an island, and she was fascinated by the fact that once the land had been at the bottom of the river, with the waters swirling above it. It was somehow magical and mysterious and she felt sometimes, when she was alone, that the quiet murmur of the deep waters wrapped around her, protecting and comforting her.

'What do you want to ask your gran?' Matthew asked as they reached the other side and he jumped out onto the bank to make the boat fast.

'Something,' she said, but wouldn't be drawn and they walked in silence away from the haven and towards Patrington village.

'I'm not sure if I should come in.' Matthew hung back as they reached Miss Dingley's door. 'They might not want me to.'

'It's all right,' she assured him. 'Gran won't mind, besides she knows you, doesn't she? It's Aunt Bella you've to be careful with.'

Flo opened the door to them. 'Why, Matthew! What you doing here? Hello, Rosa, come to see your gran? And where's our Maggie?'

'We've come on our own,' Rosa confessed. 'Maggie was busy.'

'Oh, you're a caution! Does Ma know you're here?'

Rosa shook her head. 'We'll be back before we're missed,' she explained.

Flo opened her mouth in astonishment, then closed it only to say, 'I wouldn't want to be in your breeches, Matthew, if Da finds out.'

Matthew shuffled his feet. 'He'll onny give me 'strap. Anyway,' he said defiantly, 'I'm entitled to time off. I don't have to be working all of 'time.'

'Come on through, Rosa. Matthew, you stop here a minute and then we'll go into 'kitchen. You can have a piece o' cake,' she added, smiling at him. 'By, it's good to see somebody from home and just look at you, how big you are!'

She took Rosa into the parlour where her grandmother was sitting knitting, and Miss Dingley was asleep in her chair. Her gran looked up and smiled and then put her finger to her lips. 'Don't waken her,' she said softly. 'It's onny bit o' peace I get, when she's asleep!'

Miss Dingley had her head back against the chair and her mouth open; each time she took a snorting breath the ribbons on her cap blew gently up and down about her chin. Rosa put her hand to her mouth to restrain a laugh and her grandmother shook her head in smiling admonishment.

'Where's Maggie?' she asked quietly. 'I look forward to her visits. Who's brought you?'

'I've come with Matthew. At least, I asked him if he wanted to come with me. He doesn't go anywhere much.'

'And what if 'lad gets into trouble for bringing you?'

'I'll say it was my fault. That he came to look after me.'

'And you'd have come alone if Matthew hadn't come?' Mrs Jennings put down her knitting.

'Yes, I'm big enough,' Rosa said. 'And I wanted to ask you something.'

'What did you want to ask me that's so important and couldn't wait?'

Rosa glanced at Miss Dingley, who was stirring

86

in her sleep. 'I wanted to ask you – was my da a proper prince, or was Ma just making it up?'

Her grandmother's face clouded and she turned to look into the fire.

'Because you see,' Rosa went on, 'I met this Irishman by the river and when I told him that my da was a Spanish prince, he looked at me and said, Sure and,' she hesitated as she tried to remember exactly what he had said. 'Sure, and with those eyes and dark hair, your daddy couldn't be anything else.'

Mrs Jennings took up her knitting again. 'Who was this man? What was his name?'

'Seamus,' she said. 'That's what he told Henry anyway. He said he used to work for Mr Drew.'

'Seamus!' Mrs Jennings nodded. 'Your da knew a Seamus, though why a Spaniard and an Irishman should know each other, I never could work out.'

'So, was he?' Rosa asked. 'A prince, I mean?'

'I don't know, my dear.' Her grandmother sighed and looked across at her cousin, who was just waking. 'I think it was some tale he spun your poor ma. He was a prince in her eyes anyway.'

'What! Who?' Miss Dingley woke with a splutter. 'What did you say?'

'Nothing!' Mrs Jennings said cheerfully. 'You've been dreaming again, Bella. Here's our Rosa come to see us.'

Miss Dingley humphed and stared at Rosa as if she had never seen her before. Then she said abruptly and accusingly, 'Your grandmother will say you've grown, I expect, and I daresay you

87

have. Who's that out there?' she demanded as the doorknob rattled.

'Onny Flo with 'tea things,' Mrs Jennings pacified her, 'and you'd better fetch young fella in here for us to look at,' she said to Flo as she came in through the door with a tea tray.

'Fellow! What fellow? I know of no fellow,' Miss Dingley cried. 'Who is it? Who is it?'

'Onny my brother, Miss Dingley,' said Flo placatingly. 'He's come wi' Rosa. I'll fetch him in.'

She brought in a restrained and blushing Matthew who didn't raise his eyes but kept them firmly on his boots.

'A boy!' Miss Dingley exclaimed. 'What's a boy doing here?' She leant forward and glared at Matthew. 'Your brother, did you say?' She directed her questions at Rosa. 'How is he your brother and why is he here?'

'He's not my brother, Aunt Bella,' Rosa explained. 'He's Flo's brother. He's brought me here cos I'm not supposed to come on my own.'

Matthew's head got lower and lower as he tried to hide his blushes.

'Humph,' Miss Dingley said. 'Well, take him away,' she demanded. 'I've seen him now and that's quite enough. I never did care for boys; nasty, noisy creatures.'

Matthew hastily backed out of the room towards the kitchen, and Flo poured the tea and gave Rosa a thick slice of cake. 'Matthew's had a piece already,' she whispered. 'But I shouldn't stay long if I were you. We don't want you getting into trouble at home. Not like our Henry.'

'What did Flo mean,' Rosa asked as she and Matthew walked back to the haven, 'about Henry being in trouble?' She worried that it might be something to do with that day when Henry shouted at his father for punishing her for missing school.

'He and Da are not talking to each other,' Matthew said, 'apart from giving and tekking orders. Henry says he's no more'n a labourer.'

As they climbed into the boat, he said, 'I'll row back, we'd better be quick afore we're missed.' Now that they were on the way home he was starting to get nervous that they might be found out.

'Are you scared of your da?' Rosa asked.

'No,' he said angrily. 'I'm not! But I don't want you to get 'strap.'

'Nobody said I hadn't to go to see Gran on my own,' she retorted hotly. 'And why shouldn't I?'

''Cos we're supposed to be looking after you, that's why. Da says it's our Christian duty.' He stopped rowing. 'Onny I think there's another reason.'

'What?'

'I don't know, just a feeling I've got.' He looked across at her. 'You wouldn't understand, you're onny a bairn.'

'You mean you can't explain,' she ridiculed.

'Mebbe.' He pulled to the opposite bank. 'I can't remember 'name it's called.'

'What's called?'

'Name given to – sort of meaning.'

'I don't know what you're talking about.' She climbed out onto the bank and looked up to see Henry striding towards them.

89

'I said, didn't I?' Matthew tied the rope. 'I said you wouldn't understand.'

'Hey, you young varmints! Where've you been wi' my boat?' Henry stood above them with his arms folded. 'You should have asked. I might have been waiting to get across.'

'Sorry, Henry!' Rosa lifted her eyes to his. 'We – I've been to see my gran.'

'On your own?'

'With Matthew.'

'Good,' he said, surprisingly. 'Glad somebody's got some mettle. Go on then, get off home – and you've not seen me, do you hear?'

They both nodded. They knew where he was going and that he probably wouldn't get home that night.

'Be careful, Henry,' Matthew shouted to him as he pulled away. 'Don't tummel in.'

'It'll not be 'first time if I do,' Henry answered. 'Don't worry about me!'

'I'm not going back yet.' Rosa stopped suddenly. 'It's not tea time is it?'

'Well, it might be.' Matthew looked up at the sky. 'Sun's a bit lower. Where you thinking o' going?'

'To our old house. Marsh Farm. I want to see what they're doing to it.'

Matthew pulled a face and took a deep breath. 'I'd better come with you then. It's all clarty round there where they've been digging drains. But they've not done owt to 'house.'

'Well, I still want to go,' she said, and set off in that direction.

The sun was lower and it was also hidden

by cloud. The fine day they had enjoyed was darkening with the threat of rain. 'We should go another day,' Matthew said. 'I've got pigs to see to when I get back.'

'Well, go then,' she said calmly. 'You don't have to come. I know my own way.'

He didn't answer but trudged at the side of her. 'There's nowt to see,' he said, after a moment or two. 'Our Jim's not got settled in.'

She didn't answer but walked on.

'You're 'most infuriating lass I know,' he burst out. 'Our Delia's right. You onny wants to do what you like.'

She shrugged. Then she relented. 'I'll give you my piece of cake at tea time, if you like.' She gazed up at him and placed her hand in his. 'I don't like it when *you* get cross with me, Matthew. I'm not bothered about what Delia says.'

A warmth gathered over him as he felt her small hand in his. He didn't know why but he only ever wanted to please her. He didn't feel the same towards his sisters, except perhaps Maggie, who was almost like a second mother to him.

'Come on then,' he said gruffly. 'Let's hurry up afore it rains.'

But the skies opened in a sudden pelting shower of rain as they reached the farmyard and they dashed towards the shelter of the house. 'Will Jim be in, do you think?' Rosa asked as rain ran down her hair, making it look blacker than ever. 'Try 'door sneck, see if it's open.'

Matthew lifted the sneck and it yielded. 'Give it a push, it sticks a bit,' Rosa said. 'It allus did.'

Matthew put his hand on the kitchen door and pushed. He whispered, 'Our Jim might be here.'

He was. Jim was sitting by the dead fire with his head in his hands, staring into the space where the flames should have been. The room was in darkness, no candle or lamp was lit and the sky outside was leaden grey. The door creaked as they pushed against it and Jim jumped to his feet.

'Who's there? Who is it?'

'It's onny us, Jim. Matthew and Rosa.' Matthew said urgently. 'What's up?'

'God in heaven!' Jim put his hand to his brow. 'You frightened me to death. I thought – I thought—' He stared at Rosa and took a deep breath, then shook his head. 'Doesn't matter. It's nowt. Nowt at all.'

CHAPTER EIGHT

As the seasons passed, when summer followed spring and cold winter followed mellow autumn, Rosa gave up the thought that her father might come back in his ship with golden sails. I was just a dreaming child, she thought on her seventeenth birthday, my head was filled with stories from my mother's imagination.

It was ten years since she had come to live with the Drews and although she was accepted as part of the family, she still felt apart from them, and as she gazed into her bedroom mirror, she also knew that she looked different from them. Her hair was black and glossy and almost to her waist, but it was her dark eyes which she knew marked her as foreign, large and lustrous with thick lashes, within her ivory skin.

Mrs Drew had told her and Delia that Mr Drew had agreed that one of them could go into service. Delia had not wanted to make the first decision and Rosa, knowing her so well, speculated that Delia would try to find out what Rosa desired and then put a spoke into her plans and say that that was just what she wanted to do.

Delia had a spiteful nature and sly ways, but was no match for Rosa who announced that she would like to go into service somewhere along the coast if she could find a place. 'I like being by the water,' she said eagerly. 'I don't want to be inland. Perhaps Hornsea?' she questioned, speaking of the coastal village. 'It's quite a long way but I've heard it's very pleasant.'

'Oh, no,' Delia wailed. 'She knows that's where I wanted to go! I've allus said so.'

'Now, now, girls! You can't both go. Mr Drew said one of you must stay at home to help Maggie.' Mrs Drew wasn't well. She had constant backache and had difficulty walking without pain and Maggie was effectively running the house.

'Well, not me!' Delia grumbled. 'I don't see why I should be a servant in our own house. I can earn some money if I go to Hornsea. Let her stop here and earn her keep!'

'Delia!' her mother admonished. 'Rosa is like a sister to you, just as your other sisters are, she doesn't have to earn her keep.'

'No, she's not.' Delia glared at Rosa. 'You've onny to look at her to know she's not one of us.'

'Any more of this and you won't go anywhere.' Mrs Drew was upset at this exchange and Rosa stepped in quickly. Hornsea was the last place she wanted to go to. She wanted to stay here on Sunk Island.

'It's all right, Aunt Ellen. I don't mind, honest. If Delia wants to go I'll stay here and help you and Maggie,' and she gave Delia a compassionate forbearing smile.

'You're a young minx,' Maggie said later as

94

they prepared supper. 'You didn't want to go anywhere, did you?'

Rosa gave a low laugh. 'No, I didn't. What I'd really like to do is go to my gran's old house and clean it up and make it liveable again.'

So whilst Delia went off to work as a housemaid in one of the large houses in Hornsea, Rosa, when she had finished her chores at Home Farm, took herself off to Marsh Farm to make some kind of order out of the chaos which Jim had lived in over the years.

'Seventeen?' her grandmother had exclaimed when she visited her on her birthday, going alone and across the new bridge that had been built across the north channel. 'Seventeen! I can hardly believe it. I've lost track of 'years. Such a bonny babby you were, Rosa. Black hair, black eyes.'

'Brown, Gran,' Rosa smiled. 'Not quite black.'

'Who is it?' Miss Dingley was very old and very forgetful and needed constantly reminding about most things.

'Rosa,' Mrs Jennings said. 'You remember? Our Mary's daughter.'

Miss Dingley, whose skin was as dry as parchment, gazed at her uncomprehendingly from clouded eyes. 'She's got raven hair. Who is she, did you say?'

Mrs Jennings didn't answer her. 'You get more and more like your da, Rosa. You've got that foreign look.'

Rosa knew that. She knew by the heads that turned when strangers saw her at Patrington market, and if foreign seamen came into Stone

Creek where she sometimes walked on a Sunday, they would smile and speak to her in a foreign tongue and she wished that she could have understood.

'I feel like dancing sometimes, Gran,' she said, 'and that must be my father's blood. But there's never any music at Home Farm. Mr Drew says it's sinful unless we're singing hymns and praising the Lord.'

Her grandmother tutted. 'Well, I do believe that foreigners sing and dance and they're believers too, so it can't be all that sinful! If you want to dance, Rosa, then dance!' Then she looked thoughtful. 'There's an old squeeze box somewhere. Your grandda used to play it and your ma used to try and get a tune out of it when she was a lass. Now where did it go? It wasn't in 'sale.'

Rosa shook her head. She didn't remember it.

'No,' her grandmother said. 'When I think about it, she put it away afore you were born – when your da went away and didn't come back. She said there was no music in her life any more.'

Poor Ma, Rosa thought. How she must have loved him.

'Is it in that old chest I gave you?'

'What? Sorry, Gran! Which old chest?'

'I gave you a chest with your ma's things in it – when we sold up.'

'I don't remember.'

'Aye, it had a few trinkets belonging to your ma, and my best linen for when you meet some-body and set up house. Have you met anybody?'

She gazed quizzically at Rosa. 'You're old enough now you're seventeen.'

Rosa laughed. 'No, Gran, I haven't. Though Henry keeps saying he's going to marry me when I'm older.'

'Henry? Henry Drew? Why, how old's he?'

'Twenty-eight or so, not yet thirty anyway. But I'm not going to marry him. He's like my brother!'

'I should think not! I've seen him in Patrington, coming out of yon inn.' She inclined her head towards the window and down the street. 'He's allus worse for drink. I don't know how he gets home sometimes.'

'Sometimes he doesn't,' Rosa admitted, and kept to herself how she and Matthew sometimes had to half carry, half drag Henry home, and it was in this state of inebriation that Henry always asked her to marry him and Matthew always got angry.

'Aye, that chest,' her grandmother had continued. 'It might be in there – 'squeeze box I mean. Have a look when you get back. Ask Mrs Drew, she might know.'

Mrs Drew was lying down on the parlour sofa when Rosa arrived home. She'd had a nasty turn, she said, and Maggie was making her a hot drink. Rosa sat down beside her and took her hand. 'I don't like to see you ill, Aunt Ellen.' She felt compassion for this kindly woman who had always treated her as one of her own.

'You're a good girl, Rosa,' Mrs Drew gave her a weak smile. 'I don't know what we'd do without you. Even Jim says what a difference you've made to Marsh Farm since you started cleaning it up. Yet he still spends more time at home than he does there.'

'It only needed a warm fire and 'cobwebs brushing down, Aunt Ellen. Nothing else much.'

'I know. Your gran allus kept it nice and homely. But Jim never liked going there, not even on errands when he was a lad. He used to ask Henry to go instead.

'Me and Mr Drew were talking, Rosa.' She spoke hesitantly. 'And he said I should put it to you, well, for you to think about, nothing more, cos you're still onny young.'

Rosa's brows furrowed. What was she going to say? Or rather what was it that Mr Drew had asked her to say?

'It's just that – ' Mrs Drew eased herself up on the sofa and winced as if in pain. 'Our Jim, well, he could do with a wife. Mr Drew wants him to have a wife anyway. One who would look after him at 'farm. He can't expect our Maggie to keep looking after him when I'm gone.'

'Oh, Aunt Ellen. You're not really ill, are you?' Rosa grasped her hand tightly.

'No. No,' Mrs Drew assured her. 'Just a bit put out at the moment. But we have to look ahead and if owt should happen to me, why, our Maggie will have all on to look after her da and Henry and Matthew as well, though I expect our Matthew will wed eventually. He's a handsome lad and I hear tell that there's a few lasses been mekking sheep's eyes at him.'

Rosa suddenly felt cold at her words. She had seen Matthew talking and laughing with girls on

Patrington market days. She had seen how they listened to his every word, how they flashed their eyes and tossed their hair and petticoats to attract his attention. He was handsome, no doubt about it. He was tall and broad with thick dark hair and a pleasant open face and blue eyes which laughed when his mouth did.

She always ignored him when she saw him away from the farm, she would cross the street rather than let him think she had seen him with his crowd of admirers, though she felt as if his eyes were following her. But when they were at home they were easy with each other, even though he no longer asked her to go fishing with him as he had done when they were children.

'So, what Mr Drew thought – what we thought, I mean, was – would you ever consider our Jim for a husband? He's a fair bit older than you, of course, gone thirty is Jim. Not that that matters in a husband.' Mrs Drew went pink in the face. 'He'd – he'd still be – well, I expect he'd like a family. That's what Mr Drew would expect anyway, and I'd like some grandbairns too. I allus thought that Henry would be married by now,' she sighed. 'But it seems my lads don't want to leave home.'

Rosa was aghast. Marry Jim! She'd rather throw herself in the Humber. He had become more morose as he got older. He never smiled. Hardly ever said thank you, and when he'd stood back on first seeing Marsh Farm after she had swept and cleaned and got rid of his rubbish and made a fire in the grate, he'd only said

99

begrudgingly, 'By heck, Rosa, I thought I'd got in 'wrong house.'

Jim was a man of few words, unlike Henry who was a man of many, especially when he'd been drinking.

'You look after your lads too well, Aunt Ellen.' Rosa stood up and went to open the door wider as Maggie struggled with the tea tray, and so avoided answering the question. 'That's why they don't want to find a wife and leave home.'

'There can be no other reason,' Maggie said grimly. She had plainly heard most of the conversation and shook her head at Rosa.

'So will you think about what we've asked, Rosa?' Mrs Drew said. 'There's no rush, but if you'd keep it in mind.'

'What does Jim think about it?' Rosa said, although she had already made up her mind.

Mrs Drew looked doubtful. 'I don't think Mr Drew has mentioned it yet. He thought we should put 'idea to you first. He said Jim wouldn't object.'

'Wouldn't dare to, you mean, Ma,' Maggie muttered. 'He does owt Da tells him. He's right under his thumb.'

'Now, Maggie,' Mrs Drew began, but Rosa poured the tea and interrupted, anxious to change the subject. 'I've just remembered,' she said. 'When I went to see my gran, she said that when I came here to live, she gave me a chest with some linen in it, for if I ever get wed,' she added, giving Mrs Drew some hope. 'I can't remember seeing it.'

'There was a chest. We brought it across from

Marsh Farm.' Mrs Drew furrowed her forehead. 'Now where did it go?'

'Up in 'loft, I expect, Ma,' Maggie said. 'That's where most stuff goes that we don't need.'

'Ah, well, you won't want it just yet, will you, Rosa?' Mrs Drew looked at her and raised her eyebrows.

'I shan't need 'linen.' Rosa dashed her hopes. 'But Gran thought there was an old squeeze box in it. I'd like to have a look at that. See if I can play it,' she added, taking a sip of tea.

Mrs Drew had misgivings, but Maggie frowned at her mother. 'Why not, Ma? Why shouldn't we have a bit o' music now and then? Other folk do. I remember when we had 'party for 'Queen's coronation, our family was onny one not allowed to dance.'

Rosa remembered it too. Only she had danced. Henry had whisked her away behind a barn and swung her around in time to the music they could hear coming from the field, where they were having the feast. A fiddler was playing and then someone else joined in with a penny whistle. She'd clapped her hands and tapped her feet and Henry had spotted Matthew watching them and made him dance too. She had laughed at his blushes; Matthew had been prone to blush at most things then, but as if in defiance of her laughter, he had seized her hands and clumsily whirled her off her feet.

'So can I go up into 'loft and have a look?' she asked. 'Gran said there were some of my mother's things in the chest as well.'

'Ask Matthew to go up. It's a bit tricky up

101

'ladder,' Maggie advised. 'And it'll be full o' cobwebs and birds' nests.'

She asked him at supper. 'Matthew,' she said. 'Will you help me to look in 'loft? There's an old chest of my gran's somewhere and Maggie thinks it might be up there.'

'A chest? What's an old chest of Mrs Jennings's doing here?' Mr Drew brusquely interrupted Matthew's reply.

'It's one that came with me when I moved in.' Rosa looked across at him. Why does he have to constantly question everything? she wondered. 'It's got some linen and things in it.'

'Ah!' he said, and looked significantly at his wife. 'Did we mention that little matter to Rosa, Mrs Drew?'

'Yes,' she said nervously. 'But nothing has been decided.'

He nodded, a satisfied look upon his face. 'No hurry, no hurry. Well, not too much anyway.'

His three sons looked at him, but he didn't speak further, tucking into his meat pie. They glanced at Maggie but she kept her head down.

'Excuse me.' Henry got up from the table, obviously annoyed at being kept in the dark over whatever the little matter was. 'I'm going out.'

'Sit down,' his father thundered. 'Have 'manners to wait until we've all finished.'

Henry crashed down into his seat again and glared at his father. His supper was left on his plate.

'Can I have your pie if you don't want it, Henry?' Matthew reached across and scooped the remains of his brother's supper onto his own plate. 'Nice pie, Ma.'

'Maggie made it,' his mother said quietly. 'She's got a good hand at pastry.'

Maggie gazed across the table, not catching anyone's eye. Rosa thought that tears were not far away, as her eyes were glistening and she chewed hard on her bottom lip.

'So will you, Matthew?' Rosa asked again.

He looked up from his plate. 'What?'

'Go up into 'loft.'

'Aye. After supper and when I've finished putting 'pigs to bed.' He glanced at Rosa and for some reason which he couldn't fathom, the thought of being up in the loft with Rosa made him blush, which he hadn't done for a long time.

'I'll give you a hand with 'pigs if you like,' she said and smiled at him, and he nodded and looked down at his plate.

She looked so eager, her dark eyes animated and bright as if the prospect of searching the loft was the most exciting thing she had ever done. But then, Rosa made most things exhilarating, he thought. Finding a plover's nest with the chicks in it, seeing a lamb born or watching a sparrowhawk in flight. She had the gift of making ordinary events seem special and in spite of himself, whatever she wanted him to do, he always knew that he would do it.

As she walked across the yard to the pig pen to help Matthew, Henry called to her. 'Come here, I want you.' From the tone of his voice he was still angry and she knew that she would have to soothe away the rage which was simmering over his father's behaviour.

'I can't stand it any longer, Rosa. I'm sick to death of him.'

'Henry!' she said. 'You know the answer. You must get a job somewhere else. You're an experienced farmer, you could get a job as a foreman or hind anywhere in Holderness.'

'I know.' He grabbed her hand. 'Will you come wi' me?'

She was startled. 'What do you mean?'

'You're seventeen!'

She nodded, looking puzzled.

'Well then? You're old enough to wed. We could ask your gran.'

'To wed?' She almost laughed, but her laughter died for he looked so serious.

'Aye.' He stared down at her. His eyes were very blue, like Matthew's, she thought, though he was not so handsome. 'I've allus said that I'd marry you, haven't I?'

'But I was a child and you were joking, Henry! And you only said it when you'd been drinking ale.'

'Aye. It was onny time I dared say it, and I knew that folk would think it was 'drink talking. But it wasn't, Rosa. I allus knew that I'd marry you one day, when you'd grown up. So will you?' He took hold of her other hand. 'We'll get wed and go away from here and set up a new life, away from *him*.'

She gazed up at him and felt sad. He was so unhappy and yet, in spite of his bravado, he dared not leave alone.

'You've been like my brother, Henry,' she said softly. 'How could I be your wife?' Besides, she thought, I would never have any freedom if I were married to you. I'd be forever at your beck and call, just the same as I would if I married Jim.

'Well, that's 'best thing, isn't it? We know each other so well. You know what I like and you understand farming life. Besides, I'm right fond of you, Rosa.'

'I can't, Henry.' She squeezed his hands, which were still holding hers. 'It wouldn't be right. I love you as a brother, I could never love you as a husband.'

He put her hands to his lips and kissed them, but dropped them as Matthew came around the corner with a feeding bucket in each hand. Matthew stopped abruptly. 'What's going on?' He stared at them. 'Have you nowt to do?'

'I might have,' Henry replied. 'But I'm not going to do it. I'm going to 'hostelry. I'm going to get drunk.'

Matthew barely spoke to her as they fed the pigs and swept out the pens, then as they were almost finished, he said brusquely, 'Was Henry bothering you?'

'No,' she answered. 'He wasn't. Not at all.'

'You'd tell me if he did?'

She stopped what she was doing and leaned against the broom handle. 'And what would you do? Fight him?'

He looked away from her. 'If necessary. Yes.'

She smiled and said gently, 'I've nothing to

fear from Henry. He's just asked me to marry him.'

He lifted his head and she saw the startled apprehensive expression. 'And,' his voice was husky, 'what was your answer?'

'What would you think? I said no.' She gazed at him and saw the flush on his cheeks. 'Just as I shall say no to Jim.'

He gasped. 'Jim has asked you? Jim! Never!'

'Well, not exactly Jim! Your da asked your ma to ask me on his behalf.' She continued to watch his expression, which seemed to be changing from anxiety and concern to doubt and incredulity. 'I don't think Jim knows yet, so don't tell him or Henry.'

'But why?' He raised his voice. 'I can understand Henry, but why Jim? He's not 'slightest bit interested in getting married. He'll never leave home!'

'Your da wants him settled at Marsh Farm and he won't do that without a wife.'

'So – what did you tell Da? He doesn't like to have his plans upset.'

'I'm not afraid of him,' she said simply, and watched a pale shadow cross his face as she gave him the answer. 'I'll just tell him that I can't possibly marry the men who have been like brothers to me.'

CHAPTER NINE

'Mind where you put your feet. Walk on 'joists. Don't go falling through 'ceiling or we'll both be for it!'

'I won't.' Rosa trod carefully, following Matthew along the huge loft and holding up the lantern. 'Maggie was right, it's full of old birds' nests. Phew!' She shook her head as a disturbed bat flew across her face.

'Look, there's our old rocking horse! Ma had it made for Jim when he was a babby and we all played on it.' Matthew crawled on his hands and knees into a corner where the rocking horse sat alone. He patted the horse's head sentimentally. 'He's not got much mane left. Ma said that its hair came from one of our shire hosses.' He moved further along. 'How big is this chest that we're looking for?'

'I don't know. I think – yes, I vaguely remember putting clean paper into a box of sorts, but I can't remember 'size. It would have been my grandda's farm chest, I expect.'

'Ah, this might be it.' Matthew's voice was

muffled as he moved further along the loft. 'Bring 'lantern over here.'

There were other old boxes perched on the wooden joists, and old rag rugs and surplus pieces of furniture, stools and chairs with broken cane bottoms. Behind all of these was a wooden chest.

Matthew lifted the lid. The chest was full, the contents covered over with brown paper.

'That's it,' Rosa said excitedly. 'I remember it now.'

'We'll never get it down on our own,' he said. 'I'll have to ask Jim or Henry to help me.'

'It doesn't matter about getting it down,' she murmured, lifting up the top layer of paper and rummaging underneath. 'I can look up here for what I need.' She suddenly thought that she didn't want all of the Drew family to see her looking through the contents. This was hers, brought from home, part of her heritage and that of her mother's.

'Shall I stop and help you?'

She gave him a quick smile. Matthew was an exception. She didn't mind him looking. 'Won't you be bored?' she said. 'It's only old stuff.'

'No, I like rooting amongst old things, but I won't touch anything, honest.'

'All right.' She gave him the lantern and he fixed it to a nail on one of the top spars where it shone a halo of light upon them. She pulled off the layers of paper and handed them to him. He carefully folded them and placed them on the joist.

The first thing she found was her mother's

shawl. She remembered it, an exotic rich dark blue with a peacock-feather design embroidered on it. She put it close to her face, shut her eyes and breathed in. She could smell her mother, a faint perfume of lavender and rose water. Tears gathered in her eyes and she felt her throat tighten.

'Are you all right, Rosa?' Matthew asked quietly. 'It might be upsetting for you looking at your ma's things.'

At his gentle words, she started to weep. 'Ma said that my da had given her this, before he went away,' she cried, and Matthew drew nearer and put his arm around her.

'Don't cry, Rosa,' he said softly. 'I don't like to see you upset.' She put her head against his shoulder and he bent his head to feel her silky hair against his face.

'I'm all right,' she said, her voice muffled against him. 'Really I am.'

He wanted to kiss her cheek but reluctantly drew away from her. 'Let's see what else is in there.'

She rummaged again in the chest and brought out the crisp white cotton sheets, which she looked at and then wrapped up again. 'Shan't need those just yet.' She gave a shaky laugh.

'Not till you find somebody special?'

She raised her eyes which were still bright with tears, and looked at him. 'Not till I'm ready,' she said.

In a corner at the bottom of the chest was a small box tied with ribbon. She opened it and blinked her eyes as the gold of her mother's wedding ring glittered in the dull light of the lantern. 'Gran must have put it there,' she said huskily. 'But I'd forgotten.'

'Will you wear it?' he asked softly.

'Not yet,' she whispered. 'One day I will,' and she returned it to its box and put it back into the chest.

She found the squeeze box and they laughed as it made a shrill squawk as they pressed it in and out. 'Couldn't dance to that.' Matthew grinned in the shadows. 'No matter how we tried.'

'What's this?' Rosa pulled out a bundle of papers and peered at them. 'It's foreign writing.'

Matthew took them from her and held them under the light. 'It looks sort of official,' he said. 'As if it's legal jargon. Here's a signature,' he said suddenly. 'Look, at 'bottom of this page.'

Rosa peered over his shoulder and then took the papers back. 'It says Decimus Miguel Carlos. They're my father's!' she gasped. 'I don't remember being told his name. Gran just called him – your da. *Decimus Miguel*,' she repeated. 'Decimus Miguel.' She smiled. 'Now I feel as if I know him.'

Maggie's voice called from below. 'Are you going to be all night up there? There's a right old draught coming from 'trap door. It's blowing 'fire out and Da's complaining.'

'We're just coming,' they both called, and Rosa closed up the chest, putting the papers back underneath the linen, but leaving the squeeze box and the shawl out to take downstairs.

'I'll come back up another day,' she said. 'I'll be able to get up 'ladder on my own. Thank you, Matthew,' she murmured.

'It's no trouble,' he muttered. 'Just tell me when you want to come up and I'll get 'ladder out for you.'

'No, I meant – thank you for understanding, when I was upset. For not minding and thinking me silly.'

'I do mind,' he said gruffly. 'I don't like to think you're unhappy.'

'I'm not,' she said, and touched his arm. 'It was because of finding Ma's shawl. It stirred me up. I'm not unhappy.'

He helped her to her feet. They were standing on the same joist and were very close. He bent his head low to avoid the roof trusses and touched her face with his fingers as if wiping away her tears. 'That's all right then,' he said hoarsely and reaching up for the lantern, he turned away. 'We'd better go down.'

'So what did you find?' Maggie asked when they went into the kitchen. 'Any treasure?'

'No,' Rosa said quickly. 'Just 'linen as Gran said, and the squeeze box, and this shawl which belonged to my ma.'

'I remember it!' Mrs Drew reached for it. 'She said it was a present from your da.' She held it up to admire it. 'How beautiful it is.'

Mr Drew put down his newspaper and stared at the shawl, then reached across to finger it. He said nothing and returned to his paper, only didn't turn the page.

'It's foreign, isn't it?' Maggie said. 'You'd get

nowt like that round here. He must have brought it from Spain.'

Mr Drew cleared his throat and rattled his paper.

'Put it on, Rosa,' Maggie said. 'Let's see it on you.'

Rosa draped it around her shoulders. It felt lovely, soft and silky, and she whirled around to show it to advantage.

'That's enough!' Mr Drew barked. 'We'll have no shaming vanity, no ostentatious behaviour in this house.'

Rosa stood still, the shawl slipping off one shoulder, but said nothing, only stared at him. Maggie and her mother remained silent too, but Matthew oppposed his father as Henry usually did when he was here. 'It's onny thing she has of her ma's,' he declared. 'She's doing no harm, Da.'

Mr Drew gazed in astonishment at Matthew, who rarely crossed him, then picked up his paper again. 'I'll say nowt more about it,' he muttered.

Presently Mr Drew put down his paper. 'I'm off to bed.' He consulted his pocket watch. 'It's late. Half past nine. We've to be up early, Mrs Drew. I'm going into Hedon. There's a farmers' meeting.'

'I'll come with you, Fayther,' Maggie said. 'We need some things from 'haberdashers.'

'Aye, but you'll have a wait. Meeting generally goes on overlong when they start yammering away.'

'I shan't mind,' she said. 'I can look around 'town or sit and listen, can't I?'

'If you've a mind to.' He took himself off to bed and the atmosphere immediately lightened.

'Aunt Ellen!' Rosa said. 'Did you know my father's name? His first name, I mean?'

Mrs Drew considered. 'Yes – it was something like Michael, I think. I could never quite understand his accent, he seemed to talk so quick, but Mary, your mother, called him – now what was it?' She frowned in concentration. Then her face cleared. 'Miguel!' she said. 'That's what it was. Miguel.'

Rosa cast a surreptitious glance at Matthew, who smiled at her. She didn't want to tell anyone else yet about the papers, and she knew that Matthew wouldn't. I'll find out what they are, she thought. But I'll have to go to someone who understands languages, and there's no-one on Sunk Island who can do that.

Maggie took the reins of the mare as she and her father rattled along in the trap down the long straight road off Sunk Island and on to Ottringham in Holderness. There were no large towns in Holderness, just a scattering of small villages and hamlets across the wide agricultural plain. The people of Holderness were known for their straight-talking, unpretentious, no-nonsense ways, similar in fact to the inhabitants of Sunk Island who in years gone by had come from the mainland.

But the isolation of Sunk Island had given the people who lived there a sense of exclusiveness from the mainlanders. They had little need for outside assistance; they grew their own food, milked their own cows, made butter and cheese, killed their own pigs and gathered eggs from their ducks, geese and hens, and for their needs of household pots and pans, needles and thread, these they bought from the pedlars who came, bringing such requirements and the gossip from Holderness.

Mr Drew and his sons made occasional visits into Holderness and sometimes into the port of Hull, when the business of farming, the shipping of wheat and the buying of animals necessitated it, but for Maggie, who was always busy around the home and farm, a trip into the small market town of Hedon was a rare treat.

She was restless, and had been since the conversation she had overheard between her mother and Rosa about the possibility of Jim marrying Rosa. Ridiculous, she'd thought. To think of a bright young girl like Rosa marrying such a dull fellow. For although she was fond of her brother, she often grew impatient at his tardy ways.

But then she had listened to the quarrelling of Henry and his father and knew that nothing would resolve the differences between them, and her spirits had sunk when it struck her that that was to be her life for as long as she could foresee. Her mother was ill and not likely to improve, and I'll be left, she'd brooded in her lonely bed, with three men to look after, for she discounted the personable Matthew, who would no doubt marry in time; three men who will never agree: an oppressor, a melancholic and a drunk. And they will all always want their supper on the table.

Her father was silent for most of the journey

into Hedon, with just an occasional comment on the state of the land about them. The harvest was gathered in and women could be seen in some of the fields gleaning the stubble.

'That silk shawl,' he said suddenly. 'Was that where she found it? Up in 'loft?'

'What?' Maggie was lost in her own thoughts and at first didn't understand his meaning. 'Rosa, do you mean? Yes! Is it silk? I didn't realize.'

He shuffled on the bench. 'Aye, I reckon it is. Not cotton anyway.'

Silk! she thought. I've onny ever seen silk in 'haberdashers and that was when I went into Hull, years ago.

'Her da must have brought it from Spain,' she said. 'Did he go back there? I mean, after he'd first come to Sunk Island?'

'I don't know. I hardly knew him,' he muttered, adding abruptly, 'was there owt else up there?'

She shook her head. 'I don't think so. Just linen and a tea service, and that old squeeze box which you saw.' She couldn't help but add the latter with a hint of spite, for she felt he had been unfair to Rosa.

He grunted and remained silent until they reached the town where she dropped him off at one of the inns, where the meeting was to be held, and he told her to meet him later. She drove the trap into the marketplace and although it wasn't market day there was a busy crowd of women who, like her, had come into the town with their menfolk. They were gathered in small groups gossiping and laughing, and some greeted Maggie. Because there were few of them, most of the Sunk Islanders were known in Hedon and the surrounding district.

'How's thy ma?' one woman called to her.

'Middling,' Maggie said. 'Her back's bad.'

'Just you at home now?' asked another. 'I hear as how your Delia's gone to Hornsea. Cold draughty place is Hornsea,' she added, pursing her lips. 'Though I dare say it's healthy. Not so damp as Sunk Island anyway!'

Maggie smiled and moved on. It was a fallacy that always followed them. Because Sunk Island had come up from the river, it was generally believed by others that the land was damp and that the population would never thrive, even though the crops did.

'G'morning!' A bearded man in a tweed jacket and cord breeches touched his cap as he went by and she nodded in response. He looked familiar but she couldn't place him. She collected a few items of shopping and then went to have a cup of tea in a tea shop, and joined some of the other women who were gathered there.

Mrs Brown, a farmer's wife from Keyingham, moved up at a table to make room for her. 'Don't have 'fruit cake,' she whispered. 'It's not a patch on what you can make at home. But 'scones are not bad, they'd be better for a bit more fruit but they're today's baking.'

Maggie ordered tea and a slice of bread and ham and whilst she was waiting for it the woman chatted, giving out information about her family and how well they were prospering.

'I hear that your brother's making great strides at Marsh Farm. Good crops are they?'

Maggie agreed that the harvest had been good.

'But he's not got wed? Still relying on his ma for his home comforts?'

'Yes,' Maggie agreed again. 'He is.'

'He's getting ower old,' Mrs Brown said. 'If he doesn't look sharp all young women'll be gone. Though I daresay there'd be somebody who'd tek him if he looked about him. He'd be a good catch, any road, with all that land to his name.'

She sized Maggie up and down and remarked, 'You'll not be bothered now, I expect – about getting wed, I mean? You're leaving it a bit late anyway,' she laughed. 'And there's nobody else at home now to tek over, is there? Except that foreign lass. She's still with you, I reckon?'

'She's not foreign, Mrs Brown.' Maggie hid her fury at the woman's slight of her marriage prospects, and poured her tea. 'She was born on Sunk Island same as all her family, except for her da.'

'Aye.' The woman frowned. 'Well, that's what I meant. He were foreign, weren't he? I used to see him on 'odd time or two wi' Mr Drew.'

'You saw him with my da?' Maggie was amazed. Her father had said he hardly knew him, and however would Mrs Brown have remembered from so long ago? 'When?' she asked. 'When did you see him?'

'A few times. I used to go wi' our Jack on his waggon when he was loading corn onto 'boats at Stone Creek and I saw 'em then. Handsome, he

117

was, foreigner I mean, not your da! Aye, and I saw his ship once, moored out on 'river. Fine-looking vessel.'

Maggie considered this information and thought how odd that her father had never mentioned it, especially when Rosa was a child and so eager to hear stories of her father.

'And,' Mrs Brown waved a finger at her, 'tell you what I've allus thought peculiar! That day he disappeared, when he was supposed to be riding into Hull. Well, we were out in 'fields all that day and into 'evening, every one of us, bairns an' all, and he'd have had to pass our farm on 'road out. Couldn't avoid it, 'cos Ottringham road wasn't fit to travel on in them days. Well, nobody saw him pass, though we saw Mr Jennings's hoss go t'other way a week later.' She took a deep drink of tea. 'I've allus thought it odd, that. A mystery. It's as if he niver left Sunk Island.'

When Maggie had finished in the tea shop she walked along the main street towards the inn where she hoped the meeting might be finished, but she could hear the sound of raised voices inside and guessed that it was still continuing. She hesitated outside. Her father wouldn't be pleased if she went in to look for him, he was adamant that his daughters should never frequent such iniquitous places.

She was feeling a little cold, having left her warm shawl in the trap, and was just debating whether to go and get it and wait there for her father, when a figure brushed past her.

'Beg your pardon.' It was the same man she

had seen previously, the one who had seemed familiar. He took his cap off, revealing thick dark hair with greying sideburns. 'It's Maggie Drew, isn't it?' he said, giving her a wide grin. 'I thought I recognized you.'

'It is,' she replied, feeling embarrassed and shy of speaking to a man out on the street, especially when she hardly ever spoke socially to other men except her brothers or the farm labourers. 'I'm sorry, I don't remember—'

'No, you won't. It was quite a few years back. I was about seventeen at 'time and came to help with 'harvest on my uncle's farm on Sunk Island – Ben Lambeth's. You called in one day when I was there. I remember you.' Again he gave her a wide grin and she blushed.

Yes, now she did remember. She remembered the tall thickset youth who had spoken to her and commented that he liked the bonnet she was wearing, when usually the young lads or farm hands avoided speaking to a young girl unless they had to.

She smiled at him. 'Fred, isn't it?' she said. 'Fred Lambeth?'

'You do remember me!' He looked delighted that she had. 'Are you still on Sunk Island? Or – you'll be married, I expect?'

Again she blushed. 'I'm not married,' she confessed. 'I'm at home still. I have to help my ma,' and she wondered why she felt the need to defend her unmarried state. 'She's not well.'

'I'm sorry to hear that,' he murmured and looked thoughtful. 'I've been away for a year or two so I've not caught up with all 'news. I'm a blacksmith, I've been working all over 'country. I can in this job. But I've come home to Hedon now. I'm setting up shop here, there seems to be plenty o' trade.'

'Good,' she murmured. 'You'll do well. Our old blacksmith has just finished. He's left Sunk Island and gone to live with his daughter in Beverley. I'll tell my fayther.'

He nodded. 'I've just been talking to him, and to some of 'other farmers. I need to get 'word round.'

The door of the inn opened and some of the farmers spilled out. One or two clapped him on the shoulder and said, 'Don't forget now, Fred. Next week!'

He raised a hand and said that he wouldn't and then Mr Drew came out. Maggie moved back away from the door and stood by the wall so that he had to turn before he saw her.

'There you are, Maggie!' he said.

'I've just arrived,' she pronounced. 'What good timing!'

Fred Lambeth stepped forward. 'I'll see you on Friday then, Mr Drew? Glad to do business with you.'

'Aye,' Mr Drew said. 'Don't be late.' He walked on and Maggie turned around to nod goodbye. Fred Lambeth put his cap on again and gave her a warm smile which lifted her spirits and made her long for Friday to come quickly.

CHAPTER TEN

'Rosa!' Maggie was extremely animated with barely concealed excitement. 'There's a new blacksmith coming this morning.'

'Oh?' Rosa was bringing in a basket of logs which Matthew had left outside the door. 'And?'

'He'll be in one of 'barns I expect, so – well – will you see to Ma's morning drink whilst I take tea out to 'men?'

Rosa smiled and raised her brows at Maggie's flushed face. She brushed the wood dust off her hands. 'Who is he, then, Maggie? Is he handsome? Can I take a look?'

'No!' Maggie replied swiftly. 'If he sees your bonny face he won't look at anybody else!'

'Maggie! What are you talking about? There's nobody bonnier than you!'

'Aye, but I'm getting on. Twenty-seven. I'm past my prime.'

Rosa laughed. 'Course you're not! Who is he anyway? Why haven't we seen him before?'

'He's been working away. I met him in Hedon when I went in wi' Da. He recognized me,' she said, anxious not to give the impression she had been talking to a stranger. 'We met when we were young.' She gave a huge smile which lit her face and dimpled her cheeks. 'He's right grand, Rosa. I've never seen anybody I've been so taken with afore. He's got such a nice smile.'

'And he's not married or spoken for?'

Maggie's face paled and she clutched her face with both hands. 'Oh!' she said. 'I never asked! He wanted to know if I was, but I never thought to ask him.' Her voice trailed away.

'Well!' Rosa consoled her. 'He wouldn't have asked if you were, if he had been, would he? He wouldn't even have stopped to talk!'

'No, mebbe not,' Maggie agreed reluctantly, but she was rather deflated and as a result, made her way more demurely then she would have done an hour later, when she took out a tray of tea to the blacksmith and his apprentice.

'Morning, Miss Drew!' Was it her imagination or was he much less friendly than he had been, but then her father and Jim were both there watching him work.

Henry called from the door. 'Can you come, Jim? A wheel's come off a waggon and I can't fix it meself. How do, Fred? Come back to earn an honest living, have you?'

Fred gulped down his tea. 'Aye,' he said. 'I've done my share of travelling. Time to settle down.'

'Not wed, then?'

Fred shook his head. 'No, not yet. I need an East Riding lass to look after me.'

'You'd best tek our Maggie then,' Henry grinned and winked at his sister. 'She knows how to look after folks *and* meks best pastry in Holderness.'

Maggie's face went scarlet and she rebuked Henry. 'Don't talk such nonsense!'

'Our Maggie can't get wed,' Jim butted in. 'Who'd look after us?'

'You could look round for somebody to wed yourself, Jim Drew,' Maggie said angrily. 'Don't think I'm stopping at home just for your convenience, cos I'm not!' She stormed out of the barn with the men staring after her.

Fred Lambeth looked from Henry to Jim and then said, 'Now there's a woman with spirit.' He gave a grin. 'And a good hand at pastry as well?'

Maggie plonked herself down at the kitchen table and put her chin in her hands. It had all gone wrong. She had slept in curl papers all night so that her hair looked pretty, and dressed so neatly this morning, even pinching her cheeks so that the line of her cheekbones would stand out, and what good had it done? She'd shown her temper in front of Fred Lambeth and the last thing he would want was an ill-tempered wife.

She brought herself up short and mentally slapped herself. What was she thinking of? She'd only just met him! Why ever did she imagine that he would be looking for a wife, especially on such a short acquaintance? And he was surely only joking when he said he was looking for an East Riding lass?

'Those stupid brothers of mine,' she wailed to Rosa. 'They've ruined everything!'

An hour later Rosa was crossing the yard and saw through the open door of the barn that the blacksmith was packing up to leave and the boy was loading up the cart with his tools. 'Hello,' she called to Fred Lambeth and he looked up. 'Maggie's just boiling 'kettle if you fancy another cup of tea before you go.'

'Aye,' he said. 'Thanks, this is thirsty work,' and she watched as he brushed himself down before knocking on the half-open kitchen door.

'I heard as there might be a cup o' tea going.' He put his head around the door. 'Or will it be a bother?'

'Oh! No. No.' Maggie became flustered. 'It's no bother, don't think it. Sit down, do.'

'I'll not sit down,' he said. 'I'm a bit dusty. Perhaps if I can just wash my hands?'

'Of course.' Maggie moved to the stone sink and put her hand towards the pump to draw water.

'I'll do that,' he said, and brushed against her arm as he reached for the pump handle.

'It's a bit stiff,' she said awkwardly. 'I keep asking 'lads to fix it but they never get round to it.'

He pumped the handle several times. 'Seems as if 'valves have got dry,' he said. 'It's not drawing water up as it should. 'Leather's got cracked I should think.' He glanced at her. 'I can fix it, but I'd rather come back on another day, if that's all right?'

'Oh, yes!' She beamed at him. 'That's perfectly all right. Thank you.'

She poured him tea and offered him a scone which she had baked that morning and spread it with plum jam.

'By, them's grand, Maggie. Just like my ma used to make.'

'Do you live by yourself?' she ventured.

'Aye, I've rented a cottage in Souttergate. A woman comes in to clean once a week and my sister drops in with a batch of baking now and again. I tell her not to bother, cos she's enough on with her own family, and I can manage. I know how.' His eyes twinkled as he said, 'I didn't really mean I needed an East Riding lass to look after me. I know how to look after myself.'

'Not like Jim and Henry, then?' she said. 'Or my da? They don't lift a finger. Ma's run around after them all of their lives.'

'And now they expect it of you?' he asked. 'You shouldn't let them put upon you. You deserve a life of your own.'

Her eyes stared into his. Nobody had ever said that to her before. Women looked after their menfolk. What else should they do?

'Are you walking out with anybody, Maggie?' he asked quietly. 'Any young fellow calling on you?'

She swallowed. 'No,' she murmured. 'There isn't.'

He smiled. 'But you wouldn't mind if somebody asked?'

'Depends who it was.' She smiled back at him, her spirits rising.

'What about your ma and da? Would they object?'

'Ma wouldn't. I'm not sure about Da, he doesn't like his routine changed.' She looked out of the window, seeing Henry and their father apparently locked in an argument. She took a deep breath. 'My father likes to make all 'decisions around here. He doesn't like anybody else making them.'

Fred came and stood beside her, following her gaze out of the window. He was much taller than she was, his shoulders were broad and his arms beneath his rolled-up shirtsleeves were hard and muscly. She felt fragile and womanly beside him.

'Doesn't he?' he murmured. 'But you're of age.' He looked down at her questioningly. 'If you wanted to walk out wi' somebody, you can!'

'Yes,' she breathed. 'I can. And I will.'

'Good,' he smiled. His eyes were gentle, his manner assured and she felt as if her heart gave a skip. 'I'll be back next week, then?'

Their courtship proceeded at a swift pace in spite of Mr Drew's objections. 'Your ma's ill,' he said, when Maggie announced that she was walking out with Fred Lambeth. 'Don't be getting ideas about getting wed! You're needed here.'

Mrs Drew made a great effort to run the household affairs again, though she was plainly not well. 'We can manage, Aunt Ellen,' Rosa assured her. 'Sit down and put your feet up. Perhaps you could do the mending?' She brought a pile of socks that needed to be darned, and some working shirts that needed repair, and Mrs Drew didn't feel quite so useless.

'If Maggie should marry Mr Lambeth,' she said. 'If he should ask for her, I mean, we could ask Delia to come back. I don't think she cares for Hornsea.'

'I could manage,' Rosa interceded swiftly. She had no wish for Delia to return to the household for she only caused trouble, but, to the family's surprise, on Delia's next visit she was remarkably chirpy and merry. On hearing that her sister Maggie was walking out with the blacksmith, she gave a saucy smile and remarked that she needn't think she was the only one with an admirer and that Hornsea was a grand place to be.

'Catch me coming back to Sunk Island!' she said to Maggie and gave a sly glance in Rosa's direction. 'There's nowt going on here. Anyway,' she lowered her voice, 'I've swapped jobs. I'm not at 'big house now. I'm general maid at an inn that teks in lodgers and guests. I heard they were looking for somebody and I applied. It's much more lively and I get more time off.'

Maggie was shocked. 'An inn! Is it respectable? Da won't be pleased.'

Delia shrugged. 'I shan't tell him. There's no reason why he should know.' She looked scornfully at Rosa. 'Unless anybody here tells him. Anyway, it's perfectly respectable, and it's nice to have company and to be able to chat with customers instead of being below stairs and having to keep my place all of 'time.'

'Don't worry about her,' Rosa said to Maggie later, when she brought up the subject of Delia once more. 'She seems so much more cheerful.'

'Yes.' Maggie was thoughtful. 'That's what's so worrying. I just hope that she doesn't get into bad company.'

'She won't,' Rosa assured her. 'Hornsea's a

very respectable place. She's as safe there as on Sunk Island.'

Fred asked Maggie to marry him. 'I'm asking cos I knew when I met you that day in Hedon that you were the one for me. I don't want a wife to cook and clean for me. I want a wife I can talk to and have a laugh with, and it seems to me, Maggie, that we can do that. And if you want to have bairns, then that's all right as well, and if you don't, well I shan't mind that either. So what do you say?'

He looked at her rather anxiously as she remained silent. They were walking away from the farm and alongside a deep dyke. There had been a slight frost overnight and the grass had a silver rime upon it. 'You do care for me, Maggie? I've not been mistaken?'

She stopped and turned towards him. 'I thought you were never going to ask!' she said. 'I've been waiting and waiting ever since that day you fixed our pump handle.'

He put his arms around her and drew her towards him and kissed her full on the mouth. 'Why did you wait?' he asked. 'Why didn't you ask me?'

'Ask you?' She put her mouth close to his. Being kissed was so much more pleasant than she had ever imagined. 'How could I? I'm a woman, we have to wait to be asked.'

He kissed her again. 'No, you don't. If you'd asked me we could have been wed by now. I was onny waiting cos I wasn't sure how you felt.'

'Couldn't you tell?' she asked. She was sure that everyone in the community would have been able to tell from her demeanour and happy countenance that she was in love with Fred Lambeth.

He shook his head and laughed at her. 'So when do you want to be wed, Maggie?'

She gave a deep happy sigh. 'Next week,' she said.

'Next week! Everybody'll think it's a rush job!'

She put her arms around his neck. 'I don't care,' she said softly. 'I don't care what anybody thinks, except Ma, that is,' she added. 'I just want to be with you and I want to be with you now.'

'I'm not sure that she can be spared,' Mr Drew said when Fred approached him formally for Maggie's hand in marriage. 'Her mother is not well and—'

'We'd like to be wed before Christmas,' Fred interrupted. 'There's no need for us to wait. Maggie's of age, I'm earning good money and I've got a house ready and waiting.'

Mr Drew opened and closed his mouth, his objections overruled. 'Her mother—'

'Is pleased for us! Maggie's spoken to her. They're already planning all 'cooking and baking for 'wedding feast.' Fred held out his hand and took Mr Drew's and shook it. 'Thank you very much, sir. I'm glad you've no objections.'

Mrs Drew sat in her chair and rubbed fat and flour to make pastry and sliced apples from the store, she beat eggs and mixed fruit for cakes, whilst Maggie and Rosa cleaned the house from top to bottom, washed curtains and chair covers and polished the already shining brass and copper.

'Is there going to be a wedding or summat?' Matthew grinned as he came in and sat down to his supper. 'There's a dozen sheets on 'line outside.'

'Oh!' Rosa got up from the table. 'I'd forgotten them and it's starting to rain! We must have them aired before Saturday.'

'I'll give you a hand.' Matthew rose from the table and followed her outside, whilst Jim and Henry and their father looked from one to the other.

'You're doing too much,' Matthew said as Rosa piled the sheets into his arms. 'There's no need for all this fuss.'

'I know,' she said, a wooden peg clenched between her teeth. 'But we're doing it for your ma. She's so bothered that the house won't look nice for the wedding.' She took the peg out of her mouth. 'Fred's sister and relations will be coming as well as all of 'neighbours, so she wants to put on a good show.'

'Will you be able to manage when our Maggie's gone?' he asked. 'You'll want to stay with us?'

She gazed at him. 'Of course I want to stay! But there'll be changes, Matthew. I won't be at everybody's beck and call 'same as your ma and Maggie are.'

He smiled. 'I know that. You're a free spirit. We couldn't tie you down – even if we wanted to.'

She nodded. 'I always knew that you understood me, Matthew.' She stood on tiptoe and kissed him on his cheek and he just stood there looking at her, and thinking that there never would be any chance of capturing her, that she would be just like her mother, who, it was said, waited for someone special to come along and claim her.

CHAPTER ELEVEN

All the family were coming for the wedding. Flo had been given the whole weekend off by Mrs Jennings, so she arrived on the Friday afternoon and was able to help with last-minute baking and the making up of extra beds.

The twins, Lydia and Nellie, and the young men they were affianced to were coming just for the day. Delia was coming on the Saturday and staying until Sunday, whilst Mrs Drew's sister and her family were due to arrive from Beverley at any time.

'We've got cousins we haven't seen in years,' Flo said cheerfully as she and Rosa made up an extra bed in Rosa's room.

'Will you sleep in here with me, Flo?' Rosa asked, 'and we'll put your aunt and uncle in Henry's room, and Becky and Susan in the box-room.'

'What about Delia? Where shall we put her?'

'Well, as Matthew and Henry are going to Marsh Farm with Jim, Delia can have Matthew's room if she wants. Or I can,' she said. 'Yes, perhaps Delia would prefer to be with you rather than on her own. She won't want to be with me anyway.'

'Still not friends?' Flo asked. 'Still at daggers drawn after all these years?'

Rosa nodded. 'I don't know why. She doesn't like me. Never did.'

'But you don't mind?' Flo said curiously. 'It doesn't bother you?'

'No,' Rosa answered matter-of-factly. 'I don't even think about it. I know who I care for and who cares for me.'

'You're a strange lass, Rosa.' Flo scrutinized her intently. 'I'd have thought being half Spanish you'd have been allus laughing and singing, but instead you're as deep as a well. We don't really know you. We never know what you're thinking.'

Rosa gave a slight smile. 'That's because my other half is Sunk Island. I've been influenced more by that and by 'river that runs by it.' She looked thoughtful. 'It's a sort of magnetism that's constantly pulling at me.' Then she laughed. 'But sometimes I want to dance and sing, but I can't, can I? At least not here. Your da says it's a sin.'

Flo nodded. 'Aye, he does. But it doesn't mean that he's right. Maggie says that Fred plays a penny whistle and he's going to show her how to dance, and then they can go to Assemblies in Hedon.' She gave a satisfied smirk. 'That'll be one in 'eye for Da.'

The Saturday morning dawned bright and sharp and they were all up early, except for Maggie who was allowed to have an extra half-hour in bed as it was her wedding day. But she came downstairs, flushed and looking pretty and saying that she might as well be up for she couldn't sleep anyway.

'I can't wait to meet Fred,' said Flo. 'Is he handsome? Is he jolly?'

'He's both of those things.' Rosa spoke up as Maggie suddenly went shy. 'And he really deserves Maggie.'

Maggie started to cry. 'I shall feel so strange being on my own without everybody. I've allus been used to having 'family about.'

'I felt 'same when I first went to Patrington to work,' Flo admitted. 'I missed everybody, but now I like being independent and having my own money, although – ' she stopped and looked at Maggie and Rosa. 'Well, I wasn't going to tell anybody just yet, but I've met somebody as well.' She laughed. 'Tom. He's a hind over at a big farm in Welwick. He's a widower with a five-year-old son; Tom's ma looks after 'little lad just now, but Tom wants him to live with him, he's fond of 'lad.'

'Well I never!' Maggie said. 'Does Ma know?'

'Not yet,' Flo said. 'I'll tell her later. But we shan't want a fuss and it won't be yet. Tom'll look for another place next year mebbe, somewhere that we both like, and I don't want to leave Mrs Jennings just yet, she'd have a hard job finding somebody to put up with Miss Dingley. Poor old soul,' she said. 'She doesn't know if she's coming or going.'

'Not Gran, you don't mean?' Rosa said anxiously.

'No, not Mrs Jennings, she's hale and hearty. No, Miss Dingley, she's gone soft in 'head, bless her. Doesn't know if it's night or day. I couldn't go off and leave your gran with her on her own. No, I'll stop for now and see how things are.'

Rosa thought how kind Flo was to be so considerate about the old lady, as indeed Maggie was too. She would have given up her own chance of happiness to stay with her mother if she hadn't met Fred.

Henry had hitched up one of the farm waggons and Matthew had decorated it with holly and evergreen. Rosa and Flo had draped the waggon with red ribbon and put yellow ribbon on the harnesses of the two shire horses, and Maggie drove off in style with Henry at the reins and her mother and father sitting beside her whilst the rest of the family walked behind to meet everyone else at the old church.

Practically everyone from Sunk Island was there to see the first of the Drew girls married and there was much smiling and glances between other young women when they saw Fred Lambeth drive up in his trap, with his beard neatly trimmed and wearing a dark suit with a grey cravat at his neck, and carrying a pair of grey gloves. He looked very handsome indeed.

'My word!' Nellie turned to her twin. 'Yes,' Lydia nodded. 'He was worth waiting for, wasn't he?'

After the ceremony all those who had been invited to the wedding breakfast ambled about and chatted to each other, and made their way to the big barn where the food had been laid out and covered with cloths and sheets. As they walked in there was the sound of music as two fiddlers struck up a merry tune.

Rosa stood still and looked round for Matthew. She saw him and he was smiling and tapping his feet. She went up to him. 'What will your da say? Did you know about this?'

'I did. Fred asked me what I thought. He said it was no wedding without music and I agreed with him.' He looked around. 'Da isn't here yet and by 'time he gets here it'll be in full swing.' He took hold of her hand. 'Do you remember when we danced behind 'old barn when it was 'coronation?'

She nodded. 'Yes. Shall we do it again?'

He put his hand on her waist. 'I've not danced since and I don't know how, but—'

'Let's just skip to 'music,' she laughed. 'It sounds like skipping music,' and as the fiddlers played a jolly jig they skipped and hopped around the tables, only stopping as the crowd came in, who clapped and cheered.

'Now my turn, Rosa.' Henry stepped towards her.

'I have to help with 'food,' she said, but laughingly took his hand and whirled around and came to a stop in front of Mr Drew.

His face was like thunder as he saw the dancing and heard the music, but everyone else was laughing and clapping their hands, or stamping their feet in time to the tune, so he turned on his heel and went towards the house.

After the wedding breakfast Fred made a speech in which he said he was pleased to have joined the Drew family and welcomed all of them to his. 'Though there's fewer of us,' he said, amid laughter. 'Just me and my sister and her husband and their bairns, and an uncle and aunt and a cousin or three. But you're welcome to call on my wife – ' he glanced down at Maggie, who was by his side and lowered her head shyly, though a smile played on her lips. 'On my wife and me at any time. Isn't that right, Mrs Lambeth?' he added to cheers and the raising of glasses.

At the end of the afternoon, the newly married couple left to go back to Fred's house in Hedon. 'We'd best get off before dark,' Fred said humorously and everyone cheered. Lanterns had been lit around the barn and a fire made in a tin trunk so that people might warm themselves. Two of the farm dogs stretched out in front of it and a cat curled up on one of the beams catching the rising heat.

Matthew looked round for Rosa. There were still a few groups of people gathered around talking. Lydia, Nellie and Delia were chatting to those they had known at school but most of the older Sunk Island residents had gone, leaving the younger ones to make their own way home.

'Cheerio, Matthew.' John Gore, a farmer from one of the neighbouring farms, was ready to leave. 'It's been a right good do. Your Maggie looked real bonny. I don't know why I hadn't noticed afore.'

His wife plucked at his arm and urged him homewards. 'That's because you notice nowt but colour o' 'corn. But she did look grand, and so did Rosa,' she added. 'Somebody'll snap her up afore long, I shouldn't wonder.'

Matthew nodded in agreement and wished them goodnight as they set off across the track towards their home, John Gore walking rather unsteadily, for he had drunk a fair amount of ale from the barrel which Henry had brought in the day before in the back of his waggon, knowing that his father wouldn't supply any.

'Can't have a wedding without ale,' he'd said to Matthew. 'Give us a hand,' and they'd hidden it under a bale of straw so that their father wouldn't see it.

He found Rosa in the back kitchen up to her elbows in soapy water. Flo was drying the dishes and putting them in the cupboard. 'Come on, both of you. Come outside, everybody is ready for going home and just having a last natter.'

'You go, Rosa,' Flo said. 'Go get a breath of air. You've been busy all day. I'll finish off here and help Ma to bed when she's ready.'

Mrs Drew had been very animated all day, enjoying the chat with her relatives who rarely came to Sunk Island. 'Such an outlandish isolated place, Ellen,' her sister had said on arrival. 'I don't know how you can bear to live here. I thought we were going to drown on them marshes at Keyingham. Wheels on 'trap kept getting bogged down.'

'Is it still bad?' Mrs Drew had asked. 'I haven't been over that way in a long time.'

'And you haven't got a shop or a butcher's!' her sister had sniffed. 'I don't know how you manage.'

Mrs Drew had given a weak smile. 'But we do.'

Rosa took a deep breath as she came out into the yard to join Matthew, and wrapped her shawl around her shoulders. The air was crisp and sharp to her nostrils. 'We'll have snow tomorrow,' she murmured. 'A white Christmas maybe.'

Matthew nodded but didn't speak, thinking of what Mrs Gore had said about Rosa.

'It'll be strange without Maggie,' she added. 'I'll miss her, and so will your ma.'

'Mrs Gore said that somebody'll snap you up next.' They'd moved away from the barn and towards the farm gate, which they leaned on. There was a full moon, shining clear and bright in a cloudless sky which glistened with stars.

'Did she?' She turned towards him. 'Did she say who?'

'No,' he laughed. 'But you know how women are!'

'I know how some women are,' she said. 'Always wanting to marry somebody off to somebody. But Aunt Ellen's not been like that with her daughters. She's never pressed them to marry and they've found their own husbands. Nellie and Lydia, they seem happy with their young men. And as for Maggie, well she couldn't have found anybody better than Fred.'

'But what about Delia? She seems very spirited and full of herself since she went to Hornsea.'

'She does, doesn't she?' Rosa said thoughtfully. 'I hope she's all right. You know that she's moved positions and is working at an inn?'

'I didn't know.' Matthew seemed disturbed at the news. 'I don't like 'idea of that.'

Rosa felt the cold wind on her face and she

shivered. 'Let's walk a little, it's chilly standing still. Then I must go in and help.'

'No,' he insisted. 'You've done enough for today. There's always tomorrow.'

They walked down the track away from the farm and along the wide dyke which glistened in the moonlight. There were rustlings and splashing in the water as they approached. 'Water rats,' he murmured. 'Or water hens,' then added, 'tide must be high, see how it flows.'

They heard the sound of singing. 'Henry!' they both said. 'He's drunk!' Matthew muttered. 'He can't hold his ale.'

Henry came towards them, swaying on his feet. 'Hello, Matthew. *Hello*, Rosa. What you doing out here then?'

He shook a finger at Matthew. 'Jus' – jus' remember that Rosa isn't yours, so don't go thinking it jus' cos you're out in 'moonlight with her.'

'Don't be silly, Henry,' Rosa protested.

'I'm not being silly,' he blathered. 'But if I can't have you then Matthew can't either, nor Jim, old misery Jim. Do you know what he said today after our Maggie's wedding!' He put his face next to hers. 'He said – he said, that Da says he has to marry you.' He put his fists up to his face. 'And I said that I'd flatten him if he even thought it.'

He hiccuped and turned towards Matthew. 'And that goes for you as well. I'm going to marry Rosa. I gave her her first kiss when she was jus' a little lass. You remember, don't you, Rosa? And nobody else can have her. If I have to stay on this blasted land for ever, I will, as long as Rosa's here.'

'Get off to bed, Henry!' Matthew was angry but trying to contain his temper. 'Where's Jim? Has he gone on?'

Henry nodded. 'He's gone.' He belched. 'Whoops, manners! He's gone on to light a fire across at Marsh Farm. I said I'd catch him up after I'd had another little drink.'

'A few little drinks, I should think.' Matthew grimaced. 'You've had plenty anyway.'

'Finished off 'barrel.' Henry grinned, then patted his nose. 'And a few more besides, that I had hidden. *And* a drop o' brandy that I found.'

'Brandy!' Matthew said. 'Where did you find brandy?'

'Ah ha! That would be telling, wouldn't it? But somebody had hidden it away where it couldn't be found. Onny I found it,' he said gleefully. 'Long time ago. Lots of it.'

'Medicinal brandy!' Rosa said. 'It's not that bottle we keep for if anybody's ill? Henry! How could you?'

Henry shook his head and laughed. 'Not medicinal! This is real good stuff. Or was. I've drunk it now and thrown away 'evidence.'

'You've drunk a whole bottle of brandy?' Matthew exclaimed, adding in a low voice to Rosa, 'He'd better stay here tonight. He'll never get back to Marsh Farm in 'state he's in.'

'Don't worry about me, young Matthew.' Henry started to stagger away. 'I know my way across this island better than anybody, specially when I'm drunk.' He giggled. 'I've done it more times than I remember, and most times when I don't remember!'

'I'll catch you up,' Matthew called to him. 'Wait for me. I'll just say goodnight to Ma.'

They saw him put up a hand in a wave and then he turned back and came towards them. 'Give us another kiss, Rosa. Just so's that I know you care for me a bit.'

She put her hand on his face, it was cold to her touch. 'I do care for you, Henry,' she whispered. 'But I don't want to marry you. I can't, can I?' She put her lips against his and gently kissed him. 'You're my brother.'

She saw tears glisten in his eyes, but he nodded and turned away and seemed to be walking quite soberly.

'I'd better go after him.' Matthew stared after Henry. 'I'll see you inside first.'

'There's no need,' Rosa said. 'Go with him.'

He looked at her. 'I'll go and say goodnight to Ma. She looked tired I thought, too much excitement.' He seemed reluctant to leave and continued to gaze down at her.

'What is it?' she asked.

He shook his head. 'I was wondering – well, if I was in my cups and maudlin, whether you'd kiss me like you kissed Henry?'

She gave a self-conscious laugh. 'No. Of course I wouldn't.'

'Why not?' His voice was sullen.

'Because you're not Henry!'

She lay that night in Matthew's bed and thought about the three brothers. Dour Jim, never at ease with himself or anyone else, poor unhappy Henry who couldn't pluck up courage to leave the farm, and Matthew, tall and strong and sure of himself, but not of her. She looked towards the window and saw the moon's rays pouring in and thought of how the waters of the dyke had rippled and shone beneath its beams as she and Matthew had stood there. The water had been flowing quite fast, the undercurrent from the river making the waters eddy and gurgle.

She curled up against Matthew's pillow. It smelt of him, of soap and horses, of hay and grain, and she smiled to herself. No, she wouldn't have kissed Matthew in the way she had kissed Henry. She would kiss Matthew quite differently. But not yet.

CHAPTER TWELVE

Rosa fell asleep quite quickly even though the day's events muddled through her head: the wedding and how lovely Maggie had looked in her blue sprigged gown and pleated bonnet, the party afterwards, the food they had prepared and consumed, the music and the dancing, the laughter and the shouting. The shouting echoed through her dreams.

'Henry!' The calls were loud and persistent. 'Henry!' and she remembered in her dreams how sad Henry had been as she had kissed him. But then she was kissing someone else and he hadn't looked sad, but tender and romantic and he had held her close.

There was a rattle of stone upon glass. Someone was throwing pebbles up at the window! Or was she still dreaming? She sat up urgently, then climbed out of bed and looked out. The night sky was still bright and there was a hard frost riming everything with silver. Matthew was standing below in the yard, his shadow dark and long. He waved his arm for her to come and she hurriedly draped a shawl over her night shift and ran downstairs.

She had to stretch to reach the top bolt which was stiff and awkward, and she made a mental note to put some grease on it in the morning.

'What is it?' she said. 'Why aren't you in bed?'

'We can't find Henry! He wasn't with Jim when I got back to Marsh Farm. He hadn't seen him. Did he come back here?' His words were fast and breathless.

'No!' she said, confused. 'I don't think so. But I locked up before I went to bed, so he would have had to knock. Perhaps he's in the barn?'

'Yes.' Matthew swung round. 'I'll go and look.'

'Matthew?' she said fearfully. 'You don't think that something's—?' Her voice trailed away.

'I don't know.' He ran towards the barn and pulled open the door. He quickly searched. There was little in there, they'd cleared it ready for the party. Only a few bales of straw which they'd sat upon, but Henry wasn't lying there drunk and asleep as he'd hoped.

She followed him in and saw the anxiety on his face. 'Jim's still searching but I'll have to fetch more help,' he muttered. 'Will you get Da up and I'll go and wake John Gore and some of his lads.'

'Matthew—!' she began.

'He'd been drinking,' he said brusquely. 'And it's enough to freeze your ears off out here. If he's fallen and is lying somewhere – he onny had his jacket on!'

She felt sick and weak as she thought of a worse alternative. 'Yes.' Her voice sounded faint in her head. 'I'll wake your da and then get dressed and help you look.'

He didn't tell her that she needn't, that the men would manage, and that increased her fears even more and she stifled a sob as she watched him run back down the track.

Flora got up and dressed. Delia said that she would stay with their mother, who shook with anxiety. Mrs Drew's sister's husband, Arthur Johnson, also got dressed and although he didn't know the area and might well have become lost himself, he volunteered to search with Mr Drew.

They didn't need lanterns as the night was so bright with moonlight, but they put on warm mufflers and mittens and Rosa took a blanket in case they should find Henry cold or wet and in need of warmth.

'We'll spread out,' Matthew said, when he came back with John Gore and three of his farm lads. 'I've been along this track to Marsh Farm twice already and haven't seen him. We'd best fan out across 'fields to each side of 'dyke. Rosa, you come with me, Flo, you go with Jim and Arthur, you'd better stick with Da so's you don't get lost.'

Rosa was trembling, not with cold, but with fear as she stood by Matthew's side. Matthew had a stout stick with him and a rope slung around his shoulders. She put her hand to her mouth and dared not ask him why he carried them.

The water in the wide dyke that she and Matthew had walked beside earlier was much higher, as the tide reached across from the estuary and ran into the marshland and mudflats, filling the ditches, dykes, sluices and drains of the island.

'Another half-hour and 'tide'll be on the turn,' Matthew muttered. Then he raised his voice. 'Go careful, everybody, and shout if you find him. This way, Rosa.' He led her back to the farm gate and across the brick bridge which crossed the dyke, and climbed the fence to the other side. He held out his hand to help her over. She clung to his hand as she stepped down. 'You think he's fallen in, don't you?' she said in a low voice.

'I'm thinking on 'worst possibilities so that I can give him a tongue-lashing when he turns up nursing a hangover,' he said, not very convincingly, then added, 'Don't worry, Henry'll turn up all right. He always does.'

Only he didn't, and although they searched and shouted his name, it was as dawn was breaking, when the moon and stars slid away and white streaks appeared in the sky over the river and the land was white with frost, that Rosa pointed to a dark shape in a dyke, half hidden by a clump of tall reeds, and knew that they had found him.

She screamed his name. 'Henry!' The others turned at the frenzied sound which carried across the still and silent land, and as one they ran towards them. Rosa sank onto her knees at the side of the dyke and reached out unavailingly towards him.

'No!' Matthew pulled her away. 'No! I'll get him.' He edged down the side of the dyke and someone took hold of the other end of the rope whilst Matthew eased it out, for the water, though having gone down, was still deep enough to cover a man.

'Too late!' Matthew choked back a sob as he turned his brother over and pulled him towards the steep bank. 'I'm too late!'

John Gore slid down the bank and took charge. 'Ease him this way, lad. Come on now, bear up, we've got to get him out.' He took the rope from Matthew and slid it under Henry's inert form and knotted it, then signalled to the men who were standing at the top of the dyke. Mr Drew stood as if made of stone and Flo clutched his arm. Arthur Johnson knelt down and prepared to pull on the rope.

Gradually they eased Henry out of the water and up the bank and laid him on the grass. Rosa and Flo knelt weeping over him, patting his face to try to revive him, but Matthew and Jim just stood and stared in shocked disbelief.

'What'll we tell Ma?' Jim whispered, and turned to his father.

'We'll tell her,' his voice grated, 'that this is what happens when drink gets 'better of a man! A life wasted!' he censured, and turned towards home.

They all stared after him, then Matthew urged, 'Don't let him tell her! Flo! Rosa! Go after him. Get there first, before he does.'

'Aye,' Jim muttered. 'Cos owd bugger'll say it's her fault that this has happened. He'll blame anybody but himself.'

Flo and Rosa both rose to their feet and, gathering up their skirts, raced after James Drew and overtook him to break the news to Henry's mother, leaving Matthew and Jim to bring their brother home.

Mrs Drew, though ashen-faced and trembling, was stoical in her grief, at first not comprehending the disaster which had befallen them. As awareness overtook her she countermanded her husband's insistence that they pray for Henry's lost and wandering soul by her supplication to God that He should give them strength to understand that His need for Henry's life was stronger than theirs.

Messages were sent and Maggie came back to the home which she had left so full of happiness and was returning to in such grief and sorrow. Flo stayed and the twins came back, but Delia escaped to Hornsea as fast as she could, unable to cope with the trauma of death, with the weeping and recriminations.

Matthew blamed himself for not following Henry more swiftly, and his conscience troubled him for being angry with him over Rosa. 'I should have known it was only the drink talking,' he muttered, when Rosa, looking for him to come for his supper, found him sitting morosely in the barn where previously there had been such jollity.

'It wasn't only the drink,' she said quietly. 'I told you before that he had asked me to go away with him. He was very unhappy, Matthew, yet he wouldn't leave on his own. If anyone should have a conscience it should be me.'

'No.' He rose to his feet and took hold of her hand. 'He wouldn't have made you happy, Rosa.'

'No, he wouldn't,' she agreed. 'Besides, I can't leave Sunk Island.'

'Why not?' he asked curiously.

'I don't know,' she whispered. 'I only know that I can't.'

Christmas came and went without celebration. It was a long cold hard winter, the roads and tracks in and out of Sunk Island were impassable, the rainwater in the tanks froze and had to be smashed open each day, and the hens, ducks and geese were kept under cover in the shelter of the barns. March was wet and the dykes were full and overflowing and some of the banks broke under the pressure of water. The atmosphere in the house was strained and Mr Drew found fault with everyone and everything, and not until spring, when new lambs were born and birds began building their nests, and coltsfoot and cowslips started to appear on the banks, did their spirits rise once more.

'We must give thanks for a new beginning,' Ellen Drew said one morning at breakfast. 'It is what Henry would have wanted.'

Rosa nodded in agreement. Henry did want a new beginning, but had been afraid to take it. Matthew, who had been out since early morning attending a difficult lambing, sat down at the table and said, 'We're a man short, Da. We could do with some help.'

'We'll manage,' his father muttered. 'We've finished ploughing and sowing, we'll be all right until June.'

'But we couldn't have managed without John Gore's men giving us a hand,' Matthew argued.

'We've a lot of acreage to cover now that 'land at Marsh Farm is ready.'

'We'll manage, I said,' his father growled. 'I make 'decisions about labour.'

Matthew's face flushed. 'We'd do better to employ somebody on a permanent basis,' he persisted, 'instead of casual labour. Jim doesn't live at Marsh Farm, we should get a family man to live in, somebody with a wife who can help at harvest—'

'I said no!' his father bellowed. 'I'll have nobody who isn't family working that land.' He stopped abruptly, as if he had said too much. 'I'll have nothing more said about it.' He got up from the table and walked to the door, then turned to address his wife, ignoring Matthew, whose face worked in anger, and Rosa and Jim, who sat silently looking down at their breakfast plates.

'I'm going into Hull first thing tomorrow morning, Mrs Drew,' he stated. 'I'll be away a day or two.' He glanced towards Matthew and Jim. 'I'm going to find another grain merchant. I'm not happy with 'one we've got.'

When he'd gone out of the room, Jim said in a low voice, 'There's nowt wrong with 'merchant we use! What's up wi' him?'

'Hush, Jim,' his mother said quietly. Her face was pale after the acrimonious exchange between Matthew and his father. She swallowed and looked down, then folded her hands together as if in prayer and closed her eyes for a moment. 'Your father has his reasons,' she murmured. 'It's not for us to question him.'

Matthew got up from the table. 'Not for us

to question him? I'm sorry, Ma, but if we can't question him, who can?' He was angry and spoke quickly. 'This farm is our livelihood, mine and Jim's. We're no longer children who must be told what to do and when!'

'*Fathers, provoke not your children to anger, lest they be discouraged,*' Jim recited glumly. 'I once read that in 'bible after Da had given me a beating for summat. He made me go upstairs and read 'bible and it opened on that page. I never forgot it.'

His mother looked distressed. 'Your father has a lot of worries,' she began.

'And we could take some of them from his shoulders,' Matthew maintained.

Jim shook his head. 'Onny some of 'em.' His expression became impassive and defeated. 'There's some worries we all have to live with for 'rest of our lives. There's nowt nor nobody can help us wi' some o' them.'

'Whatever do you mean, Jim?' Rosa stared across at him and Mrs Drew put her hands to her mouth as if she had witnessed a revelation, but Jim said nothing more and rose from the table, pushed past Matthew and stumbled through the door.

CHAPTER THIRTEEN

James Drew rose at four thirty the next morning, dressed in his grey breeches, black leather boots and black jacket, and taking his stovepipe hat off the chest in the corner of the bedroom, crept quietly downstairs.

Ellen Drew, wide awake for some hours with the pain in her back, watched him from half-closed eyes, ready to feign sleep in an instant should her husband turn towards her. But he didn't, so intent was he on dressing and going downstairs. He hastily ate the bread and curd cheese which had been left for him on the kitchen table, and throwing his heavy cape over his shoulders stole out of the house towards the stable, saddled his sturdy mare and started his journey.

Rosa heard him, as did Matthew, but both lay in their bedrooms, one on either side of the narrow corridor at the top of the stairs, and waited until they heard the bolt on the door being drawn back. Rosa then turned over, no need yet to get up, but Matthew rose from his bed and pulling on a shirt and breeches padded downstairs. From the kitchen window he watched his father mount his horse and ride away.

James Drew crossed his land and turned on to the rough track which led to the new turnpiked road to Ottringham. This new road cut the journey into the town of Hull by at least an hour, but it would still be mid-morning before he arrived.

He was churned up with self-reproach and condemnation, guilt and contrition, yet he urged his horse on into a canter as his mind dwelt lustily and wantonly on matters which had to be resolved before he descended into madness. He prayed aloud for help to overcome his weakness, yet his urges grew stronger as he rode, and he finally absolved and discharged the demons which he fought and let them capture him in fulsome and carnal chains.

Sweat was pouring from him as he crossed the old bridge into Hull and he turned into the High Street and trotted down to the George Inn, where he gave his lathered horse to a stable lad, went inside the inn and ordered a glass of ale and a slice of beef.

'Ridden far?' the landlord asked as he drew his ale.

'Holderness.' He replied briefly, for to give the name of Sunk Island always drew curiosity, and sometimes misplaced humour when men in their cups would stare down at his boots and ask if his feet were webbed.

'Ah!' The landlord's interest waned. Holderness wasn't a place he knew, although he had heard of the isolated countryside which grew good corn. 'You'll want a room then?' he asked. 'You won't be going back tonight?'

'That's right.' James Drew was relieved that he didn't have to make the request himself. He felt his guilt always showed when asking for accommodation. 'Two nights,' he said briskly. 'Your best room. I've a deal of business to attend to.'

The landlord nodded. He had a good memory for faces and he remembered this man from a previous time. The countrymen stood out amongst the seamen and foreigners who frequented his inn. They were ill at ease, unused to being away from their quiet lands and plunged into the industrial hustle and bustle of town life. He remembered that his man had barely used his room, he'd staggered in late at night, not drunk with ale, but definitely inebriated and satiated with something heady.

'A single room, sir?'

'What? Oh! Yes! But a double bed if you please.'

'I'll have to charge extra.' The landlord looked solemnly at him.

'It doesn't matter,' he replied.

The landlord grinned. 'Quite right, sir. I allus say there's nothing like a bit o' comfort when you're away from home.'

James Drew didn't answer this remark but after inspecting the room gave the landlord a deposit, asked him to be sure that the fire was kept in and the bed well aired, and stepped out into the High Street. He walked past the Corn Exchange and into the wide thoroughfare of

Lowgate. He hurried through shabby streets and past crowded courts, keeping his head averted from the women lounging in inn doorways, and on towards Leadenhall Square. He was in pursuit, not of a grain merchant, but of a different establishment where he knew, from previous visits, that he would be made more than welcome.

It was a square of ill repute. He had, on the first occasion, followed a young woman who had smiled at him and provocatively lifted her skirts to show her ankles. Like a man sleepwalking he had followed her, down narrow streets and alleyways until he was completely disorientated and quite lost. Then the girl had entered an alley and looked back at him over her shoulder. 'I'm lost,' he said. 'Can you help me to find my way?'

'Course I can,' she'd said. Her voice was low and guttural. 'Come down here wi' me and I'll put you right.'

He had followed her down the alley, and around the corner she had leaned against the wall and lifted her skirts revealing grimy naked legs and a young rounded body, and the man he thought he was had disappeared, leaving behind what he now knew to be his real self, a debauched and sinful monster in human shape.

The girl had finally cried out and tried to push him away but a violent lust was up and wouldn't be satisfied, and not until they were disturbed by others coming down the alley had he desisted. 'That'll cost you,' the girl had panted. 'You've had more than my regulars have.'

Breathing heavily he had turned out his

pocketbook and given her what she asked. 'Can I see you again?' he'd pleaded.

She'd agreed, for a price. 'But not here,' she'd said slyly. 'If you carry on like that, I want a bed to lie on.'

Over the years she had been replaced by other women, each giving more than the last, and he expecting more each time; he had also on occasions suffered infections from these women, which dulled his ardour and caused him pain. He silently vowed he would resist temptation, but his lascivious nature did not remain dampened for long and at last he found a brothel with 'clean' women, where he could indulge himself all day and sometimes all night, staggering back to his hostelry debauched and dissipated. His conscience only rose up in admonishment as he rode home to his patient wife, who, he was sure, if she knew, would forgive him his lustful sins as she forgave him all of his others.

He knocked on the door of the house in the corner of the square and a girl opened it. 'Hello, Mr Brown,' she smiled. 'Long time since we last saw you!'

He had given that name on his first visit, but had discovered subsequently that all the customers were given the same name. What he didn't know was that the ladies of the establishment had their own way of knowing who was who. Consequently he was Mr Country Brown; there was Mr Beverley Brown, Mr Hessle Brown, Mr Magistrate Brown, Mr Black Brown and Mr Toff Brown. Others were given names according to their physical attributes, Mr Fat Belly Brown,

Mr Big Brown and Mr Nothing Much Brown. Each Mr Brown was convinced that he was anonymous and incognito.

'So pleased to see you again.' Madame Emerald floated towards him. She had thick red hair and was dressed in diaphanous blue which revealed her ample bosom. Around her neck she wore a huge emerald on a gold chain and she smelt of heavy exotic spice.

'I have someone here who would suit you perfectly, Mr Brown,' she whispered. 'She has such stamina!' She gave him a knowing smile and clutched his arm with strong fingers. 'Not quite as unquenchable as you,' she purred. 'But if she tires, don't worry, there are others who can take her place.'

He felt powerful and mighty at her words, like Hercules or Atlas, and he couldn't wait to climb the stairs, to fecundate and impregnate his chosen partner with his virility, and he closed his mind to the bible's disapproval of wasteful seed and consigned to oblivion the truth that these women were there only for his pleasure and not conception.

It was dusk as he left the house with the promise that he would return the next day. His legs were weak and his back ached and he cursed his aging body. I'll have supper and an early night, he promised himself, and perhaps I won't go back tomorrow, but will go home, calling first at the Corn Exchange to chat with some of the merchants.

By thinking on this, he almost convinced himself that that was the reason he had come to the town, as he had told his family, and not just for his bodily pleasures. But his inflamed senses knew that his needs were not yet satisfied and that he would return to the women in the house who had pleasured and tormented him, and who in turn had succumbed to his gross and rampant demands.

He had almost reached the High Street when he saw two men walking towards him. There was something about their swagger and their laughter that struck him as familiar, but before he could turn a corner away from them they had seen him, and he was confronted by two people he had hoped never to meet again.

'Mr Drew!' said the older one. 'How grand to see you again. Just look who's here, John! Who would have expected it, here in the middle of this fine town?'

James Drew nodded his greetings and reluctantly took the proffered handshakes of Seamus Byrne and his brother John.

'So what brings you to town, Mr Drew?' Seamus asked. 'A spot of business?'

'A meeting at 'Corn Exchange,' Drew said quickly. 'I'm thinking of changing my merchant.'

'Ah!' Seamus Byrne touched the side of his nose. 'Legitimate business, eh?'

'Of course,' Drew replied huffily. 'Of course legitimate.'

'Still dealing out of Stone Creek?' the younger man asked quietly. 'Much shipping, is there?' His face was pallid as if he had not seen much sun.

James Drew shuffled his feet. 'Yes, more now that Patrington Haven is silting up.'

'Patrington Haven is silting up?' John Byrne queried. 'And it was such a busy haven when I was a young fellow.' He stared at James Drew, not taking his eyes from his face. 'That's a few years ago, of course.'

'Eighteen at least.' His brother glanced at him. 'Eighteen since you were last in Holderness, John.'

'How is your son – Jim, isn't it?' John Byrne continued. 'We were about the same age if I remember. We had some good larks together, him and me, and—'

'He's all right,' Drew interrupted. 'We're busy on 'farm. No time for larks now.'

'I met your other son, Henry, a few years back,' Seamus said casually. 'I was working on the river-bank and saw him with a little black-haired colleen.' He rubbed his hand over his beard. 'Bonny child she was, put me in mind of somebody but I can't think who!'

'Henry's dead,' James Drew muttered. 'Drowned just afore Christmas. I must go,' he pronounced. 'I have things to do.'

Seamus expressed his shock and gave his condolences. 'He was a fine-looking fellow. You won't remember Henry, John.' He turned to his brother. 'And neither did he remember me, for he was only a little lad in school when I first saw him. But of course we remember Jim. He was a great help to you, wasn't he, Mr Drew? Your right-hand man wouldn't you say, just as John was to me.'

Drew agreed that he was and again tried for departure, but Seamus Byrne delayed him by saying, 'Is there any chance of doing business again, Mr Drew? We know of a good ship with an English master.'

'No, I don't think so.' Drew looked warily from one brother to another. 'I only deal in corn.'

'That's a pity, Mr Drew,' John Byrne said softly. 'We'd dearly like to make up for our losses.'

'I can't help you, I'm afraid. It was unfortunate, but we all lost money when—'

'When our friend disappeared?' Seamus asked. 'And his ship was confiscated with John and me on board.'

'It was nothing to do with me,' Drew said hastily. 'He set off to warn you, but he just disappeared into thin air. Nobody saw him again. Not his wife. Nobody.'

'And how is his pretty wife?' John asked with a sneer in his voice. 'Playing the grieving widow, or did she join Carlos in Spain, like he always said she would?'

'She's dead,' Drew said hoarsely. 'She waited years for him to come back.' His voice shook. 'Her mind went in the end. She drowned herself off Spurn peninsula some years ago.'

Seamus crossed himself, but his brother still glowered at James Drew and scoffed, 'But they never found him? How do we know that he didn't escape across to Holland on another ship?'

'We don't know,' muttered James Drew, aware that he was sinking further into a deep pit of deception. 'There were plenty of ships going out from Stone Creek and Patrington Haven, foreign ships too. He could have hidden on board.'

'I'd have trusted him with my life,' Seamus said softly.

'I'd trust nobody.' His brother's voice was harsh. 'I've met enough villains in my life to know that.'

'Such a young man to be so bitter, isn't he, Mr Drew?' Seamus locked his gaze into Drew's. 'Would your own son be so bitter if he had had a life of adversity?'

James Drew thought of Jim, so dour and life-less, and knew that he would be so.

'You see, John was arrested as I was when the ship was taken by the Customs. I managed to escape and live a life on the run. But John here has spent most of the last eighteen years in and out of English jails. Not a good place to be if you're an Irishman, Mr Drew. You take the blame for everything that goes wrong and not a man to speak up for you.'

'I'm sorry. I must go,' Drew said again. 'I hope things go better for you in 'future.'

'You may see us again, Mr Drew.' Seamus gave a half-smile which made Drew shudder. 'There's always work for an Irishman on Sunk Island. Give us a pickaxe or a spade and we're happy. They're still draining and embanking I expect?'

'Yes,' Drew said reluctantly. 'Yes, of course.'

'Then we look forward to meeting again soon,' Seamus once more put out his hand to shake it. 'May God go with you.'

'And the Devil be not far behind.' John Byrne had no smile on his face as he muttered the words and turned away.

'A spot of business, eh, John!' Seamus said as they walked down the street.

'He was lying. He was coming from the wrong direction if he'd been to the Corn Exchange,' his brother replied sourly. 'The Corn Exchange is in the High Street. I don't trust the man.'

'Ah! He's had an assignation!' Seamus laughed. 'Did you not see the flush on his face? He's been treating some little wench to a few favours.'

'And using our money!'

'Or a dead man's?'

'We don't know that,' John Byrne griped. 'Why should he be dead? More likely he escaped when he heard the Customs were looking for him.' He clenched and cracked his knuckles. 'I'll find out,' he said grimly. 'One way or another, I'll find out what happened to him. 'Tis a pity his wife is dead.'

'Sure it is,' Seamus agreed. 'And that's why I think he's dead too. If ever a man was besotted with a woman, he was. If he'd gone away he'd have taken her with him.'

'There's still the daughter,' John Byrne murmured. 'Maybe we'll have a little talk with her.'

'She wasn't born when he disappeared,' Seamus objected. 'She'll know nothing!'

His brother gave a thin smile which creased his mouth but his eyes were cold. 'We'll talk to her all the same.'

CHAPTER FOURTEEN

Matthew was out in the fields when he saw the trap with Maggie and Fred approaching. The land was so flat and the roads so long that it wasn't possible for anyone to arrive without them being seen from a great distance.

He waved and walked towards them. 'No work to do, Fred?' he joked. 'Taking 'day off?'

'Just that.' Fred grinned. 'What's 'use of having a fine wife and not enjoying her company? Besides, she wanted to see her ma.'

'How is she, Matthew?' Maggie asked anxiously. 'She's been on my mind for a week or two.'

'She's all right,' Matthew assured her. 'She doesn't complain anyway. Da's gone into Hull,' he added. 'Says he wants a new grain merchant.'

'Why? What's wrong with 'one we've got?'

Matthew shrugged. 'He's just taken it into his head to go, that's all. You know how he is. Can't budge him once he's made his mind up. He went off in a hurry anyway, first thing this morning.' He moved off. 'I'll be up for my dinner afore long. Put 'kettle on when you get home,' he called.

'Is Rosa home?' Maggie called back.

'Aye, she is. She's singing.' He laughed. 'And playing her squeeze box.'

Rosa had stoked up the fire, made porridge for Matthew's breakfast and for Jim when he arrived, and taken Mrs Drew her breakfast in bed. Before she sat down for her own breakfast she ran upstairs again and brought down the old squeeze box. She put her thumbs through the leather loops at each side and squeezed it in and out. 'I wish I knew how to play it,' she'd murmured.

'Well, just practise with it,' Matthew had suggested. 'Then maybe you'll get 'hang of it. Onny do it after I've gone!' he added jokingly.

He'd looked at her from across the table. We're alone and she doesn't think of me any differently from the way she does of Jim or did of Henry, he thought. Yet I never think of her as my sister, even though we have lived in the same house for over ten years. He watched the way her dark lashes touched her cheekbones as she looked down, the way her mouth softly smiled as she concentrated on finding a note on the instrument. It's hopeless, he reflected dismally. She told Da that she couldn't marry any one of us, as she thought of us as her brothers.

She'd looked up and given him a brilliant smile as she found a right note, then gave a small frown. 'What is it? You look sad!'

'It's nowt,' he sighed and got up from the table.

She touched his bare forearm and it was as if he had been given a powerful magnetic shock.

For a moment neither of them spoke, then she said huskily, 'It's 'first time there's been any kind of music since Maggie's wedding. You're thinking of Henry, aren't you?' she said. 'I'm sorry.'

'Don't be sorry,' he'd said quietly. 'Henry wouldn't want us to mope and he liked a bit of music anyway.' As he went out of the door, he said, 'I'll see you at dinner time,' and had reflected that Henry was the last person on his mind and the only one who filled his thoughts day after day, hour after hour, was Rosa herself.

'I'll show you how to play it.' Fred took the squeeze box from the side table after they had had their midday meal. Mrs Drew had joined them and was very cheerful now that Maggie had come, and wanted to know all that was happening in the town of Hedon.

'Don't tell Da, will you, Ma? But Fred and me went to a dance.' Maggie's face lit up with delight. 'Fred bought me a new dress, pale grey muslin with sprigs of flowers on it. Mrs Winter, who lives just a few houses down from us, made it up for me.'

Mrs Drew gave a deep sigh. 'Oh how lovely, Maggie! And where did you buy 'material? Not in Hedon?'

Maggie leaned forward towards her mother. 'No. In Hull! I went with Mrs Winter by carrier and we did some shopping, and she helped me choose 'fabric, and then we caught 'carrier back.' Maggie's face was bright as she described her shopping trip and her mother exclaimed on her exciting life since she had married Fred.

'Maggie!' Fred was bent over the instrument

and showing Rosa how to finger it. 'It don't matter whether your fayther knows or not about us going to a dance. You're my wife now and if we want to dance, or sing in 'market square we can do! We don't have to ask anybody's permission.'

He looked across at her and smiled, yet he was perfectly serious.

'I know,' she said fervently. 'It's just that—'

'Old habits,' Rosa murmured. 'Maggie can't help it, Fred. She's always been an obedient daughter.'

Fred laughed aloud. 'Not like you, eh, Rosa? You wouldn't be playing this forbidden instrument if you were obedient, would you?'

'It's different for me,' she objected. 'I'm not Mr Drew's daughter.'

'Yet you wouldn't disobey Ma, would you?' Matthew interrupted.

Rosa shook her head and turned to smile at Mrs Drew, who was watching her with a calm expression on her face. 'No, but then Aunt Ellen has been like a mother to me. She probably understands me better than my own mother did,' she added. 'And she doesn't hold me back but gives me my freedom.'

Mrs Drew smiled gently. 'You would have flown from us long ago, Rosa, if I hadn't. You're like a wild bird that flies in for shelter and food.'

Rosa came across the room and bent and kissed her cheek. 'And love,' she whispered, so that no-one else could hear. 'I come for that too.'

Mrs Drew stroked Rosa's face with her thin

fingers. 'I know,' she said softly. 'I know. That's why I wanted you here.'

'We're going into Hull next week,' Fred announced. 'I'm going to see a lawyer. Now that I'm a married man,' he winked at Maggie, 'I've got to see my wife's provided for if owt happens to me.'

'There's a lawyer in Hedon that Da uses,' Matthew said. 'You don't need to go into Hull.'

'Aye, but this one in Hull, Somerville, he looked after my affairs when I was working away, so I'll use him again. So,' he looked around him, 'if there's owt anybody wants while we're there?'

Rosa put her fingers to her mouth and contemplated. 'Is he a learned man, this Somerville? I mean – would he know languages, do you think?'

Fred considered. 'Don't know. Mebbe. Aye.' He shook a finger. 'He mebbe does when I think about it. He's got a bit of Latin up on a wall in his room at any rate. I noticed it last time I was there. Why?'

Rosa looked enquiringly at Matthew and wondered if he remembered the foreign papers they had found in her box. He frowned for a moment as he caught her eye, then his face cleared and he nodded. 'Yes,' he said. 'Why not!'

'I've got some foreign papers in my box up in the loft,' she said, in answer to Fred. 'I don't know what they are.' She looked towards the door as it opened and Jim came in. He was wet and muddy and late for his dinner. 'Jim!' she said. 'We'd given you up. I've kept your dinner hot.'

'No hurry.' He leant against the back of a chair and nodded towards his sister and Fred. 'I need to get this muck off me first.'

Rosa turned again to Fred. 'I think they might have belonged to my father. His name was on them anyway.'

Jim straightened up. 'Your da? His name on what?' His eyes flashed piercingly between Rosa and Fred.

Rosa blinked and thought what an odd question when Jim had only caught the tail end of a conversation.

'Some papers I found,' she said briefly. 'They had my father's name on them.'

'Oh!' Jim ran his hand over his whiskery chin. 'I see. I'll just go and get cleaned up,' he muttered, and went out of the room.

'What's 'matter with him?' Maggie began. 'He allus looks as if he's just lost a shilling!'

'Shall we bring the chest down from 'loft and put it in your room?' Matthew interrupted to ask Rosa. 'Seeing as Fred and Jim are both here.'

Rosa looked at him, remembering that they were going to ask Henry to help them bring it down, and merely nodded as she realized that Matthew's thoughts were elsewhere and not on his dead brother.

'By heck, but it's heavy. What's in it?' Jim stood halfway up the ladder with his back to the trap door whilst Matthew eased it down from the loft space onto Jim's back, with Fred waiting with arms at the ready to balance it and take some of the weight.

'Only linen and china,' Rosa said from the bottom of the ladder. 'My gran packed it, she said she'd put in things I might need one day.'

Jim grunted. 'She put in 'stone sink by 'weight of it, and her smoothing iron.'

'We'll shift it into your room, Rosa,' Matthew said, once it was down, 'then you can look for your papers again.'

She smiled her thanks. 'I know where they are.' She had been up into the loft several times on her own, when the men had been out on the farm and Mrs Drew asleep. She had fetched a ladder from outside and climbed up, pushing the heavy trap door open, and had sat by the side of the chest with a lighted candle in her hand, fingering the linen or holding the sheets of parchment with the foreign lettering up to the candle flame, trying to decipher what the words meant. Then when she had finished she had always carefully tucked them away again under the folds of linen, so that she would know where to find them the next time.

She thanked the men for their efforts and closed her bedroom door to take the papers from the chest in private, and wondered why Jim was shuffling his feet and hovering around when she'd said she would only be a minute.

'I'll take care of 'em,' Fred said, when she gave them to him. 'They look official.' He glanced through them and Jim came to peer over his shoulder. 'Might be a last Will and Testament like I'm going to do.'

'That's what we thought, didn't we, Matthew?'

Rosa said vaguely, wondering if she was doing the right thing by letting them go.

'Why, have you seen 'em afore, Matthew?' Jim asked and when Matthew said that he had, commented, 'You never said owt!'

'Why should I?' Matthew rebuked sharply. 'They're not mine to discuss. They belong to Rosa.'

Jim lowered his eyes. 'I didn't mean owt. I just wondered why they'd not been mentioned afore, that's all. Squeeze box was brought down and talked about.'

'I forgot about them, Jim.' Rosa suddenly felt sorry for him. He seemed such an abject forlorn figure. 'We were going to bring 'chest down and then, what with Maggie getting married and Henry—' she faltered. 'It didn't seem so important.'

'Ah!' Jim turned away. 'Da's not seen 'em, I suppose?'

She stared at him in surprise. 'Why no. Of course not! No-one has, not until today.'

'Ah!' he said again and stood pondering, one hand on the doorknob. 'Not worth mentioning really,' he mumbled. 'He wouldn't be interested. Not in some old papers.'

Rosa stared at him. What was he trying to say? She glanced enquiringly at Mrs Drew, who in turn was watching Jim with such a look of grief etched on her face that it was as if tears were not far away.

'I hadn't thought of mentioning them, Jim,' Rosa said. 'As you say, your da wouldn't be interested.'

Jim went out of the room, muttering something about seeing to the horses, and there was a sudden potent silence.

'He's a funny fellow, that brother of mine,' Maggie declared. 'I never could make him out. Except when I was very young,' she added. 'When I was just a bairn. He used to look after me then, didn't he, Ma? It was after he left school that he changed.'

Mrs Drew gave a deep deep sigh. 'Yes,' she said softly. 'When he started work with your father and when the Irish were here working on 'embankments and digging dykes and drains and laying sluices. It was a period of great change on Sunk Island.' She looked at Rosa. 'It was during 'time when your ma met your father and brought him here to meet Mr Drew.'

'To meet Da?' Maggie exclaimed. 'Why ever would she want to do that? Da is hardly welcoming to strangers.'

Her mother suddenly became nervous and confused. 'I have often wondered that myself,' she said. 'But she did. I remember distinctly, when I went to answer 'door as she knocked. "Mrs Drew," she said. "This is Mr Carlos from Spain." Her eyes were shining like stars and I could see that she was very taken with him by 'way she looked at him. "I've brought him to see Mr Drew." That's what she said.'

Mrs Drew looked around at them all. At Maggie sitting with Fred, at Rosa and Matthew. 'It was later that Jim became moody.' She sighed again and her fingers played distractedly around her mouth. 'I think his father worked him too hard. He forgot that he was just a boy and he gave him a man's responsibilities.' Then she lowered her head as if in contrition that she had unwittingly criticized her husband.

Fred broke the tension. 'Come on then, Rosa, I'll play this old squeeze box and you can give us a dance before Maggie and me make tracks for home.'

She gave him a swift smile and asked him to wait a moment, and dashing out of the room returned a few moments later with her thick plait unbraided, and her mother's silk shawl which she draped not around her shoulders but around her waist, so that as she swayed to the rhythm the fringes around the edge of the shawl rustled and whispered against her skirt.

'Make her some castanets, Matthew,' Fred laughed as he urged a tune out of the old music box. 'She'll look like a proper Spanish dancer then.'

Rosa closed her eyes and clicked her fingers high above her head and her black hair drifted around her shoulders, and Matthew, watching her, knew that he had lost her; that she was gone elsewhere, to her father's mythical castle in Spain, to a dreamland that was warm and colourful, full of flowers and music and happy laughing people who sang and danced and kissed.

CHAPTER FIFTEEN

James Drew prayed all the long way home. He prayed for forgiveness and for salvation. He also prayed most fervently that he would never see the two Irish brothers again, particularly the younger one.

He had almost forgotten the existence of John Byrne over the years, and only when Henry had told him that he had met Seamus, on the day when Rosa had played truant from school, had he even thought of them. He had the ability to forget conveniently anything that was abhorrent to him, able even to convince himself that any wrongdoing on his part was not his fault at all but due to the negligence of others.

For a month after his visit to Hull he was in good humour, the weather was fine, the drilling and sowing were finished and he and Jim and Matthew went out rook shooting. Though there were few trees on Sunk Island, the rooks flew in daily from Holderness to peck and pull at the burgeoning growth of corn. On the salt marsh a colony of black-headed gulls were breeding, and cormorants and herons were a frequent sight flying across the land.

Along the divisions of farmland, the few hawthorn hedges were smothered with creamy white blossom which filled the air with its sweet scent and provided shelter for hedge sparrows, wrens and fieldmice. Bees buzzed in the blossom and butterflies, peacock, tortoiseshell and white, opened their wings and fluttered on the warm air.

Early one morning after he had eaten his breakfast, Drew stood at the farm door looking out at the greening acreage, listening to the bleat of lambs and the incessant call of a cuckoo. There was a feeling of renewal, of reanimation, and he gave a silent prayer of thanks that they had survived the harsh winter.

He had lost a son, it was true, but he considered grimly that Henry wouldn't have died if he hadn't been drinking and lost his way. They had also lost a cow which had strayed and fallen into a dyke, but there had been no flooding, most of the dykes had held and the roofs of the house and barns were secure. But even as he contemplated the coming summer, he felt the stirring of his own blood, a physical energy and agitation which was setting him on fire.

He went back inside and climbed the stairs to the bedroom he shared with his wife, opened the door and stared down at her. 'Ellen,' he murmured. She didn't stir, her face was white and her lips were bloodless and he knew that she was in pain. 'Ellen!'

She opened her eyes and gazed at him. 'What

is it?' She attempted to rise but the effort was too much and she fell back against her pillow. 'Is there some trouble?'

He sat on the side of the bed. 'No. No trouble.' He stared out towards the window. He could see the gleam of brown river beyond the pasture-land. 'I might have to go into Hull again. I – I need to get this business of 'corn merchant sorted out.'

'Yes.' She gazed at him, her pale eyes expressionless. 'If you must.'

'I thought I might go today. Lads can manage without me for a couple o' days.'

She didn't answer but continued to gaze at him.

'They're both out now. Will you tell them when they come back at dinner time? Or tell Rosa to tell them. Where is she anyway? She's not in 'kitchen or in 'yard.'

His wife shook her head. 'I don't know. Maybe helping with 'milking or collecting eggs.' Her voice was low, as if it was an effort to speak.

'Are you very sick?' he said suddenly, turning towards her. 'Shall I send for 'doctor?'

'No. Not yet,' she breathed. 'I can manage for a bit.'

'All right.' He stood up and looked down at her. 'If you're sure? I don't mind 'expense.'

She shook her head again and he felt a guilty sense of relief that he didn't have to make a diversion to Patrington to call the doctor. He quickly changed his clothes into something suitable for the ride and to wear in town and hurried downstairs. His breathing was rapid and he stumbled as he went out of the door.

Rosa came across the yard towards the house. She was carrying a basket of eggs. 'Going somewhere, Mr Drew?'

'Aye.' His voice was terse and defiant. It was nothing to do with her where he was going. 'You'd better get inside,' he said. 'Mrs Drew isn't well.'

'I know that,' she said boldly. 'She needs the doctor.'

'She can have one,' he said angrily. 'As soon as I get back I'll send for him.'

'It might be too late,' she muttered and turning towards the door she went through it and closed it behind her.

She put the basket down beside the sink and pumped in some water, then carefully laid the eggs into it to wash them. She raised her eyes to the ceiling as she heard a sound and listened intently. She ran swiftly upstairs, holding up her skirt hem so that she didn't fall, and into Mrs Drew's bedroom.

'Are you all right, Aunt Ellen? I thought I heard—'

Mrs Drew was sitting up but with her head bent low over the bed and her hands clasped together. She looked up and Rosa saw the pain in her face and saw too that she had been weeping. 'Are you hurting?' she said anxiously. 'Shall I send Matthew for 'doctor?'

'No, my dear,' she said softly. 'The doctor can do nothing for 'kind of affliction that I've got, and there's a sickness in my heart that he can't cure.'

177

Rosa sat on the bed and took hold of her hand. 'Shall I send for Maggie to come? Or Flo? They can be spared I'm sure and they would cheer you up.'

'No, don't bother them. They have enough to do.' Mrs Drew attempted a smile. 'I'm quite happy with your company, but – but I would like to talk to 'parson. I haven't been to church in a long time and there's something I'd like to discuss with him.'

Rosa went in search of Matthew or Jim and found Matthew saddling up a horse in order to visit John Gore. 'Can you go on to Patrington after you've been there?' she asked. 'Your ma wants to talk to the vicar.'

Matthew's face changed colour. 'She's not worse, is she?'

'I'm not sure,' she admitted. 'She's been crying, but doesn't want 'doctor to come.'

He came and stood in front of her. 'But do *you* think 'doctor is needed?'

'Yes,' she said, 'I do, but your da said he would send for him when he gets back.'

'Gets back? What do you mean? Where's he gone?'

'He didn't say, but he was dressed 'same as he was when he went into Hull last month.'

Matthew lashed his whip in the air with a sudden spurt of anger. 'Damn and blast him! What on earth is he doing?'

Rosa remained silent for a moment, then said, 'When you're in Patrington seeing 'vicar, will you call on Flo? See if she can come over for a day. Gran won't mind.'

He said that he would and, digging his heels into the horse's flanks, rode off to Patrington to ask the vicar to call.

The incumbent of the church on Sunk Island also served the parish of Patrington and had made the journey on horseback across the marshes for many years. It was no hardship for him therefore to saddle up immediately and set off to visit one of his most faithful parishioners.

'Dear lady,' he said, when he arrived that same afternoon and was shown upstairs, 'I should have called before!'

'Not at all.' She smiled, for she was fond of this gentle man. 'I know how busy you are and I know that I was in your thoughts.'

'Indeed you always are, my dear. You are one of my most steadfast parishioners, as is Mr Drew. Is he not at home today?'

'He has had to go into Hull, on private business,' she said softly, 'and it is of my husband that I wish to speak.'

She folded her hands together and murmured, 'I am dying, Mr Metcalf,' and she raised her hand to grasp his as he exclaimed in dismay. 'But I don't wish to speak of myself. Not yet at any rate, though your prayers will be welcome when 'time comes.'

The vicar put his hands together and closed his eyes.

'I want you to pray for Mr Drew,' she said quietly. 'He is in great need of salvation. His soul is in peril and I am afraid that he will descend into Hell without the power of prayer.'

The vicar opened his eyes and gazed at her in

astonishment. 'Dear lady!' he said. 'He is a most devout man. A regular worshipper at church!'

'He is a hypocrite,' she whispered, 'and he must not be allowed to influence others. He pays lip devotion only and you must relieve him of his duties as churchwarden. Please,' she said earnestly. 'I beg you, he has committed many wrongs. Pray for him now before it's too late. I pray for him every day, but I'm getting weaker and I'm afraid that when I'm gone he will be past redemption.'

Her eyes filled with tears. 'I once had great love for him, even though I knew he was a sinner. Now I have to make my own peace with God, to ask forgiveness for my sin of overlooking my husband's weaknesses.'

'You cannot take on the burden of another's sins,' he urged. 'Your husband must take the responsibility of exculpating them himself.'

'You won't tell him that I have discussed this with you?' she begged. 'He will deny everything.'

'Then if he has sinned so grievously as you say, and yet denies everything, he is lost,' he murmured, and knelt at the side of the bed. 'But we will pray together now that he sees the error of his ways, and for the mercy of his soul.'

Flo came later that evening and said that Mrs Jennings insisted that she should stay for a day or two. 'She said you must visit her, Rosa, she hasn't seen you for weeks.'

'I know,' Rosa said. In spite of her telling Matthew that there would be changes after Maggie had gone and that she wouldn't be at everyone's beck and call, she found that she had so little time to spare now that Mrs Drew was ill that the days just flew by. She hadn't been to the riverbank or walked along the side of the dykes to watch for frogs and newts, nor had she seen her favourite bird, the heron, for weeks, and her grandmother must feel sorely neglected without a visit from her, she thought.

'Go on, go out for some fresh air. Take a walk. I know that's what you like to do,' Flo urged.

Rosa fetched her shawl and said that she wouldn't be long.

'No hurry. I'll see to Ma and to supper. It's a lovely evening. Make 'most of it.'

Rosa saw Matthew and Jim coming towards her. 'Flo's here,' she called. 'She's seeing to supper, but not yet. You'll have to wait till she's had a chat with your ma.'

'Is Da coming back tonight?' Jim asked. 'Do you know where he's gone?'

'No, I told Matthew he was dressed as if he was going to Hull. Perhaps Aunt Ellen knows, but I haven't asked her as the vicar was here most of the afternoon.'

'Why?' Matthew asked Jim. 'Did you want him for summat?'

'It's just one of 'dykes at Marsh Farm. I need to speak to him about it. It needs shoring up.'

'Well, see to it then! You don't have to ask Da about that. Get one of 'labourers to do it.' Matthew frowned at his older brother, wondering why he needed to speak to their father about such a simple thing.

Jim shuffled his feet. 'No, I'd better ask.

It's one we had trouble with afore. It's been weakened, I think.'

'Then it needs fixing.' Matthew was sharp. 'If there's a high tide it might fail.'

'I'll go and ask Ma what he said.' Jim moved towards the house. 'He'll mebbe be back later tonight.'

'I don't think so,' Rosa murmured. 'He took an overnight bag with him.' Then she shrugged. She didn't want to waste the evening discussing Mr Drew. 'I'm going for a walk,' she said to Matthew. 'I need to stretch my legs.'

'Would you like company?' he asked. 'Or do you need to be alone?'

She looked up at him and smiled so that he wouldn't take offence. 'I need to be alone,' she said softly. 'Just this once.' She put her hand into his. 'Your mother is very ill, Matthew. I think you should go to her. Sit with her and Flo and Jim, and tomorrow send for Maggie and Delia and the twins to come.'

The reality of what she was saying hit him hard and he swallowed as a lump came into his throat. He was sad for his mother, but he had been expecting it. Only, what would Rosa do if – when – his mother died? Would she stay here with them? This is why she wants to be alone, he pondered. She's going to think about her future.

CHAPTER SIXTEEN

The Irish brothers had been looking for work and they had found it. They found it in an inn by the river which the sea captains and merchants frequented when they had goods to sell or move on. This inn, however, was not one in which legitimate trade was bargained for or exchanged. This was an inn where men spoke in whispers and money changed hands furtively, and where if a man spoke to the law, he would be found in the river the next day with his throat cut.

Seamus Byrne had a solid reputation known to those who were in a similar line of business, sea-going enterprises in which foreign goods were brought ashore and no duty was paid to Her Majesty's Customs officers. Seamus Byrne was both sailor and landsman: brought up in a fishing community on the west coast of Ireland, he knew how to handle a boat and how to dig a dyke. He was strong physically and alert mentally and he was known as a man of honour by those who did business with him. A likeable, honest rogue is how he would have been described had the men he dealt with been given to voicing a description, which they were not, being of the opinion that the least said the better.

His younger brother, John, though, was still an unknown quantity. Having spent so many years in jail, only just missing transportation, few as yet knew him or were willing to trust him completely, even though he was given a full recommendation by his brother. But he cared not for anyone else's opinion, what he cared about was that his youth had been wasted inside a prison cell and doing hard labour, when he could have been sailing the seas in a high-speed cutter or experiencing the thrill of a chase by a revenue boat. The blame, he thought, lay with a certain Spanish gentleman who owned a ship, and who on the last voyage brought goods into the port of Hull and then went off to arrange the transport and was never seen again, leaving him and Seamus on board ship to be arrested by the Customs men.

John Byrne was so embittered that he would not listen to his brother's reasoning as to why Carlos should disappear, leaving behind his beloved ship and his beautiful wife who was pregnant with their first child. Someone had to be blamed for his years of incarceration. That someone, as he lay in his prison cell, had always been the Spaniard. If he was dead, and reluctantly he now conceded that it was looking that way, then someone else must take the blame.

It was one o'clock in the morning when the brothers left the inn; neither of them was drunk although they had imbibed a little as they discussed the possibility of a deal with a ship's captain. This ship's captain was anxious to discharge goods ashore on his next trip, only not in Hull he emphasized, where, he said, the owner of the ship had many contemporaries who would notice if crates and casks were disappearing into plain-sided waggons and carts which did not bear the owner's name.

'What we need is a small port, like Patrington or Stone Creek,' Seamus murmured. 'Or even an inlet which would take a coggy boat.'

'But what we need more than anything is someone local who can store the goods until such time as we can sell them.' John Byrne pondered. 'That fellow Drew, if he could be persuaded again. Or his son.'

The streets were quiet, most law-abiding citizens being long in bed. But there were the usual street women hanging around dark corners and tramps sleeping in doorways. They walked on past them towards their lodging house which was situated in a street occupied mostly by the Irish community, of which there were many in the town.

Seamus clutched his brother's arm and drew him back towards the wall. 'Speak of the devil,' he whispered.

'And an angel appears,' added his brother with a grin on his face. 'Got him!'

James Drew was leaving the doorway of a house across the street. A lamp shone in the hall of the house, illuminating the interior. Women were at the door, dressed in gaudily coloured clothes, shouting raucous goodbyes to Drew. There was the sound of music and laughter and there was no doubt what kind of establishment it was.

'Follow him,' John Byrne said urgently. 'See where he's lodging. I'll catch you up.'

'Where are you going?' Seamus called softly as his brother moved stealthily down the street and started to cross the square towards the house.

John pointed to the door which had now closed and ran towards it. James Drew was moving unsteadily down the street. 'He's had a drop or two,' Seamus murmured to himself. 'He'll have a head in the morning.'

John Byrne knocked boldly on the door of the brothel, for he was convinced that that was what it was, he had visited them himself on occasions when he had money to spare. A large woman opened the door. She had a mass of dyed red hair and was wearing a deep red velvet gown with an emerald necklace around her throat.

'Ah!' He feigned surprise. 'I must have the wrong house! I'm looking for Mary Patrick.'

The woman smiled invitingly. 'There's no-one of that name here. Do you want her especially or could someone else take her place?'

He sighed. 'She's my sister! She's giving me lodgings for the night. Now isn't that just my luck! When I need a nice-looking woman like yourself I haven't a shilling to my name to treat her.'

The woman's smile faded. 'We don't give credit and we only deal in cash. Come back when your ship comes in!' She half closed the door. Then she opened it again. 'And I'd cost you more than a shilling, and so would my girls.'

He sped down the street with a rare grin on his face. The old devil, he thought. The pious old hypocrite! I remember him quoting the scriptures at me even when he was unloading run goods with Carlos. And he associates with whores too! He gave a silent whoop of satisfaction. I reckon we've found our harbour!

He caught up with his brother, who was making slow progress as Drew kept stopping to lean on a wall or a bollard. They could hear him moaning and muttering to himself. 'He's not drunk,' Seamus whispered, 'I thought he was, but he's not. I think he's worn out.'

'There's no wonder,' John whispered back. 'You should have seen the Amazon of a woman who opened the door to me. She could squeeze the breath out of you by just shaking your hand.'

They followed Drew down the High Street and he turned into the stable yard of the George Inn. 'Never again,' they heard him mutter. 'Dear God, forgive me. I'll never go again. I'm too old.'

John suppressed a laugh. 'He's not penitent over his sins, he's just sorry that he's old!'

'Ah, sure you'll be old yourself some day, God willing!' Seamus rebuked him. 'We'd all like to keep a young man's body and virility. The mind doesn't always grow old at the same pace.'

His brother wasn't listening. He was watching Drew as he lifted the latch of the inn door. 'Mr Drew!' He stepped forward. 'We meet again.'

James Drew started in shock as John Byrne came up behind him. 'What! Who? Oh!' He put his hand to his chest. 'You startled me – I wasn't expecting—'

'Of course you weren't!' John shook a finger at him. 'You weren't expecting us at any rate, were you? Come on,' he said cheerfully and took hold of Drew's elbow. 'We'd like to buy you a drink!'

'No, no,' he objected. 'I rarely drink. I've just been out for a walk. Couldn't sleep. I'm off to bed now. Got an early start in 'morning.'

John Byrne gave him a conspiratorial grin and pushed open the inn door. A flood of noise and light hit them. 'We'll ask for a quiet room,' he said. 'Somewhere we can talk.'

'We've nothing to talk about,' Drew insisted. 'And I'm really very tired. I've had a busy day.'

'And a busy night!' John winked. 'My word – those ladies! Especially the one with red hair. Sure, she's too much for me. She needs an older man – with experience. Someone such as yourself, I suspect, Mr Drew.'

'I don't know what you're talking about,' Drew blustered, but he was being propelled forward by John Byrne's firm hand as Seamus spoke to the innkeeper, who pointed to a door up the stairs.

Between them they pushed him upstairs and the innkeeper brought a lamp and placed it on the table and lit candles on the mantelpiece. A low fire burned in the hearth beneath.

'I don't wish to speak to you.' Drew turned towards them as the landlord went out of the room. 'I've nothing to say and no business to discuss.'

'We have business to discuss with you, Mr Drew.' Seamus spoke up in a reasonable, soft tone. 'We heard of something today which we think will suit you very well.'

'I told you last time, I only deal in corn now. That episode with the run goods, which I regret, I must tell you, is over. Over!' he repeated.

'We need a small haven,' John Byrne continued as if Drew had not even spoken. 'Somewhere like Stone Creek, if Patrington is no longer suitable.'

'The men who work that haven are all honest men, they wouldn't touch run goods,' Drew insisted.

'They did before,' Seamus said.

'They were not Sunk Island men,' Drew said. 'They came from downriver.'

'I'm not bothered where they come from.' John Byrne stared at him. 'And we can get men ourselves if necessary. We only need them to unload and move the goods to somewhere safe. We need you to tell us when the time is right, when the harbour is safe.'

'No!' Drew said. 'I've told you.'

'You've told us nothing.' John Byrne smiled thinly. 'But we'll tell you something! What would your friends say if they knew what you got up to when you were away from home? What would your wife and daughters say?'

'I don't know what you mean.' Drew's face flushed. 'I've been here on business at 'Corn Exchange.'

'That's what you said last time.' John Byrne tipped his chair back and studied him. 'Only this time we followed you. We saw you go in.' He stretched the truth a little. 'And we waited for you to come out. We had a long wait, Mr Drew. You took your time.'

James Drew bent over the table and put his

head in his hands. They both watched him for a moment, then Seamus put up a warning finger to his brother to silence him.

'We don't wish to upset you, Mr Drew,' Seamus said persuasively. 'And it might only be just this one little job.'

'You're blackmailing me.' Drew's voice was muffled.

'Yes,' Seamus agreed. 'It could be construed as that. But we would prefer it if it was just called a little business between old friends.' His voice was soft and smooth. 'We just want to make up for wasted years. John here is particularly bitter about that. He feels very badly done by. I wouldn't like to think what he might do if he was thwarted again.'

'I told you,' Drew raised his head. 'It wasn't my fault. I don't know where Carlos went.'

'Would your son know?' John Byrne asked. 'Jim?'

There was fear in Drew's eyes. 'No. No, don't ask him. He was onny a lad, he wouldn't remember.'

'I was only a lad too, Mr Drew.' John Byrne's voice was cold. 'And I remember very well. I shan't ever forget. I shan't forget being dragged off the ship, nor being thrown into an English jail, nor breaking up great lumps of stone. How did Jim spend the rest of his youth, eh? Being out in the fields, listening to the songbirds, sowing corn and reaping its harvest? A bit different from mine.'

'Just this once, you say?' Drew muttered in a defeated voice. 'There'll be no more after that?'

'Can't make any promises,' Seamus said. 'It'll depend on how much we make. And if it's easy we might want to do one more run.'

'But nothing will be said? Not to my wife or anyone? My wife is very sick,' he said, as if he might elicit some sympathy from them.

'Sick, is she?' Seamus Byrne now looked at him as coldly as his brother had done. 'And no loving husband at home to take care of her?'

'My sons are there and the girl – Rosa.'

'Rosa?' John Byrne breathed. 'Lovely name. Sounds foreign. Is she very pretty? I'd like to meet her.'

'She's very pretty. You remember, John, I told you I had met her. Yes,' Seamus agreed. 'It would be nice for you to meet our old friend's daughter.'

'She knows nothing of her father,' Drew interrupted. 'Except what her mother told her when she was a child. She always believed he would return and filled 'child up with nonsense of him coming back for them – in a ship with golden sails!'

'How charming!' John Byrne's voice was cold.

The two brothers got up from their seats. 'We'll see you in a week or two, Mr Drew,' Seamus said. 'We'll get work on the embankments until the ship arrives. You'll let us know about Stone Creek and who might be willing to help us? Oh, yes,' he said, as if he had just thought of it. 'And we'll need a barn to store the crates.'

'Not at Home Farm,' Drew objected. 'They would be seen.'

'Where then?' John Byrne frowned.

'Marsh Farm,' Drew said reluctantly. 'It belongs to me now. No-one goes there, only me and Jim.'

They nodded and moved towards the door, but Drew called them back. 'You haven't said what I'll get out of this. What's my cut?'

They both stared at him, then John Byrne started to laugh. The laughter was without any humour. 'Your cut? You've forgotten already, Mr Drew? Your cut is silence! Remember?'

'I should have summat,' Drew muttered. 'I'm risking everything.'

'Brandy then.' Seamus grinned and conceded. 'An anker of brandy.'

Drew sat on in the small room after they had gone, staring into the ashes of the fire. Brandy! He was risking his livelihood for an anker of brandy. He could go to jail for such a trifle. He had, as the Byrnes suspected, conveniently pushed to the back of his mind the real reason why he was in this predicament. But an unwanted image kept reappearing in his head and though he tried to banish it, it was persistent. An image of Henry lying on the top of the dyke, all life gone from him and the distinctive smell of brandy mingling with the river water which lingered on his cold dead lips.

CHAPTER SEVENTEEN

Matthew rode off to Hedon early the next day to ask Maggie to come, and then travelled across country towards the coastal village of Hornsea to see Delia and ask her to come home as soon as possible. He arrived in the afternoon and was perturbed to see the shabbiness of the inn where she worked. It stank of stale ale and the flagged floor in the entrance was in much need of a scouring brush. He was also dismayed at the manner of the woman who ran the house, when he asked to speak to Delia.

'She's not in.' She stood behind the wooden counter dipping pewter tankards into grey and greasy water, then drying them on a thin cloth. She narrowed her eyes at him. 'What is it you want?'

He was reluctant to give her the bad news. 'I'm Delia's brother. Could I wait?'

She shook her head. 'It's her afternoon off, she'll not be in till late.'

'Do you know where she's gone? I could perhaps look for her.'

The woman humphed disparagingly. 'She

could be anywhere. I don't know. I'm not given to asking questions about my staff, they're entitled to their privacy.'

He sighed. He'd go and look, there were not so many places she could be in this village. 'If I miss her, could you ask her to come home as soon as possible. Her mother is ill.'

'It'll be another month before she has time off,' she interrupted sharply, 'or else I'll have to dock her wages.'

He nodded. 'It's urgent,' he emphasized. 'You'll be sure to tell her?'

'I'm not in 'habit of forgetting messages.' She was curt and offhand. 'I'll tell her.'

He walked away but on reaching the door turned and asked, 'What kind of work does Delia do here?'

She gave a short laugh. 'Anything! Cleaning. Making beds. Serving customers. Whatever needs doing.'

'In here?' he asked, looking around the low-ceilinged smoky room where men were sitting at tables or on benches near the fire.

'Course in here!' she said. 'Where else?'

'I just wondered, that's all. She didn't say.'

'Well, no!' She raised her eyebrows. 'It's not 'sort of job that you'd boast about. But then, when young lasses come without a reference they have to take what they can get.'

He wished her good day and left. No reference! That meant that Delia had been dismissed from her previous employment. But why? What misdemeanour had she committed? It was a respectable house that she had been at, one of the best in Hornsea, owned by a gentleman and his family.

He rode down the quiet streets towards the sea. Perhaps she was walking on the sands. It had been a lovely day, sunny and bright, though now there was a sharp wind blowing. He would look along there first and if he couldn't find her he would ride to the Mere, the lake close to the village with its pleasant walks around the perimeter, before setting off on the long ride home, and trust that the innkeeper would give Delia his message.

He saw her down on the sands. She was alone and pacing up and down as if thinking or pondering on something. Her head was lowered and her arms clutched around herself. He called to her and she looked up, startled.

She ran towards him.

'Matthew? What is it? What you doing here?' Her face was pale and blotchy as if the wind had scoured it, or as if she had been crying.

'I've come to fetch you home,' he said. 'Ma is ill.'

'I'll lose my job,' she complained. 'Mrs Groves won't let me have any more time off.'

'I'll speak to her,' he said. 'If I explain?'

She shrugged. 'You can try.'

The innkeeper said, when asked, that if Delia returned the next evening, she would take her back, but that she would lose a day's wages.

'That's all right,' Matthew accepted. 'I'll bring her back, unless,' he glanced at his sister. 'Unless – our mother is worse. Is there a stable nearby? Can I hire a horse?'

The woman nodded. 'Just up 'street. 'Farrier has horses for hire.' He thanked her and wondered how Delia could bear to work for such a disagreeable woman. He said as much to her and she replied that it was better than the other place and that Mrs Groves was better for knowing.

'Why did you leave your other employment?'

'Didn't like it,' she said briefly, and as they approached the farrier's yard, she said, 'You know I don't like horses, can't we hire a trap?'

He gave a sigh. Delia could be so awkward and he wanted to get home as soon as possible. 'I'll ask, but we really mustn't delay,' and he realized that she hadn't asked one single question about their mother's state of health.

Matthew hitched his horse to the hired trap and they drove in silence out of Hornsea. Then he said, 'Ma's very poorly, Delia, I don't think she'll recover from this.'

'What is it she's got?'

'I don't know!' he said uncomfortably. 'I think it's a woman's thing and I don't like to ask.'

'She's had it a long time then,' she submitted, and lapsed into silence. After a while she said, 'I suppose I'll have to come home! Maggie can't now that she's married, Flo won't and 'twins'll be getting wed soon.'

'You've forgotten Rosa,' he said quietly.

'No I haven't.' She stared straight ahead. 'She can't stay if anything happens to Ma.'

'Why can't she?' He looked at her in astonishment. 'She's family.'

'No she's not! She's no relation. And she's

same age as me so she can't stay with you and Da and Jim. It wouldn't be right. Folks would talk.'

He gave a short humourless gasp. 'I don't believe what you're saying! Folks! What folks? Have you taken leave of your senses?'

She turned to look at him with cynicism written all over her face. 'You allus was sweet on her. She can do no wrong, can she?'

He refused to be drawn on the subject and simply said, 'You wouldn't want to come home after enjoying your freedom and independence. You've forgotten what it's like under Da's thumb.'

'I haven't forgotten,' she said, 'and I might decide to come home.' She paused, and there was a note of uncertainty in her voice when she spoke next. 'Or I might not. I'll let you know when I've decided.'

The next morning Rosa got up early and left Mrs Drew to the ministrations of her daughters and set off to walk to Patrington to see her grandmother. She would, she knew, miss having Flo there to help her with Aunt Bella. As she crossed the bridge over the channel she looked back towards her former home, Marsh Farm, and wondered why Mr Drew had been so eager to have it. The house is wasted, she thought, echoing Matthew's former words to his father. Jim is never there, and I can't think why he wanted such a small parcel of land.

Her grandmother was struggling to dress Aunt Bella when she arrived, but it was an impossible task, for each time Mrs Jennings put an item of clothing on her, such as a shoe or a stocking, the old lady took off the other one. She refused to have her hair brushed nor would she wear her cotton cap.

'Flo manages her so well.' Mrs Jennings sighed. 'I can't do anything with her!'

'Why not leave her in her night robe, Gran?' Rosa suggested. 'It doesn't matter for once and she's quite comfortable and respectable. Then perhaps later she'll let me brush her hair.' Aunt Bella's fine white hair was standing on end. 'Why don't you make us a nice pot of tea and I'll sit with her.' She guessed rightly that her grandmother would be glad of a few moments of peace pottering in the kitchen.

She picked up the fire tongs and put another piece of coal on the fire, then draped a shawl around Aunt Bella's shoulders and tucked a blanket around her knees. The old lady said something unintelligible to her and Rosa nodded and smiled back.

'Gran,' she said, when Mrs Jennings brought in the tray of tea and scones. 'Why do you think that Mr Drew wanted our farm after Grandda died?'

'Now you're asking me summat! I never could fathom it out,' her grandmother answered. 'But he was forever hovering about looking over it, even afore your grandda was took ill.'

'You mean – when Ma was still alive?'

'Bless you yes, when she was carrying you, and your da had disappeared. Why, he even searched our land himself when a search party was sent out.'

'You mean a search party went out to look for

my father?' Rosa remembered a search party looking for her mother. 'I didn't know.'

'Well of course you wouldn't. You hadn't been born then! But your ma was so distraught when he didn't come back that she made every farmer and cow keeper search their land and barns and sheds, and Mr Drew insisted on helping your grandda in looking over ours.'

'My da could have drowned,' Rosa said thoughtfully, thinking of Henry. 'He wouldn't have known 'layout of land. He could have fallen into a dyke.'

'They'd have found him then, wouldn't they? But they looked along 'dykes,' her grandmother said. 'Even on new embankments. He'd just disappeared.'

'I found some papers with his name on them,' Rosa murmured. 'They were in that old chest that you gave me.'

'Did you?' Mrs Jennings was astonished. 'What sort of papers?'

'Foreign,' she said. 'Fred, Maggie's husband, has taken them into Hull. He knows a lawyer who might be able to read them.'

'Well, well.' Mrs Jennings clicked her tongue. 'Fancy that. They must have been with your ma's things, were they? Cos I don't remember seeing them.'

Rosa said that they were. 'His name was Miguel, did you know that?'

Her grandmother nodded and looked wistful. 'Aye,' she said. 'I did. Decimus Miguel Carlos. That was his full name. Michael, the tenth child. That's what he told us it meant.'

'The tenth child?' Rosa exclaimed, her voice rising. 'He had nine brothers or sisters! That means then – that means that I have aunts and uncles, maybe cousins even, in another land!'

'Aye, I suppose it does!' Her grandmother was startled and gazed at her. 'I never thought of it afore!'

Tears sprang to Rosa's eyes. 'Another family, Gran, who know nothing about me!'

If James Drew had felt any remorse when he arrived home to find his eldest, middle and youngest daughters at his wife's bedside, then he didn't show it. Matthew was tired and irritable after his long ride to Hornsea and back to fetch Delia, and he hardly spoke to his father, not even to ask if he had found a new corn merchant. Jim was his usual dour self, Delia spoke little and it was left to Flo and Maggie to try and keep up their spirits.

'You got out just in time, Maggie,' Flo said as they washed the breakfast dishes the following morning. 'You'd be stuck with Da and 'lads if you hadn't wed.'

'Yes, I would,' Maggie agreed and mused on how pleasant it was having her own home where she could do whatever she wanted. Fred was a most agreeable husband and generous too. He had bought her a horse and trap of her own and he insisted that she drove to Sunk Island in it when she received the call from Matthew to come.

'You'll be all right,' Fred had said. 'I wouldn't let you go in 'dark or in bad weather, but it's fine and dry now so off you go and stay 'night or as long as you're needed.'

She'd kissed him and thanked him for being so understanding for she was worried about her mother, but she had felt embarrassed about arriving in such style at her old home, and was glad that there had been only Flo and Rosa to greet her, who both exclaimed in delight when they saw the smart conveyance.

'I'm bothered about Rosa though,' she said now to Flo, as she stacked the dishes in the cupboard. 'When Ma—' She stifled a sob and Flo put her arms around her and hushed her.

'Don't worry about Rosa,' Flo consoled. 'She can take care of herself.'

'What about Rosa?' Matthew walked in through the open kitchen door. 'What's up?'

'Nothing.' Maggie sniffled. 'I was just wondering what she would do if – when Ma—'

'She'll stay,' he muttered. 'She said that she would when I asked her, onny – onny—'

'What?' Flo said. 'Onny what?'

He looked towards the stairs. Delia was upstairs sitting with their mother, and he lowered his voice. 'Well, when I brought Delia back yesterday, she said that she might come back home, and you know what that means!'

'Oh,' Maggie said. 'Rosa and Delia don't get on. There'll be a right rumpus then!' Matthew nodded in agreement, then asked, 'How do you think Ma is this morning? Should I go for 'doctor?'

'Won't he call?' Maggie asked.

'He hasn't been sent for yet,' Matthew

answered. 'Rosa said that Ma wouldn't have him. Not yet, she'd said.'

'But you should have insisted!' Maggie complained. 'Or Da should.'

'Da was supposed to be calling on him when he came back from Hull, onny he didn't. When I asked him last night he said he wanted to see how she was before he called him out.'

'Go then,' Flo said. 'Though there's not much he can do, it'll put our minds at rest.'

So Matthew mounted his horse once more and this time set off to Patrington in search of the doctor, who said he would come at the end of the afternoon when he had finished seeing his other patients. Matthew hesitated in the main street, before turning for home. Rosa was staying with her grandmother, and on a sudden impulse he wheeled around and set off towards the small house which he remembered from all those years ago. That was when Rosa had come to see her grandmother and he, accompanying her and visiting his sister Flo, had been closely scrutinized by Miss Dingley.

He knocked on the door and Rosa answered it. She seemed aroused and stimulated about something, he thought, and her eyes were bright. She greeted him with pleasure and invited him in. It seemed strange to him to see her in a different setting from the one they were usually in.

'Your ma's not worse?' she said anxiously, when he said he had been to fetch the doctor. 'I'd better get back!'

'No, no.' He was emphatic. 'There's no need.

It's just that Maggie is worried, so Flo said we'd better send for him.'

'It's too late,' she said softly. 'You know that, don't you Matthew? I told your father before that he should send for him.'

He nodded miserably. 'I think Ma knows that. That's why she wouldn't have him visit. She doesn't want to be told what she already knows.'

Mrs Jennings invited him to have a cup of tea, which he refused, but he shook hands with Miss Dingley and asked her if she remembered him. She just gazed at him with tired eyes and said nothing.

'She'll not remember you,' Mrs Jennings said. 'She doesn't remember anybody, onny Flo, and she clings to her, calls her her bonny lass, when she can get it out, which isn't often.'

Rosa pondered as she watched her grandmother giving Aunt Bella her drink and breaking up pieces of scone to place into her mouth. What will Gran do when Aunt Bella isn't here? she wondered. Though her grandmother was elderly she was still very sprightly and alert. Will she stay on here in Aunt Bella's house? Will she have any money to live on?

'I'd better get back,' Matthew said. 'I've to take Delia back to Hornsea. It's been nice seeing you again, Mrs Jennings.'

'And you too, Matthew.' Mrs Jennings smiled. 'You're not 'shy tongue-tied lad that I remember!'

'No,' he agreed, and looked at Rosa. 'I'm not.'

'I'll see you at home.' Rosa let him out of the door. 'I won't be late back.'

He nodded. At home! It was her home and had been for a long time, but would she still want to stay if Delia was there?

She put her head to one side. 'Matthew? Are you all right?'

He gave a small sad smile. He would be more all right if he could place his hands around her face and kiss her lips. As if she was reading his thoughts she reached up and kissed his cheek. Her face was soft against his. 'Try not to worry about your ma,' she whispered. 'She's a good woman. God won't let her suffer.'

'I know,' he said, and waved goodbye.

'He's made a handsome young fellow, hasn't he?' her grandmother remarked as Rosa went back into the parlour.

Rosa agreed that he had.

'And he's sweet on you, Rosa. Anybody wi' half an eye can see that.'

Rosa smiled. 'Yes, he is. Always has been.'

CHAPTER EIGHTEEN

Matthew took a silent Delia back to Hornsea and Flo returned to Patrington, insisting that they send for her if their mother worsened.

'She seems all right at the moment,' Maggie said to Rosa hopefully as the two of them sat at the kitchen table. 'Mebbe 'doctor was exaggerating when he said it was bad!'

Rosa nodded and said nothing, not wanting to upset Maggie further, but Mrs Drew had called her to her side when she had returned from her grandmother's, and had taken her hand in hers. 'I know you'll do what's right for everybody, Rosa,' she'd said in a dry whisper. 'But you must do what's right for yourself too. You've been cheated out of what should have been yours.'

'I don't understand, Aunt Ellen!' Rosa was puzzled. 'Cheated out of what?'

Mrs Drew had turned her head to look out of the window. A fine grey drizzle was falling, splattering the panes with raindrops and darkening the room. 'Out of your ma and da,' she said. 'I did what I could to replace them, but it wasn't enough. A child needs its parents.'

'You've been as good as a mother to me, Aunt Ellen. Gran must have known that when she asked you to take me.' Rosa had a lump in her throat as she reassured the sick woman. 'As for my father, well I never knew him, so I don't know how he would have been.'

'He would have loved you,' she'd answered softly. 'There's no doubt about that. He was a warm and loving man. He had his faults, but no more and much less than some I can think of.'

'Rest now,' Rosa had implored her. 'Don't worry about what might have been.'

'No,' Mrs Drew sighed. 'It's too late for that. But you'll remember what I said? And – and if anything should happen – if you should discover something which causes you pain, then will you try to forgive?'

Rosa had gazed down at her. What was she trying to say? But she declined to question Aunt Ellen further for she appeared so very weary, and only said that she would try.

She lit the lamp and left it low. 'Would you like Maggie to come up and sit with you?' she'd asked and Mrs Drew had said yes, but that she also wanted to speak to Jim and to Matthew when he returned from Hornsea. 'Never mind if it's late,' she said. 'There's something I want to say to him.'

Rosa had turned to leave the room but Aunt Ellen called her back. 'You know that Matthew loves you?' she whispered.

Rosa smiled. 'Yes.'

'He'll make up for what has gone before,' she murmured. 'If only you'll let him.'

It was late when Matthew returned and he was in ill humour, for he was wet through and said that Delia had barely spoken on the journey and seemed only concerned about losing a day's wages. 'Have you no thought for our mother?' he'd asked her angrily. 'She wanted to see you.'

Delia had had a sullen expression on her face as she answered. 'I've got worries too. It's all right for all of you. I'm stuck out here on my own.'

'But you wanted to go into service,' he'd retaliated. 'You said before that you wouldn't come back to Sunk Island!'

'Well, so I wouldn't,' she'd muttered. 'Given 'choice. But I might have to,' and she lapsed into silence again, and he couldn't be bothered to argue with her any more.

Matthew seemed calmer after talking with his mother and when he came down, Maggie and Rosa were sitting by the parlour fire. Maggie asked if she could make him a hot drink. 'Thanks, Maggie,' he said, 'and then I'm off to bed. It's been a long day. Where's Da?' he asked Rosa. 'He's late.'

'He went with Jim across to Marsh Farm,' she said. 'He said he wanted to check if 'hayloft was dry.'

Matthew frowned. 'Why would he want to do that at this time of night? And why isn't Jim staying here when he might be needed?'

Rosa shook her head and said she didn't know. 'Your da went off some time ago. Maybe he's talking to Harry or somebody.'

'That's not like Da,' he murmured. 'He likes to

be in his bed afore ten.' He looked perturbed. 'I'd better go and look for him.'

'He's just coming,' Maggie called out from the back kitchen. 'I can see him pottering about in 'yard and Jim's with him.'

Matthew leaned towards Rosa and lowered his voice. 'I don't think it'll be long.' He indicated upstairs. 'I'll fetch 'doctor first thing in 'morning.'

She nodded and grasped his hand. 'Yes,' she said softly. 'But don't tell Maggie. Let her have a good night's sleep.'

He turned her hand over and kissed her palm, then dropped her hand as they heard the outer door open and his father's voice. She smiled gently, then looked away as Maggie, Mr Drew and Jim came into the room. Mr Drew was short-tempered and irritable and Jim seemed even more morose than usual.

'Your ma wants to speak to you, Jim,' Rosa said.

'It's late,' he replied half-heartedly. 'I'd better not disturb her now.'

'Go on up,' Matthew broke in. 'She's still awake. She wants to see you.'

Maggie looked anxiously at Rosa and then at Jim, who was hovering as if uncertain what to do. 'You'd better go up then, Jim.' She had a catch in her voice and her eyes were moist. 'Rather than disturb her in 'morning.'

Jim slowly climbed the narrow stairs and knocked on his mother's bedroom door. The lamp burned dimly though the fire was bright and sent a glow around the room.

'How you feeling, Ma? Any better?' He was never a man of words and as he stood by his mother's bedside he was lost for anything to say. 'It's still raining. Young corn's getting flattened.'

'It'll spring up again.' She gave a weak smile. 'It always does, and we'd have no corn at all without rain.'

'Aye,' he agreed, and lapsed into silence.

'I wanted to talk to you, Jim.' She eased herself up higher in the bed and asked him to adjust her pillows. 'Come and sit here by me.' She patted the patchwork coverlet on the bed. 'We don't often have 'chance to talk together.' Her throat rasped and she coughed and beckoned for the glass of water on the table by the bed.

She took a sip and handed the glass back to him. 'I know that you've not had a happy life,' she began. 'There's been something bothering you since you were just a young lad.' She lifted her hand and turned his face towards her, for he had looked away as she spoke.

'I'm your mother, Jim,' she pleaded. 'Why couldn't you confide in me?'

He shook his head and looked down. He could feel his throat tightening and tears welling at the back of his eyes. There was nothing he could tell her, and why should he share his misery and torment with her, especially now when she was so ill?

'You won't tell me because someone else told you not to?'

He looked at her, then put his hand over his eyes and sobbed. Sobbed as he had done all those years ago.

'You were only a boy,' she said softly. 'Whatever happened, you were not to blame.'

'I was.' He felt a low drooping of spirits, a great heaviness of heart. 'It was my fault.' He lifted his head and looked at her through his tears. 'You don't know. Nobody knows.'

'Do you want to tell me about it?'

He shook his head. 'I can't. I can't tell anybody. I onny know that I'm damned.'

'No.' She took his hand and stroked it as if he was a child again. 'God will forgive us if we repent.' She paused, then said softly and wearily, 'I don't know what happened that night, I only know that something dreadful did. I believe you to be innocent and someone else guilty. Neither,' she added, 'do I think that you could possibly have guessed at the consequences.'

He took a handkerchief from his pocket and wiped his eyes, then blew his nose. 'Is that why you took Rosa after her ma died?' he croaked, and when she nodded, he added, 'It was like salt in a wound when she came to live wi' us. A constant reminder.'

She sighed. 'I thought it might be. But it was for her I did it. To try to make up for her loss.'

'But she was such a bright little lass and seemed to fit in, so after a bit I persuaded myself that she wasn't likely to find out.' He spoke almost to himself, forgetting that his mother didn't know what had happened either. 'And I got fond of her same as 'others, Maggie and all of 'em.'

Then his face tightened and a note of bitterness crept into his voice. 'Until Da said I should marry her. That was wicked, Ma. Really wicked. How can I ever marry anybody with this sin hanging over me? Least of all Rosa?'

The rain woke James Drew as it hammered against the window and he sat up in bed and looked out at the grey morning. He hadn't slept well and wished that he had gone into the spare room as Rosa had suggested, in order to give Mrs Drew some rest. But when he had said to his wife that he would sleep in another bed, she had put up her thin hand to him and said, 'There'll be many nights when you'll sleep alone, James. Sleep with me tonight.'

She had put her hand on his as they lay side by side, but he didn't clasp it or turn to her, and when she whispered would he pray with her he had grunted and feigned sleep. He looked down at her now. She was quite still with no breath in her. He touched her face and it was cool to his touch and he knew that she had left him.

He slid out of bed and knelt at the side of it, clasped his hands and closed his eyes. 'Dear God,' he murmured, but got no further in his prayers. She's gone, he thought, and taken my conscience with her, for he was in no doubt that she had been his saviour watching over him, gently and silently chastising him for his sins and praying for his redemption. I shall go to Hell now, without her to save me, he pondered. The Devils of Darkness will capture me for their own, for I have an evil worm inside me which is devouring my soul.

A tear ran down his cheek, but he knew in his heart that he was crying for himself who was lost, and not for his wife who lay still and silent in the bed which they had shared for the last time, and who had asked for comfort and had been refused.

He tapped sharply on the door of the bedroom which Maggie and Rosa were sharing for company. 'Go to your mother,' he said, when one of them sleepily answered, and then went to wake Matthew, but he found his bed was empty already, and looking out of the window saw Matthew saddling up one of the horses. He rattled on the windowpane and Matthew looked up. He indicated that he should come inside and wearily plodded down the stairs to begin another life.

'I'm glad that you were with her, Da,' Maggie wept. 'It would have been a comfort to her, knowing that she wasn't alone at the last.'

Her father didn't answer, but it seemed that a knife slid further into him and twisted in his entrails.

'Will you go and tell Flo, Jim?' Rosa asked. 'Matthew's worn out with all the travelling yesterday. And call on 'doctor and parson, and tell them, whilst you're there.'

Mr Drew looked sharply at Rosa as she made the arrangements, but said nothing. Jim agreed. He seemed weary, as if he hadn't slept. 'Aye, I don't mind. I'll do owt, but I'll see to 'pigs first and old Harry can look to hosses.'

'We'll send for Delia and 'twins when we know 'date of 'funeral,' Mr Drew butted in, attempting to assert his authority. 'No sense in cluttering up 'house with too many folk.'

'And Mrs Drew's sister too,' Rosa said quietly, 'and 'neighbours. They'll all want to come.'

The tiny church was packed with mourners, for Ellen Drew had been a much loved friend and neighbour as the parson confirmed in his address. He asked the congregation to pray for her soul and for her family's courage in continuing without her. 'Pray particularly for her husband James,' he intoned. 'For he will feel the loss of her devotion, her bounteous goodness and compassion.'

James Drew opened one eye and peered between clasped hands as the cleric spoke. It seemed to him that every expression of sympathy he had received had had a double edge to it. Following the interment in the churchyard where the birds sang in full-throated chorus and the perfume of summer flowers, the dog rose and narcissus, and the heady scent of syringa drifted over them, the parson drew him to one side.

'A word, dear sir,' he said. 'It will be difficult for you, I know, adjusting to the loss of your dear wife.' He patted James Drew on the shoulder. 'So I have decided to withdraw your name as church-warden – for the time being,' he added. 'You will need time to reflect and to pray privately, you do not need to be involved with the weight of church affairs.'

'But—' James Drew stared at the parson. It was what he did need. Whilst he was involved in church matters, he felt that the hand of God had a tentative hold on him, if not guiding, at least pulling in the opposite direction to that in which he was inclined to drift. With Ellen gone and the church too, then he was damned for sure.

The parson moved away, murmuring that he was available at any time should he feel the need of comfort and prayer or confession.

Mrs Drew's sister and her husband left that afternoon and Maggie, staring after them, stated flatly that that was probably the last time they would ever see them. 'They don't like coming to Sunk Island,' she said. 'They do nothing but grumble every time they come.'

The twins went back to Ottringham and Flo asked Rosa if she would like her to stay until the next day, as Maggie and Fred were leaving that evening.

'No, you get off,' Rosa said. 'Gran needs your help with Aunt Bella more than I do.'

'Aye,' Flo said softly. 'There'll be another funeral afore long.'

Delia was sitting by the kitchen table biting her nails. She looked across at Flo. 'Why you asking her whether you should stop? You should be asking Da or Jim or Matthew.'

They all stared at her. Her face was flushed and she glared angrily back at them.

'Rosa's been running 'household for months,' Maggie broke in. 'You don't seem to realize just how long Ma has been ill.'

'Don't let's have any recriminations,' Matthew warned. 'Ma's onny just gone.'

'Aye, and she thinks she can step into her shoes,' Delia snarled. 'And she can't.'

'I don't think that,' Rosa said quietly. 'No-one can replace Aunt Ellen, least of all me. She was good and kind and irreplaceable.' She glanced at Mr Drew, who was sitting watching and listening to them. He seemed apart from them, as if what they were saying was nothing to do with him.

'Anyway, you were keen enough to get back to Hornsea and leave Rosa to it,' Flo said sharply. 'I can't hear you offering to come back to help!'

'Well, that's where you're wrong, Miss clever monkey.' Delia gave her a black look. 'I might come back and if I decide to, I'll work my notice and then come home.'

James Drew got up from his chair. 'I'm going for a lie-down,' he said abruptly. 'When you've all decided what's happening, be good enough to let me know.'

Rosa was dismayed. She didn't know if she could live in the same house as Delia. Mr Drew was difficult enough to deal with and without Mrs Drew there to mediate in disputes it would be worse. Now if Delia with her bickering quarrelling ways should come back, there would be no pleasure here.

'Just why have you decided to come home, Delia?' Matthew asked curiously. 'What's happened to make you want to come back, when before, when I took you to Hornsea, you hadn't made up your mind?'

She hesitated. 'Nowt's happened,' she said. 'I just thought that as I was 'onny daughter that could come home, then I'd better. Even if I don't want to,' she added in a martyred tone. 'But I know that Ma would want me to look after Da.'

'If you don't want to come home, Delia, you don't have to,' Rosa said. 'I can manage – and I was going to ask your father if we could have a girl in to help in the house. So that I've more time to help with 'animals – with 'milking and with 'pigs.'

'Da would never agree to it,' Flo said dismally.

'That he wouldn't,' Matthew sighed. 'I'm going to get on to him again to get extra help with haymaking. A regular lad I mean, not just casual labourers. But I don't suppose he'll agree.'

'Aye,' Jim muttered. 'A young lad to do fetching and carrying and some of 'heavy work, that's what we need. Owd Harry's past it, he's that slow.'

There could be no agreement on extra help until their father had been consulted and an uneasy silence hung over them. Then Fred stood up, having kept quiet whilst all the discussion and bickering had been going on. 'Well, Maggie, it seems there's nowt more we can do here, so we'll be off.'

Maggie stood up by his side. 'Yes,' she said, rather nervously. 'You're sure there's nothing else we can do, Rosa?' She deferred to Rosa and ignored Delia, who flashed a spiteful sneer at her.

Rosa swallowed. She felt as if she hadn't had time to grieve for the woman who had been like a mother to her, she had been so busy making arrangements, comforting Aunt Ellen's sons and daughters in their loss. The house would be empty without her and too full if Delia came back. 'No,' she said, hardly trusting herself to speak. 'There's nothing more to be done.'

CHAPTER NINETEEN

A month passed and nothing had been heard from Delia as to whether she was coming home, and Rosa began to feel that perhaps she wasn't returning after all. Mr Drew had reluctantly agreed that they could employ a lad for the farm and they had found Bob Hargreaves, a willing youth from Patrington who had missed the chance of employment because he had fallen and broken his arm the week before the November Hirings, and no-one would take him on. 'But it's mended now,' he'd said eagerly. 'It's as good as new.'

But Mr Drew had not agreed to Rosa having help in the house. 'If Delia comes home,' he said, 'pair of you'll be sitting at 'kitchen table gabbing all day 'cos you've nowt to do.'

Nothing to do, she'd thought grimly. I've now got five men to feed, for young Bob was to live in with a bed above the stable, and old Harry had his dinner with them every day and went home to one of the workers' cottages each night.

'I'm sorry, Rosa,' Matthew said one day. 'You've such a lot to do.'

'But so have you,' she said. 'You work very hard. But that's the life we lead. What else can we expect?' And as she spoke, a remembrance came into her head of her mother's words from so long ago. What was it she had said? Where the river is constantly beating at our door and we do nothing but work every day that God sends! What was it that her mother was looking for? A new life? Sunshine? Music? And she had been denied all of those things.

'What is it?' Matthew touched her arm, for she had become silent and meditative.

'I was thinking about the river,' she said softly. 'My mother didn't like it, but I do. And I never walk there now because there isn't time, but I want to, Matthew. It renews me, gives me energy. I seem to draw strength from it.'

He looked down at her. There was no-one else in the house. They had finished their dinner, Jim and Bob were out and his father had ridden off as he was apt to do without telling anyone where he was going.

'Then go and get a wrap and we'll go.'

She laughed. 'What, now? I haven't collected this morning's eggs yet.'

'They'll be there when we get back. Come on, there's no reason why we shouldn't.'

'You're coming too?'

'Would you rather go alone?' Once before she had said that she wanted to be alone.

'No, of course not. I'd like your company.'

She fetched her shawl for although it was a fine day, the wind was always constant on the river. They walked along the Humber bank in the direction of Stone Creek, which marked the boundary of Sunk Island and linked the watery marshes of the island to the mainland. There were a few small ships in the creek and a ship moored out in a deep channel on the river. 'Oh, look,' she said, pointing to it. 'There's the Dutch fluyt come back again.'

Matthew looked at her questioningly. 'What about it?'

'It's a very old ship.' She stared across the water towards the graceful vessel. It evoked such poignant sensations in her.

'I can see that it's an old ship. But how do you know about it?' He laughed, and pulled gently on the single black braid which hung down her back. 'I didn't know you were an expert on ships!'

'I'm not. Henry told me about it, years ago. Do you remember, it was that time when I played truant from school and Henry came to look for me?'

'Yes, and Da gave you 'strap.' A veil of sadness drifted across his face. 'Poor old Henry. He always wanted to leave home, but never dared. I miss him.'

'I know,' she said softly. 'I miss him too.'

He turned to her. 'I was always jealous of him, you know. I always thought that he was special to you.'

'He was,' she replied and smiled. 'He was special. He made me laugh. He took care of me.'

'Is that all? I mean – not special in any other way?' His mother had said to him the night before she died that he mustn't rush Rosa. That everything would come right if only he was patient.

She tucked her arm into his. 'Were you jealous of Jim too?' she teased. 'Your da wanted me to marry him.'

'No,' he acknowledged. 'Not of Jim. He's such a sobersides. He'll never marry.' He stopped abruptly as they approached the creek. 'Look,' he said. 'Is that Da?'

In the distance they could see a short stocky man, holding a horse by its reins and talking to someone, possibly a boatman by his apparel of thick jumper and breeches tucked into long waterproof boots.

'I think it is!' she said. 'I wonder why he's down here? Not arranging for corn to be carried, surely?'

'No. That's not till later.' Matthew mused. 'Perhaps something is being delivered.' He gave an exasperated exclamation. 'Da only tells us what he wants us to know, but I'll ask Jim,' he determined. 'Mebbe he'll know.'

Jim hedged and said he knew nothing when Matthew asked him, but he seemed uneasy and jittery and wouldn't look Matthew in the eyes. 'What's up with you?' Matthew enquired. 'I'm onny asking a simple question. I'd ask Da but he'd want to know why I was wasting time down at 'river instead of working.'

'And why were you?' Jim asked. 'Nowt better to do?'

'I went with Rosa,' Matthew said bluntly. 'She gets no time off with looking after us. We just went for a walk, that's all.'

Jim gave a sudden grin. 'Nowt better to do then, had you?' Before Matthew could reply, he said, 'I don't know why you don't marry her! You wouldn't have to tek her walking then.'

'What! And have poor lass still live at home looking after all of us?' Matthew joked at the suggestion.

'Why, aye! Course. Who'd look after us if she didn't?'

'Delia?' Matthew raised his eyebrows.

'Heaven help us!' Jim groaned. 'No thanks.'

The following week, Rosa decided that she would go again to the riverbank. Just for a short walk, she thought. The men were out and she had finished all of her tasks.

It was a warm afternoon, a gentle wind was blowing, scattering the few clouds in the wide sky, and in some of the meadows flocks of sheep were grazing. As she gazed on the tranquil scene and felt the pull of the breeze in her hair, and the salty smell of the estuary touch her senses, she knew that she never wanted to live anywhere else.

I belong here, she mused. Even though I have foreign blood. I'm bound by this river that once ran around the land, and even though the boundaries are silting up, there still seems to be an invisible rim around the island separating us from the mainland. Generations of family who had been born here, she felt, were holding her fast.

Yet I'm curious, she thought, as she strode out along the long embankment. Where did my father come from? Why did he come here?

What did those foreign papers say? Fred had not yet been to collect them from his lawyer, though he had said he would be going into Hull again soon.

She was walking towards Hawkins Point, the isolated place where Henry had found her when she was a child, and she saw gangs of men working on the drainage channels beyond the salt marsh where vegetation had flourished and trapped the silt, building up the growth of land that was only covered at high tide. The field drains drew off the water from the land and returned it to the Humber by the drainage channels, leaving behind a rich and fertile earth.

She knew she would be visible to the men as she approached; her figure would be etched against the skyline, no trees or hedges here by the riverbank to conceal her. One of the men straightened up and looked in her direction and then another did the same and they both stood watching her. As she drew near, one of them threw down his spade and walked across towards her.

He touched his hat and looked up at her, for she was on the embankment and he was on the lower ground. 'Grand day, miss,' he said in a soft Irish accent. 'Just the day for a walk.'

She nodded and agreed.

'But be careful how you walk, miss.' He seemed to look at her keenly. 'The ground is muddy – wouldn't want you to slip into the marsh!'

'It's not muddy up here,' she said. 'It's quite dry on the bank. Besides,' she added, 'I'm used to walking along here. I've always lived by the river. I'm used to it.'

'I seem to know you, miss,' he said. 'Did we meet some years ago when you were just a little lassie?'

'I don't know. Did we?' He did look vaguely familiar and she thought that he might be the same Irishman she had met with Henry.

'I believe we did.' He smiled and he had a twinkle in his eyes. 'Did you not tell me that your daddy was a prince?'

She laughed. 'I might have done. That's what my mother used to tell me.'

'And you're still here on Sunk Island?' he queried. 'Has no fine young man wanted to carry you off to a more civilized place?'

She bridled slightly at his personal question, yet it was asked in an easy and friendly manner.

'I like it here.' She only half answered him. 'It's my home.'

'Ah, yes, of course. And I suppose you know the island well? There'll be no secrets out here in this flat land?'

Puzzled, she shook her head. 'None,' she stated. 'Everyone knows everyone else and what they are doing.'

Another man detached himself from the group of workers and came towards them. 'Seamus,' he called. 'The foreman is grumbling about you not working. You're giving the Irish a bad name.'

'Sure and don't we have one already? I only came to warn this young lady about slipping on the mud, but born and bred here, she is, and doesn't need my advice.'

'Ah!' The other man, who was younger, in his mid-thirties, with red hair which curled on his collar, stared up at Rosa. 'Begging your pardon, miss, but you put me in mind of another young woman who used to walk along by the river. Do you remember her, Seamus? When you first brought me to Sunk Island?'

'That's a lot of years ago. You were only a lad then,' Seamus interrupted and folded his arms across his chest. It seemed to Rosa that neither of them were in the least concerned about getting back to work or about the foreman's opinion of them.

'I'm Seamus Byrne, miss,' the older man introduced himself. 'And this is my brother John. I brought him to Sunk Island on his first trip out of our mother country. Now who was that young fella you were friendly with?' Seamus turned to his brother. 'I wonder if he's still here?'

'Jim?' John Byrne creased his eyebrows as if trying to remember. 'Jim – something? Brewer? Drewer?'

'Drew!' Rosa said. 'Jim Drew. Yes, he's still here. I live with his family, although Jim farms Marsh Farm where I used to live. But who,' she asked quickly before they could interrupt again, 'who was 'young woman you saw? It might have been my mother!'

John Byrne pulled himself up the steep bank to stand level with her, and his brother with a wave of his hand went back to the gang. 'Perhaps it was,' he said softly. 'She was married to a Spaniard that we had business with.'

'My mother,' she whispered. 'And father.'

'So what happened to him? Did he go back to Spain?'

Rosa gave a sudden shiver. A dark cloud had drifted over the sun, blocking out its warmth. But it wasn't just the sun's disappearance that had made her feel cold. There was something in this man's eyes and in his voice which seemed threatening, and chilled her through to her marrow.

'I don't know.' She swallowed. 'I never knew him.'

John Byrne gave her a sudden warm smile and her doubts melted away. 'Then you missed a grand fellow,' he enthused, and his voice was engaging and his grey eyes appealing. 'And if you could have seen him at the helm of his ship with a goodly breeze blowing and the sails billowing and a fast cutter chasing us, well there *was* a prince of a man to admire.'

She gazed at him with her lips apart. 'A ship?' she breathed. 'He had a ship?'

'Sure he did. Did no-one ever tell you? A fine vessel it was. Sometimes—' He dropped his voice. 'Now don't be telling anybody for they'd be laughing at me, but sometimes, with the sun setting on the horizon, the sails looked as if they were made of gold!'

She suddenly wanted to cry at his words. Here was a man who knew her father and he said he was a prince of a man. But – 'Why was a cutter chasing his ship?'

John Byrne shook his head. 'Well now, there's a story that would take some telling, Rosa, and I'd need a promise that you wouldn't repeat it, for what we were doing was scarcely legal!' His face hardened slightly. 'A man can go to jail for what we did.'

'Did my father go to jail?' she asked. 'They say he disappeared, but perhaps the law caught him?'

He shook his head. 'We would have heard. We would have shared the same cell.'

His voice again was cold and she asked cautiously, 'Did you go to jail?' and when he nodded, she said, 'I'm sorry. Was it my father's fault?'

He appeared to hesitate and his mouth tightened, but then he answered light-heartedly. 'Not a bit of it. Why, he wasn't here, was he? He'd disappeared. Gone to ground.'

He turned round to look at the men working on the channels and said, as if reluctantly, that he had better be getting back. 'They'll stop my wages if I don't, but my word it's been grand talking to you, Rosa. Can we meet again?'

She smiled. 'Yes, I'd like that.' He was handsome and engaging even though he seemed to have an undercurrent of tension within him. But then, she considered, if he has been in jail it would make him distrustful of strangers. But she wanted to hear more about her father and his ship. And she would also like to know why he was here on Sunk Island in the company of two Irishmen.

He waved goodbye and she watched him as he

made his way back down to the group of men. He was not tall, but broad-shouldered and lithe, and she thought that she could imagine him with his feet steady on the deck of a ship. Yes, she thought, I would like to talk to him again. But as she walked back towards home, a thought struck her. He called me Rosa! I never told him my name! Then she remembered speaking to his brother Seamus that day with Henry, and Seamus had asked her name. How odd that he should remember it after so long, and when did he tell his brother, for him to remember it too?

As she walked back to the farm, she saw Jim travelling home on a waggon and he drew to a halt to give her a ride. She climbed up and he said dryly, 'Been playing twag again, Rosa?'

'Yes,' she said. 'I have. I've been for a walk. I saw someone who used to know you, Jim,' she added. 'He said you used to be friendly when you were young lads.'

She furrowed her brows as she wondered what the two brothers had been doing on Sunk Island. Were they digging field ditches and channels then? They must have been desperate for work to come such a long way.

'Mm?' Jim stopped by one of the dykes and got down to look at the water. 'Dyke's full,' he commented as he got back in the waggon. 'Must be a blockage further back. Who knew me? One of Holderness labourers was it?'

'No, an Irishman. Two in fact. One is called Seamus and I've seen him before – when I was a child. The other one who knew you is called John Byrne.'

She had turned to Jim as she spoke and was startled to see his sudden change of expression. The colour had drained from his cheeks and he had a look of extreme fear.

'He's come back, has he?' he muttered. 'I allus knew that he would, sooner or later.'

CHAPTER TWENTY

Rosa had gone into the dairy to escape the heat. The dairy cows which they kept for their own use were producing gallons of thick creamy milk. The churns, buckets and jugs containing it were covered with muslin cloths to keep the flies away. After rearing the calves, butter and soft cheese were made and the surplus milk or cream used in cooking and baking, for custards and breakfast gruel.

She wiped her forehead. She was tired, there was too much to do for one person. Next week haymaking was to start and she would have to provide food for the itinerant workers as well as the men of the family and young Bob and Harry.

She looked at the basket of eggs which she had placed on a shelf that morning and which she still hadn't had time to wash, and determined that she would put up with it no longer. 'No matter how he grumbles,' she muttered to herself, 'James Drew is going to have to get me some help or I shall tell him I'm leaving and going to live with Gran and Aunt Bella.'

She picked up an empty bucket to fetch some

water from the rainwater butt. That too was a worry, for the spring and early summer had been dry and they had to be sparing with the use of water, the tubs and butts beneath the gutters and drainpipes were getting lower, and the brick well which had been built beneath the yard to catch the rainwater from the house was half empty. They could use river water for washing and cleaning, but it was brackish and unfit for drinking.

Rosa turned towards the door and gave a startled gasp. A woman stood there, her bonnet and long skirt outlined in silhouette against the brightness of the day outside. 'Flo? Is that you?'

'No.' The unmistakeable carping voice of Delia answered. 'Not Flo. It's Delia. Where's Da?' she asked abruptly, without greeting Rosa.

'Out somewhere.' Rosa went towards her. 'However did you get here?'

'Carrier, and walked some of 'way.' Delia's eyes were shadowed and she looked tired and dirty. 'I'm desperate for summat to drink and I'm that hungry.'

Rosa took in her dishevelled appearance and turned back into the dairy and ladled some milk into a small bowl. 'Here,' she said. 'Drink that. You look all in!'

Delia quaffed it in one gulp and licked her lips. 'Where's Da?' she asked again. 'Is he likely to be in yet?'

'No, not yet. Not until supper. All of the men are out. Jim's over at Marsh Farm and Matthew's gone over to Patrington. You'd better come in to 'kitchen and sit down.'

She led the way across the yard and into the kitchen. Has she come home to stay? she wondered. And why does she look as she does, as if she's been sleeping out in the open? Delia's skirt was muddy and torn at the hem and she was carrying her winter cloak even though the weather was so warm. But what bothered Rosa more than anything was that she was also carrying the leather bag which she had taken with her when first going into service.

Delia sat down in a chair with a huge sigh and started to pull off her boots. 'Oh,' she groaned. 'My feet!'

Rosa cut some bread and cheese and put it on a plate and handed it to her. She took it without a word of thanks and started to eat ravenously. 'Mek us some tea, will you?' she said, with her mouth full.

'Ever heard of *please*?' Rosa said sharply, but lifted the kettle off the fire to warm the teapot.

Delia didn't answer and went on eating until she had finished all that was on her plate. She reached to put it on the table and muttered, 'Thanks,' as Rosa handed her a cup of steaming tea.

Rosa sat down opposite her. If Delia had come home for good, then there had to be some rules laid down. She would not tolerate rudeness or aggravation from her. Absolutely not, she decided. So the rules must be decided now.

'You said you'd walked some of the way?' she said. 'Why was that?'

'I got a lift with a carrier to Aldbrough, and then I thought if I kept to 'coast road, I'd mebbe get another lift to Withernsea, but a farm hand came along in his cart and said he'd give me a lift as far as Lelley mill which was where he was going, and then I could cut across country to Keyingham.'

She glanced sideways at Rosa and shifted in her seat. 'Well, that was all right for a bit, and we'd gone a few miles when he started hinting that I'd have to pay him for 'ride. When I said that I'd no money, he said that that was all right, I could pay him in some other way.'

Rosa took in a deep breath of horror and stared at Delia. 'So what did you do?'

'I jumped off 'cart.' She wrinkled her nose distastefully. 'He was an old fella and smelt of pigs.'

'What did you do then?'

'I ran.' She sniffed and rubbed her nose with her hand. 'I thought he might come after me, but he didn't. But I got lost cos I didn't know which road to take. Then I saw a sign for Humbleton and I'd heard of that, so I walked there and got lodgings for 'night.'

'I thought you said that you hadn't any money?' Rosa said curiously.

'That's what I told 'farm hand, but I had my wages,' Delia said reluctantly. 'So I paid for my bed and a cooked breakfast. I asked directions, and I walked all yesterday.'

She leant forward and cupped her chin in her hands. 'I thought I'd get home in the day, but it was that hot on Holderness Plain I could barely find energy to walk, and there were hardly any farms where I could ask for shelter or a drink, so

I just kept on walking till nightfall and then I slept under a hedge. I got up at daybreak and started walking again, then I saw a sign for Keyingham so I knew it wasn't much further.'

'Why?' Rosa asked. 'Why didn't you send a message and Matthew or Jim would have come for you?'

Delia turned her head away. 'I couldn't stand working for that woman any longer. She treated me like a slave. Do this. Do that. So I asked for my wages and left.'

'Were you given notice?' Rosa asked quietly. There could be no other reason why Delia should suddenly depart from her employment, even if the landlady was as obnoxious as she and even Matthew had said she was.

'No,' Delia replied sharply. 'I just said, didn't I? I couldn't stand it any longer.'

Rosa stood up. 'Well, as you're here, you might as well make yourself useful. I've been wanting some help. There are five men in for supper. You can start scrubbing 'potatoes while I chop up 'mutton for the stew.'

Delia glared at her. 'Don't think you can give me orders about what's to be done. This is my father's house, not yours. I hardly slept last night, I'm going to have a lie-down.'

'Then you'll get no supper,' Rosa replied calmly, even though she was seething inside. 'Everybody has to work for a living here and if you're staying then you have to share the load. There's too much for one person to do. I was about to tell your father that I needed some extra help.'

'Tell him?' Delia said scornfully. 'You'll not get far doing that. Nobody tells him anything!'

Rosa faced her. 'I was going to tell him that if I didn't get help then I was leaving. If you're staying, the two of us can manage 'work between us. If you're not willing, then I'll leave anyway and you can stay on your own.'

Delia stared back at her, her face defiant. Then suddenly her expression changed and her features crumpled as she started to cry. 'I can't,' she wailed. 'I can't stay on my own. I'm in trouble.' She screwed up her eyes but the tears poured down her cheeks.

'In trouble?' Rosa's words were abrupt. 'What sort of trouble?'

'I've got caught,' she sobbed. 'I don't know what to do!'

'Caught?' Rosa's hands went to her mouth. 'How? What do you mean?'

Delia shot her a contemptuous glance. 'Don't you know owt?' she almost shouted. 'Caught wi' a babby. I'm expecting.'

Rosa sat down again. She felt as if all the breath had been knocked out of her. 'Who—?' she whispered. 'What about the man—? Won't he—?'

'Marry me?' Delia mocked. 'When I asked him, he just laughed and said his wife would have summat to say about that!'

Rosa groaned. 'But—!' She was lost for words. How could Delia have become involved with someone so deceitful, so vile as to take advantage of her innocence. 'Did you not know anything of him?' she asked. 'Of his family? His background?'

Delia wiped her eyes. 'No,' she muttered. 'He used to lodge at 'inn every month. He travelled all over 'county, selling stuff.'

'A pedlar?' Rosa was aghast. It was getting worse and worse.

'Not a pedlar!' Delia sneered. 'A salesman. He sold goods from manufacturers. You had to order them and then he delivered 'following month. Not like 'pedlars that come here!'

It seems like the same thing to me, Rosa pondered. But what would I know about it? And if he was travelling the county he could have any amount of vulnerable young women in trouble. 'Did your employer find out?' she asked. 'Is that why you left?'

'Yes,' Delia admitted. 'She heard me being sick. She didn't seem to care until she found out who it was, then she said I had to go. She said she needed his custom more than she needed me. I think he was carrying on with her anyway,' she divulged, seemingly without shame. 'I could tell by her face that she was nettled about it.'

'He was carrying on with her!' Rosa repeated. 'And you knew?'

Delia shrugged. 'I thought I could get him off her. She was too old for him anyway!'

'I think you are a disgrace,' Rosa said slowly and deliberately. 'If you had loved this man and he loved you, then I could have understood. But it seems to me that there was no love there at all and therefore your behaviour is inexcusable. I'm only glad that your mother isn't here to witness this.'

Delia put her chin up and there was a suggestion of bravado in her expression, but her mouth trembled and there was anxiety in her eyes. 'I'm not bothered about what you think,' she started to mutter. She bit her lips together. 'But what's Da going to say when he finds out?'

'You should have thought of that before,' Rosa said coldly, and getting up from her chair left the room.

She went back to the dairy and sat down on a stool. It was cool in there and she put her hands over her eyes and tried to think. Mr Drew would be outraged. He might not even let Delia stay. He was such a righteous, religious man, although, Rosa mused, he doesn't go to church so often since Mrs Drew died. And he is no longer a churchwarden. But I'm sure he will send Delia away to have the child elsewhere so that the shame doesn't reflect on him.

Poor baby, she thought. It will have no father's name.

'Rosa!' She heard her name. 'Rosa!' Matthew was calling from the yard.

She went to the door. 'I'm here.'

He smiled when he saw her and she thought how brown and strong he looked. His shirt-sleeves were rolled back showing his tanned muscular arms, and the sun had bleached his brown hair in golden streaks. 'What you doing?'

'Oh – just cooling off,' she said lamely. 'It's so hot in the kitchen.'

'It is,' he agreed. 'I went in to look for you. Listen,' he grinned. 'I went to see Flo when I was in Patrington and she's told me of a girl who she thinks would come over to give you a hand with 'housework. She'd have to live in, of course.'

She gave a low laugh. It might be just too late.

'I haven't told Da yet,' he said. 'I thought we'd give him an ultimatum. I've been dropping hints that you were thinking of going into service in Patrington!'

'Wasn't there anyone in the kitchen when you went in, Matthew?' she asked.

'No. Don't tell me you've hired somebody already?'

'No. No I haven't.' She wanted to tell him that everything was about to change. That from now on, their lives were going to be different. Hers, Matthew's, Mr Drew's. Delia's behaviour would be the talk of the island. There were no secrets here, nothing could be hidden. Their lives were as open as the landscape they lived in. But she couldn't tell him. Delia would have to do that.

'What is it?' There was concern in his voice. 'There's something wrong?'

She took a deep breath. 'Delia is here. She's left her employment and come home.'

He frowned, drawing his dark eyebrows together. 'To stay?'

'Ye-s. I think so.'

'She's taken her time about it, but I suppose she had to work her notice?'

She nodded. 'I expect so.'

He looked at her and there was pleading in his voice. 'Don't leave, will you, Rosa? Please don't.'

She gazed at him, at his anxious blue eyes. You know that he loves you, his mother had said, and she'd answered yes. Slowly she went towards him. She was trembling, her emotions in turmoil, and as if he knew, he drew her to him. She bent her forehead onto his chest and he folded his arms around her and softly kissed the top of her head. 'Rosa – !' he whispered. She lifted her head and placed her finger on his lips to silence him. 'Ssh,' she murmured. 'Not now.'

He gazed down at her and she saw the love in his eyes, but how could she return it when there was so much conflict ahead?

'Rosa – !' His eyes searched her face, looking for the truth. 'You're leaving, aren't you, and you daren't admit it?'

She shook her head. 'I won't leave,' she said softly and reaching up she kissed him tenderly on his lips. 'How could I?'

Delia looked up from the sink when they went into the house. She had made a start on the potatoes. She had also washed her face and combed her hair and looked altogether more presentable than she had done when she had first arrived.

She greeted Matthew and glanced at Rosa as if wondering whether she had disclosed the reason why she was here, but she visibly relaxed when Matthew asked her what had made her change her mind and come home. She told him the same as she had told Rosa, that she couldn't bear to stay any longer.

'I'm not surprised you left,' Matthew

commented. 'She was a dowly woman. Did you come by carrier's cart then?'

'Yes,' she answered swiftly. 'Practically all 'way.' He expressed surprise, but then added, 'There's more folks coming through Holderness now that 'roads are being improved, and especially now it's dry. Though you'd have to walk from Keyingham, I expect. Is that 'way you came?'

She was saved from answering by Jim coming in to ask if there was a cup of tea. 'What you doing here then, Delia? Been given time off?'

Rosa handed him a cup of tea and gave one to Matthew. 'She's left,' she answered for Delia. 'Now, can we keep 'questions until later or we'll never get your supper on 'table.'

'Who's left? Left what?' Mr Drew stood in the doorway. 'Delia! What you doing at home?'

Again the question was asked of her.

'I've come home to help,' she answered nervously. 'I knew Rosa couldn't manage on her own and none of 'others can come.'

Her father stared at her. 'Never known you to think of anybody else! So why didn't you come afore?'

'I'd to work my notice,' she mumbled.

Jim took a sup of tea. 'They haven't finished you, have they?' he asked. 'You'll never get another job if they have. Not without a reference.'

'I just told you,' she said sharply. 'I've come home to help. All these questions, I'm beginning to wish I hadn't come.'

James Drew's eyes had narrowed as he heard Jim's comment and he asked abruptly, 'Have you been finished? Is that 'reason why you've come? That was a good house you were at, you wouldn't give up a job like that and good money just to come home. Did you do summat you shouldn't?' His voice became sharper as he cross-examined her.

Delia started to shake. 'No. No,' she denied. 'I didn't. It wasn't my fault.'

'What wasn't your fault?' he roared. 'You have been up to summat! What was it? Did you break some china or summat valuable? You allus was clumsy.'

He turned to Rosa. 'What's up with her? What's she done?' He shook a finger at Delia. 'I'll get to bottom o' this, my lass. If you've scarred my name at yon house!'

'Delia left that house some time ago, Da,' Matthew interrupted. 'She took employment elsewhere.'

'Elsewhere? Where elsewhere? How is it I didn't know about it? Your sisters have stayed in 'same employment, why haven't you?'

'I didn't like it,' she whimpered. 'We didn't get on.'

'Didn't get on! Didn't get on! And now you've left this other position and I suppose you didn't get on there either?'

She shook her head and looked down at the floor. Her face was ashen. 'No,' she muttered. 'We didn't.'

'So they asked you to leave?' His voice dropped and it seemed more threatening than when he was shouting. 'Where is this other place? I'll ride over to Hornsea myself and speak

241

to them. I'll not have this. Sullying my name! Sending you off without a reference as if you're a nobody! I'll find out 'reason why.'

'No,' she gasped. 'Don't. I'll tell you. I'm sorry.' Tears ran down her cheeks. 'I'm sorry, Da, really I am.' She glanced at them all in turn and finally at Rosa. 'I can't,' she sobbed. 'I can't tell them.'

Rosa took in her blotchy face and shaking body and knew that Delia couldn't disclose the news to her father, that she was too afraid of the consequences. But the confession must be made. There was no doubt that he had to be told before he found out for himself.

'Delia's expecting a child,' she said quietly and unemotionally. 'And the father can't marry her.'

There was a sudden hush. Even the fire seemed to stop its crackling and the kettle its hissing.

'What? What did you say?' Mr Drew stared at Rosa and then at his daughter. 'Expecting a child! A bastard?' His face grew scarlet and sweat stood out on his forehead whilst Matthew and Jim rose simultaneously and gazed numbly at Delia.

'You strumpet!' Disgust lined Drew's face. 'Can't marry you? Who is he? I'll have him horse-whipped!'

'He's gone,' she wept. 'You'd never find him. I've not seen him for weeks.'

'Gone, has he?' His tone was harsh and bitter. 'And that's what you can do, young woman. Go! I'll not have any fornicating trollop living in my house.'

Rosa drew in a sharp breath at his coarse language and Matthew started to object.

'Be quiet!' Drew bellowed. 'I'm master in this house and I'm telling you I'll not have her here. Get your bags and go!'

CHAPTER TWENTY-ONE

Delia collapsed sobbing into a chair and the only sound in the room was of her weeping, until her father turned towards the door. 'Ten minutes,' he barked, as he brushed past her. 'I'll give you ten minutes to get your things together, then be off wi' you.'

'Da!' Matthew started to say. 'Let's talk about this.'

'Mr Drew,' Rosa began.

He put up his hand to silence them but as he came towards Jim, who was blocking his way, Jim stopped him. 'Hold hard a minute, Da,' he said quietly. 'Don't be hasty. She's your daughter and our sister and you can't just turn her out.'

'Can't I though?' his father said savagely. 'She might be your sister but she's no daughter o' mine.'

'She is your daughter and you know where she'll finish up if you turn her out?' Jim stared him in the face. 'She'll finish up in 'streets of Hull – or in a brothel!' His last few words dropped to a whisper so that Rosa, who was contemplating Delia's future if her father refused to have her at home, didn't quite catch what he was saying.

But James Drew did and he blinked rapidly and opened and closed his mouth. Then he composed himself. 'She can go to 'devil for all I care,' he muttered.

'Aye,' Jim said softly. 'Well, isn't that where we'll all meet up? It'll not be in heaven, that's for sure.'

His father pushed past him and went out of the room, but Jim followed him, giving a quick glance at Matthew as he did so, and putting up his hand to stop him following.

'Where shall I go?' Delia moaned. 'Who'll have me?' She appealed to Matthew. 'Do you think our Maggie'll let me stop with her?' Her face was blotched with crying and her eyes red and swollen.

Rosa's eyes were drawn towards the window. Jim had his hand raised in a fist as he was talking, and although she couldn't hear what they were saying, she could see that his father was angry as he too was waving his arms about.

Presently Jim returned to the house. 'You can stop for a bit till we decide what's best to be done.' His voice was shaky but he had a set determined look on his face.

Delia started to cry again and Rosa said to her, 'Why don't you go up to your bedroom until things calm down. Of course your da is angry. He's had a shock. He's upset.'

She nodded and rushed upstairs and Matthew asked Jim quietly, 'How did you manage to make him change his mind?'

'He hasn't changed it!' Jim gave a deep sigh and sat down and started to drink his now cold tea. 'I've just reminded him of a few things. It's a temporary reprieve, that's all.'

'Reminded him of what things?' Matthew asked curiously.

'Nowt that concerns you.' Jim's face was creased with tension. 'Just summat that happened a long time ago. I needed to refresh his memory that none of us is perfect.'

'I thought Da was,' Matthew said cynically. 'At least that's 'impression we were always given.'

'Jim!' Rosa butted in. 'It seems that your da will listen to you, more than he'll listen to Matthew and certainly more than to me. So I was thinking. Will you tell him that if he won't let Delia stay, then I'll leave because there's too much for one person to do, and he'll have to get a housekeeper and a girl in to do for you. He won't like that,' she added. 'He won't want strangers in the house.'

Jim nodded. He appeared strained after the heated discussion with his father. 'Aye, I'll tell him when he's cooled down a bit.' He looked up at her and his eyes searched her face. 'But don't think that he won't listen to you. He will. He has you on his conscience.'

'On his conscience? Whatever do you mean?' She was totally puzzled. James Drew had never shown her any concern.

'Never mind,' Jim said abruptly. 'I've said too much already.' He rose from his chair. 'Come on, Matthew. We've work to do before supper.'

'Conscience!' Matthew exclaimed with sudden

enlightenment as Jim went out of the door. 'Yes. That's it! That was 'word I was searching for that day we went to see your gran – years ago, don't you remember, Rosa? And then we went to Marsh Farm and frightened Jim out of his wits? I said there was another reason why Da said you should live with us, but I didn't know 'word for it then. I couldn't explain myself!'

She vaguely remembered, but it was a very long time ago and somehow it didn't seem important. Not when there were so many difficulties looming ahead.

Yet, strangely, there was never any further discussion on Delia's future and so she stayed. But her father didn't speak to her, neither would he eat at the same table. Delia took her food alone, either before or after everyone else had eaten. Rosa felt sorry for her but tried not to show it and Delia never commented on her exclusion, but grew silent and discreet in her father's presence as if trying to be invisible.

'Should I take her to see 'doctor?' Matthew asked Rosa one day, some weeks later. 'I'll drive her over in 'trap. And mebbe we should tell Maggie and Flo?'

Rosa agreed. No-one else had been told and Delia had kept to the house and yard, never venturing even into the fields during harvest time in case anyone should see her and comment on her being at home.

'I'm going to ride into Hedon tomorrow,' she told him. 'The pedlar hasn't been and we need some things for the house. I'll call on Maggie and tell her myself.' She didn't know what was needed for a pregnant woman when she began in labour, but thought that Maggie being an eldest daughter might know. She would ask her anyway. They needed to be prepared.

Maggie was in sparkling form and delighted to see Rosa, who had not visited her in her neat little house before. 'Come in and I'll show you round,' she said, and took Rosa into her tidy kitchen and cosy parlour. Then she led her through the staircase door and up the wooden stairs to the bedroom. There was another door in the bedroom and through it was another very small room. It smelled of new paint, and Maggie showed her the flowered curtains she was making for the windows.

'Can you guess why we're preparing this room, Rosa?' she asked, and half covered her face with her hands as she hid a smile.

Rosa shook her head. 'Expecting visitors?'

'Not visitors,' Maggie said. 'Someone permanent.'

'Permanent? Who? Oh! Not a baby?' She gazed at Maggie, who was oozing suppressed delight. 'Oh, Maggie! I'm so pleased for you.' And how can I tell you now of Delia? she reflected. I can't spoil your happiness by bringing you news of your sister's disgrace. 'When?' she asked. 'When will it be?'

'Sometime in January, 'doctor thinks. I would have come over to tell you but Fred has been busy and he won't let me drive 'trap on my own, not now. He's like a dog with two tails, Rosa! Though he said he wasn't bothered one way or another when we wed, he's that proud now and he runs around after me, won't let me do a thing and makes me sit with my feet up!'

'I'm so glad for you, Maggie, and for Fred.' And so sorry for Delia, she considered, who has no-one to love her or think well of her baby. 'And of course you must take great care of yourself.'

'I know. 'Doctor says I'm in good health and very strong and even though I'm old for a first babby, he says if I rest a bit each day, I'll be all right.

'I'm scared though, Rosa,' she confessed. 'I remember when Ma had Matthew, she nearly died, and then she went on to have Delia. I wish she was here,' she said, suddenly tearful. 'She'd tell me what to do.'

'She would have been so glad for you,' Rosa said, and added, 'So what kind of things do you need? I mean, perhaps I can get them for you?'

'Oh, bless you, that's all arranged. I've got lying-in sheets and a crib, and ordered a layette, though I haven't collected it, it's supposed to be unlucky to do that before 'babby is born. And 'midwife has been to see me already.'

'A midwife! Of course!' Rosa pondered. She hadn't thought about a midwife and she doubted if Delia had cither. But then Delia hadn't discussed her forthcoming confinement at all. And of course she wouldn't. She couldn't discuss it with her brothers or her father. So there's only me, and she has never liked me. But there, she thought. We will both have to forget our differences and plan for the future.

She had tea with Maggie and then set off back on the long road to Sunk Island. As she reached the village of Ottringham a waggon was coming towards her. As it drew near she saw that Fred was driving. She greeted him and gave him her congratulations.

He beamed. 'Aye, it's grand news. Best yet. So! What news from Sunk Island? Or have you given it all to Maggie?'

She hesitated. Should she give Fred the news of Delia, so that he could tell Maggie at a suitable time? She decided that she would, she had always found him to be a responsive man. He drew into the side of the road when she said she wanted to talk to him, and she slipped down from the saddle and with the horse held on a long rein, she climbed onto the waggon seat next to Fred.

'It's not good news,' she began. 'And I didn't tell Maggie because she's so happy and I didn't want to spoil things for her, but—' She told him as plainly as possible of Delia and her trouble, and that she was at home, on Sunk Island.

Fred's expression hardened. 'And this man won't marry her?'

'Can't.' Rosa's voice was low. 'He's married already.'

'She's been consorting wi' a married man?' he said heatedly. 'Did she know he was married?'

'I don't know,' Rosa confessed.

'Well, if she did, I've no sympathy for her! None at all and I'm not sure that I want my wife to be in her company!'

Rosa was taken aback. She had not expected sympathy for Delia, but some compassion at least.

'Shameful behaviour such as this reflects on everybody, Rosa.' He was quite emphatic. 'It brings disgrace on 'whole family.'

'That's what her father said,' Rosa answered. 'He won't talk to her, won't let her eat at 'same table with him.'

'But he's let her stop? He hasn't turned her out? There's many a father wouldn't have her in the house. But then, he's a good church-going man is Mr Drew.'

'He said at first that she had to leave, but Jim persuaded him to let her stay,' she explained. 'He said that he'd reminded him that none of us is perfect.'

'Well, that's true,' Fred admitted. 'But it doesn't alter 'fact that what she's done is wrong.'

'And what about the man?' Rosa asked. 'Hasn't he done wrong too?'

'Well, yes, of course he has, and if it was my daughter I'd search him out and give him a beating.' Then he became thoughtful. 'It's funny, you know, but when you're about to be a father your ideas change. If I have a daughter and she goes astray—'

'Yes,' Rosa said. 'What would you do?'

He was silent for a moment. 'I don't know. I really don't. I'd need to be sure that I'd allus been honourable and just, in order to cast 'first stone. And I know that I haven't allus been.'

He gave a deep sigh, then said, 'I'll not tell Maggie yet. Like you say, she's very happy right now and I don't want to spoil that. But in a week or two I'll bring her over to visit and Delia can tell her for herself. It's her disgrace so she can impart it.'

After Rosa had left that morning, Delia cleared the breakfast things, washed the dishes, built up the fire and fetched in more wood. She only half filled the basket for it was heavy if it was filled to the top. Jim had caught her carrying it one day and had told her not to, that she had to ask him or Matthew to bring it in for her. But she knew that Rosa filled it and carried it every day and she didn't want to be beholden to her, or for Rosa to think that she was shirking.

They hadn't had much conversation, she and Rosa, but Delia admitted to herself that she wasn't patronizing or condescending towards her as she had thought she might be. She didn't care for her any more than before. She didn't like Rosa's efficient manner, nor the way she was so independent and would go off on her own whenever she wanted to. Delia had never been interested in the river and its moods nor in gazing at the swaying corn in the moonlight, as she had seen Rosa do. But I'm going to need her if Da lets me stop at home to have 'bairn. I can't have it on my own so I'd better try and be nice to her, she thought.

She prepared the midday meal for when her father, brothers and the two farm hands, Bob and Harry, came in. She set the table ready so that they could help themselves, and she would disappear out of sight when they arrived. She knew that in her father's eyes she was a fallen woman, no longer fit to be included in his family. But she would abide by his rules. She would put up with his moralizing and hide from his sight, if only he would let her stay. For where else could she go?

There was a knock on the back door and she stiffened. No-one was expected, so who could it be? She had not answered the door since she came home, Rosa always did that, and not all of the families on Sunk Island knew that she had returned. She peered out of a corner of the kitchen window. A man was standing there. A youngish man, not anyone she knew. Should she answer or let him go away? But what if it was someone with a message for her father? She had seen and heard his wrath on previous occasions when her mother had not been there to take a message for him.

She smoothed her apron and hoped that her swelling waistline didn't show too much, patted her hair and went to the door.

'Good day to you, miss.' The man took off his hat, his hair was a deep warm shade of red. 'And a fine morning it is.'

Nervously she agreed that it was. 'What can I do for you?'

He gave her a cheeky grin. 'Well now, I'm sure there would be plenty that I could think of, but today I'm looking for Mr Drew.'

Delia smiled back. It had been a long time since she had had a flirtatious conversation with a man. But then her smile faded, as she thought of where such conversations had brought her. 'He's not here. He's out somewhere.'

'Ah!' He seemed disappointed. 'And when will he be back?'

She shrugged. 'Dinner time, I expect. They'll all be in then.'

He meditated, then said, 'All?'

'My brothers, and 'farm hands.'

'Ah, so you're one of Mr Drew's lovely daughters?'

'I, er – yes.' She hadn't meant to say.

'Well, I have to say that the ladies of Sunk Island are a grand sight to behold. I met Rosa not so long ago. She lives with you, I believe.'

She frowned. Who was he? 'Yes. Yes she does.' She looked across the yard and saw her father and Matthew, leading two of the shire horses, coming down the track towards the house. 'Here's Da coming now,' she said abruptly. 'You'll have to excuse me, they'll be wanting their dinner.'

Matthew was surprised at his father's curt attitude towards the stranger. He didn't introduce him, but merely told Matthew to see to the horses and took the Irishman, for undoubtedly that was what he was, judging by his accent, to the other side of the yard, away from the house.

He washed his hands in the sink and could hear Delia clattering pans over the range in the middle kitchen and he called to her, 'It's all right, Da's not in yet. He's talking to somebody.'

'Who is he?' Delia kept a wary eye on the window so that she could scuttle away when her father appeared. 'He sounds Irish.'

Jim came bursting through the door. 'Who's Da talking to?' he asked sharply.

'An Irishman,' Delia and Matthew answered simultaneously. 'Never seen him before,' added Matthew, and wondered at the grim expression on his brother's face.

Their midday meal was taken in silence, broken only occasionally by young Bob or Harry, commenting on what needed to be done that afternoon. 'Get on and do it then,' Mr Drew growled, 'no use in just thinking on it.'

'Thanks, Delia,' Matthew called as he left the table and put on his coat to go out. He glanced at his father and Jim, but neither of them said a word.

'Thank you, miss,' young Bob called also, and Harry said in an aside that they didn't see much of Miss Delia even though she was living at home.

It won't be long, Matthew thought, before Harry puts two and two together. It would have been better if Delia had shown herself each day. Her weight increase would not have been as obvious as it will be if Harry catches sight of her now. And then it will be all around the island, especially if he tells his wife.

Out in the yard when they were alone, Jim confronted his father. 'You were talking to John Byrne! Why has he come back? What did he want?'

'He wants some help and came to us.' His father didn't look at him. 'It's just a small job! We won't be involved. Just storing 'goods, that's all.'

'No! Not again!' Jim's face had lost all its colour. Defying his father wasn't easy. But he had to make a stand. 'We can't. I won't. You can't bully me same as when I was a lad.'

His father looked up at him. 'Bully you? Of course not. You must make your own mind up on such matters.' He seemed to hesitate, and Jim felt there was a nervousness in his manner. 'I'm not telling you that you have to help me, but I'm asking if you will. They – them two, they said they'll go to 'law if I don't help them with this job! They said,' Drew took a deep breath, 'that they'll think up some cock and bull story about Carlos's disappearance. They said that they'll implicate us both if we don't help with this job.'

'How can they? They know nothing.' Jim felt a terrible fear as his past confronted him.

His father pursed his lips. 'Insinuation. A whisper that Carlos didn't disappear of his own free will.'

Jim stared at his father. He was afraid. He would die if he was locked up.

'They said . . .' His father's voice dropped low. 'They said that they'll accuse us of murder!'

CHAPTER TWENTY-TWO

Delia refused Matthew's offer to take her to Patrington to visit the doctor. 'I can't,' she wailed. 'Everybody will see me and gossip about who the father is.'

Rosa stayed silent for a moment, then she asked, 'Will you have 'doctor here, if he'll come? You'll have to see him sooner or later. I know nothing about babies. Suppose it comes early, what would we do?'

Delia pouted and Matthew grew impatient. 'You can't pretend that it isn't going to happen, Delia,' he pointed out. 'Rosa's right. You'll need some help.'

With very little grace Delia said that she would see the doctor at home. 'Onny make sure that Da's not about,' she said. 'And who'll pay him?' She started to cry. 'Da won't and I haven't any money.'

Rosa hadn't any either. Only the housekeeping money, and Mr Drew went over her housekeeping bills meticulously.

'I'll pay,' Matthew said. 'And I'll ask Jim to chip in. I'll go tomorrow to Patrington and ask him to call.'

'I'll go,' Rosa interrupted. 'I want to see Gran. Flo sent a message to say that Aunt Bella is ill and won't last much longer.'

I'll also tell Flo about Delia, she thought. She ought to know, and perhaps she'll write to the twins and tell them.

She thought of Maggie, who had come with Fred just a few days earlier. Rosa hadn't told anyone of Maggie's forthcoming confinement, for she guessed that Maggie would want to tell her father and brothers herself, but the first person Maggie saw as she entered the house was Delia, and Delia was stretching her back after putting the kettle on the fire in the very same action that Maggie herself used. Her pregnancy was obvious, and Maggie had drawn in her breath and held onto the back of a chair.

'Delia!' Maggie gazed at her sister and then across at Rosa, who was folding sheets. 'Delia! You're—!'

'Yes,' Delia said rebelliously. 'I am. And it looks as if you're in 'same boat.'

'No,' Maggie said slowly. 'I don't think so! I'm carrying my husband's child. Whose child are you carrying?'

Delia hadn't looked at Maggie, and she thrust her chin in the air as she'd replied, 'Somebody else's husband's.'

Maggie had lowered herself into a chair. 'You never told me, Rosa,' she accused. 'Why didn't you?'

Rosa came and knelt beside her. 'How could I?' she'd said softly. 'How could I spoil your joy?'

Maggie had wept and then Delia, in her shame

at ruining her sister's tidings, cried also, and Maggie, after having a cup of tea, was driven home again without seeing her father or brothers. It was left to Rosa to give them the news that Maggie too was expecting a child.

Only Matthew seemed to be glad to hear of it. Mr Drew merely grunted and said that the event was predictable, whilst Jim seemed so preoccupied, it was as if he wasn't really listening.

Rosa looked across at Marsh Farm as she passed it on the way to Patrington. The roof on the barn had had some new tiles fitted and she saw that there was an empty waggon in the yard, and wondered why it was there, when usually the waggons were kept at Home Farm.

Flo opened the door at Aunt Bella's house and put her finger to her lips. 'Doctor's here,' she whispered. 'It doesn't look too good for Miss Dingley. She's sleeping a lot, we can barely wake her up to feed her.'

Rosa wondered what her grandmother would do when Aunt Bella died. Flo, she knew, would marry her faithful Tom and leave Patrington, but Gran is getting old, she thought, will she be able to live alone?

They were talking in the parlour when the doctor came downstairs followed by Mrs Jennings. 'You'll know my granddaughter, Rosa?' she said to the doctor. 'She lives with 'Drew family on Sunk Island.'

'Yes, of course I do.' The doctor nodded to her. 'Mrs Drew sang your praises – said you were like a daughter to her. Well, I must be off, Mrs

Jennings,' he said. 'I'll look in tomorrow. There's no more to be done, I'm afraid.'

'Doctor—' Rosa hesitated. 'Could you call at Home Farm some time soon?'

'Who's sick? Not Mr Drew?'

'No.' She pondered. Now it would come out. 'It's Delia. She needs to see you.'

'Delia?' Flo said in astonishment. 'She came home then?'

'Will you come?' Rosa asked the doctor again. 'It's urgent.'

He asked what was the matter with Delia and why couldn't she come to see him?

Rosa looked at Flo and then at her grandmother. 'She's not sick,' she said in a low voice. 'She's expecting a child. She doesn't want anyone in Patrington to see her.'

The doctor lowered his head and gazed at her solemnly and then said he would come as soon as he could, within the next few days.

'Delia expecting!' Flo exclaimed when he had gone. 'I can't believe it! Who's the father? When is she to be wed?'

Mrs Jennings tutted. 'Dearie me. One poor soul on her way out to mek room for another coming. 'Good Lord knows what he's about, I expect, even if we don't. She doesn't know who 'father is?' she queried. 'Is that it?'

'She does know who he is,' Rosa defended. 'But she won't say. He can't marry her. He's married already.'

'Aye, well. Of course he is.' Mrs Jennings sighed. 'They allus are. Poor young lass. She'll have a rough life from now on.'

'What does Da say about it?' Flo was aghast. 'Is he letting her stay?'

'For the moment,' Rosa said. 'But he won't speak to her and she can't eat at 'same table as him. And I don't know what will happen when 'babby is born.'

'An outcast! A pariah, that's what she'll be.' Mrs Jennings nodded sagely. 'And babby as well. But those who shut 'gates on pity must first look to see that their own hands are clean.'

'Gran! What will you do when – if – anything happens to Aunt Bella?' Rosa asked.

'It'll be when, not if,' her grandmother said. 'Her time's almost run out, like it does for all of us eventually. And – well, I don't rightly know what I'll do. I should have planned things better, but summat will work out I expect.'

'Yes.' Rosa was thoughtful. 'I expect it will. Gran, do you think – that is, if I can arrange it with Mr Drew, would you come and live with us at Home Farm and help with Delia's baby?'

The days were getting shorter and a chill wind whipped around the island, heralding the winter which was to come. On most days, if Rosa finished her chores early and whilst Delia prepared supper, she put on her cloak and walked along the river embankment.

The onset of winter held no fears for her. She loved to watch the turbulent waters of the Humber as it lashed across the salt marsh, its foamy spray dashing against the high embankment as if trying to claim back its rightful habitat. The migratory birds were flying in from their long journey overseas, and mallard and teal were to be found hanging in many larders of the farmsteads.

Today, as she walked along the high river wall, the tide was out and the saltmarsh and mudflats were thronging with vast flocks of wading birds: dunlin, plover, shelduck and redshank were feeding on the prolific supply of crustaceans. She stood still for a moment, watching, and not wanting to disturb, the long-legged curlews as they dropped onto the flats to burrow with their curved bills into the mud, searching out lugworm and ragworm.

As she watched, Rosa deliberated that she still hadn't approached Mr Drew about her grand-mother coming to stay for Delia's confinement, but she could put it off no longer. Aunt Bella had died the previous week and Mrs Jennings was sorting out her cousin's possessions and had to make a decision about her future. I'll ask him today, she determined. No, I will tell him! There is no alternative that I can think of.

She walked on until she came to Stone Creek, where she stood looking down at the boats moored in the harbour. Fishermen were sitting on upturned barrels mending their nets, men were unloading coal from a seagoing vessel and another group of men standing apart from the others were in a serious discussion. One of them was James Drew. Two others were the Irish brothers.

Rosa realized that if they turned they would see her standing there and she pulled her hood over her head and turned around, wondering at herself for not wanting to be seen by Mr Drew, for she was entitled to be out if she wished. She started to walk back along the track watching the river and its traffic and saw a cutter, midway in the river, drop its anchor almost opposite to the Stone Creek harbour.

She heard a voice from behind her hail '*Hello*,' but she kept on walking and saw in the distance a figure coming towards her. A man with a gun and a dog which wagged its tail in acknowledgement of her.

'Rosa!' The voice called her again and she recognized it as John Byrne's. She turned and he was running along the track towards her. His brother and James Drew were out of sight. 'Rosa!' This time the call came from the other direction, from the man with the dog. Jim.

John Byrne reached her first and he smiled. 'Are you running away from me?'

'No. Why should I be?'

'From James Drew then?' There was a hint of a laugh in the question but his voice was probing.

'No need for me to run away from him either,' she answered calmly. 'I'm free to do as I wish.'

'Ah,' he sighed. 'If that were only true. We are none of us totally free.' He looked up as Jim drew nearer and dropped his voice. 'The man yonder looks familiar. One of Drew's sons?'

She didn't answer but turned to Jim as he approached. 'This is a busy thoroughfare today,' she said lightly. 'Stone Creek's as busy as Patrington market day and I was expecting to be alone.'

'There's allus somebody about when you least

263

expect 'em.' Jim spoke to her but stared at John Byrne, who returned his gaze.

'Jim Drew?' John Byrne asked. His voice had a hard edge to it.

'Aye, 'same.'

It seemed to Rosa that the men were like two dogs sniffing and circling as they gave their greetings.

'John Byrne?' said Jim.

'Indeed. Sure and I never thought that we'd meet again.'

'Nor I,' Jim answered. 'It's been a long time.'

'Too long.'

'I wouldn't say that,' Jim said slowly. 'I'd no wish to see you or your brother again.'

Rosa was startled. Jim was often blunt and plain-spoken but never uncivil, as she felt he was being now.

'Your father is glad to see us.' John Byrne had a cynical smile upon his lips. 'We have a little business venture going.'

'He doesn't need any other business,' Jim said abruptly. 'We're farmers.' He glanced at Rosa as he spoke. 'Neither should it be discussed here. It's not right or proper.'

'Oh, but I think it is.' The Irishman turned to Rosa as if he was including her in the discussion. 'It's as if we've come full circle. The second generation!'

'No! Not on any account.' Jim's voice was full of suppressed fury.

'You wouldn't want your father's name dragged in the mud?' There was a threat in John Byrne's voice.

'I'll not have Rosa brought into it.' Jim shifted his hand on his gun.

'But she is in it,' Byrne said smoothly. 'When her father disappeared and she was born, she surely took on his mantle?'

'You're talking rubbish,' Jim snarled. 'You were always full o' damned moonshine and me, young fool that I was, used to believe it.'

'What are you talking about?' Rosa broke in. 'What mantle? What about my father?'

'Nowt!' Jim said. 'Get off home, Rosa. I'll not have you involved in his shady business.'

'Protective, aren't we?' Byrne sneered. 'Why's that, I wonder? And I also wonder why your father took her under his wing? He's hardly got the milk of human kindness in his blood. Not from where I'm standing anyway.'

'Get off home, Rosa,' Jim repeated. 'I'll sort this out once and for all.'

'No!' Rosa had seen his fingers shifting on his gun and was afraid that he might fire. 'I want to know what all this is about.' She turned to John Byrne. 'The last time we met you said that my father had a ship. Was he a smuggler? Is that why you were here on Sunk Island?'

He gave her a lazy smile. 'What a clever girl. Brains as well as beauty!' His eyes appraised her and she felt herself blushing. 'We were smuggling sure enough. Had a good business going too until we came to this lonely land.' He grimaced. 'Then your daddy fell in love and became senseless. We don't know what happened next, except that Carlos disappeared and Seamus and me got caught by the Customs.'

He looked at Jim, who was eyeing him with loathing.

'As for Jim here.' John Byrne shook his head. 'He did whatever his father told him, didn't you, Jim? Just as you will this time.'

Rosa watched Jim's face. He seemed to be struggling with fear, defiance and humiliation.

'He doesn't have to do anything he doesn't want to,' she said boldly. 'Especially if you're planning something else that is against the law.' She looked back towards Stone Creek and couldn't believe that Mr Drew would become involved in something illegal. 'I'd have thought you would have learned your lesson if you've been in prison already.'

Byrne stiffened. 'It's because I've been in prison that I've come back! Somebody has to pay for those years.' His words were harsh. 'I was only a boy when I was caught. I grew up in jail. I want some answers and I'm going to get them.'

Jim defied him. 'You're full o' bluster, Byrne. An ass, that's what you are. An ass in a lion's skin! There are no answers! Can't you get it into your head? It's finished! Over! We should all get on with our lives as best we can.'

There was a burning obsession in John Byrne's eyes as he spat out, 'Never! Never while I live. Whilst I have breath in my body I'll find out the truth and somebody will pay.'

CHAPTER TWENTY-THREE

'Mr Drew! I need to talk to you.' Rosa took her courage in both hands when she met him alone out in the yard. 'It's about Delia.'

'I don't wish to discuss her.' His manner was abrupt.

'It can't be easy for you.' Rosa thought she would try placating him. 'It's been a shock to you. Not what you would expect from one of your daughters.'

His face was like thunder and he opened his mouth to bellow at her, but she quickly forestalled him. 'I think there is a way out of the present difficulty.'

'The only way out is for her to disappear off Sunk Island and out of my sight,' he snapped. 'I want nothing more to do with her.'

'She's carrying your grandchild,' she implored. 'She has done wrong, but that can't be undone now, and none of us is without sin.'

His face, which had been scarlet with fury, drained of colour and he stared at her.

'The child will be born out of wedlock, I know,'

she went on, 'but her mother wouldn't have turned her away.'

'What? What did you say?'

She gazed back at him. 'Her mother wouldn't have turned her away,' she repeated.

He licked his lips and took several shallow breaths and she thought that he was like a man drowning. 'Are you ill?' she asked. 'Do you want to go inside and sit down?'

'No,' he gasped. 'I just want all of this to go away. I need some peace.'

There's something more than Delia bothering him, she thought. He's shaking! 'I've asked my gran to come and stay,' she said firmly. 'We've enough room and she knows about these things. I don't,' she added, 'and you wouldn't want a stranger coming here to deliver the child.'

'No,' he said. 'I won't have that.' He stared defiantly at her. 'I'll not pay her for coming!'

'She wouldn't expect you to,' she said coldly. 'Just her keep, that's all.'

He turned away. 'Another mouth to feed,' he muttered.

She couldn't resist a barb. 'You had a wife and five daughters to look after you before, Mr Drew. Now there's only me, and Delia. Besides, my gran's a good cook.'

He grunted, but said nothing more and she turned and went into the house, feeling satisfied. It would be so much easier with her grandmother there, she was a comforting, steady soul, and she wouldn't put up with any tantrums from Delia.

'You're not a very good colour,' was the first thing Mrs Jennings said to Delia on arrival. 'You should be blooming! Are you eating? You're eating for two, don't forget.'

'I wish I could forget,' Delia muttered. 'I wish I could just forget about it and it would go away.'

'Well it won't,' Mrs Jennings said cheerfully. 'You should have given more thought about it before. You can't undo what's done, so you must make 'best of it.'

She put the kettle on the fire. She seemed to have taken charge of the kitchen already. Turning to Delia she added softly, 'You'll feel different about it when you hold 'bairn in your arms, mark my words if you don't.'

She ran her fingers over Delia's cheekbones. Her face was thin and her skin had a greyish tinge to it. Mrs Jennings gave a slight nod of her head. 'Best rest from now on,' she said. 'A walk every morning to get some fresh air and then a lie-down in 'afternoon. No lifting coals or wood.'

Tears came into Delia's eyes at the kind words and she blinked them away. 'I don't feel well,' she mumbled, 'but I'm scared of what my da will say if I don't pull my weight.'

'You leave your da to me.' Mrs Jennings patted her arm. 'I'll make sure he's nowt to grumble about.'

To Rosa she expressed her fears. 'That young woman doesn't look good. I'm not happy about her. We'll have 'doctor here to take another look at her.'

The doctor, when he came, pursed his lips. 'Rest,' he said to Delia. 'I think it won't be long before your confinement.'

Delia turned even paler. 'I think I'm going to

be sick,' she whispered to Mrs Jennings after the doctor had left. 'I'm that frightened.'

'Nowt to be frightened about,' Mrs Jennings said soothingly. 'It's happening to women all over 'world, every day, perfectly natural. Just think on all animals that just get on with it: hosses, cows, sheep, pigs.'

Delia gave her a look of disgust. 'That doesn't give me any comfort at all!'

'Well, that's 'way it is.' Mrs Jennings was blunt, her patience rapidly disappearing. 'So remember if ever you're tempted again.'

'I'll not be tempted,' Delia said bitterly. 'I'm finished wi' men for good.'

But she realized she would change her mind on the morning she took a gentle walk across the pastureland and met the red-haired Irishman again. He greeted her so politely and asked, with a charming lilt to his voice, how she was, and offered her his arm to escort her back home.

'Miss Drew,' he said quietly. 'Forgive me – perhaps it's Mrs?'

'No,' she mumbled. 'It isn't, I'm Delia – and I'm not wed.'

'So!' He gave her a smile. 'A chance for some of us?'

She tossed her head. 'I don't think so.'

'Can I ask you a question?' His voice was soft, like velvet, she thought.

She shrugged. 'If you want.'

'You might slap my face!'

She didn't answer, for he was gently stroking her arm with his fingers.

'Are you unfortunate enough to be in the family way? Has some cowardly lover left you?'

She stared straight ahead. It showed, then. She had thought if she didn't eat much and wore loose clothes that no-one would notice, but she had felt the eyes of Harry, the farm hand, on her the other day, and he had dropped his gaze when he saw her looking back at him.

'Yes,' she said. 'I am. And he did.'

'Did your father and brothers not go after him?' he asked.

'He's left the area,' she lied. 'They couldn't find him.'

'But you've got the support of your family? Your father is taking care of you? You're very lucky.' He gave her a compassionate glance. 'If you had been an Irish girl so afflicted, she would have been abandoned by her family and the baby sent to an orphanage.'

She shook her head, feeling that she could confide in him. 'No. Da would have turned me out. He's so righteous. He said I had sinned, which I know I did.' Tears, which came so easily, flushed her eyes. 'But Matthew and Jim persuaded him to let me stop.' She didn't mention Rosa or the effort she had made.

'Ah,' he said softly. 'Of course. It must have been hard for your poor father, being a religious church-going man. So God-fearing! He would expect his sons and daughters to be as strong and virtuous as he so obviously is.'

She thought she detected a laugh in his voice, but when she turned to face him, he was straight-faced and solemn.

'Someone will come along, Delia,' he murmured. 'Someone else will see your worth and charm.' He smiled and looked into her eyes, then reached to kiss her cheek. She blushed and drew in her breath. 'They will forgive that they are not the first to capture your maidenhood.'

She stood with lips parted. Was it true? Did some men not mind if a woman isn't pure when they marry her?

'I'd like to think that there'd be someone—' she began.

They were close to the farmhouse, but he didn't even give it a glance as he stepped nearer to her. 'There'll be someone, be sure of it,' he murmured, and turning her face up towards him he kissed her on the lips. 'Be sure of it, Delia.'

He stroked her cheek, then blowing her a kiss he moved away. 'Go home now,' he urged. 'Take care of yourself and your baby.'

She smiled. She hadn't felt so good in months. There was hope after all. She watched him as he walked away. He had such a spring in his step. He looked so lively. He turned and waved and she saw the smile on his face. He seemed very happy. Was it because of her?

Mrs Jennings had seen them from the window. She tried to warn her. 'There'll be some men will try to tek advantage,' she said. 'They'll think cos you've fallen once, you'll be willing. Don't be tekken in,' she advised. 'They'll sweet-talk you, but they won't marry you, girl. They'll not tek on another man's child.'

Delia listened and nodded in agreement but as she went upstairs for her rest she smiled. What did that old woman know? When had she last felt the sweetness of a man's lips on hers? She felt a restlessness inside her. She wanted to get on with life now that there was some hope, and the Irishman had given her that hope. Mrs Jennings might be wise, but she was quite wrong.

She lay on her bed and ran her fingers around her breasts, which were full and round, then smoothing them across her belly, she considered that she hadn't felt any movement for some time. She sighed. She hoped now that it wouldn't be long. Better to be over and done with and she could make a fresh start. A picture of the Irishman came into her head and she etched her fingers around her mouth where he had kissed her.

She played out a little scene where he and she and the baby left Sunk Island. Taking his arm, she turned her back on her family and especially on Rosa, and they rode away in a neat trap, like the one which Maggie had. I'll show them all, she thought drowsily. I'll teach them to look down on me. For that was what she felt. She had fallen from grace, not able to eat at her father's table, nothing more than a lowly servant.

If Rosa hadn't been here, Da would have been glad to have me back, even with the babby. If she hadn't been here I might never have gone away in the first place, and none of this would have happened. And so she absolved her guilt and transferred it to someone else. To Rosa, whom she had never liked.

'Is yon young woman expecting?' Harry asked Rosa as he sat down at the table for his midday meal. The others hadn't come in yet and Mrs

Jennings had gone to the dairy to fetch some butter.

'She is. But please don't mention it in front of Mr Drew.'

'Can't disguise it, though.' He took a sup of ale that she had poured for him. 'Can't hide summat like that.' He gave a sniff. 'And 'chap won't marry her, I suppose, otherwise we'd have seen a wedding by now. I expect her da'll be preaching in 'church about sins of 'flesh, being sort o' man that he is. But she'll not be 'first and she'll not be 'last either. Why – I remember when I was a young chap—'

Rosa hushed him as she heard the sound of footsteps entering the house and Mr Drew was followed in by Matthew and Jim.

'Dinner not on 'table?' Mr Drew barked.

'It's ready,' Rosa said. 'I didn't put it out as I know you like your rabbit pie straight from 'oven.'

'Rabbit pie! Aye, it has to be hot – or else cold. Never just warm.' He sat down in his chair as Mrs Jennings came in and took the pie out of the oven, and Rosa dished up the floury potatoes.

'Carrots! Mrs Drew allus did carrots with rabbit,' he muttered, but appeared mollified as, without a word, Mrs Jennings put in front of him a dish of carrots with a knob of melting yellow butter on top.

'Tha's allus had a good hand at pastry, Mrs Jennings,' Harry said appreciatively as he ate. 'I remember it well when I used to work for Mr Jennings. We allus knew where we would get good grub and where we wouldn't, and yours was allus one of 'best places.'

'Ah well,' said Mrs Jennings. 'Feed a man well and he won't stray far.'

'Aye,' he cackled. 'Or at least he'll allus be home in time for his dinner.'

Mr Drew glared at him. A red spot burned on each side of his face. 'Let's have less talk, we've work to do this afternoon.'

'Where's 'other young lass?' Harry ignored the admonishment. 'She never eats with us at dinner time. I hope she's feeding herself up. Babby'll tek her strength if she doesn't.'

There was a momentary silence and Rosa tried to catch his gaze that she might implore him to be silent, but he ate and gossiped garrulously about somebody's pregnant daughter who didn't eat, and the baby took her nourishment until she was as thin as a skeleton.

'That's enough,' Matthew began, but Mrs Jennings butted in. 'You're talking rubbish, Harry Miller. Now, no more of this for you know nowt about it. If you must know, Delia has eaten her dinner already and is resting upstairs. More pie, Mr Drew?'

'Well, now it's out,' Rosa said to her grand-mother as they washed the dishes and dried them. 'Now that Harry knows, everyone else on Sunk Island will hear about it before the week's out. He's a proper old woman for gossip.'

'So we can stop pretending, can't we?' Mrs Jennings said. 'It should have been told afore and it would have been over and done with. I'll go into Patrington tomorrow and buy a few things that she'll need – and some knitting wool for a start.'

'And the day after I shall go to Hedon and visit Maggie,' Rosa determined. 'I haven't had time to go and see her, I've always been so busy.' She reached across and kissed her gran on the cheek. 'I'm so glad that you're here,' she said. 'I know everything will be all right now.'

Maggie was a picture of health. Her skin was clear and her extra plumpness suited her. She was seated on a sofa with her feet up when Rosa arrived and she greeted her warmly. She showed her the baby clothes that she had knitted and the linen she had stitched for the crib, then eventually she asked about her sister.

'How is Delia? Is she well?'

'Not so well as you, Maggie, and your father still won't speak to her. It's as if he's pretending that she isn't there.'

'Poor girl!' Maggie commiserated. 'I'm so sorry. I was angry with her to begin with, but she won't have much of a life if she and her babby are to be hidden away.'

'It's much easier now that my gran has come,' Rosa said. 'She's so sensible. She's making Delia rest every day now, but,' she added, 'she doesn't look as you do. Her skin is grey and sometimes she's sick. Gran thinks that 'babby will come soon.'

'She's earlier than me then?' Maggie pondered. 'And I thought we were 'same time. I've a month to go.' She gave a happy smile. 'I just can't wait and neither can Fred.'

A few days later Delia started to be sick. She retched morning, noon and night and complained of pain in her back. 'Ride for 'doctor, will you, Jim,' Mrs Jennings said late on the third afternoon. 'Summat's not right.'

Mr Drew heard Delia crying and wailing and pacing the floor up in her room as he was downstairs in the parlour trying to read his paper before supper. 'Tell her to mek less noise,' he bellowed to Mrs Jennings. 'Tell her it's her just punishment for 'sin she's committed and she must bear it quietly.'

'And what of 'fellow who put her in this state?' Mrs Jennings answered sharply. 'It teks two to mek a bairn. He's not suffering, is he? Men tek their pleasure and don't suffer consequences.'

He threw down his paper, got up from his chair and marched towards the kitchen door. He turned. 'Men have bodily needs that are stronger than women's,' he cried in a tight hoarse voice. 'Women must have 'strength and courage to resist them, not indulge them in their depraved sins. They must show them 'error of their wicked desires, not pander to them.'

He banged the door behind him and Mrs Jennings stared after him. 'Well, well, well,' she exclaimed.

Jim was about to mount his horse to ride to Patrington when his father stormed out of the house and into the stable, bringing out his mare. 'I'm going for 'doctor, Da. There's no need for you to go.'

His father mounted. 'I'm not going for 'doctor,' he bellowed. 'I'm going out, away from that Hades racket.'

'But where are you going? It's late!'

His father wheeled his mount around and headed for the gate. 'Never you mind. I'll be back in 'morning.'

It was a long dark ride and when he reached the town of Hull, instead of booking a room in the inn, he rode on to Leadenhall Square and tied his horse up outside the house. He rang the doorbell and a young woman he hadn't seen before answered it. He was very dishevelled after the ride and she half closed the door.

'Tell Miss Emerald it's Mr Brown,' he barked at her.

She smiled and opened the door. 'You'd better come in, Mr Brown. You've had a long journey by 'look of it.'

'Aye. I need a bath.'

'I'll see to it,' she said soothingly. 'It will help to relax you.'

Miss Emerald appeared a few moments later. 'How good to see you, Mr Brown. We thought you had forsaken us!'

'No.' He felt exhausted. 'Just busy.'

'And now you need to unwind?'

'Aye, I do, but I have to be off early in 'morning.'

'I understand.' Her voice was soft and pleasant. 'Just a brief visit this time?'

He was bathed and towelled and dressed in a robe and taken to a room, dimly lit and heavily swathed with hangings which smelled of exotic perfume making him feel quite dizzy. The women who were sent in to him were in turn vivacious, tender, rampant or provocative. They

278

whispered promises of so many delights, but they all failed to rouse him to sensual pleasure or gratification.

Each fair face and comely body which lay beside him on the crisp perfumed sheets shifted and transposed into the sad face and swollen body of his youngest daughter. The daughter who had fallen to the desires of a man as these women had fallen.

'I'm a sinner,' he moaned, as they ran their sensuous fingers over his collapsed and drooping impotence.

'Of course you are,' they murmured. 'We all are. That is why you are here, so we can enjoy sinning together.'

One sat astride him and lowered herself so that her breasts were brushing his face and her nipples close to his mouth. He turned his head away. No. No, he groaned inwardly. She's with child! But he opened his mouth and sucked and sucked until the girl cried out that he was hurting. But still his body was flaccid and useless.

He blamed them, the women. 'I'll not pay in full,' he told Miss Emerald as he prepared to leave. 'They're not as good as they used to be.'

'Perhaps you are a little tired?' she suggested, but her eyes were cold. 'They are my best girls.'

He grunted and gave her only half of what she asked for and as she closed the door behind him, she slipped the money into the folds of her dress and called to a man sitting in another room, 'Cross Mr Country Brown off our list. He'll not be coming back.'

CHAPTER TWENTY-FOUR

The doctor was out attending an emergency. 'But *this* is an emergency,' Jim told the housekeeper. 'My sister's babby is coming.'

She nodded her head. 'Then it'll keep on coming whether 'doctor's there or not,' she said calmly. 'There's no stopping 'em once they've started. I'll tell him,' she assured him, 'just as soon as he gets in.'

There's no sense in me rushing back then, he thought, and headed for the nearest hostelry in the marketplace. There's nowt I can do. Though I expect it's similar to delivering a calf or a lamb, and I've done plenty of them. He ordered a glass of ale from the landlord. I wonder what she'll get and if da will let her stop? He realized that although his father had been persuaded that Delia should stay until her confinement, he hadn't said that she could stay after the child was born.

There'd be no harm in it, he pondered. Folks will talk, but not for long, and it'd be nice to have a little nipper around, 'specially if it's a lad and I could teach him about farming.

He turned to look around the room. It was an old hostelry, dark and smoky and lit by firelight and candles held in brackets on the walls. As he peered to see who else was in the room he saw a man leaning against the hearth wall watching him. It was John Byrne.

Jim turned away, but Byrne came across to him. 'Don't often see you out here at night,' he said.

'No, there's allus work to be done until late,' Jim replied briefly. 'Not much time for socializing when you're a farmer.'

'You could give it up.' Byrne dropped his voice. 'There are other ways of making money.'

'Illegal ways!' Jim muttered. 'No thanks, I like to sleep with an easy conscience.'

Cynicism crossed Byrne's face. 'And can you do that? There are few men who can say that they do.'

'I've made a few mistakes,' Jim admitted tersely. 'No need to add to 'em.'

Byrne gave a small shrug. 'Your father is willing to take another chance.'

'He's not willing. You've threatened him that you'll spread rumours about us.' Jim's voice was low and bitter. 'Rumours about Carlos. Insinuations that he was murdered!'

Byrne looked astonished, then he laughed. 'Is that what he said? That we'd spread rumours about somebody who went missing nearly twenty years ago?' He laughed again. 'The old devil!'

Jim frowned. 'Then what did you say? You put 'wind up him over summat.'

'Well, it wasn't that! Although . . .' he added

slowly and gazed at Jim intently. 'It's worth considering as a possibility. Why? I wonder—' He tapped his mouth with his fingers. 'Why would he say such a thing to you if it wasn't true?'

Jim shuffled his feet. He didn't like the way the conversation was going. Byrne was too tricky for him, always had been. 'There's no reason why he should say it,' he hedged.

'Except that he didn't want you to know the real reason.' Byrne gave a sly smile. 'Your precious da! So holier-than-thou! He wouldn't want his sons and daughters to find out why he'd agreed to go along with us in our little schemes.'

Jim stared at him. 'And we don't want to know,' he vowed. 'There's no reason to sully 'waters when they seem clear enough.'

'Even though there's foul sediment lying beneath?' Byrne sneered.

'Even then!' Jim put his glass down on the counter and turned towards the door, but was almost knocked over by a gang of local youths coming in.

'There's one of 'em,' one in the crowd shouted. 'Here! Irish!'

Byrne turned lazily towards them. 'Would you be speaking to me?'

'*Sure and that I would!*' another mimicked, then changed his tone to one of menace. 'Some of you Irish have been making up to our lasses. And we'll not have it!'

Byrne looked him up and down. 'Maybe you'll not, but the lasses are willing enough to have it. I speak from experience, I assure you of that.'

The fellow lunged towards him but was

restrained by several hands. 'Leave it, Greg,' someone else said. 'That's one of Byrne brothers. They're nowt but trouble.'

The man pointed a finger. 'Just let me catch you messing with any of our women and you'll be sorry.' He looked around the room for moral support and caught sight of Jim. 'I'm surprised to see you in such company, Jim Drew,' he said. 'Thought you'd have had more sense!'

'I'm not in anybody's company but my own,' Jim maintained. 'I came in for a quiet drink of ale. Nothing more. Now if you'll let me pass I'll be on my way home.'

As he unloosed the horse's reins from the ring on the outside wall, he heard shouts and the sound of breaking glass coming from within the inn. He gave a grimace. He hoped it was John Byrne getting the worst of a fight but in spite of the numbers against him, he didn't think that it would be.

His thoughts were confirmed a few minutes later as Byrne sauntered out with his hands in his pockets and a smile on his face. 'By the way, Jim,' he called. 'How is your sister? Delia, isn't it? Give her my regards and say I hope all goes well with her.'

Jim glared down at him from the saddle. 'Don't come bothering her,' he warned. 'She's got enough trouble without you mekking more.'

'I wouldn't make trouble,' he replied easily. 'I'm not so careless. At least – not usually!'

How does he know Delia? Jim deliberated as he rode across the bridge and on to Sunk Island. When has he met her? She hardly ever goes out.

He gave a deep sigh. There's no let-up, allus summat to worry about. As he rode along the embankment, he looked about him as he always did. The sky was light although it was late, and his sight was keen. He glanced towards one of the old drainage channels and saw that the water was high, almost to the top of the bank. He looked along it and saw, further down, that part of the bank had crumbled, so blocking the water from running along it.

That one's allus been a problem. He stood looking down the channel. We'll have to dig it out or we'll have trouble there at high tide.

He continued on home, to be met at the gate by Matthew. 'Did you see 'doctor? Is he coming?' Matthew looked anxious. 'She's having a terrible time. I can't bear to stay in the house.'

'He was out,' Jim confessed. 'His housekeeper said she'd tell him as soon as he got back. I doubt he'll come tonight, it's nearly eleven.'

'So where've you been? And where's Da? I've not seen him for hours.'

'I had a tankard of ale in Patrington, and Da's gone off somewhere.'

'Where?' Matthew persisted.

'I don't know! He said he'd be back in 'morning.'

'In 'morning!' Matthew was incredulous. 'And he didn't say where he was going? Do you think he's gone to stay at our Maggie's? Mrs Jennings said he was grumbling about 'row Delia was making.'

'I said, I don't know.' Jim was sharp. 'I'm not his keeper!'

'No, but he's yours, isn't he?' Matthew answered back. Both were short-tempered and irritable.

'I don't know what you're on about.'

'I think you do. You can't step out of place but he's on to you. You shouldn't stand for it.' Matthew faced his brother. It was the nearest they had ever come to a quarrel. 'You're just like Henry. He never defied him, even though he argued with him.'

Jim took a deep breath. 'I don't want to fight wi' you, Matthew, but there's a reason for most things. Just keep out of it wi' Da and me. We'll sort things out sooner or later.'

He turned away, then as if in afterthought turned back and said, 'Have you seen that Irishman hanging around here? Younger one wi' red hair. John Byrne?'

Matthew pursed his lips. 'I saw him walking along one of 'dykes not long ago.'

'Let me know if you see him again, and don't let him near Delia – or Rosa.'

Rosa sat down on a kitchen chair, 'I wish 'doctor would come. Is it always so bad, Gran?' She was exhausted after walking up and down with a weeping Delia, who had at last dropped off to sleep on her bed.

'He'll not come tonight. Not now. He won't risk riding over here in 'dark.' Her grandmother poured them both a cup of tea. They'd been taking it in turns to be with Delia. 'She's frightened. That's why she's so tense and in pain. If she would relax she wouldn't feel it so much.'

285

'Maggie says she's got another month to go yet. I hope Delia doesn't tell her how bad it is.'

'It might not be so bad for her. She's looking forward to having her babby, she knows there's joy to come at 'end of her pain. Young woman upstairs hasn't got that joy.' She raised her eyes to the ceiling as they heard again Delia's plaintive voice calling for someone to come.

'But she will have when it's born, won't she?'

Mrs Jennings got up from her chair and turned towards the stairs. 'Mebbe.' There was doubt in her voice. 'If all goes well.'

The doctor came early the next morning, arriving shortly before James Drew. He greeted him after attending Delia, and accepted the offer of a cup of tea from Rosa. 'Your daughter is in considerable pain, Mr Drew, and I fear for the child. It's lying very awkwardly and—'

'Don't tell me for I don't want to know,' Drew replied brusquely. 'I want nowt to do with her or 'bastard she's carrying.' His lips tightened. 'If she's suffering then it's punishment for her sins. We'll all have to suffer on 'Day of Judgement.' His expression became blank and he stared into space. The doctor looked at him keenly as he continued, 'And some folks will go through fires of hell even afore then.'

'Come, come, Mr Drew.' The doctor drank his tea. 'I didn't see you as a zealot!'

Then you don't know him, Rosa thought as she listened to their conversation through the open kitchen door. It doesn't bode well for Delia. She felt sorry for her. She was going through physical

286

and mental pain as she walked the floor, crying out querulously what was to become of her.

The doctor finished his tea and, giving Drew a cursory nod, went outside, signalling Rosa to follow him. 'I'll come back tonight,' he said. 'I've left a potion with Mrs Jennings to give to Delia which will calm her, but tell Mrs Jennings, out of Delia's hearing, that the child may not survive.'

Rosa gazed at him. He's coming back tonight! Does that mean that Delia has to suffer all the rest of the day?

'The child is very still,' the doctor continued. 'I can't find any sign of life. I may be wrong, we can't always tell, but it is very still.'

So what will happen then? Rosa sat down on a mounting block in the yard and pondered. Will Delia stay here if she loses her child? Will she be able to live under her father's uncharitable gaze? And if she does, can I?

'What is it, Rosa? What's up?' Matthew came out of the fold yard leading two waggon horses.

'Doctor says that Delia's baby is very still.'

'What does that mean?'

'He's bothered about it.' She looked up at him. 'What's going to happen to her, Matthew? Will your da let her stay? Will she want to?'

He looked across the yard to where Harry was coming in through the open gate, and signalled to him to take the horses. 'Hitch them to 'waggon, Harry,' he said. 'We'll shift some muck into 'top field. I'll be with you in a minute.'

He turned to Rosa. 'I don't know what will happen.' He looked down at his feet and scuffed the dust, making long lines with the side of his boots and then crossing them to make squares. 'How would I know? Da never tells us anything, Jim never tells me anything; so how would I know about Delia? She isn't the young girl I knew as my sister.' He looked up at her and she saw misery on his face. 'I don't know anything about anybody, not even you.'

She gave a half laugh. 'Of course you know about me! You know that you do.'

'No. No, I don't.' He took a step towards her. 'I'm always here and yet you never see me. I'm just part of the landscape, a wall, a hedge, a chair, and if I wasn't here, you wouldn't even notice that I'd gone.'

She took in a short sharp breath. Surely he understood? 'That isn't true and you said that you didn't know *me*,' she said, 'and yet you are talking about *you*.'

Mrs Jennings knocked from an upstairs window and called her urgently.

Matthew turned away. 'It comes to 'same thing,' he muttered.

'Be quick!' Mrs Jennings called again. 'I need you, Rosa. She's going off her head!'

Delia did seem to have a madness on her and she struggled against Mrs Jennings and Rosa as they tried to give her the tincture which the doctor had left for her. She spat it out at Rosa and clutched Mrs Jennings's arm in an iron grip as she tried to administer more.

'I don't want this babby,' she screamed. 'I never wanted it. How will I live with a bairn to bring up? What'll I do for money?'

'Whether you want it or not, miss, makes no

odds.' Mrs Jennings forced the spoon into Delia's clenched lips. 'It'll not go away.'

'It's your fault,' Delia bellowed at Rosa. 'If you hadn't come here, I needn't have gone to work in Hornsea and this wouldn't have happened. I'd have stayed with my da and Jim and Matthew.'

'That's enough, that's enough!' Mrs Jennings pushed her onto the bed. 'Tek no notice,' she murmured to Rosa. 'It's pain that's addled her brain. She doesn't know what she's saying.'

Delia's eyes started to close and her fingers loosened their grip on Mrs Jennings. 'By!' she said, rubbing her bruised arm. 'He's given her a strong dose of summat, but she should settle for an hour or two. Come on.' She rose from the side of the bed. 'Morning's getting on. We've dinner to see to or else *he'll* have summat to say.'

Rosa looked down at Delia who, even though drugged, tossed her head and murmured incoherently.

'Why does she hate me so, Gran? None of the others resented me, not Maggie or Flo or any of them.'

'Jealous,' her grandmother said, 'though why she should be, I don't know. You were never treated any different, were you?'

'No.' Rosa continued to stare down at Delia. 'Why should she be jealous? There was no favouritism. I got 'strap more often than Delia ever did.'

She sighed and followed her grandmother out of the room, down the stairs and into the kitchen.

'But whatever she says doesn't matter to you,

does it, Rosa?' Her grandmother looked at her keenly.

'No,' she said softly. 'I hear her, but it doesn't seem to matter. I don't know why.'

'I do.' The old lady gently patted Rosa's arm. 'I've onny just realized. You've grown a shell around you so nothing touches you. You don't cry. I've never seen or heard you cry since you were a bairn.'

Rosa didn't answer but poured potatoes from a bucket into the sink and started to scrub them. That's so that nothing can hurt me, she thought. I won't let it.

'But then it's just as well.' Her grandmother was still talking. 'Some folks are allus wailing and moaning about summat and it doesn't do a bit of good. You've just got to get on wi' life.'

They heard a thump from upstairs and Mrs Jennings sighed. 'She'll have to wait. I'll put 'taties on to boil when you've finished 'em. 'Meat's almost ready.'

A leg of pork was sizzling on a spit over the fire and Mrs Jennings stirred a pan of apples and added a scraping of nutmeg. 'There, sauce is ready. He likes it cold, doesn't he?'

Rosa nodded. How quickly her grandmother had picked up Mr Drew's idiosyncrasies. Hot rabbit pie with carrots. Cold apple sauce with pork. She occasionally put in some of her own favourites and Mr Drew never commented, but she was careful to prepare other recipes in the same manner as Mrs Drew had always done them.

'I'll go up, Gran.' Rosa put the potatoes into a

heavy pan as her grandmother lowered the pork over the flame to crisp it. 'And Mr Drew'll have to be content with cabbage today.'

'Aye, go on then. I think I can hear her moaning. Mebbe poor lass has started up wi' pains again.'

Rosa ran upstairs to Delia's room and quietly opened the door. Delia was lying half on, half off the bed and Rosa gasped. 'Gran! Gran! Come quickly,' she shouted. 'Babby's coming. It's coming now!'

CHAPTER TWENTY-FIVE

Matthew heard Delia's cries and came running into the house. 'Shall I fetch 'doctor?' he called up the stairs.

'Tell him no,' Mrs Jennings said to Rosa. 'It's too late, but ask him to put pan o' water back onto 'fire.' She turned back to Delia, who had taken a deep breath and was about to shriek again. 'Now that's enough! Just concentrate on what I'm saying and it'll all be over.'

'You stupid old woman,' Delia railed. 'What do you know about it? And tell her to get out!' She turned a flushed tormented face to Rosa, who was standing near the door.

'Fetch a bowl o' warm water, Rosa. Now push, girl!' Mrs Jennings urged Delia. 'Come on, it's nearly here.'

Matthew was hovering by the kitchen fire and Rosa went to fetch a bowl and a clean towel from the linen cupboard. Jim came in. 'No use asking if there's a cup o' tea going? I've never heard such a row! You can hear her right across 'farm.'

'It must be terrible.' Matthew was ashen-faced.

'I don't remember Ma making such a fuss,' Jim

commented. 'I can remember 'twins being born and you and Delia, and not a murmur from Ma.'

'Mebbe it's worse with 'first one.' Matthew lifted the pan from the fire shelf and poured the water into the bowl which Rosa brought in. 'How would we know?' His face tensed. 'I'd like to horsewhip 'fellow who brought her to this. Pass me 'teapot,' he said to Jim. 'I'll make some tea.'

His father strode into the room. His face was livid. 'Tell Mrs Jennings to shut 'window up-stairs,' he commanded Rosa. 'That girl is letting 'whole of Sunk Island know of her wicked sins and retribution.'

'Best that they all know,' Jim muttered. 'Better than letting a sin be hidden. Better that than a canker consuming you day by day.'

Matthew glanced from his brother to his father, and then to Rosa. She turned away and went upstairs carrying the bowl of water. 'What you talking about?' Matthew asked, his voice raised. 'She's having a babby and isn't wed! She was tempted and fell. She's not killed anybody, for God's sake!'

Jim's face drained of colour and his father stared at him, breathing heavily, his mouth working.

'What's going on?' Matthew asked, but neither answered, and after a pause he pressed further. 'Is there summat I should know?'

'No.' Jim's voice was strained. 'There isn't. Are you going to make that tea or not?'

Matthew brought out the cake tin and placed it in the middle of the table, but no-one took any cake. They sat at the table and drank the tea in

293

silence, Matthew staring in the direction of the stairs and Jim and his father towards the window. It was quiet now above them, until they heard the sound of footsteps on the stairs.

Mr Drew rose hurriedly from his chair and headed towards the door as Mrs Jennings came panting into the room. Her face was flushed and hot and her hairline beneath her cotton cap was wet. 'Don't you want to know about your daughter, Mr Drew?' she asked, detaining him.

'She's no daughter of mine,' he muttered, his hand on the doorknob. 'I've said afore I want nothing to do with her or her child.'

'Her son,' Mrs Jennings butted in. 'She's had a son.'

Matthew and Jim both gave an audible sigh and their father stared at the old lady.

'Will it live?' His question was terse and without emotion.

'I don't know.' Mrs Jennings sat down in his vacated chair. 'He looks sickly, he's not breathing properly. Will one of you fetch 'doctor back?' She turned to Jim and Matthew.

'I'll go.' Jim got up, and Matthew asked, 'What about Delia? Is she all right?'

'Aye. Exhausted, but she'll recover. My,' she exclaimed, 'but she's got an ill temper on her.'

Jim and his father left the room without speaking and Mrs Jennings reached for the teapot. 'Is this fresh?'

Matthew said that it was. 'Who made it?' She lifted the lid and peered into the teapot.

'I did.'

'And was 'water in kettle boiling when you poured it onto 'leaves?'

Matthew nodded. 'I used it from the pan after Rosa had finished with it.'

'You never made tea from warm water!' Mrs Jennings pulled herself up from the chair and swung the kettle back onto the fire. 'Did nobody ever tell you that water has to be boiling!'

He shook his head. 'I've never made it before. I thought I'd done well,' he grinned.

'Useless,' Mrs Jennings grumbled. 'Men can plough and sow and bring harvest home, but they're not much good at owt else; except mekking babbies,' she added. 'Aye,' she gave a great sigh. 'They can do that all right.'

Jim hadn't got back from Patrington, but at midday Rosa dished up the meal for Mr Drew and Matthew and urged her grandmother to sit down and eat also. 'Delia's sleeping,' she said. 'Take a rest now.' She didn't mention the child in front of Mr Drew, for he had a dark sullen expression about him.

'We usually have turnip with pork,' James Drew muttered. 'Not cabbage.'

'Cabbage was quicker,' Rosa said sharply. 'Turnip takes too long and I didn't want to keep you waiting. I knew how busy you were.'

'We'll have it tomorrow with cold pork and stuffing,' Mrs Jennings attempted to pacify, 'and a plum duff to follow.'

'Why should we always have to humour him?' Rosa said after Mr Drew and Matthew had finished their meal and gone out again. 'Why should it matter so much whether he always has the same as before?'

'It's his house,' her grandmother said patiently. 'He makes the rules. It's not our place to change them. Well, not mine anyway.' She gave a little smile. 'Your grandfer allus said I cooked just like his mother did. But I didn't, onny when we were first wed, then little by little I did things the way I wanted and he never noticed 'change.'

She nibbled on a piece of apple-pie crust as she cleared away. 'But yon fellow is too set in his ways to change. He's got a rod of iron in his backbone and a stone for his heart.' She pondered for a moment. 'But he must have a weakness somewhere. He wouldn't be human if he hadn't.'

They were about to take a few minutes' rest by the fire when they heard the sound of horses in the yard. 'That'll be Jim with the doctor.' Rosa got up from her chair. 'Will you go up with him, Gran, and I'll give Jim his dinner? He won't want to waste any more time, they're repairing 'dairy roof and cow byre, and want to finish before dark.'

'Aye.' Mrs Jennings nodded and, as the doctor came in, she asked, 'Will you tek a look at babby, Doctor? He's small and not a good colour and his breathing isn't regular.'

'And the young mother?' the doctor asked. 'Has she recovered? Her brother refers to her labour as sounding like a wildcats' concert!'

'It's true she didn't suffer silently.' Mrs Jennings glared disapprovingly at Jim, who had the grace to look abashed. 'But population would soon die out if roles were reversed and men had to give birth! But she's well enough now, or will be when she's rested.'

She led the doctor upstairs and Rosa raised her eyebrows at Jim as she served him his meal. 'Didn't mean owt,' he started to say, when they heard a muted cry from Delia's room.

Rosa went to the bottom of the stairs and listened, then slowly climbed the steps and opened the bedroom door. Delia was standing by the window with her back to the room, whilst the doctor had his ear over the baby's chest, listening intently. Then he straightened up and shook his head. 'I'm sorry, my dear,' he said. 'I'm afraid he's gone.'

Delia didn't move, but Mrs Jennings, who was sitting on the side of the bed, put her hand to her mouth and stifled a sob. 'But he was all right,' she gasped. 'He was wheezy as if his tubes were blocked, but—'

She stopped as Delia turned towards them. Her face was white and her eyes glittered. 'It wasn't meant to be, then, was it?' she breathed. 'He wasn't meant to have a life. I'll dig a little grave for him at 'bottom of 'garden.'

'No, no,' the doctor said soothingly. 'That will be taken care of. Come back to bed, my dear. You really shouldn't be on your feet yet.'

'He'll have to have a proper burial in 'church-yard,' Mrs Jennings told her. 'With a service and everything.'

'No,' Delia said. 'Da won't allow that. If we bury him here on 'farm, nobody will know.' Her words were whispered as if she was confiding a secret. 'Matthew will make him a little box.' She glanced towards Rosa as she spoke and Rosa had the distinct impression that Delia was goading her, but then she immediately dismissed the notion. Why would Delia do that? She was upset, bound to be, having lost her baby, perhaps her mind was distracted.

'Let me help you back into bed, Delia,' she said, as Mrs Jennings took the still form of the child and wrapped a sheet around him.

'I can manage on my own,' Delia snapped. 'I don't need you to help me.'

Rosa exchanged a look with her grandmother, who indicated with a slight movement of her head that she should go. 'See 'doctor out, Rosa, and then put 'kettle on 'fire.' She sighed. 'And is there any brandy? I reckon a drop in hot water wouldn't do any of us any harm.'

As Rosa took the brandy bottle from the cupboard downstairs she suddenly thought of Henry, who had imbibed too much brandy and drowned in the ditch. She leant her head against the cupboard door and blinked away hot tears. A picture of her mother came into her mind and she wondered how she had felt when giving birth to her, not knowing where Rosa's father had gone, or if she would ever see him again. Did her mind turn? Was that why she eventually went down to Spurn and didn't come back? She thought of Delia and how her eyes had glittered with a kind of madness.

'Rosa?'

She hadn't heard the door open and when she

turned, she saw Matthew standing there. 'What is it? What's wrong?' He came towards her. 'Who's having brandy?'

She put out her hand to him. 'It's for Delia, I think – or for Gran – I don't know. Oh, Matthew!' She stifled a sob. 'It's the baby. He was such a sweet little mite. And he's gone! He's dead.'

Matthew put his arms around her and held her. 'I don't understand,' he mumbled into her hair. 'I thought everything was all right.'

'It was,' she whispered, and thought how steady and strong he was. 'Or seemed to be. But he stopped breathing.' She drew away reluctantly and lowered her eyes as he gazed down at her. 'Delia wants you to make a casket for him.'

'Me?' he said. 'Jim's the carpenter! He'll do it better.'

She shook her head. 'She said you. You'd better go up and see her, she was talking non-sense – about burying him in the garden, so that no-one would know about him.'

'I'll not have that.' There was anger on his face and in his voice. 'That's because of Da! But he's an innocent child, he'll have a decent burial.'

James Drew made no comment when told of the child's death, but simply left the room and sat alone in the parlour for an hour. Then he came out, went up the stairs and, after rapping sharply on Delia's door, opened it. Standing in the doorway, he announced that the parson wouldn't bury the child in the churchyard as he had been conceived in sin, hadn't been baptized and had no father's name.

'Nay, Mr Drew,' Mrs Jennings, who was in the room with Delia, objected. 'That wouldn't be Christian! He's a good parson. He'd not deny an innocent bairn.'

Mr Drew didn't answer but turned around and went down the stairs again.

Delia lay awake until the early hours, her eyes wide open. It was not yet dawn, the skies dark and grey. She ran her hands over her breasts, which were tender and swollen, and then down to her navel. Nobody else need know, she pondered, only those of us here at home. She forgot about Harry and the farm lad, she forgot about John Byrne: they had all known. She forgot too about her sisters, who had also known and who might have spread the news. Except that she hadn't actually forgotten, she simply pushed them to the back of her mind as being irrelevant to the present situation.

She rose from her bed and, taking a shawl from the back of the chair, wrapped it around her. Her child, whom she hadn't named, was in the wooden casket which Matthew had hastily made for him, beneath the window. She averted her eyes from it and stole out of the room and along the landing to her father's room.

Gently she turned the brass knob. It yielded and she slid in through the door. She saw, by the light from the small fire which still burned in the grate, that her father was fast asleep in the bed which he had once shared with her mother. She took in a deep shuddering breath as she thought of what she was about to do, but even though in a confused and muddled state, she was determined.

She leant over her father's sleeping form and put a hand on his flannel-clad shoulder. 'Da,' she whispered. 'Da, wake up!'

'Huh!' He gasped and opened his eyes with a start. 'Ellen? No! Who is it?'

'It's Delia. I need to talk to you, Da.'

He sat up in bed and peered at her in the gloom. 'Get out!' he said in a guttural voice. 'How dare you come in my room? You're a wanton woman bringing shame on our name.'

'I know.' Tears thickened her voice. 'And I'm sorry, Da. But I've thought of something, and the others and 'doctor and Mrs Jennings said I couldn't do it, but I know that you'll say I can.'

He leaned on one elbow and stared at her. 'What are you talking about? I want you out of this house. You're not stopping!'

She started to weep. 'I've nowhere to go, Da, but babby's dead! If we bury him quietly, nobody else need know, onny 'family and Mrs Jennings and her – Rosa, and they won't say anything if you tell them not to.'

He frowned. 'What are you trying to say?'

She sniffled. 'If you'll help me, Da, we can bury him in 'garden. I can't dig, I'm not strong enough yet, but we have to do it soon – afore parson comes. Tonight even! And then, and then, if nobody else on Sunk Island knows, perhaps I can stop at home?'

He kept his eyes on her face. 'You'd not have to tell anybody where he was, and I shall deny it if I'm questioned.'

'Yes. Yes! And then I can stop at home? I'll not go wrong again, Da!' As she made the vow, the words of the Irishman came into her head, that someone would care for her. If it was him, she thought, I would make him wait until we were wed. I'd not be tempted again.

'Fetch him then,' her father said abruptly. 'We'll do it now. Onny be quiet. Don't waken anybody.'

The wooden box was surprisingly heavy, but Delia carried it as her father refused to. She trod carefully in her bare feet down the stairs and into the middle kitchen, and waited for her father to unbolt the rear door. When she heard the bolt slide back she tiptoed into the back kitchen and her toes curled as they touched the stone flags.

The wind whistled around her as she stepped outside and it pulled on her shawl, sliding it down her back. She shivered, she should have put some outer clothes on, but there hadn't been time, although her father had put on a pair of breeches over his nightshirt and even now was pulling on his boots which he always left inside the back door.

He collected a heavy spade from the lean-to where the tools were kept and led the way to the bottom of the garden, past the small orchard and towards the kitchen garden, but then he stopped. 'This is no good,' he said in a low voice. 'Somebody'll turn it over, ready for winter frost. They'll find him once they start digging.'

She saw that there was one row of potatoes and

only a few cabbages and winter sprouts left in the ground.

'We'll have to go over to 'other side of 'hedge,' he said. 'Nobody'll find him there.' He pointed to the low hawthorn hedge which had been planted to keep the rabbits out of the garden, and strode towards it.

There was a bank of grass beyond the hedge and then a ditch which was half filled with water. He strode over the hedge and stood on the bank waiting for her.

'I can't get over,' she said. 'You'll have to take it.'

A second's hesitation and he took the wooden casket without a word and laid it on the ground, whilst she struggled to scramble over the hedge, catching her night robe and scratching her legs on the sharp thorns.

He started to dig on the bank whilst she stood shivering. She was so cold that her teeth were chattering. I should have given him a name, I suppose. But if I had, he would have been a real person and I would remember him. Should I ask Da to say a prayer? But will he?

'There,' he said. 'That should be deep enough. Put it in!' His voice was brusque and she knelt down, the hard ground scraping her knees, and lifted the casket into the hole. Without a word he started to shovel the earth back in again, and it rattled against the wood.

She hoped in her own silent thoughts that the child wouldn't go to hell if there was one, even though he couldn't go to heaven as he hadn't been baptized before he died. If there was a hell she would undoubtedly go there, for she had been wicked. But then, she thought, I don't believe in hell or heaven either.

Her father finished his shovelling and brushed the soil from his hands, then he wiped them on his breeches. Then he brushed them together again as if he couldn't get rid of the dirt. He stamped down the newly dug earth and then pulled over a few clumps of grass and stamped those down as well.

'There,' he said. 'Nobody will see that's been dug.' He faced Delia and stared her in the eyes. 'And don't forget, I shall deny any knowledge of this. You've done this on your own. It's another sin to add to your wickedness.'

'But I can stop at home now, can't I?' She was so afraid he would change his mind.

'Providing nobody finds out that I've been a party to this.' His face was set and hard. 'Then you can stop.'

CHAPTER TWENTY-SIX

Rosa hadn't slept well, disturbed by sounds which she couldn't identify. It must have been the wind howling against the side of the house and rattling the windows, she decided. She must get out the heavy winter curtains and fill in the gaps between the window frames with strips of cloth to exclude the draughts. She had helped Mrs Drew to do it in other winters, and last year she had done it alone and made long sausage-like draught-excluders to put against the doors. The wind was always prevalent on Sunk Island but in winter it was ferocious, blowing across the open land from the river and the sea, with nothing to bar its way.

She rose early and after washing and dressing she hurried downstairs and put the kettle, which was always kept filled with water, onto the hook over the fire. She riddled the low fire with the poker and added more fuel, then stirred the pan of porridge oats which had been on the fireside shelf overnight.

The milk jug in the larder was almost empty, so she poured the remains of the milk into the porridge, rinsed out the jug and turned to the door to go out to the dairy to fetch more. The bolt was unfastened. Someone else must be up. Must be Gran, she thought, though I didn't hear her.

She went out to the dairy but there was no-one about and the door was closed. She drew in a deep breath. It was very cold. A damp fog lay over the land and the sound of ships' horns drifted eerily from the river. Winter was on its way.

I'm sure that I bolted the door before I went to bed, she pondered as she added more milk to the porridge and gave it another stir. But it was such a harrowing day, perhaps I forgot or maybe someone else went out after I'd gone to bed.

'Rosa!' her grandmother called downstairs. 'Come here, quickly, and bring up some more blankets.'

Blankets! Why blankets? She pulled two out from the cupboard and hurried upstairs. 'Why blankets, Gran?'

'It's Delia. She's shivering with cold or fever, we'll have to have 'doctor back again. He'll be sick of coming backwards and forwards to Sunk. But summat's happened.' Mrs Jennings was still in her night robe and cap. By her feet were bloodstained sheets which she had stripped from Delia's bed. 'I looked in to see how she was before I got dressed,' she explained, 'and found her in this state.' Delia was sitting in a chair with a blanket wrapped around her, visibly shaking.

'Fetch me some thick flannel sheets and a couple more blankets, some old sheets and then some hot milk, and we'd better have a hot brick for 'bed as well.'

Rosa rushed to do as her grandmother bid and helped her to make up the bed, then together they lifted Delia back under the covers.

'She's feverish.' Mrs Jennings put a hand on Delia's forehead. 'Now what's brought that on? Mebbe shock of losing 'babby.'

Rosa glanced towards the window. Perhaps the baby shouldn't have been left in Delia's room, perhaps the sight of him in his little box was more than she could bear. 'Where is he?' she murmured. 'Where have you put him?'

Mrs Jennings wrapped another blanket around Delia's shoulders and plumped up a pillow behind her. 'What?' she enquired. 'Where's who?'

'The baby!' Rosa said in an urgent whisper. 'Where have you put him?'

Her grandmother turned towards her and then looked over to the window. 'God in heaven! I haven't moved him. Why would I?'

They both looked towards Delia, but she had her eyes closed. Her face was flushed but she was shivering violently.

'I'll get Matthew up,' Rosa said. 'If he sets off now he'll catch 'doctor before he goes off on his calls.'

She knocked on his door and called urgently. He opened the door, buttoning up his breeches and without his shirt. 'I'm sorry, Matthew. You'll have to fetch 'doctor again,' she said breathlessly. 'Delia is feverish and – and have you moved the baby's casket?'

'Why would I do that?' he said in an astonished tone.

'I – I don't know,' she stammered and wondered why she should feel embarrassed at seeing him bare-chested and with his hair tousled from sleep, when she had often seen him without his shirt when he washed at the sink. 'He's not there, in Delia's room, I mean.'

'But why should anybody want to move him?' He gazed at her in amazement. 'If you haven't and your gran hasn't, it onny leaves me and Da and he wouldn't—' His voice trailed away. 'I mean – he doesn't want anything to do with Delia or her babby.'

'And Jim left early last night, so it wasn't him,' Rosa added. 'Look, never mind now. It's 'doctor who's needed. Delia is really sick. Tell him it's urgent, Gran is worried about her.'

'We'll have to tell Da,' Matthew said when he returned later. His hat and hair were soaked for the rain was sleeting down, but his face was flushed for he had ridden as fast as he could into Patrington and back. 'He'll have to know. Doctor said he'd called to see 'parson yesterday and told him there'd be an infant burial. He'll probably come over today.'

'Well, there'll be no burial without a body,' Mrs Jennings said grimly. 'I've never come across owt like this in all of my life. Where can poor bairn be?'

Rosa remembered the back door. 'Matthew,' she said, 'did you bolt 'back door last night?'

'No! You did. I heard you.'

'Then somebody's been out, perhaps your da. I

forgot to ask him earlier.' Mr Drew had been exceedingly grumpy when he came down for breakfast and although Rosa had told him that Delia wasn't well, he had appeared quite indifferent and she hadn't dared to mention the child's disappearance for fear of incurring his further ill temper.

Delia was delirious when the doctor arrived and couldn't be questioned about the baby. 'She's got childbed fever,' the doctor pronounced. 'She shouldn't have got out of bed when she did. I said as much at the time.'

He fastened up his leather bag. 'Just keep her quiet, plenty of cool drinks, we can do nothing more than that.' He shook his head. 'Foolish girl!'

He followed Mrs Jennings downstairs. 'So what do you think has happened to the child? It will have to be reported to the authorities of course.'

Mr Drew came in for his morning drink. 'What! You here again, Doctor?' He glanced at Rosa and Mrs Jennings. 'So who's paying 'fee?'

'Well, presumably not you, Mr Drew,' the doctor answered coldly. 'But if there is any difficulty I can waive it. It wouldn't be the first time!'

James Drew sat down in his chair and Rosa hurried to make him a hot drink.

'We're concerned about the disappearance of the child's body,' the doctor said. 'A report will have to be made if it isn't found.'

'Disappearance? I don't know what you mean.' Drew gazed unwaveringly at the doctor.

'The child's body has disappeared—' the doctor began. 'Surely you were told?'

'I know nothing of it,' Drew interrupted. 'But it can't have a Christian burial as it wasn't baptized – so if it has disappeared—' He shrugged nonchalantly as if the matter was of no consequence.

'A report will have to be made to the authorities.' The doctor's voice was icy. 'A child was born, has died and has now disappeared. Someone must know where it is! It is an offence,' he added, 'to conceal a body, even that of a newborn child.'

As Rosa gave Mr Drew his drink she thought that he paled, and he brushed the palms of his hands together. 'Surely not a bastard child?' he questioned, sarcasm in his tone.

'Even so.'

'Then you'd better question its mother,' James Drew said abruptly. 'She's onny one likely to know about it.'

The doctor gave him a withering glance and, nodding to Mrs Jennings and Rosa, went out of the room. Rosa followed him. 'He won't want any fuss,' she began. 'Mr Drew's a very private man.'

'Whether he wants a fuss or not is of no consequence! For that is what he'll get if the child isn't found,' the doctor interrupted. 'My views of James Drew are changing rapidly. I always thought of him as a devout religious man, but it seems that he has no compassion.' He gazed thoughtfully at Rosa. 'He must be very pure himself to be so critical of others!'

Rosa made no immediate answer. James Drew was rigid and unbending in his self-righteous rules, but, she considered, she couldn't condemn him. He had given her a home when she was a child and she had always tried to remember that. He didn't have to take me, she thought, not when he had so many children of his own to bring up. He had never reminded her of the obligation and asked nothing more of her over the years than he asked of his own daughters, that they went about their tasks and were obedient. He had given her no affection, no friendly pat on the shoulder or kind word, but neither did he with his own.

'He's God-fearing,' she answered finally. 'I do believe he's afraid to show weakness.' But as she spoke, doubts were pressing on her as she remembered his involvement with the Byrne brothers.

'I am not a religious man, myself,' the doctor said as he mounted his horse. 'But it is said that God is love. Perhaps Mr Drew might do well to remember that.'

Delia lay ill for a week. She thrashed around in her bed, mumbling and muttering, and Rosa and her grandmother took turns to sit with her, to cool her forehead and give her sips of water. Jim and Matthew looked in at her every day, but her father did not.

'I don't understand him,' Mrs Jennings commented. 'His own daughter. It doesn't seem natural.'

The parson came, but he agreed, when Matthew and Jim persuaded him, that any decision regarding the law and the missing child should be left until Delia could be questioned.

'We ought to look about,' Matthew urged his brother. 'If Delia has hidden him, she can't have taken him far from the house.'

Jim agreed and so they searched the barns, the cow house, the tool shed and the rooms above the dairy which would have been easily accessible to Delia, even in her weakened state from child-bed. They were both tidy men and knew as they looked in every possible place that nothing had been moved or hidden.

Matthew cast his eyes over the spades and forks and sludge tools which were hanging on hooks on the wall of the lean-to. There was just one, an open spade, which still had wisps of grass and earth clinging to it. But it was heavy, if Delia had thought to bury the child herself, she wouldn't have been able to handle it. Rosa had a small spade and fork for the vegetable garden which he had had made for her when he saw that the others were too unwieldy. They too were hanging from the wall and were quite clean.

Rosa was sitting by the bedside when Delia woke. She gave a slight cough, stared at Rosa and then glanced towards the window where the child's casket had been. 'Have I been ill?' she said in a husky voice.

'You have, you've had a fever. 'Doctor said you'd got out of bed too soon.'

'Out of bed?'

Rosa nodded. 'After 'birth of the baby,' she said softly. 'You must have caught a chill.'

Delia grimaced and took in a deep breath. 'Have I – have I been talking in my sleep? I've had such funny dreams.' Her eyes narrowed and she bit her lip. 'Really strange dreams about 'babby being taken away.'

'The babby died, Delia,' Rosa reminded her gently. 'Don't you remember?'

'I'm not sure.' Her voice was cautious. 'Did he?'

Rosa called her grandmother. She didn't want to be the one to question Delia, but Mrs Jennings was brisk when she realized that the invalid had recovered. 'Now, young woman,' she said. 'What happened to that babby? He's got to have a proper burial with 'parson and all.'

'I don't remember,' Delia began sullenly. 'I've been very ill.'

'And why have you been ill? It's because you were out of bed hiding that poor bairn! I could understand it,' Mrs Jennings went on, 'if nobody had known about 'birth, but what's 'point in hiding him when we all knew?'

'But nobody else on Sunk Island knows, Mrs Jennings,' Delia whispered. 'Onny us here, onny family and you and Rosa.'

'And 'doctor and parson and 'woman at 'Patrington shop where I bought 'knitting wool, and Harry and young Bob and no doubt dozens of others!' She leant towards her conspiratorially. 'And all 'world'll know when 'constable comes to ask you where he is.'

Delia shrank back onto her pillow. Her eyes were yellow and her face pale. 'But if they don't find him they'll go away—' she began.

'They won't go away and you'll go to court.' Mrs Jennings was blunt. 'And then what will your father say?'

'Da said I could stop.' She looked wildly from Mrs Jennings to Rosa. 'I promised I wouldn't stray again and he said I could stop at home.'

'And I'm sure you can.' Mrs Jennings drew her arms across her bosom and waited. 'Just tell us where you've put 'poor babby.'

'Get Matthew to come up,' Delia said petulantly. 'I'll tell him.'

'I can't fetch him now,' Rosa said. 'He's behind with his work.' She didn't say because he had been travelling backwards and forwards to Patrington to fetch the doctor or to see the parson on Delia's behalf, but that was the reason why Matthew was now trying to make up for lost time. 'When he comes in for his dinner I'll ask him to come up.'

When Matthew had eaten his meal she detained him. 'Delia says she'll tell you where she's hidden 'babby.' She glanced towards Jim and Mr Drew. 'She wants you to go and get him.'

Jim hung back but his father went out, his eyebrows beetling together and a black look on his face. 'Why Matthew?' Jim asked. 'Why not us? Matthew's going to tell us anyway.'

But he didn't. 'I can't tell you,' he said after talking to Delia. 'She's made me swear that I wouldn't say where he is.' He ran his fingers through his hair and looked baffled. 'I think she's gone a bit soft in her head.'

He went out into the yard and whistled for his

dog. Jim followed him into the lean-to. 'You don't have to tell me where you're going,' he said. 'I'll just follow you and watch.'

Matthew gave an ironic grin. 'We must seem to outsiders to be an ordinary family—'

'Aye,' Jim's voice was bitter. 'But open up Pandora's box and see what's inside! She's never buried him?' he added sharply as Matthew lifted a spade from the wall.

Matthew shrugged. 'She said that she did. There's no wonder she was so ill. Rosa said that 'back door was undone night after 'babby died, and it was a bitter cold night.'

Jim fell silent but followed Matthew to the bottom of the yard and towards the kitchen garden. Matthew with an easy stride went over the hedge and Jim followed him. The dog jumped over too and Matthew called to him. 'Come on, lad. Find!'

The dog rushed to and fro, his tail wagging and his nose to the ground as they searched up and down looking for any disturbance by the hedge, then he whined and started to scrabble with his paws. 'Come off,' Matthew commanded, and bent down. He swallowed hard. 'I think this might be it,' he murmured and then looked up at Jim, who had made a strangled cry. He had his hand clutched over his mouth and there was horror in his eyes.

'It's all right,' Matthew said softly. 'She said she'd buried him in his casket. She must have planned it all along, that's why she asked me to make it for him.' He straightened up and put his foot on the blade. The soil yielded, soft after the rain, and he pushed down. 'It's there,' he said. 'I can feel it.'

He looked around. Jim had moved away. He was kneeling on the ground, his body hunched low, weeping and retching into the hedge bottom.

CHAPTER TWENTY-SEVEN

Rosa put on her heavy cloak and fastened up her outdoor boots.

'Where do you think you're going?' Delia's voice came from behind her.

'Out!' She was brief. She had no wish to enter into an acrimonious conversation with Delia.

'Be back in time to help with supper!' was Delia's parting shot as she went out of the door, but Rosa made no answer.

She heaved a great sigh as she set off across the side of the meadows towards the river. Delia was being so tedious. Since she had recovered from childbirth and the fever, she had been petty and mean and slowly and insidiously had tried to take control of the household. She had not succeeded where Mrs Jennings was concerned, for after a bout of ill temper from her, Mrs Jennings had packed her bag, put on her bonnet and told Mr Drew that she was leaving.

'You don't need me now,' she'd said. 'I onny came temporary till yon daughter got over her trouble. Well, she's over it, so I'll be off!'

Mr Drew had looked at her in dismay. 'But—!

Delia can't cook! Rosa can, but not as well as you, Mrs Jennings. Besides, where will you go?' He'd attempted to show concern for her future well-being. 'You'll not get a position at your age!'

'That is perfectly true!' she had admitted. 'I shall have to go on 'parish when bit o' money my cousin left me runs out.'

'We can't have that,' he insisted, and she had known perfectly well that he had no interest at all in her prospects, but was only concerned that his meals should be on the table.

She agreed nevertheless that she would stay and let Delia know in no uncertain terms that she would not put up with her ill humour. 'You're lucky to be here at all, young woman,' she lectured. 'Just remember that and be humble!'

The doctor and the parson had implicitly agreed that as the body of the child had been found, no further action regarding the law need be taken. Delia had been temporarily unhinged after the long labour, they decided, and a quiet blessing had been given at the churchyard and the small casket laid to rest for a second time, next to the graves of Henry and his mother.

'What name shall we give the child?' the cleric had asked Delia, but she had stared vacantly at him and shaken her head.

Rosa had been gazing down at Henry's headstone. 'Henry?' she murmured.

Delia had glared at her. 'Martin,' she muttered and there were sidelong glances from Jim and

Matthew, who were also present, each wondering if that was the name of the child's father.

'I'll make him a little wooden cross, if you like, Delia,' Jim muttered. 'He should have some kind of marker.'

Jim had been ill, too, since the finding of the child's body. He had stayed alone, in bed, at Marsh Farm for two days until Mrs Jennings had walked across carrying a jug of soup, and persuaded him that whatever was troubling him would go away much more quickly when aided by hard work.

It's so odd how Jim was affected, Rosa thought as she strode along. He had been all right until he and Matthew had found the casket. And then he had become so morose, barely speaking to anyone, and towards her in particular he had seemed troubled and ill at ease.

She reached the embankment and climbed it, looking up and down the estuary. The light from Spurn Point gleamed through the fog but the banks of Lincolnshire were obscured on the other side of the estuary. Traffic still flowed along the Humber, coal barges and fishing cobbles, homeward bound to the port of Hull. It was getting too late for her to walk far as dusk was coming in fast and the fog was drifting in towards the land, but she was reluctant to go back yet.

Delia's presence had changed the mood of the house, which, although never one of calm or comfort due to Mr Drew's cold demeanour, had at least been tolerable. Now Rosa wondered whether she should finally make up her mind to leave Sunk Island.

The thought of it made her sad. She had spent her life here, her mother was buried here in the churchyard and her father – well, where was he? she wondered. And her grandmother, would she stay on at Mr Drew's without her? And Matthew? He, too, was so much part of her life. The idea of leaving them all seemed like a betrayal.

A three-masted ship appeared out of the fog and trimmed its square sails as it came upriver in the direction of Stone Creek. It was a long ship with a steep deck and a rounded stern, and as she watched its progress towards her she felt the same sensation she had felt twice before. It's the Dutch fluyt here again! Why do I feel this stirring of my blood when I see it? Why does it bring about this excitement within me?

The ship anchored out in the river and she saw the crew moving about on board near the aperture which housed the stern rudder, and on a sudden impulse she picked up her skirts and ran along the embankment as far as she could until she reached the marshland which bordered Stone Creek.

Two horsemen were on the stone bridge, one, a stockily built man, was leaning down talking to someone. She could see his booted legs but not his face as he was obscured by the horse, but she could see an arm pointing out towards the ship. The other horseman, who had his back to her, appeared to be staring out into the estuary.

She was intrigued and yet didn't know why. The harbour was well used by local fishermen and farmers, especially now that little trade was done at Patrington Haven, but she wondered why anyone should be down there now when it was late.

She turned homeward. She would have to hurry if she was to get back to the house before dark. There was no light from the night sky because of the fog and it would be so easy to fall into a dyke. She shuddered and thought of Henry, too drunk to pull himself out of the water. If she should be so unfortunate as to fall in, she would be hampered by her boots, her heavy cloak and woollen skirt. But I'm not going to fall in, she told herself, I'm an island girl, used to the land of drains and ditches.

Matthew was shrugging himself into his coat to come and look for her as she arrived back. He was angry with her. 'Where've you been? Delia said you'd been gone ages. Your gran was worried about you!'

'Sorry. I walked further than I meant to.' She followed him into the house. 'Are you finished outside? Shall I lock up?'

He shook his head. 'No. Da and Jim are still out somewhere.'

'Are they on foot?' she asked, as a thought struck her.

'No, they've taken a couple of hosses. Something to pick up at Stoney, Da said.'

Mr Drew came in about half an hour later, saying that Jim had gone straight back to Marsh Farm.

'Doesn't he want his supper then?' Mrs Jennings asked in surprise.

'No.' There was no explanation given. Just the one bald word.

After supper, Rosa cleared away, Delia went upstairs to her room and Mrs Jennings sat darning a pair of socks until her eyes started to droop. 'That's me finished then,' she said, putting the darning wool and the socks back into her workbox. 'I'm off to bed. Goodnight, everybody.'

'Goodnight, Gran.'

'Goodnight, Mrs Jennings,' Matthew said, and she smiled at him.

Mr Drew grunted. He didn't look up, but continued to stare into the fire which Matthew had just banked with coal and slack to keep going all night.

Rosa was about to sit down and start some stitching herself when Mr Drew said, 'Get off to bed then, girl. It's getting late.'

She looked at him in surprise. She didn't usually go to bed so early. Matthew, too, gazed at his father enquiringly.

'I – I haven't locked up yet,' she said.

'I'll do it,' he grunted. 'I have to go out into 'yard.'

She thought he meant to the privy, so she put away her sewing and said goodnight. He nodded, but didn't answer, and she glanced at Matthew who shrugged and pursed his lips and said, 'Goodnight, Rosa. Sleep well.'

As she climbed the stairs she heard Mr Drew telling Matthew that they had to be up early and that he ought to go to bed too.

'We're up early every morning,' Matthew replied. 'What's special about tomorrow? Anyway,' she heard the assertion in his voice as she paused to listen, 'I'm not ready for bed yet. I'd as soon sit here by 'fire as lie awake in bed.'

She heard his father grunt something in reply and then the back door banged as he went outside. She lit the lamp in her room, keeping it low, and didn't undress straight away, but sat by the window. The fog had drifted inland and the waggons in the yard and the fruit trees in the kitchen garden beyond were shrouded in shadowy misty outline. Then she saw James Drew cross the yard. He was wearing his thick dark coat, had a muffler around his neck and a woollen hat on his head. He looked up and she drew back behind the curtain.

She went downstairs on the pretence of looking for a book and found Matthew still staring into the fire, his feet stretched out in front of him.

She picked up the book from a shelf and stood hesitating. 'Matthew! I've been thinking—'

He looked up at her and wrinkled his brows. 'You're not going to leave us, are you, Rosa?'

'Why do you think that?' She gave a short laugh of denial, but it was just the subject she had been about to broach.

'I've seen how things are with you and Delia. You don't work well together, not like you and Maggie did.'

She smiled. How perceptive he was. 'We don't,' she admitted, 'and I had thought of moving away.' She saw a look of pain in his face, and quickly continued, 'But if I left, then Gran probably wouldn't stay either and Delia couldn't manage on her own. It's very hard,' she said, 'I know. There's too much to do for one person.'

He got to his feet. 'I'm not bothered that there's too much for her to do.' His words were harsh. 'Da would have to get extra help.' He looked at her with appeal in his eyes. 'I just don't want you to go. I couldn't bear it if you went away. Rosa.' He reached for her hands and said softly, 'You know how I feel. You've always known, even though no words have passed between us.'

She nodded. You know that he loves you, his mother had said with her dying breath. He will make up for what has gone before if you will let him. But what had gone before? She didn't know. She only knew that there was a void, an emptiness within her. She felt tears pricking her eyes, but she mustn't cry. It wasn't the time for crying, for she never did. She also knew that it wasn't the time for Matthew to speak out or her to respond. There would be a right time, but it wasn't now. There would be other issues, other circumstances to unfold first. She didn't know what they were and didn't understand the consciousness within her. It was some instinct, a presentiment perhaps, that they must wait, and she felt that Matthew understood that too.

'Please. Don't go.'

There was a sound behind them and as they looked up, Delia was on the stairs staring down at them. 'What's going on?' she demanded.

'Nothing that concerns you, Delia.' Matthew's words, though blunt, were not unfriendly.

She stepped into the room. 'Is she going behind my back about something?' Then she saw Matthew's hands still holding Rosa's, and looked from one to the other. 'You're not planning owt?' She addressed Rosa. 'I know you've allus been after Matthew. But he's too good for you. You're not worthy of him!'

There was hostility written on Delia's face and Rosa tried to release her hands from Matthew's grasp, but he held them fast.

'Don't say things like that, Delia,' he admonished harshly. 'Rosa is worthy of a better man than me.'

Delia sneered. 'She's allus wanted you. She wants our farm and that's how she thinks she'll get it. Through you. She thinks she belongs here. Well, she doesn't. She's a foreigner, like her father was.'

That hurt Rosa and she drew in a breath before saying, 'I belong on Sunk Island, just as you do, Delia. My father was foreign, but I was born here, as my mother was and my gran and grandfather and generations before them.'

As she spoke she felt an empathy with those past generations who had come to this once waterlogged land and who had sweated and died in their efforts to make it cultivated and habitable, and she wasn't sure that Delia even thought about that or would understand it. But Matthew did, of that she was sure.

'It doesn't make any difference,' Delia glared at her, 'whether you were born here or not! It doesn't make you entitled to it. It's good land, that's why folks want it. If they can stand the isolation and solitude they can make a good living out here, and that's what you're after.'

'You're wrong, Delia,' Matthew interrupted, his voice sharp. 'You don't have a feeling for Sunk Island and that's why you went away. You wouldn't have come back if you hadn't been in trouble and needed help.'

'I went away because of her,' Delia said bitterly. 'I knew I couldn't stop under 'same roof. I had to get away.'

Rosa pulled her hands from Matthew's grasp. 'But why, Delia?' she appealed. 'What did I do? Your ma and da took me in when I was only a child. Why do you feel this way?'

Delia stared at her with hatred in her eyes, then her face started to crumple. 'I haven't got anybody,' she grieved. 'I was youngest and expected to tag along after everybody else. But Matthew was my friend. At least he was until you came along, then he forgot about me and it was Rosa this and Rosa that, and it didn't matter about me any more.'

'I don't understand,' Matthew said. 'You had all of us, me, Henry, Jim, four sisters – Rosa was the one who had nobody else.'

'But you were 'onny one who took any notice of me.' She sniffled and her eyes filled with tears. 'I was just a nuisance to everybody else. A runt,' she declared hotly. 'An unwanted bairn, even by Ma.'

'That's unfair, Delia,' Rosa broke in. 'Your ma loved all of her children. Even me.'

'Aye, and that was 'worst of it! I saw that she

was fond of you and I saw from 'start that she was making plans for you and Matthew.' She wiped her eyes. 'And I couldn't bear that. Matthew was *my* brother, *my* friend, and *you*, who I hated, were taking him away from me.'

CHAPTER TWENTY-EIGHT

Rosa lay fully dressed on her bed until midnight. How could she resolve this impasse with Delia? One of them would have to leave, and Matthew had said to her, when Delia had turned her back on them and run upstairs, that if she, Rosa, should think of leaving, then he would follow her.

She gave a great sigh. I'll have to talk to Gran, she thought. She's old and wise, she'll know what I should do. Unable to sleep, she rose from the bed and stood by the window. The mist was lifting, swirling around the yard as the breeze caught it. It hung over the roof of the barn, hovered cobweb-like across the tiles and, drifting down to the orchard, floated over the tops of the old apple trees. From the river she could hear the haunting cry of ships' hooters reaching out in warning and she suddenly thought of the Dutch fluyt, moored out in the Humber, and again wondered why it was there.

I'm curious. I'll go! I'll go right now to see if it's still there. It's not so dark now that the mist is lifting. I'm wide awake, I'll not sleep if I get into bed. She argued with herself as to why she should go. It was no business of hers, there were ships up and down the river all the time. What was so special about this one? But it *was* special. She felt strongly that it was, and not least because she was sure that it had been Mr Drew and Jim and one of the Byrne brothers who had been at Stone Creek, also looking towards it.

She put on her shawl and another pair of warm stockings and stealthily crept downstairs and into the kitchen, where her cloak was hanging behind the door. She put it on and another shawl around her head, and laced up her boots.

The door was still unfastened and she hoped that no-one would lock her out. The door creaked as she opened it and she stood and listened for a moment. It was quiet, no sound of movement from upstairs, and she wondered if Matthew had been able to sleep after the dispute with Delia.

The hens in the coop stirred and cackled quietly as she went past and the dogs, tied up in their kennels, thumped their tails slowly and sleepily. She bent down to pat their heads and moved on quietly until she reached the gate, which was open, and hurried along the familiar path by the side of the dyke towards the river.

She was breathless by the time she reached it for she had half run, half scurried in her eager-ness to get there. The ship was still moored, silent, with the mist drifting about it and the water slapping against the hull, and no sign of life on board but a low light showing on deck, to warn other shipping of its presence. A red flag with a white circle in the centre flew from the masthead, but she didn't know what it represented.

What was I expecting? she wondered. Why have I come? She looked down towards the creek and her attention was caught by another ship, a cutter, moored on the edge of the tiny harbour with no light showing, and a coggy boat low in the water, being rowed away from it towards the shore. As she watched, she heard the rattle of chain on a capstan, the anchor on the cutter was hauled and the vessel prepared to make sail. Two seamen were at the midships wheel and they steered a course to give a wide berth to the Dutch fluyt which rode gently on the current.

She climbed down from the embankment and walked below it, along the edge of the fields towards the creek. The ground was muddy and pulled squelchily at her boots, yet she plodded on. Who was rowing the coggy boat, she wondered, and why at this time of night? It had to be illegal, and smuggling was the first thing that came to her mind. Was this why my father came to Sunk Island? And if so, why did he choose to come here and not the port of Hull?

The ground was becoming more marshy and the water was lapping up to her ankles. She knew that she would soon have to stop and climb the embankment again and risk being seen by whoever was down by the water's edge. She scrambled up on her hands and knees and peered towards the harbour. Three men with their backs to her were unloading goods from the coggy boat and, judging by the number of crates

that were already stacked there, they had un-
loaded more than one consignment. Now they
were lifting barrels off the coggy boat and trans-
ferring them to a nearby waggon.

She crouched, better to see the activity, and
drew in her breath as they turned their heads.
James Drew was one of the men, Jim was another
and the third, she was sure, was Seamus Byrne.

'Well, little lady. Have you seen enough?' a
voice whispered in her ear and she gave a sudden
cry of fright as John Byrne grabbed her around
the waist.

'Oh! You frightened me!' Her heart hammered
furiously and she tried to pull his hands away from
her waist. 'Let go of me, please.'

He lifted her to her feet and turned her so that
she was facing him. 'Not until you tell me why
you are here,' he said softly. 'You're spying I
think?'

'No.' She caught her breath. 'I'm not. I wasn't.'

He gave a little chuckle. 'You wanted to know
what your precious Drew family were up to,
didn't you? You were curious about this pious,
God-fearing, hypocritical preacher by the name
of James Drew, and his lily-livered son, weren't
you?'

Before she could deny it, he brought her closer
to him and stared down into her eyes. 'Is Jim
your lover? Is that why you were watching? Did
you wonder what he got up to at night when he
should be sleeping the sleep of the just?'

'No! No. How dare you! Let go of me.' She
struggled to get out of his grasp, but he held her
fast.

'I told you. I'll let you go when you tell me why you are here. If it is not curiosity, then what is it? Hah!' His eyes lit up with a sinister light. 'You want to be part of it, don't you? You want some of the excitement! You're tired of the mundane life you are leading!'

'No. No. No!' She raised her voice. 'If you must know I came to look at 'ship out yonder.'

'The ship?' A wariness came into his voice.

'Yes.' The word came out in a sob. 'The Dutch fluyt. I wondered why it was here. I've seen it before.'

His fingers eased on her waist and she pulled away a little. 'It's an old ship,' she started to explain, but he interrupted her.

'I know it's an old ship, but how do you know it?' His words were rough and demanding.

'I – I've seen it here before,' she said. 'I saw it for 'first time when I was just a child. Henry told me that it was a Dutch fluyt.'

'Henry?'

'Jim's brother. He's dead now. He drowned in a dyke.'

'Ah, yes.' He dismissed Henry with a shrug. 'When did you next see it?'

It was when I was with Matthew, she remembered. When he insisted that we went walking because I said I was missing the river. 'It was a while ago,' she said. 'Just before I met you and your brother at Hawkins Point.'

'Hmm.' His eyes pierced into hers. 'Do you know whose ship it is?'

She shook her head. 'No! Why should I? I know nothing about ships.'

He gave a cynical smile. 'Even though your father was a sailor?'

Her eyes opened wide. 'I don't know if he was a sailor,' she said. 'I only know that you told me that he was a smuggler! You probably know more about him than I do. He's a mystery to me and to others on Sunk Island.'

'But not to James Drew or his son?'

'I believe that they met him, yes. But they don't talk about him.'

'And they don't talk about his ship? The ship that was confiscated with me and my brother and the run goods on board!'

As he spoke he turned towards the river and the fluyt, which was clearer to see now that the mist was lifting. Rosa glanced at him and saw how his eyes narrowed as he gazed at the vessel.

She drew in a breath. 'What are you trying to say? That isn't—? But how? If it was—' Her words dried up. Was this why she had such a strange sensation each time she had seen the ship?

'That's it, all right. I'd know it anywhere, I spent enough time on it.' His voice dropped. 'I loved that ship as if it was my very own.' He nodded his head as if lost in thought, then said, 'Revenue men must have sold it on, probably to a foreign buyer. But now it's back on its old hunting ground, but who, I wonder, is its captain?'

She gazed across at it. Was it true what he said? Could she believe him? Was this really once her father's ship? She felt her lips trembling and she was full of emotion, but she was suddenly rudely jostled by Byrne, who took her arm and marched her along the embankment.

'Come on, enough of this reminiscing,' and she knew that he was speaking of his own memories and not of hers. 'We'll go and meet the rest of the family.'

Jim and James Drew straightened up and looked round as John Byrne approached, then, as Jim saw who was with him, being so roughly mishandled, he charged forward.

'What do you think you're doing,' he yelled. 'Get off her! Let her go.'

Byrne gave a mocking smile and kept hold of Rosa's arm. 'Yours, is she, Jim? She's just denied it!' But his words were cut short as Jim hurled himself towards him and aimed a blow at his face. Rosa fell to the ground as Byrne released his grip, but was brought to her feet by Seamus Byrne who surveyed her coldly, no ready smile in his eyes as there had been on other occasions when he had greeted her. James Drew just stood as if made of stone, his hand on a wooden cask.

'You beggarly heathen!' Jim aimed another blow at John Byrne, who retaliated with a fist to his chin. 'Why bring her into it? I warned you before.'

Seamus Byrne stepped aside from Rosa and with a swift movement made to separate the brawling men. He put his arms between them, a hand on each chest, and said quietly, 'Will you leave your fighting till we get this stuff away! It'll be light before long and the fishermen will be here.'

The two men drew back, breathing heavily, and eyed each other. 'He'd no right to bring her here,' Jim said bitterly. 'This isn't woman's work.'

John Byrne smirked. 'I didn't bring her here. She was here already. I found her up on the embankment watching what was going on.'

Jim turned to Rosa. 'Is this true, Rosa?'

Her mouth trembled. 'I came to see the ship.' She pointed out to the river. 'I wanted to see if it was still here.'

'Why?' Seamus Byrne asked, his haste to be away seemingly forgotten. His eyes focused steadily on her.

'I don't know why,' she confessed. 'There's something about it that intrigues me.'

'The little woman is fey!' Seamus said cynically. 'A visionary perhaps? Do you see spirits within the shadows? Do you see your father on the ship, his dark hair blowing in the breeze and a gold ring in his ear?'

She shook her head and glanced towards Jim, who was clenching his fists together.

'No.' She was frightened. 'I don't know what you mean.'

'I mean,' he drew nearer to her, 'that we are all intrigued by that ship. That ship that was once your father's.'

'Can we get on?' James Drew spoke for the first time. 'Let's get 'waggon away. You can talk later.'

John Byrne strode across to him. 'You don't like to discuss our friend Carlos, do you, Mr Drew? Is that because he's still around? Because you are still doing business together? Is it unfortunate that his ship should sail in just when we happen to be here?'

'You're talking rubbish!' Drew spluttered. 'It's nearly twenty years since Carlos was here. That

335

ship has probably been sold half a dozen times since 'Customs requisitioned her. Besides, that's not Carlos's flag. It's a house flag.'

'We know it isn't his flag!' John Byrne's voice cracked in a sudden explosion of virulence. 'But I'm going to tell you and your precious son something, Mr Drew! I don't trust you! I didn't trust you before and with good reason, and I don't trust you now. I wouldn't put it past you to have informed the authorities about my brother and me!'.

James Drew started to protest and Jim moved forward towards John Byrne. But he, with a swift movement, leaned towards Rosa and pulled her to his side. 'So, what I aim to do, if we can't have Carlos, then we'll have his daughter.'

With one hand he smoothed Rosa's head, with the other he held her fast. 'She's our hostage in a sense, until the goods are safely on their way.'

'You can't.' Jim defied him. 'She'd be missed. 'Constables would be all over 'island if word got out that she was missing.'

'She won't be missing,' he replied softly. 'She can stay at home and I'll come every day to make sure that all is going as we planned. The waggons will come from Hull in a week's time to collect the goods.' There was a threat in his smile as he turned to Rosa. 'And I'll come a-courting my lovely. If there's a whisper gets out to the law,' his eyes glittered and fell on Jim, 'she comes with us when we flee and you'll not see her again.'

Rosa was sent on her way home alone and each time she turned her head, John Byrne was watching her. She slipped and stumbled as she ran along the embankment and floundered and splashed through the marsh in her desire to put a great distance between herself and him. He had put an icy fear into her, for she was in no doubt that he would have no pity on her if, as he suggested, the constables had been warned.

Would Mr Drew do that? Would he pretend that he was helping the Byrnes when all the time he was tricking them so that they would fall into the hands of the law? And he has been involved with them before! A previous conversation with John Byrne and Jim came jumbling into her mind and she shook her head to clear it. Mr Drew is not what he seems. Yet he is such an upright, uncompromising man! He surely would not tolerate unlawfulness. But yet he is there now, unloading smuggled goods!

The answer came clear as the strike of a bell as she stumbled through the gate and into the farmyard. The Byrnes have something against him, or something against Jim, and they are forcing them to help them. I know it. She felt a great heaviness come over her as she lifted the sneck on the door. It's something to do with my father.

CHAPTER TWENTY-NINE

Rosa crept into the back kitchen and hung her cloak and damp shawl behind the door, then sat on a chair to unfasten her bootlaces. Her feet and stockings were soaked and her hands trembled as she pulled her boots off.

'They'll take some drying.' A quiet voice came from the inner door and she jumped as she saw Matthew leaning against it.

'Matthew!' she gasped. 'You startled me.'

'And you startled me when I saw you walking along 'dyke side an hour or more ago.' He spoke in a low, terse manner, and his expression was rigid. 'Where've you been?'

'I – I couldn't sleep,' she mumbled awkwardly. 'I – I was upset over Delia.'

His face was tense. 'Don't be,' he pleaded. 'We'll resolve it one way or another. She won't want to stay anyway, she's just being awkward. I know her only too well. Once she's feeling well again, she'll be wanting to be off.'

He came towards her and put out his hand to pull her up from the chair. 'Come on,' he said. 'Go to bed. You look frozen stiff. You're crazy to go out there in this weather.' He ran his hand over her wet hair and against her cheek. 'You'll catch your death,' he said softly, 'and then what would I do?'

She looked up at him and felt a lump in her throat. I wish I could tell him. But I can't. I should be betraying Jim and his father. But what will he say when John Byrne comes calling?

He wasn't there when the Irishman knocked on the door, but Delia answered it and stared open-mouthed when he asked for Rosa. He glanced up and down at Delia and said quietly, 'I see you've got over your trouble! So you're a mammy now?'

'No. I'm not,' she said sharply. 'My bairn died.'

'Ah!' He expressed his sympathy, then nodded his head thoughtfully. 'And here I was thinking you'd be so busy with maternal matters that you'd have no time for anybody else.' He gave a great sigh. 'And I asked your sister to come walking with me.'

'She's not my sister,' she snapped and Mrs Jennings, who had come through from dusting the parlour, lifted her head at her words.

'No, of course she's not. Anybody can see that,' he said softly. 'She's dark-haired and young and innocent, whilst you're—' he hesitated. 'Well, you have a grown beauty about you, a maturity, like a full ripe peach.' His eyes appraised her. 'I think perhaps I made a mistake,' he whispered. 'I prefer a fully fledged woman. One who knows what a man likes.'

He reached out and slid his hand onto her neck, stretching his thumb and fingers around her throat. She swallowed and felt the pressure of his hand, then he dropped it as Rosa appeared.

'You will excuse us, Delia,' he said. 'Rosa and I have a little business to discuss. We won't be long. Just a walk along the dykes,' and he took hold of Rosa firmly by the elbow and led her away.

'What's all that about?' Mrs Jennings came to the door and looked over Delia's shoulder. 'Where's he going wi' Rosa?'

'Don't know,' Delia said abruptly. She had been disturbed by his appraisal of her, and the sensation of his fingers on her throat had both frightened and excited her. Yet she was annoyed at the way he had walked away with Rosa. Where were they going and when had they arranged this assignation?

'I don't like it,' Mrs Jennings said thoughtfully.

'Mebbe you don't.' Delia was rude and cutting. 'But some do.' Then she added, 'I doubt if he'd make an honest woman of her, though, he has his sights set on somebody else.'

'Who?' Mrs Jennings stared at her, non-plussed. 'Not you?' She laughed. 'I've told you, girl. Be careful. You've fallen once. It'll be easy to fall again.'

'Not me,' Delia replied, but knew that she lied.

Matthew saw Rosa with John Byrne as he was cleaning out ditches with Jim. He straightened up with his foot on the narrow blade of the sludge spade and saw them in a direct line in front of him. He stopped what he was saying to Jim and stood looking towards them.

'What?' Jim asked and looked up. His lips tightened as he saw the couple.

'What's he doing with Rosa?' Matthew threw down his spade and climbed out of the ditch. 'Where does he think he's going?'

'Leave it,' Jim muttered. 'It's nowt.'

Matthew glanced at him. 'Nowt! What do you mean, nowt?'

'I mean – he asked Da if he could walk out wi' Rosa.' Jim's face flushed as he spoke.

Matthew stared at him, speechless, then he shook his head. 'I don't believe you. She wouldn't. Not Rosa!'

'I've told you. Leave it. It means nowt.'

'It must mean summat or she wouldn't be there,' he fumed. 'And why isn't he at work? Is he still on our pay sheet?'

'No.' Jim leaned on his spade. 'He was onny casual anyway.'

'Then he's no right on our land.' Matthew picked up his spade again. 'I'm going to see him off.'

'He's not on our land!' Jim attempted to placate him. 'If you use your eyes you'll see he's on 'road. You can't stop him from being there.'

'I'm going anyway.' Matthew slung his spade into the nearby cart. 'I want to know what this is about.'

He was consumed with jealousy, not least because Byrne had his hand tucked beneath Rosa's arm. As he walked towards them, Rosa faltered and her eyes blinked rapidly as she saw him.

'Good afternoon,' Byrne said pleasantly. 'A cold damp day for ditching, is it not?'

Matthew ignored him. 'Rosa! Is this fellow bothering you?'

She hesitated. 'I – er, no. No, he's not, Matthew. You need have no fear of that. I – I'm just showing Mr Byrne the extent of your father's land.'

'Why?' he asked bluntly. 'Why should he want to know about our land?'

'Why – Matthew! It is Matthew, isn't it? Yes?' Byrne gazed at him languorously. 'I'm from farming stock myself. I've not always been a ditcher, you know. No, I've worked the land. I know of ploughing and sowing and reaping the harvest. And I know of the potato harvest – or rather I don't know of the potato harvest, for there wasn't one in Ireland when I was a boy. It failed! You might have heard?'

There was a sneer in his voice and Matthew knew instinctively that this man had many axes to grind. 'And soon,' Byrne seemed to be speaking almost to himself, 'and soon there was no land either, for my mammy and daddy were turned off theirs. The English, you know – they did that.'

'I do know,' Matthew said decisively. 'I do know that the Irish countryman had a difficult time, just as the English and 'Welsh, and 'Scots did too – as they are still having.'

'And that is why,' Byrne continued in the same soft voice, 'that is why I am looking over your father's land and thinking how very lucky you are.' He gazed at Rosa and said meaningfully, 'I think I shall have to find me a farmer's daughter to marry and settle down in this fine country.'

He then turned to Matthew. 'Well, if you will

excuse us, we must be on our way. I want to get Rosa home before dark. Though sometimes,' he playfully pinched her cheek and she turned her face away, 'the naughty girl stays out late. Come now, Rosa,' he added with a smile, as she drew in a quick breath. 'You know that you do!'

Matthew turned his back and marched away. So that was where she had been that night! Meeting him! He didn't speak to Jim, who stared as he passed him, but rushed along the road towards Home Farm.

'Cup o' tea, Matthew?' Mrs Jennings called as he stormed in through the kitchen. 'I've just made it.'

'No thanks.' He charged upstairs two steps at a time and slammed his bedroom door behind him.

'What's up wi' him?' Mrs Jennings stood with the teapot in her hand.

'Can't imagine.' Delia had a satisfied smile on her face. 'Somebody's upset him. I wonder who?'

He didn't come down to supper and after everyone else had eaten, Rosa climbed the stairs and knocked on his bedroom door.

'I said I didn't want any supper.' His voice was harsh and Rosa opened the door a crack and said quietly, 'I haven't brought you any. I just wanted to talk to you.'

He was lying on his bed, his hands behind his head. He sat up as she stood in the doorway. 'There's nothing to talk about,' he said bitterly. 'Jim said that you were walking out with Byrne and Delia confirmed it.'

343

'I'm *not* walking out with Byrne.' She was angry. 'Don't even think it. They're quite mistaken.'

He swung his legs off the bed and faced her. 'Then what were you doing with him? Jim said that Byrne asked Da if he could walk out with you.'

Her face flushed. How could she possibly explain? And Byrne would be coming back again tomorrow. 'I can't tell you why,' she said simply. 'I can only ask that you trust me. Something has happened and I became involved. But I'm not walking out with Byrne,' she repeated.

He frowned and got up off the bed and came towards her. 'Summat happened? What? Does Da know? Does Jim?'

'I can't tell you.' She gazed at him pleadingly, but his eyes pierced hers as if trying to discern what lay behind them.

'Then if you can't tell me I'll find out for myself.'

'Don't, please.' She put her hand out to him and he took it and drew her into the room and towards him.

'Rosa,' he said, his breath warm on her face. 'I have to know.' He suddenly bent and kissed her urgently on her mouth. 'If anyone should harm you or put you in danger,' he whispered vehemently, 'they'll have me to reckon with – be it brother, father or Irishman.'

She drew away, alarmed at his passion. 'I shouldn't be here,' she whispered.

'You shouldn't be anywhere else.' He gripped her arms. 'You belong with me, Rosa. You always have. I've tried to keep my distance, to treat you

344

as a sister, to give you your freedom. But it doesn't work. I need you as I need breath. I'm nothing without you and when I saw you with Byrne—' The words choked in his throat.

She knew. She had always known and she wanted nothing more than for him to take her in his arms and for her to feel safe. But there had always been a question mark hanging over her. Some mystery buried in her past which had to be resolved before she could make a commitment.

'John Byrne means nothing to me. I hardly know him. Trust me, Matthew, but I have to see him again.'

'No!' He clutched her fiercely. 'There's summat wrong. I know there is and by heavens, I'll find out what it is.' He stared at her. 'You're afraid of him, aren't you?'

She didn't answer, but closed her eyes so that he wouldn't know her feelings. Yes, she was. She was afraid of Byrne, and so she thought was Jim.

'Look at me,' he demanded. 'You're afraid of him?' he repeated.

She opened her eyes for him to see. 'Yes,' she whispered. 'I am.'

Matthew resolved to speak to Jim first thing in the morning, for when he went downstairs Jim had gone across to Marsh Farm and his father was nowhere to be found. Delia had a smirk on her face and started to say something detrimental about Rosa. He cut her short. 'Keep your nose out of this, Delia,' he said bluntly. 'It's nowt to do with you what Rosa does.'

345

Mrs Jennings, who was darning socks by the light of the oil lamp, looked up at him and gave a whimsical smile. 'She's had her nose put out o' joint.' She nodded over to Delia. 'She thought 'Irish fella had a fancy for her, didn't you, lass?' She turned the sock round and rethreaded the needle with wool. 'But I've warned her. She must watch out. Besides,' she put down the darning and gazed into space, 'there's summat not right about him.'

'What do you mean, Mrs Jennings?' Matthew turned to her. 'Not right?'

'Well, he's got a fanatical light burning in him. I've onny seen him a couple o' times but I've noticed it each time. Mebbe it's because he's Irish and feels he's been hard done by, but on 'other hand,' she pursed her lips and continued her darning, 'I'm probably just a silly old woman, but I think he's got a thorn in his breast – an old grudge mebbe, and somebody's got to suffer for it.' She looked up at Matthew again. 'So I'd be happier if our Rosa wasn't in his company. If he was asked to leave Sunk Island – if you get my drift.'

The next morning as they were eating breakfast there was a hammering on the back door. A young boy had a letter in his hand. A trap drawn by a mare stood in the yard. 'A message from 'blacksmith,' he said. He wiped his red nose with the back of his hand. 'It's been a long ride. Is there chance of a sup o' tea?'

The letter was addressed to Mr Drew, who gave it a cursory glance and then handed it to Rosa. 'Maggie's been delivered of a daughter,'

346

he said briefly to the family in general, but to no-one in particular. 'She needs some help, but you can't go, Rosa, as she asks. Delia, you can go.'

Delia's face crumpled in dismay. 'I can't go. How can I when I've just lost my own bairn?'

'Why can't Rosa go?' Matthew confronted his father. 'Maggie would be glad if she went.'

'She's needed here.' James Drew finished drinking his tea and got up from the table. He had a red spot of colour on each cheek. 'Delia can go, she's well enough.'

'I'll go.' Mrs Jennings came in from the back kitchen where she had given the boy some cold bacon and bread and a beaker of warm milk. 'She'll be missing her ma, poor lass, and though I'll be a poor substitute I can mebbe help her with 'new babby.'

'Thank you, Gran.' Rosa gave her grand-mother a smile of gratitude. She would know exactly what to do for Maggie, and it would save any explanation as to why she couldn't go her-self. She glanced at Matthew. His face was as dark as thunder as he stared at his father, but Mr Drew looked stricken as if he had received a great blow.

'Yes. Yes, you go, Mrs Jennings,' he faltered. 'And tell our Maggie – tell Maggie that I'll come and see her when I can.' His head nodded vaguely. 'She was very close to her mother.' He compressed his lips. 'She would have been glad about this bairn, I expect,' he murmured, and they all fell into silence at this first show of emotion they had ever seen from James Drew regarding his wife.

Mrs Jennings quickly packed a few things and set off with the boy in the cart. 'I'll tek 'reins,' Rosa heard her say. 'I know you young 'uns, you'll get hoss into a lather and have us tipped over into a ditch.'

'Nay, missus,' he complained as she pulled away. 'I got it here right enough without any bother.'

Rosa smiled as she closed the door. The turnpiked road to Ottringham was completed and strangers need no longer fear for their lives as they came into Sunk Island. In the meantime, the other tracks into the island were potholed and deep with water after rain, and it was easy enough to get a cartwheel stuck if you were not careful.

'I suppose you'll be skiving off this afternoon?' Delia's voice came from behind her. 'Your lover will be calling.'

'He's not my lover, Delia. Please don't say that he is.'

'What is he then?' Delia faced her. 'Why does he call on you?'

'It's a private matter,' she said, and refused to be drawn further. 'We'd better get on. There's a brace of pheasants waiting to be dressed, and pastry to be made for dinner. Gran's not here to help us.'

Delia gave a great sigh. 'I'm sick of this. There's never a minute to yourself,' and Rosa nodded thoughtfully and wondered if Matthew was right when he'd said that Delia would be off as soon as she was feeling well again.

John Byrne didn't call that day, nor the next, and Rosa felt a sense of reprieve. On the morning of the third day, Harry came bursting in with the news that there had been a riot in one of the inns at Patrington.

'Young Greg Brown had a knife stuck in him. They don't know if he'll mek it or not. His da's threatening he'll declare war on every Irish in Holderness if he dees.'

'Irish?' Rosa asked. 'Were they involved?'

'Oh, aye.' Harry warmed to the story. 'They reckon that 'Patrington lads accused 'Irish of tekking a young lass's virtue.' He ran his fingers through his beard. 'Though if you ask me, he might not have tekken it so much as been given it on a plate. Aye, I can well remember her mother being a bit free with her favours—'

'Harry!' Rosa warned.

'Oh, beg pardon, miss. Yes, well, seems like there was a big fight between 'Irish and Holderness lads, which spilled out onto 'street. Then somebody called 'constable, not that he could've done much on his own, but when it had all died down they found young Greg in an alley wi' a knife in his belly.'

Jim came in for his morning break as Harry was talking. He had already heard the news from one of the farm labourers. 'He's dead,' he said, his voice flat. 'I've just heard. They're saying it's murder. There's a group of vigilantes out searching for perpetrator already.'

Rosa felt a coldness draw over her. 'Do they know who they are looking for? There's a lot of Irish in Holderness.'

'Aye, they do.' He looked quickly from her to Delia, whose eyes were wide with curiosity. His glance flicked from them to Harry, who was looking disgruntled at being behind with the news. 'Constables have issued a warrant. They're looking for a man called John Byrne.'

CHAPTER THIRTY

The Patrington constable came to warn the farmers of Sunk Island that a dangerous villain was at large. 'It's doubtful that he'll come across here,' he said, when he came to Home Farm. 'For there's nowhere to hide on Sunk Island, but keep your doors locked just in case.' He looked at Rosa and Delia. 'He's ruined one young woman and there's others coming forward to accuse him, but apart from that he's wanted for murder.'

'But you don't know yet if he did it,' Rosa said. 'Is there proof?'

'Proof! Proof? There's a fine young fellow lying dead and this villain has disappeared. What more proof do you want than that? Besides, somebody saw him arguing with Greg Brown before 'fight broke out.' He shook his head. 'It's a bad business. Very bad and there'll be more trouble if vigilantes find him before 'law does.' He got up from his chair. 'So if you don't mind we'll tek a look over 'farm buildings and mek sure he's not hiding anywhere, same goes for Marsh Farm as well.'

James Drew had kept quiet until now, but then

said, 'Don't bother yourself. We'll do that, my lads and me. I don't want my winter feed ruining with your men tramping all over it, or my live-stock disturbing.'

'Why, we'll not do that, Mr Drew!' The con-stable was most indignant. 'We've looked over other farms and nobody has complained.'

'We'll know if owt has been disturbed,' Jim broke in. 'And we'll send for you if we think it has. And we've allus got our guns wi' us, there's a lot o' waterfowl flying in just now,' he added.

'We'll go and look right now.' Mr Drew rose to his feet, effectively dismissing the constable. 'It'll save you 'bother. There'll be nobody here on my land without me knowing about it.'

Later that morning Rosa tied a warm shawl about her shoulders. 'I'll go and dig up a row of potatoes,' she told Delia. 'Will you mend 'fire, it's getting low?'

Rosa looked about her as she went to the tool shed and, reaching for her garden fork and picking up a bucket, went down to the bottom of the garden and started to dig up the last row of potatoes. She didn't think that John Byrne would come here. As the constable said, there was nowhere to hide; but, she thought, what about the smuggled goods? And where are they hidden? He would want his share of the money from those, he wouldn't want Mr Drew to have it all. Ah, Seamus, she remembered. He would probably make the arrangements to be rid of the goods, and she felt a great sense of relief that maybe they had seen the last of the two Irishmen.

Delia had pulled a face behind Rosa's back as

she went out, and when Rosa called, 'And better lock 'door after me, like 'constable said,' she had blown a rasp of derision.

'I'll do as I like,' she muttered. 'I'll not tek orders from you.' But she brought in the wood basket and built up the fire, but perversely didn't lock the door and she didn't hear it as it slowly opened and John Byrne slid inside.

Delia had her back to him and he sidled up to her, putting one hand on her mouth and the other on her breast. She drew in a deep breath and turned her head, her eyes opening wide as she saw him. He took his hand from her mouth and turned her towards him.

'They're looking for you,' she breathed.

'I know,' he said softly. 'Silly people. I didn't kill the lad, but they had to blame someone. So I ran.' He pushed her against the kitchen wall and pressed himself against her. 'Where's the old woman?'

'She's not here.'

'Good, for I couldn't go without saying goodbye, Delia.' He put his parted mouth against hers, forcing it open with his tongue, and explored her moist and warm mouth.

She gasped. 'Somebody will come! Rosa! 'Door's not locked.'

'I know it's not locked.' He smiled, and, keeping hold of her, reached towards it and turned the key. 'There,' he murmured. 'Now it is,' and he pulled up her skirt and petticoat, lifting them above her knees and putting his hands beneath them.

She took deep gasping breaths as his hands

touched her bare flesh and gently stroked her buttocks, then moved round towards her belly. 'Oh! Oh! If somebody should come,' she panted.

'No-one will come,' he softly assured her. 'They're all out searching for me.'

His fingers gently tantalized her flesh and, utterly intoxicated, she pushed her hips towards his body, making low moaning sighs. Then he drew away.

'Don't stop.' She ran her tongue around her lips, then took his fingers into her mouth and sucked on them greedily. 'I want you!' Gone was her resolve not to fall again to a man's desires.

'Ah! I must go, my darling.' He took his hand away and kissed her mouth. 'Listen,' he whispered. 'I'll come back for you. Sure, we'll run away together. Yes?'

'Yes,' she said huskily. 'Yes. Yes! When? I'll get my things!'

'No. Not yet, we must wait till the chase dies down. Listen to me.' He ran his hands around her face and neck and she felt weak, as if she could hardly stand. 'I've found a place to hide. Pack me some food, bread and cheese, or meat. I've not eaten for two days, and I need some money, however much you've got. Then when things are quieter, I'll come back for you. Be quick now, there's a good girl. Rosa will have dug up that row of 'taties by now.'

Rosa! Yes, yes, of course. She'd be back any minute. She didn't know what to do first she was in such a fluster, and he smiled and said, 'Bring it out to me in ten minutes. I'll be behind the woodstore. If I'm not there, just leave it and I'll find it. Don't let Rosa see what you're doing.' He blew her a kiss and slipped out of the door as silently as he had come in.

I won't, she thought. She's that sharp she would probably guess. She quickly gathered up a loaf of bread and a hunk of cheese, then took a thick slice of pork from the larder and wrapped them all in a cloth and hid them at the back of a shelf. She had no money of her own, but there was housekeeping money kept in a tin on the shelf in the kitchen and she took most of it and put it in her apron pocket.

'My word but it's cold.' Rosa blew on her hands as she came in only a few minutes later.

'Is it?' Delia answered briefly. 'I'm hot with building up that fire.'

Rosa glanced at her. 'You look rather flushcd. Are you all right?'

'Yes – no, I feel a bit giddy. I'll get a breath of air in a minute and then have a lie-down.' She waited until Rosa was busying herself with something, then crept into the larder, picked up the parcel and went towards the door.

'You'll need a shawl,' Rosa called. 'It's bitter out there.'

'Yes, I've got one,' Delia said. 'Don't fuss, and don't forget to lock 'door behind me.' She gave a little satisfied smirk. What luck that Rosa had gone out for the potatoes! John Byrne must have been watching and waiting until he knew that she was alone. He trusted her, not Rosa. She wrapped the shawl around her shoulders and tucked it over the parcel and set off down the yard. Matthew was opening up the door of the woodstore and she stopped in dismay.

'What's up, Delia?' he asked.

'Nothing! I'm just coming out for some air.'

'That's not like you! Well, don't hang about. Somebody said they'd seen a fellow crossing 'fields and he couldn't recognize who it was.'

'Oh, everybody's jumpy,' she said. 'They'll all be seeing John Byrne in their dreams, but he'll be well away by now.'

'Mebbe,' he said abruptly, 'but we won't take any chances.' He went inside the store and brought out a bench, then took an axe which was hanging from the wall and started to chop up wood, throwing it into a pile just inside the door.

She watched him for a few minutes. John Byrne wouldn't come whilst he was there. What was she to do? She walked down to the kitchen garden, looking casually about her, but there was no sign of anyone. She lingered as long as she could, then walked slowly back towards the woodstore where Matthew had his back to her. At the side of the store was a pile of sacks and moving quickly and quietly she picked one up, put the parcel of food and money into it and threw it against the wall, away from the others. If John Byrne should come back, then he should find it easily enough and she would come out later to see if it had gone.

After she and Rosa had served the men their dinner, she made an excuse to go to her room. She wanted to think again about Byrne and how he had excited her – her body throbbed when she thought about him – but she wanted also to pack a bag, ready to leave when he should say so.

'I think I've left my window open,' she said. 'I'll just go up and close it. Don't want John Byrne climbing in,' she joked.

'It's no laughing matter, Delia,' Jim said bluntly. 'He's dangerous. There's a man dead, a woman raped.' He seemed nervous and edgy and had eaten very little.

His father too was restless, his eyes glistening and darting around the room and towards the door and windows. 'He'll have gone,' he said, and there was a jubilance in his voice. 'He won't wait around here, knowing that 'rope's waiting for him.'

Jim's face went white and Delia stopped on the stairs and turned around, her hand on the stair door. 'Rope?' she whispered.

'Aye, they'll hang him right enough,' Harry interrupted, chewing on a piece of meat, then removing it from his mouth with his fingers he placed it on the side of his plate. 'If they can catch him.'

'But he didn't – what if he didn't do it?' Delia questioned nervously. 'He might be innocent.'

'He'll not be innocent. Not him,' James Drew muttered.

'How do you know, Da?' Matthew stared at his father. 'What do you know of him? He came here to our farm. Why did he come?'

His father glanced at him and then at Harry, who was listening most intently. Young Bob too was watching him with his mouth open.

'He'd – er, he'd seen Rosa, wanted to meet her.

357

I told him he couldn't, but he came back.' Drew's face was set rigid and he clasped and unclasped his hands. 'He'll get a load of shot in his backside if he comes again,' he said roughly, and glanced at Rosa, who stared incredulously at him as he went on, 'I'll not have you walking out with him, Rosa, do you hear? You'll not see him again!'

He pushed back his chair and, picking up his jacket, he signalled to Harry and Bob to hurry and finish their dinner and follow him. 'There's summat wrong here,' Matthew said as Harry and Bob went out. He seemed bewildered. He looked at Jim and then at Delia, who was still standing by the stair door and looking as if she was about to cry.

'It's not true,' Delia whispered. 'He wasn't interested in Rosa. It was me. It was me he wanted to see.' She gave a small sob and picking up her skirts she ran up the stairs.

Jim pushed back his chair. 'You're best keeping out of it, Matthew.'

'Keeping out of it!' Matthew stood up to face his brother and raised his voice. 'Keeping out of what? What's going on?'

Jim didn't answer and walked out of the room. Matthew turned to Rosa. 'Will somebody tell me what's happening! What's all 'secrecy about? Rosa!'

Rosa heard the exasperation and anger in his raised voice and said quietly and decisively, 'I'll tell you what I know.' She drew a chair up to the fire and sat down. 'There's a mystery here,' she confessed, 'and it's something to do with my father, your father and the two Irishmen.'

He came and stood beside her. 'Your father and my father? But Da didn't know your father, at least not well!'

'He did! And I think that Jim did too,' she said. 'I think – and I'm only guessing – that the Irishmen are blackmailing your father into handling smuggled goods.'

He gave a short wry laugh. 'Da! Being black-mailed? Over what? He's a puritan! What could anybody possibly find to accuse him of?' He crouched down beside her. 'You have to be wrong over that, Rosa. Not Da.'

'No,' she insisted. 'I'm not wrong. That night when I went out late, I saw your da and Jim and the Irishmen loading crates onto a waggon at Stone Creek. There was a ship, a cutter, setting sail from the harbour, and a coggy boat coming in. The coggy boat had crates on it too. John Byrne caught me watching and made me go down to 'creek with him. He told Jim and your father that he would hold me hostage in case your father informed 'law.' She took a deep breath. What a relief to be able to tell him the truth. 'That's why he came to call on me, he was really checking on your father. He said if a whisper got out about the smuggled goods, then he would run and take me with him.'

She shuddered. The very thought of it made her tremble. There was such hatred in him. He would have no mercy on her, she was convinced of that. 'There's something else,' she said.

'What?' His voice was dull, as if all the energy had been knocked out of him.

'I only went out so late because I wanted to see

359

another ship that was moored out on 'river. I'd seen it before, do you remember? Henry had told me that it was a Dutch fluyt, and – ' She searched his face, wondering if he would understand her. 'And there was something about it that made me curious, I wanted to see if it was still there.'

'And was it?'

'Yes,' she whispered. 'It was, and John Byrne told me, when I explained to him why I was there, that it had been my father's ship.'

'But that was years ago,' Matthew interrupted.

She nodded. 'That's what your father said, when Byrne asked if he was still doing business with him. Mr Drew also said that it wasn't my father's flag, that it had probably had numerous owners since the Customs had requisitioned it.' She stopped, worn out by the trauma of the telling and wondering where was the sense of it all.

Matthew drew his hand over his face. 'So Da had known your father well! I can't believe that I didn't know any of this,' he muttered. 'How could they keep it from me?' Then he grew angry. 'And how could they let you become involved? My own brother. My own father!'

'Jim lost his temper,' she said. 'He fought with John Byrne and said that he should let me go. That's when Byrne said that I'd be held hostage until the goods were safely away.'

'And now he's on 'run, wanted for murder.' Matthew considered. 'But he'll not go without his dues. So where is he? And where've they stored 'run goods?'

They heard a sound on the stairs and Matthew got quickly to his feet and opened the door. Delia was sitting on the steps, tears coursing down her face.

'It's not fair,' she wailed. 'It was my chance at getting away. And now it's all ruined.'

'What?' Matthew frowned at his sister. 'You've been listening,' he accused sharply. 'What's spoilt? What are you talking about?'

'John Byrne,' she sobbed, and put her head on her knees. 'He was going to come back for me.'

Matthew took hold of her and brought her into the room. 'What do you mean – come back for you? Has he been here?'

'Yes.' She nodded and put her hand to her mouth. 'I feel sick,' she mumbled.

'When?' Matthew shook her by the shoulders. 'When did he come?'

Delia looked shamefaced and hung her head. 'When Rosa was digging up potatoes for dinner.'

Rosa gave a gasp. For him to be so close! 'But why didn't you say, Delia? Did he threaten you?'

'No,' she whispered. 'He didn't have to. He made promises to me.' Her mouth trembled. 'I would have gone with him.' She swallowed hard and wiped the tears from her face. 'I wanted to,' she admitted. 'I really wanted to. He said – he said—' She couldn't finish, and Rosa looked in alarm at Matthew.

'Did he – ? He didn't hurt you, Delia?' Rosa said softly. 'He didn't touch you?'

Delia gazed at her, then looked down and rapidly blinked away tears. 'No,' she said, and Rosa knew that she wasn't telling the truth. 'Nowt that I couldn't cope with anyway. He was onny here a few minutes. He asked me to get him some food,' she confessed, 'and some money – I took it out of 'housekeeping tin.'

'Well, Da won't be able to complain about that,' Matthew said grimly. 'Not after all he's done! But where is Byrne now?' he demanded of Delia.

'I don't know. I left 'money and parcel of food by the woodstore.' She took a handkerchief from her pocket and blew her nose. 'That's where I was going when I saw you chopping wood. He told me he'd found a place to hide.'

Matthew gave a snort of anger. 'So he's right here under our noses. Still here on Sunk Island!' He grabbed his coat. 'Well, he'll not stay hidden for long. I'll root him out. Him and his brother.'

CHAPTER THIRTY-ONE

But Matthew didn't find him, even though he searched the barns and haylofts, woodstores, stables, henhouses, cow byres and pig pens. He even searched the waggons and carts, piercing fiercely with his hay fork in every pile of loose straw or steaming manure. He also had angry words with Jim and told him that he would get to the bottom of the secrecy and web of lies which he and his father had been spinning.

Jim looked shamefaced, but only muttered something about blood on his hands and an uneasy conscience, and Matthew had glared at him, knowing that there was something more that his brother could tell him, yet he didn't feel that now was the time for confession. Not until Byrne had been caught.

He didn't come in until after dark. Jim was sitting morosely over the supper table, but his father had eaten and gone up to his room. Rosa put a bowl of soup in front of Matthew and asked anxiously, 'Is there no sign of him?'

'None.' He took a sip and then pushed the bowl away and put his elbows on the table.

'I've searched every inch of 'homestead. Every corner.'

'I've done it all already,' Jim muttered. 'And Da went across to Marsh Farm after 'constable had been. I reckon Byrne's done a runner.' He pushed his chair back and stood up. 'I'll go and make sure everything's locked up for 'night,' he said. 'Then I'm going to 'Ship for a drink afore I go to bed.' He looked across at Matthew and added, 'Do you want to come? We can have a talk.'

'Aye,' Matthew answered. 'In a bit. I'll catch you up.'

Rosa sat across from Matthew at the table. Delia had gone to her room. She had been very quiet and tearful all afternoon but had rebuffed Rosa angrily when she had asked again if Byrne had hurt her. 'Just leave it be, will you?' she had shouted. 'I'm a fool. I was tekken in by soft words and seductive promises, just like last time. But he's not got me pregnant if that's what you mean! He didn't hurt me. Onny my feelings and they don't count,' and she had rushed away upstairs and banged her door behind her.

'Matthew!' Rosa said quietly. 'I've been thinking – ' She stopped, wondering how to say what had been on her mind all afternoon. She too had gone upstairs to her room. The men were out, the fire built up, the supper was prepared and she decided that she deserved some time to herself. She sat on a chair by the window and looked towards the river.

The Humber had always been her consolation

in time of distress or anxiety. It was constant and reliable, its grey-brown presence calming and soothing, and even on its turbulent days when the agitated tides rushed and foamed, billowed and surged, she felt it was merely shaking off an ill temper. And when she walked across the land she sometimes thought she could feel its pulsating fluidity beneath her feet, as if she was treading on the *Sonke sande* of years gone by.

Today it had merged into the brownness of the flat landscape. The fields had been reaped, the pigs and sheep turned onto the land to graze, and the river was only discernible by its shining surface and the ships which showed their white sails above the fields. But the afternoon sky had been dark and ominous above it, and she had given an involuntary shudder and had turned to look in the other direction towards her old home, Marsh Farm, near the bridged North Channel. Across the wide landscape, in the fields and meadows, she had seen groups of men searching in dykes and ditches and hedge bottoms for John Byrne.

'Yes?' Matthew said, lifting his head from his deep contemplation of his fingernails. 'What have you been thinking?'

She knew that he had been angered by the revelation that his father had been involved in the smuggling with the Byrne brothers, and feared that he would be made angrier still by what she had to say now. But it had to be said. She kept her voice low, conscious that Mr Drew was in the house.

'Jim said – that your father had searched Marsh Farm for a sighting of John Byrne.'

'Yes, I know he did.' He gazed at her questioningly. 'He said there was no sign of him.'

'Why wouldn't he let anyone else search?'

Matthew shrugged. 'We were all looking elsewhere.'

'He wouldn't let 'Patrington constable look either.'

He frowned. 'What are you suggesting?' His face darkened. 'Not that Da's harbouring him?'

'No. No!' She was quick to refute it. 'It's just that – well, your da will never let anyone near the place, only Jim – and I wondered,' she hesitated and he urged her on with a gesture. 'I'm probably wrong, but do you think that the smuggled goods are being kept there?'

'Good God!' His mouth dropped open and he whispered, 'You're right, Rosa. 'Barn is padlocked and Da has the key and he's never locked it before. That's why he wouldn't let 'constable take a look!' He pondered for a moment, then rose from the table. 'I'm going over.'

'Will you ask your da for the key?'

'No,' he said grimly. 'I won't. I have a sharp axe which will split 'chain on 'padlock. I'll not be put off, which is what he would try to do. I'll not be kept out.'

'And what will you do then?' she asked. 'Report your father and Jim to the authorities? They'll go to prison if you do!'

He stopped in his tracks and stood nonplussed

for a moment, then said, 'Folks who live near 'sea or river's edge have often been involved in smuggling. An anker of brandy, a bit of baccy, and it doesn't do a deal of harm. But we're talking of more than that. You said you'd seen crates coming ashore, so that's a big venture and if Da is storing it, then he's as involved and as guilty as those who bring it in.'

'So, you'd tell?' She spoke quietly. Matthew was so straight and honest, always so open, no covering up mistakes, no subterfuge. Yet she couldn't think that he would report his father and brother to the law.

He sat down again and put his head in his hands. 'I don't know! How can I, Rosa? Why? Why does he have to do it? He doesn't need any money. Why is he taking such a risk? He could lose 'farm. We could all lose 'farm! 'Crown agents won't let any of us stay if there's 'least sniff of dishonesty.'

Rosa was aghast. The possibility of losing the farm hadn't entered her head. But it was true. The farms had to be run satisfactorily or the leases could be terminated.

'What shall we do?' she whispered.

He got to his feet again. 'I'm going anyway. I have to know. If 'goods are there I shall confront him, make him get rid of them somehow or other. I have to get to 'bottom of this, and if we're wrong then I'll apologize to him for my mistaken beliefs.'

'I'll come with you.' She hurriedly reached for her thick outdoor shawl.

'No!' he said. 'You won't.'

'I will,' she parried. 'It's dark and John Byrne might be out there.'

He gave her a quick smile. 'And you'd defend me against him, would you?'

'Yes,' she said softly. 'Of course I would.'

He looked at her tenderly. 'If he's out there, all the more reason why you should stay here with 'door locked.'

'I'm coming with you,' she determined. 'I've made up my mind.'

'Will you always come with me, Rosa?' he asked. 'Even if we have to leave Sunk Island?'

She was about to reply when they heard footsteps on the stairs and Delia came into the room looking tired and dejected. Matthew turned towards her. 'Delia. I'm going across to Marsh Farm and Rosa's coming to pick up Jim's washing,' he lied, harmlessly. 'Will you lock 'door behind us and wait up 'till we get back?'

'Now?' she griped. 'Why can't Jim bring it in 'morning? I don't like stopping on my own.'

'You'll not be on your own,' Rosa said quickly, 'your da's upstairs, and Jim keeps forgetting to bring his dirty clothes across. You know I keep asking him.'

Delia shrugged. 'Do as you like,' she muttered. 'I couldn't care less what you do. It doesn't make any difference what I say or think anyway. I'm a nobody in this house. Of no importance whatsoever.'

'That's not true, Delia,' Matthew retaliated. 'Look, I'll talk to you when I get back.'

She didn't answer and turned her back on

them and sat down by the fire, only nodding when Matthew reminded her to lock the door.

'Should we go for Jim?' Rosa asked as they hurried along, and she pulled her shawl around her. A strong chill wind had sprung up, whistling about them.

'No, he'd onny try to put me off going. There's summat Jim isn't telling me; some secret.'

Yes, Rosa agreed silently. There is, there always has been. For many years.

There was a full moon but it was hidden by dark buffeting clouds. Streaks of light appeared intermittently, giving the clouds a halo of silver but shedding no luminance on the land, and they had to take care where they put their feet. Matthew carried a lantern and also the axe which he had picked up from the woodstore. Rosa took hold of his elbow. 'Watch your feet,' she murmured. 'That's what my ma used to say whenever we went down to 'river bank.'

'Do you still miss her?' Matthew asked softly. 'I still miss my ma.'

'I can hardly remember her,' she admitted, 'but strangely I feel her presence, as if she hasn't gone. And,' she paused, 'even though I didn't know my father at all, I feel as if he is still here too. There have been so many sailors and fishermen washed up here on 'shore and yet his body was never found.'

'Mebbe you like to feel that he's still here?' he said. 'Mebbe you don't want to think that he's dead.'

'Yes.' She looked up at him. 'Perhaps that's it.' Have I inherited this forlorn hope from my mother? she thought. Is that why I can't commit myself to Matthew? 'Fred hasn't brought those papers back from the lawyer yet,' she commented. 'I hope they haven't lost them.'

As they approached Marsh Farm, Rosa took the lantern from Matthew whilst he lifted the heavy iron latch and opened up the gate. They crossed the rectangular yard containing the pig pen and straw shelter, and approached the barn which was under the same roof as the house itself. The granary was built at the side of the barn but at a slightly lower level. 'I'll take a look in 'barn first,' Matthew whispered. 'Then up in hayloft. You stay here.'

He smashed the chain holding the padlock with one swoop of his axe and opened the door. He propped the axe against the wall and taking the lantern stepped inside the timber-framed barn. The last time he had been inside they had been threshing and were choked by the dust, even though the heavy wooden doors were propped open. There had been only a small corn harvest at Marsh Farm and he remembered that his father had insisted that the threshing was done immediately, rather than wait for the winter months as they usually did. Now each of the three bays was swept clean, a box waggon and a two-wheeled hay cart in one of them, some stacks of straw in another. The flails were hanging from hooks on the wall and the winnowing baskets stacked neatly in a corner.

There were no cattle or horses kept here since Mr Drew had taken over the farm, and no hens or ducks either as there had been in Mr

Jennings's time, and Matthew thought it strange that Jim hadn't seen fit to keep any. He had some pigs, four sows in litter and a boar, but had said that he didn't want to increase the stock and always sent off the young pigs to market as soon as they were ready. His heart isn't in it, Matthew thought as he climbed the ladder to the hayloft, yet it was once a good holding.

He lifted his lantern and at a cursory glance there was nothing unusual to be seen, just rusty old tools that had once belonged to Rosa's grandfather, scythes, sickles and hay forks. A pile of rope lay coiled up in a corner alongside some corn sacks and potato baskets. There was no winter bedding as there were no animals kept there, but a number of wooden crates were stacked side by side beneath the wooden rafters, half hidden by sacking.

Rosa waited inside the door of the barn. Though the surroundings were familiar to her, she felt uneasy. She wasn't normally of a nervous disposition, but there were rattles and clatterings as the wind rushed around the yard, clanking the lids on iron buckets and blowing twigs and branches everywhere, and she could hear the creaking of the boards in the hayloft as Matthew moved about.

She kept her hand on the heavy door to stop it banging and looked up the ladder. She could just see the halo of light from the lantern, but everything else was in pitch darkness. She glanced over her shoulder: the moon was hidden again by thick cloud, and the air was heavy in spite of the wind. She gave a sudden gasp as a shadow loomed in the yard behind her. 'Jim! Is that you?'

'No, my darling.' A soft voice answered her and her mouth was covered by a rough hand. 'It's not your precious Jim. It's your old friend John Byrne.'

She tried to bite his hand as he picked her up with his other arm and carried her towards the granary, but he appeared not to feel the pain for he laughed softly and neither stumbled or panted as he took her through the open door.

'Now, promise you won't scream or shout and I'll take my hand away,' he murmured. 'If you do, it'll be the worse for that fine young fellow back there.'

She nodded. His face was close to hers and his hand was tight against her cheeks. Slowly he removed it, then gently smoothed her face. 'What soft skin, Rosa! Soft and blooming like rose petals. Is that where you got your name, I wonder.'

She shook her head. She was trembling so much that she couldn't speak.

'Why, I could die happy if I could but kiss that unblemished skin.' He whispered, yet his tone was menacing.

'Please don't,' she begged. 'I wouldn't want you to.'

'Ah!' She felt his breath on her face as he spoke, and he still had his arm around her. 'Not like Delia, then? She wanted me to.' He ran his fingers around her waist. 'Delia wanted me to do all kinds of things.' Then he drew back and, as he did, the moon came from behind the clouds and shone a bright path into the granary. She saw that his red hair was matted and his face was grimy, and she shuddered. The thought of him touching her horrified her.

'But you wouldn't want that, would you, Rosa? You'd want to keep yourself pure for someone special?'

'Yes,' she whispered. 'I would.'

He nodded. 'I respect that, Rosa, though I'd be disappointed that I wasn't the one. Still,' she saw his eyes gleam, 'if that raw youth searching in the barn amongst my things decides to cause trouble, then I might think fit to take you along with me, and who knows what might happen if we were alone together?' His voice was intimidating and she could feel her fear growing stronger. 'Men are such weak creatures, it would be more than I could bear having such beauty beside me.'

He drew her towards the door and, putting both hands around her waist, said softly, 'Now that we've had our little chat, I want you to shout to – Matthew, isn't it? Listen,' he cocked his head. 'I can hear him. Tell him to come at once.'

'You'll not hurt him? Please don't! He's done nothing.'

'He hasn't, has he? Not like some people I know. But I want him to help me. He's such a fine fellow I'm sure he'll be glad to. Go on.' His voice became rough. 'Shout!'

*   *   *

Matthew stepped across to the crates and saw that they were sealed by wooden locks. He'd left his axe below and, looking around for something to open them, found a spanner lying on top of the sacks. He swung it against one of the locks and it cracked open. He lifted the lid. In the crate, packed in cotton cloth, were rolls of fabric. He rubbed his fingers against one of them. It was soft and fine and, holding up his lantern, he saw that it was a rich red. He pulled up a fold of another roll, a cream colour and thicker in texture.

Is it silk, I wonder? He opened another crate and the sweet rich aroma of tobacco came drifting out, as it did in the third crate. There were two more larger crates. He smashed open one which had an iron lock on it and took a deep breath as he saw that it too was filled with sacks of tobacco. 'Oh, Da,' he breathed. 'What have you done?'

He called down the ladder to Rosa. 'Rosa! You were right. It's all up here.'

She didn't reply so he called again. 'Rosa!' Still no answer and he wondered if she had been disturbed by Jim returning home from the Ship. I'll have summat to say to him, he thought, as he ran easily down the ladder. The door was open but Rosa was not there beside it and he called again, more urgently, and held up the lantern as there was very little light coming in from the open door.

She wasn't there. Nor was she in the yard. He walked towards the granary and saw that the door was ajar. His heart started to beat faster as he thought of John Byrne. 'Rosa!' He lifted his voice to a shout. 'Where are you?'

'Matthew! I'm here.' Her voice sounded thin and frightened and came from behind the granary door. 'Don't come in!'

CHAPTER THIRTY-TWO

The moon slid behind a cloud again and Matthew held the lantern high. Rosa stood in the doorway of the granary and John Byrne was behind her, one hand resting familiarly on her shoulder.

'Let her go!' Matthew's voice was full of controlled anger. 'What sort of a man are you to hide behind a woman?'

Byrne drew in a gasp of fury. 'I know what kind of man I am, I've served a long apprenticeship. Not like you,' he sneered, 'just off his mammy's breast.' He put his free hand on Rosa's other shoulder, holding her fast. 'But you're mistaken, I'm not hiding behind her. We've had a little chat, Rosa and me, and if I don't get co-operation from you, then she's agreed to come with me. Isn't that so, Rosa?'

Matthew saw the fear in her face and said quickly, 'What is it you want from us? Haven't you done enough damage to this family already? Why don't you just go? The law will catch up with you if you don't.'

The moon slid out again and illuminated

Byrne's face. 'Me?' he said. 'Done damage to your family! Sure you don't know the history, do you, Matthew? Has your daddy not taken you on his knee and told you the tale of the Byrne brothers and Señor Carlos? No, I can see from your face that he hasn't.' He stroked Rosa's hair and Matthew felt his hackles rise. He couldn't endure seeing Byrne touch her.

'Well,' Byrne said softly. 'Rosa's father and the Byrne brothers and your father had a good little business going. But there was some double dealing going on and I'd swear on my mammy's head that Carlos and the eminent Mr Drew, aided by young Jim, decided to go into business together and cut us out. The Customs swooped on the ship where my brother and I were waiting and Carlos conveniently disappeared.' He gave a half smile. 'You've not heard that story before, Matthew?'

'No,' Matthew said bluntly. 'And I don't believe it.'

'Ah! It's true enough,' Byrne said pleasantly. 'I could tell you so many stories about your father, Matthew, but I wouldn't sully Rosa's ears in the telling of them. Ask him sometime, man to man, about his trips into Hull to visit the ladies of the night. Oh,' he said in mock anguish. 'I really didn't mean to tell.'

His voice hardened as he continued. 'And if your conniving dissolute father thinks that because I'm on the run now, I'm going to leave all those goods behind for him, like last time, then he's very much mistaken.'

'What do you want from us?' Matthew was

shaken by what Byrne had said, but as he spoke he heard the sound of the gate creaking and hoped that it was Jim, home from the Ship. Byrne heard it too and pulled Rosa back into the granary.

'Get inside,' he spat at Matthew. 'The girl will feel my hand round her throat if you don't.'

Matthew believed him. He wished he'd picked up the axe instead of the lantern, but he came inside as he was bid. 'It's Jim,' he urged. 'Tell us what you want and be gone.'

'I want a waggon to hold the goods and a couple of strong horses to pull it. I also need a driver, because,' he smiled at Rosa, 'I shall be under the covers, cuddling up to Rosa, making sure that we get into Hull safely.'

'You want me to drive you into Hull?' Matthew was incredulous at the gall of the man.

Byrne nodded and looked out through the door to where Jim could be seen crossing the yard. 'Yes, or Jim,' he added thoughtfully. 'We know that Jim is a good fellow. Always does as he's told.'

He leaned towards the doorway, still keeping hold of Rosa. 'Jim,' he called, and it came home to Matthew that John Byrne knew no fear, even though there would now be two men against him. Except that he still held Rosa fast for his own protection and surety.

Jim looked towards the granary. 'Who's there? Matthew? Is that you? 'Barn door's open!'

Byrne kicked open the granary door. 'Well, who in the name of heaven can have done that, for it wasn't me!'

Jim stopped. 'Byrne?' he said warily. 'I thought you'd gone from Sunk Island! They're starting another search in 'morning.'

'Is that so,' Byrne answered cheerily. 'Well, I'll be long gone by then, me and Matthew and Rosa. Why don't you come in,' he persuaded. 'We're all here and telling a few tall stories. Reminiscing, you know. We're having some real good crack.'

'Matthew – Rosa! What's going on?'

'You tell me!' Matthew was full of fury. Jim's manner towards Byrne was so familiar that it seemed quite possible that he had known the Irishman before. 'I've been hearing that you and Da and the Byrnes were running smuggled goods together.'

Jim was silent and Byrne broke in, 'And then you double-crossed us, didn't you, Jim? You and your da and Carlos.'

'Not Carlos,' Jim muttered. 'He wanted to finish wi' smuggling when he married Mary Jennings.'

'What happened to him, Jim?' Rosa's voice was quiet. Matthew put the lantern down on the floor as the clouds scudded away, and he saw her pale face in the moonlight. He must take his chance when he could to overpower Byrne.

'He's dead.' They could hardly hear what Jim said, his voice was so low.

'Hah!' Byrne was disbelieving. 'That's what you say. So what happened to his body?'

'He's dead and his body is buried.'

'Jim!' Rosa exclaimed. 'Where? How do you know?'

379

'Yes, young Jim.' Byrne was cynical. 'How do you know?'

Jim raised his head and looked at them. He was standing outside, close to the open door. He looked at Byrne, then his eyes turned to Matthew, but lingered longer on Rosa who was still held in Byrne's grasp between him and Matthew.

'I'm sorry, Rosa.' His voice was thick with emotion.

'Come on. Come on!' Byrne shouted impatiently. 'We don't want to dig him up! Just tell us how you know.'

'I know,' Jim said slowly, 'because I killed him.'

No-one spoke for a moment, then Rosa, in a shaky voice, asked, 'Why? How?'

'It was an accident.' Jim lowered his head. ''Gun went off. Killed him instantly.'

'Why didn't you tell anybody?' Matthew said harshly. 'Where's he buried?'

Jim's face was ashen and his voice strained. 'I'd have been charged wi' murder if we'd told,' he muttered. 'And nobody'll find him now, he's well buried. 'Customs had had a tip-off and were on 'lookout.' He looked up and directly at Byrne. 'He was riding into Hull to tell you, honest to God, he was! But then—' He shook his head and his voice broke. He put his hand to his forehead and covered his eyes. 'It was too late. I'm sorry, Rosa. So sorry.'

Rosa started to weep. 'How could you keep this to yourself? Why couldn't you have told me?'

'All right,' Byrne broke in. 'That's enough.' He

was agitated, as if disturbed by the revelation, and bit on his lip. 'Leave it! Seamus always believed that Carlos was honest.' Then he gave a short cynical laugh. 'But don't think it makes any difference, I still want that waggon and horses to pull it, so let's get moving.'

'We don't keep any hosses here,' Matthew said quickly. 'One of us will have to go to Home Farm to fetch them. But there's a waggon in 'barn, you can use that.' He made up his mind to settle the situation.

'Right,' Byrne said. 'Let's get into the barn, and don't try anything, either of you. I have the girl, and – ' he thrust his right hand into his belt, 'I also have a knife. I wouldn't want to spoil her lovely face or that slender neck.' He touched Rosa's throat with the point of the gleaming blade and she flinched and swallowed.

They all moved into the barn and Jim and Matthew pulled the waggon out from one of the bays. Byrne nodded. 'Good. Now get the casks out from behind the straw and start loading them into the waggon.'

Matthew looked at him uncomprehendingly, but Jim went across to where the straw was stacked in the other bay and, pulling over a couple of bales, revealed several casks lying beneath. Matthew gave his brother a hostile stare. Jim turned his face away from his glance and they both loaded the casks into the waggon.

'Leave one anker,' Byrne said with a sly grin. 'That's your father's payment for us keeping quiet about his night-time activities. He'll know that we at least keep our bargains, and,' he added, 'if the Customs men do come there'll be evidence enough to show that he was involved.'

When they had finished loading the casks, Byrne said roughly, 'That'll do, now all we need are the horses. You can fetch them, Jim, and if you try any tricks, be sure that I shall tell the law of your confession to murder if I'm caught. If I go to jail then so do you, not forgetting your father. We shall be company for each other,' he added maliciously. 'You'd like that, wouldn't you?'

Jim cast a look of misery at Rosa, then went out of the barn door. 'And be quick about it,' Byrne called after him. 'I want to be away before dawn.' He turned towards Matthew. 'Now then. Get moving. Get up that ladder and bring down whatever is in those crates. Leave the crates,' he said. 'They're too heavy and would weigh us down. Bring down the rolls of silk and the tobacco.'

'Hellbound! Son of Satan!' Matthew cursed as he climbed the ladder.

'Names don't hurt me,' Byrne mocked contemptuously. 'And look to your own when scoffing and see if you can hold your head up.'

Matthew looked down at him. Byrne held Rosa with one hand and in the other he held the knife. She seemed calm, yet her mouth worked nervously. Byrne had the advantage. He had Rosa. Jim wouldn't tell anyone that Byrne was here, not when his own life could finish in jail. Matthew's regard for his brother and father reached the lowest possible ebb. What would Rosa think of them now? She had been cheated by the Drew family, and any hopes of her joining her life with his faded rapidly. She would surely put a great distance between them.

He turned and continued up the steps. Despair and anger battled in a storm within him. But, he resolved, he would gain the day. He would outmanoeuvre Byrne. Somehow he would make retribution to Rosa for the wrongdoing of his father and brother. If it took the rest of his life he would make amends and be happy to do so. He wouldn't, couldn't, lose her.

Jim's heart was pounding by the time he reached Home Farm. He had run practically all the way, stumbling over the fields of stubble and jumping over narrow ditches to save time. He must move fast to outwit Byrne. I must make up for what I've done, he panted. Another wrong won't put it right. God in heaven, help me to be strong this time. Help me to oppose my father for he will surely be against my plan. Ma! If you can hear me, give me 'courage which I lacked when I was a lad.

Sweat streamed down his face as he hammered on the door. 'Delia,' he called. 'Delia! Let me in.'

Delia opened the door cautiously. 'Jim! It's you! I thought it was Matthew and Rosa. They've gone across to Marsh Farm.'

'I know. Listen, Delia. You've got to help me! Put on some warm clothes. I want you to ride to Hedon.'

'What? At this time of night! You must be mad!'

'I am mad,' he agreed. 'But listen to what I have to tell you. Byrne is at Marsh Farm and he's got Rosa and Matthew.' Quickly he filled in the details, or as much as he thought she should know, but leaving out his own involvement in Carlos's death.

'I want you to ride to Hedon, go to Fred and tell him what I've told you. Tell him to alert 'constable that Byrne is dangerous and not to put Rosa's life in peril cos she will be with him. Matthew will be driving 'waggon and I'll tell him to go through Keyingham marshes.'

Delia had been silenced by what Jim had told her. Now she said, 'They'll get 'wheels bogged down!'

'That's 'general idea,' Jim said. 'It'll give us more time to get men together. I'll call on John Gore and get him to ride for 'Patrington constable in case Byrne teks it into his head to go that way.' He helped her into her heavy cloak. 'Come on, there's a good lass. I'll saddle up a steady hoss for you.'

'It's pitch black!' She hung back, wavering at what lay in front of her as they went out into the yard. 'I'll tummel into a ditch. It'll take me hours – you know I'm no good on horseback!'

'You can do it, Delia,' he persuaded. 'It's onny low cloud coming in from 'river. See, it's lighter inland and 'moon's up.' He helped her mount and, looking up, took hold of her hand and squeezed it. 'Our lives depend on you, Delia. Mine and Matthew's as well as Rosa's.'

She nodded and her lips trembled. 'I've not been good to Rosa, Jim. I've allus been jealous of her.' She swallowed her tears. 'But I wouldn't want her to get hurt.'

'No,' he said softly. 'We've done enough of hurting folks, you and me. So now's 'time to make up for it. Go on, now. Ride as fast as you can. Thank God for that Ottringham road. Then stay with our Maggie and Mrs Jennings till all's done here.'

He heaved a deep breath as Delia rode away. It had only taken minutes to persuade her to go. Now he must bring out two waggon horses, not so fast that they'd make speed, but with feet used to wet ground and pulling a heavy load. He harnessed them and brought them into the yard, then with an acute sense of foreboding went back indoors to waken his father.

He was still awake and came to the bedroom door when Jim knocked. He was in his bed shirt, with a nightcap on his head. 'All's up for us, Da,' Jim began. 'Past has overtekken us.'

'What you rambling on about? Why are you here and not abed at Marsh Farm?' his father said irritably. 'You know I like you to stop there, specially now if Byrne's about.'

'Byrne's already there,' Jim said and hardened his resolve to be strong. 'So are Matthew and Rosa. Byrne's got a knife to Rosa's throat and Matthew's loading up a waggon with 'run goods.'

His father's mouth dropped open. 'Never,' he protested. 'How did they get in? I put a strong lock on that barn door.'

'You didn't hear me, Da!' Jim's voice rose angrily. 'I said – Byrne's got a knife to Rosa's—'

'Yes. Yes. I heard you,' he said testily. 'What

385

they doing there anyway? Poking their noses into what doesn't concern them!'

'It does concern them, Da. Matthew found the stuff in 'barn and Byrne told him what it was – and about us. And I told them about Carlos.'

'You did what?' His father stared incredulously. 'You idiot. You blockhead! Why did you do that? Are you completely out of your senses?'

Jim nodded. 'I probably am. But I also know that I'm sick to death of lies and deceit. I can't go on living this half life any longer. I've drunk from 'cup of regret and bitterness and I'm ready to tek my punishment if I have to.'

'Well, so you might be,' his father grunted. 'But I'm not.' He tore off his nightcap and turned to pick up his breeches from a chair in the bedroom. 'I'll do a deal with Byrne. Get him safely off Sunk Island if he keeps quiet.'

Jim shook his head. He couldn't believe his father's behaviour. Had he no thought for anyone but himself? 'It's too late for that,' he attested. 'I've already sent for 'authorities.'

'What!' His father stopped in the action of putting a leg into his breeches.

'I've sent a messenger,' Jim said. 'I've alerted Hedon.'

'But not Patrington?' His father hurriedly pulled up his breeches and buttoned them. 'We can try to get him out over 'bridge into Patrington.' He hesitated. 'That is, unless they've put a watch on it. Mebbe we'll tek him over in a waggon at first light. Then if he's caught we can swear we didn't know he was in there.'

'Swear on 'bible, shall we, Da?' Jim came into

the room and wearily sat on the side of the bed. 'Call heaven as our witness?' He put his head in his hands. 'You're not listening to me. What would Ma say if she knew?' he muttered. 'Would she forgive us?'

His father looked askance. 'Don't dare bring your mother into this! This has nowt to do with your mother!' His voice thundered, but had a shaky edge to it and Jim knew that his barb had hit home.

'I won't help you, Da. I've a scheme to catch him and I won't be put off. You've manipulated me since I was a lad of thirteen. I've had 'threat of gallows hanging over me and not once have you tekken any of 'blame.'

He knew that time was getting on and that Byrne would be waiting for the horses, yet he couldn't stop the outpouring of wretchedness. It had lain festering for so long, and now, like a foul boil, it erupted, spewing forth his regrets, griefs and sheer misery.

His father was rendered speechless and stood with one hand on the iron bedhead and the other clasped to his mouth as he gazed at him. Finally, Jim stood up. 'So, I'm telling you. I'm going to catch Byrne and his brother, cos he'll turn up too, sooner or later, and if they tell of what happened all those years ago and I go to jail, well, so be it.'

There was a sudden crack of thunder and a flash of lightning lit the room as James Drew said in a low voice, 'You won't go to jail. It'll be me.'

'Don't give me that, Da,' Jim said dejectedly.

'Don't start playing 'martyr now. It's too late for that.'

'No. No, I'm not. It was me. It wasn't you.'

Jim looked at him. His father's face seemed grey, even though the low fire in the hearth cast a glow to the room. 'What was you?' He glanced towards the window at the rosy reflection of the fire.

'I killed Carlos. It wasn't you. I was holding 'gun. You tried to knock it out of my grasp as I pointed it at him. I was the one with my finger on 'trigger.'

'Da! Look! Summat's on fire!' Jim pointed to the window. In the blackness of the night sky came a red glow and sparks flying into the air. 'God in heaven,' he cried. 'It's Marsh Farm! It's on fire!'

CHAPTER THIRTY-THREE

Matthew's legs were beginning to ache. He could only carry one roll of fabric at a time down the ladder and he had been up and down a dozen times already. Byrne sat on a bale of straw with Rosa at the side of him. He loosened his hold on her each time Matthew went up the steps and took hold of her each time he came down.

Matthew emptied one crate and started on another containing tobacco. He sniffed the pungent aroma which emanated from the sacks and put one over his shoulder. Holding the other in his hand, he shuffled carefully down the steps again.

'Ah, baccy!' Byrne said. 'I can smell it from here.'

'Customs will smell it too if they get near,' Matthew muttered and loaded the two sacks into the waggon next to the rolls of silk.

'But they won't get near, will they? They'll not be expecting me in a waggon. Come on,' he said, as Matthew took a breather. 'We haven't got all night. I told you I want to be away before dawn.'

Matthew climbed up again and picked up

another two sacks. He carried them down under Byrne's gaze, stored them in the waggon and went up again. He's tiring, he thought. Sitting down has made him sleepy. Byrne had put his head back against the wooden structure whch made up the bays and was watching him through half-closed eyelids.

Again he collected another two sacks of tobacco and took them to the top of the ladder. Byrne was having difficulty in keeping awake. His head kept jerking as he fought sleep and Matthew saw Rosa edging away from him. The knife was lying loosely in Byrne's hand. Matthew put down the sack and as Rosa looked up at him, he put his finger to his lips. He picked up the sack again and stepped silently down.

Halfway down he stopped. Byrne's eyes were closed and Rosa had managed to edge herself along so that she was sitting right on the end of the bale. Matthew indicated that she should move further away, came down another few steps, then, putting down one of the sacks, he lifted the other high and hurled it towards Bryne where it crashed against his legs, waking him. Rosa sped away, out of his reach.

Matthew grabbed the other sack, sprang down the remaining steps and, keeping hold of the neck of the sack, launched the bulk of it at Bryne, as with an oath he jumped to his feet. The weight of it caught him and he staggered and dropped the knife. Matthew launched the sack again at Byrne, hitting him on the side of his head.

'Run, Rosa. Get out,' Matthew shouted, and she ran towards the door, but hesitated, holding

390

onto it. 'Go on,' he shouted again. 'Run. Go to John Gore's. Get help.'

Still she hesitated, and Byrne, now seemingly recovered, hit out at Matthew with his fist. 'She'll not get there in time,' Byrne snarled. 'You'll be dead before she's halfway there.'

'We'll see about that,' Matthew retaliated. He was younger and stronger too, of that he was sure. Byrne might well have powerful muscles from digging ditches, but so had he. Working on a farm was no job for a weakling. His arms, shoulders and chest were hard and muscular from digging and ploughing, scything and threshing, as well as handling horses and oxen. He was also taller and more heavily built than Byrne.

He dropped the sack and punched Byrne on the nose. Byrne drew back, a trickle of blood running down towards his mouth. Fury was in his eyes and he lashed out wildly at Matthew, catching him on his cheek. Out of the corner of his eye, Matthew could see Rosa still hesitating by the door. Why doesn't she run, he thought distractedly, and took another blow from Byrne which sent him staggering.

'Matthew! Watch out.' Rosa gave a warning shout as his feet came too close to the lantern. Byrne, though, didn't see it as he lunged again at Matthew and caught it with his foot, crashing it over onto its side. The glass broke, the oil seeped out and a small tongue of flame licked the loose straw which had spilt from the bales, and ignited it.

Matthew stamped on the burning straw, but

Byrne hit out at him and he ducked away, fielding Byrne's wild blows and striking out at him. He saw the flame as it sped along the straw towards a bale, and called again to Rosa. 'Go for help,' he urged. 'Place'll go up in flames. Pax,' he shouted at Byrne. 'We've got to put 'fire out!'

But Byrne didn't seem to hear him or see the flames catching the bale of straw and licking up the sides of the wooden waggon. It was as if his blood was up and all he was intent on was wreaking revenge and right now, Matthew was the enemy.

They fought hard and furiously and Rosa screamed from the doorway for them to get out. Smoke started to billow about them as the fire took hold of the other straw bales and then the waggon, then the rolls of silk were set alight and, with a great whoosh, the flames tore through the casks and lit up the brandy, sending up spirals of blue and yellow flame which curled above them, blackening the upper storey of the barn.

Matthew took a step backwards. The smoke was thick and choking. He couldn't get his breath, his chest was heaving, and he couldn't see Byrne whom he had just sent crashing to the floor with a blow to his chin. 'Byrne,' he shouted, 'where are you? We have to get out. Byrne! Answer me!'

Rosa suddenly appeared at his side, carrying a bucket of water which slopped over her feet as she heaved it into the heart of the flame where the lantern had been.

'I told you to run,' Matthew shouted at her. 'Go fetch help.'

'I couldn't,' she sobbed. 'How could I go and leave you with that madman? He was going to kill you.'

'Fetch another bucket of water,' he bellowed. 'I'm going to try and find him—' As he spoke there was a tremendous crash and a weakened blackened joist holding the upper level of the barn pitched to the ground, bringing down the wooden ladder and part of the floor, blocking the doorway and their exit.

'Matthew,' Rosa clung to his arm. 'We're trapped!'

Jim dashed into the stable block and brought out a young mare. She was a jaunty mover, used to pulling the trap, and didn't object to having someone on her back, though she didn't travel at great speed. He sprang onto her, unsaddled, and dug in his heels. His father was left in the yard staring after him as Jim shouted, 'Go to John Gore's. Tell him to fetch as many men as he can. And a pump. We'll have to pump water out of 'ditch. There'll not be enough in 'tanks.'

As he rode, he knew that he must get there as fast as possible to save Matthew and Rosa. They were there with Byrne and he could only think that they were in very grave danger, and because of what had happened in the past, it was his fault. His and his father's.

It wasn't you. It was me. He could hear his father's words echoing in his mind as the mare cantered steadily at one speed, and no amount of urging and kicking made her move any faster. What did he mean? That incident on the night of nearly twenty years ago had been so confused and blurred that he had never really comprehended what had happened, and in order to preserve his sanity he had deliberately blocked it out of his mind.

He remembered Carlos full of smiles. He had told Jim and his father a few weeks before that he was to be a father. 'I am so happy,' he had said, when he announced the news. 'My beautiful wife, she gives me this gift. I must be worthy of them both. My wife and child. I will give up the smuggling. It was an exciting life but now I will become respectable!'

His father had been angry with Carlos, arguing that they would lose good business, but Carlos was adamant that he would give up the smuggling, he would become an honest seaman. James Drew had turned away and Jim saw that stubborn look on his face which appeared whenever he was crossed. He had been absent for several hours, missing his supper.

The sun was slowly sinking on that fateful evening when Jim came across his father and Carlos in the middle of another heated argument, on the track leading off the island. Carlos was holding the reins of a black stallion which belonged to Mr Jennings. James Drew was bound for the marshes for he had his loaded fowling gun with him, a canvas bag over his shoulder and a dog by his side. According to Carlos, a messenger had brought the news that the ship with the Byrne brothers on board had arrived in Hull with a consignment of goods, which were waiting to be taken off. Carlos was now on his way to tell the Byrnes that he was going to declare the goods to the Customs officers.

'You may find it's too late,' Drew had insinuated. 'Customs may well be on your trail.'

'Pah!' Carlos had said. 'How can they be? There is no-one who would tell.' But then he had become suspicious of James Drew's devious manner and asked him point-blank if he had told the law. Drew bluffed, but Carlos now knew that he had double-crossed them out of sheer perversity and spite.

Jim remembered now, as he rode towards Marsh Farm, that he had stood back, terrified at the anger in his father's voice and manner. It was as if he had a madness in him, a violent passion that was about to burst, and as Carlos shouted that he had betrayed them and lunged towards him, Drew lifted his gun and pointed it at him.

Jim gave a great sob of anguish, as he had on that night. 'No, Da! No!' There was a rumbling of thunder and a fork of lightning lit the sky and, like a bright light suddenly illuminating his vision, he remembered. He had rushed at his father, his hand reaching up for the fowling gun. But his father had swung away out of his reach, then swiftly turned again towards Carlos, who stood as if carved in stone. Jim saw the whole scene as if he was in a trance and moving at half speed: Carlos's horrified expression and the movement of his hand as he crossed himself, his father's determined attitude and his finger on the trigger.

'No, Da. No!' He shouted again out loud as he

neared the blazing building. All of this, the tragedies of Carlos and his drowned wife and orphaned child, the Byrne brothers making an unwelcome return for vengeance, the smuggling which his father had once again agreed to, came rushing into his head. And the reaching for the fowling piece once more, and the crack of the shot as it hit Carlos in the forehead, echoed in his mind as the timbers of the barn roof crashed to the ground.

'Look what you've done,' his father had blamed. 'Look what you've done! I was onny going to frighten him. You've killed him. That's what you've done, you've killed him!'

Jim had stared down at Carlos, at the gaping blackened hole in his head, his dead eyes wide open, and had known only terror and confusion. 'What shall we do, Da?' he'd whispered, his throat rasping with fear.

'Do? Why, we'll have to get rid of him, that's what! Come on, I'll help you. Let's get him away from here and buried before he's missed, and we'll have to hide hoss for a day or two. Otherwise it's 'rope, my lad.' He'd shaken his head reproachfully, but Jim was conscious that although he was frozen with fear and could hardly move his limbs, his father's eyes flickered and darted as if in exhilaration. 'Yes,' he'd said. 'It's a hanging offence, even if you pleaded that it was an accident.'

'It wasn't me. It wasn't me,' he muttered under his breath as he slid off the mare's back and surveyed the scene in front of him. But now it didn't matter. It didn't matter that he had lived with the threat of the rope hanging over him from boyhood. It didn't matter that his own father had transferred the guilt to him, when it was really his own. What mattered was finding Matthew and Rosa, and finding them alive and not perished in the flames.

'Matthew!' He raised his voice to a shout. 'Rosa!' The timbers and trusses on the barn roof had gone, showers of sparks were rising and falling into the midst of the fire and sheets of flame were leaping up into the night sky and creeping insidiously over towards the granary. He went as close as he dared for the heat was intense, and called again, but all he could hear was the crackle and snapping of burning timber and falling masonry.

The water-storage tank was situated in the yard near to the pig pen and straw shelter, and although he rushed towards it to fill a bucket, he knew that it was hopeless. A few buckets of water would be of no use at all. If Gore arrived with a pump in time they might be able to save the granary, otherwise what they needed was a miracle.

Another flash of lightning which lit the sky and a rumble of thunder overhead gave him hope. 'Please God, let it rain! Let it pour in torrents!' He held up his arms in furious supplication. 'I've suffered all these years, God, and for what? You've never listened to me before when I've asked for mercy and forgiveness. Listen to me now! Please!'

As if in answer, another flash and a simultaneous crack of thunder made him jump and he fell to his knees and clasped his hands together. 'I'm ready to take my punishment, God,' he wept. 'I've kept silent all these years when I should have confessed. But they're onny young – and innocent. Let them live and me die in their place.' He lifted his head as the rain started to patter down on him and raised his voice in a desperate roar. 'Matthew! Rosa!'

CHAPTER THIRTY-FOUR

'We're trapped,' Rosa croaked, her voice husky with fear and smoke. 'We can't get out.'

Matthew lifted her shawl from her shoulders and covered her head. 'We will,' he said firmly. 'But we mustn't panic and we must move fast.'

He stripped off his heavy cord jacket and moved towards the roof truss which had fallen over the exit to the doorway and was now burning ferociously. He thrashed at the flames with his jacket, pounding and beating on the long beam until he felt that the flames had subsided a little, but the door frame had now caught hold and it wouldn't be long before the door, which was half open and letting in air which was fanning the fire, would be alight too.

'We're going to have to make a dash for it,' he shouted. 'When I say jump, jump.' He put his jacket over his head. 'Get ready.'

Rosa drew a deep breath and took hold of his hand. 'Now,' he shouted. 'Jump!'

She lifted her skirts above her knees with her other hand and with a great leap and a lift from Matthew's firm grasp about her waist, they were over and running through the door with the flames dancing around them. He pulled her down onto the ground and rolled her over and over with his arms around her.

'Are you all right?' he panted. 'Rosa! Speak to me.'

'I'm all right. Yes. Are you?'

He ran his fingers through his hair. His jacket had slipped off his head but had stayed on his shoulders. 'Yes, my hair's a bit singed.' He gave her a grin and said, 'I was in need of a haircut anyway,' which made her want to cry.

'Come on.' He pulled her to her feet. 'Let's get some water onto 'granary walls. Mebbe if we dampen it down then flames won't spread.'

She looked back at the flaming barn. 'What about John Byrne?'

He shook his head. 'I reckon he's gone.' He put his hand on her shoulder. 'They say if 'smoke gets you first, then you don't feel 'pain. Let's hope that's what happened. I wouldn't like to think he suffered.'

They took bucket after bucket of water to the granary walls. Rosa filled them from the tap on the tank and Matthew rushed across the yard to throw them at the brickwork, then Rosa too took buckets over, but the iron pails were heavy and when they were full she could hardly lift them. Finally she persuaded him to stop. She could see that his legs were giving way beneath him and her arms, too, were aching with moving the heavy buckets as she filled them.

'Stop,' she implored. 'We can do no more,' and she pulled him down to sit by the tank, where he crumpled up in sheer exhaustion. She put his head against her shoulder. 'Rest, Matthew. Help will come. Everyone on Sunk Island will have seen 'flames. Jim, Mr Gore, they'll all be here.'

She gave a deep sob as she looked towards the raging fire. If only they can save the house. She felt a great despair well up inside her. Gran will be so upset if it's destroyed. She thought of her grandmother at Maggie's house in Hedon unaware of what was unfolding at her old home. She thought of her mother, who had lived her life in the house and given birth to her in sadness. A tear crept down her face, streaking a dark path through the soot and grime, as she remembered her home as it was when she had lived there as a child, warm and comforting, and not as it was when Jim had lived in it, without love or care.

Jim! He killed my father. He'll think that I won't ever forgive him. And I won't! Not if it was done in malice and with intent. But why did he? He said it was an accident. How? He was only a boy! She shivered. She could hear thunderous sounds and lights flashed in front of her. Her mind was befuddled and terrified by the deeds of Byrne, the confession of Jim, the fight between Byrne and Matthew. Together with the sheer fright of being caught in the fire it was all suddenly too much. Her heart started to flutter and palpitate, she grew hot and cold, and she keeled over on top of Matthew, her limbs limp and her mind blank, into the realms of unconsciousness.

She felt the rain pattering on her face and the sound of weeping. 'Rosa. Matthew! Can you hear me?'

Someone was patting her cheeks and she stirred and tried to sit up. Matthew too sat up and rubbed a dirty hand over his face. It was raining hard and Jim was kneeling over them.

'Thank God,' he was crying. 'Thank God. I thought you were dead.'

'Oh!' Matthew groaned. 'What happened? 'Fire? Is it out? No, it's not,' he answered himself as he turned towards the burning building. 'We must try and save the house.'

Rosa looked at him. His face was blackened with smoke and soot and the top of his hair was singed, he was exhausted yet he still wanted to try to put the fire out. She got onto her hands and knees, not trusting her legs enough to be able to stand.

'Are you hurt, Rosa?' Jim asked diffidently.

She shook her head. 'No.' Her voice seemed to have gone and she spoke only in a croaky whisper. 'I'm all right, but I seem to have lost 'use of my legs.'

Matthew helped her to her feet, but Jim stood back. It was as if he was afraid to touch her in case he was rebuffed.

'Better get you back home,' he said gruffly. 'Matthew, you too, you've done enough here. John Gore and his lads have just arrived, and some of 'other farmers. We'll manage now. Rain'll put 'fire out.'

Streams of thick black smoke were gushing from the barn and issuing into the sodden night sky, and even the rain seemed to be black with soot.

'Where's Da?' Matthew asked suddenly. 'Is he here?'

'No,' Jim answered. 'I don't know where he is. I asked him to go and fetch help, but Gore said he hasn't seen him. He'd already seen 'flames and set off here.' He told them too of sending Delia to Hedon to tell that John Byrne was on Sunk Island, and they listened in amazement that she had had the courage to ride alone and in the dark to fetch help.

Rosa looked at the crowd of men who were gathered around the blackened barn, waiting now for the heat to subside before they went in. Perhaps Mr Drew was amongst them, hoping to salvage what was left. A thought struck her that he wouldn't want anyone to see what had been stored there, not that there would be much left. The casks were well alight when she and Matthew had escaped and the tobacco would have shrivelled to nothing. His secret would be safe.

'John Byrne,' she said hoarsely. 'Will they find him?'

'Aye,' Jim said bluntly. 'I expect so. What's left of him.'

He urged them again to go home. 'You can do nowt else here tonight. We'll start clearing up in 'morning when 'heat's died down.'

Slowly they walked back towards Home Farm. They were lashed by pelting stinging needles of

403

rain which reddened their faces and soaked them through, and they almost fell through the door into the kitchen.

'I'll build up 'fire,' Matthew said. 'Soon have a blaze going. Then we'll put 'kettle on for a hot drink.' He fetched a blanket from the cupboard and unfastened her wet shawl, then, unbuttoning the back of her dress, he slipped her arms out of the sleeves and wrapped the blanket around her. She let her dress fall to the floor and as she stepped out of it, he gently propelled her into a chair and knelt to take off her wet boots. 'Then it's off to bed with you and a hot brick between the sheets.'

She shook her head and in a whisper, for her voice had no strength, said, 'No. I wouldn't be able to sleep. I keep thinking about Byrne. Do you think he got out?'

'It would be a miracle if he did! But we'll know in 'morning. I reckon they'll find him then.'

Rosa's head ached and her throat was sore and she made no answer. What was to be done now? She could no longer live here at Home Farm, not with Mr Drew and Jim. Not now that she knew the truth, or at least some of it. But she was still puzzled as to why Jim had killed her father; and what part did Mr Drew play? There was still a mystery that hadn't been resolved. And where was James Drew now?

They sat silently by the fire, feeling the heat warming their cold bones and dozing intermittently. Jim came in as a grey dawn stole through the window.

'It's still raining and more to come,' he said, his voice husky with smoke. 'But 'fire's out and 'granary's saved and 'house is secure, so thank God for that.' He didn't look at Rosa as he spoke but kept his eyes firmly down on the floor. Then he glanced at Matthew. 'Da?' he asked. 'Is he here?'

Matthew shook his head. 'Not unless he's hiding under his bed,' he said bitterly.

Jim ran upstairs to his father's room, then came slowly down a minute later. 'His fire's out and oil lamp's burned dry. So where is he? Where's he got to?'

The farmers and labourers who had come to help put out the fire trudged back home to snatch an hour's sleep before rising again to start their daily routine. As they moved away from Marsh Farm, two bedraggled figures dropped down from the rafters of the pig pen where they had lain flat and silent so that they didn't disturb the occupants below.

They didn't speak for they had a common purpose which had been agreed upon some time before. The older man of the two looked out from the door and signalled to the other, whose face and hands were red and burnt and who crouched as if in pain, that it was safe to go.

He kicked away some straw in the corner of the pen, and picked up two iron-tipped wooden sludge spades from beneath it. Together, keeping their bodies low, they hurried towards the dark and turbulent river, and found the spot on the embankment which they had marked.

'I'll do the digging,' Seamus said. 'You keep a watch.'

His brother shook his head, his voice grating as he spoke. 'I'll do my share,' he rasped with short gasping breaths. 'It'll give me the greatest of pleasure.'

They started to dig, making a deep and narrow trench in the embankment and leading it towards a dyke which was already full with rainwater. Above them thunder still threatened, giving low ominous warning growls. The sky was lightening as they finished the trench, but this was not a bright sign of a new day. The colours were dark grey with a flash of silver to show the dawn.

'We'll have to hurry,' Seamus said softly. 'Folks will be moving about before long.'

'But not out here,' John Byrne replied huskily and it seemed a great effort for him to speak. 'They'll have no business in this remote spot. They'll be home mending their waggons or fixing the leaks in their roofs.'

They moved along each side of the dyke and started to dig again, though this time at random, loosening the sides of the dyke and letting the earth fall in so that the water came gurgling to the top.

They both crouched down as they again approached Marsh Farm land and saw Jim Drew leave the farmyard and fasten the gate behind him, taking one last look at the burnt-out barn. 'They'll be mourning you, John,' Seamus said wryly. 'But Mr Drew will be sorely puzzled if he can't find your body in the morning.'

John Byrne nodded. His eyes were glazed with pain and he could hardly hold the spade in his burnt hands, but he was determined to finish off what he had started. 'It will give him something more to worry about,' he whispered. 'He'll never again have peace of mind. He'll always wonder if he'll be found out.'

They moved along towards a drainage channel which carried the water back to the Humber. This they blocked, taking the earth from the land around it and piling it into the channel to prevent the water's exit.

'That'll do it all right,' Seamus said with satisfaction. 'If the tide is high enough the land will flood. Let's get on our way.'

'No,' John Byrne objected. 'I want to see it. I want to see Drew's face when he realizes his land is flooded and he sees why. He'll know then that we're still here, that *I'm* still here to torment him.'

'Come now,' Seamus said quietly. 'We've done enough. There's a cutter in the creek. Let's get away whilst we can. There's a noose waiting for you if we're caught.'

'A noose for something I didn't do,' his brother croaked. 'That foolish boy fell on his own knife. I didn't kill him.'

'And who will believe you? Not the law! Come away now or we'll be too late.'

But John Byrne would not be persuaded. He would wait, he said, even though he was sorely in pain. He would wait for the high tide to rise as it surely would, for there was broken water and white crests on the river, and storm clouds were brewing and a strong wind blowing. He would watch the river break through the embankment and fill the dykes and channels and flood James Drew's land.

CHAPTER THIRTY-FIVE

James Drew had watched Jim ride off from the farm gate towards the red glow in the sky. They'll all know, he deliberated uneasily. Everybody will know about the run goods. Matthew and the girl know already. I didn't want him to find out. He's like his mother, straight and honest. I'll never be able to look him in the eye again. I'm not bothered about her, Rosa. I've kept her under my roof all these years. I've salved my conscience, paid back for what happened to her father.

He leaned on the gate, making no effort to chase after his son and help to put out the fire or to fetch other men as Jim had requested he should. 'Best let it burn,' he muttered to himself. 'If it all goes up in smoke, then onny family will know about 'smuggled goods. That's it. Let it burn.'

He pondered for a few moments that Matthew and Rosa might be in the burning building with Byrne, but then dismissed the thought, despite what Jim had said. They'll have got out all right, he persuaded himself, and contemplated that it would be too late for him to do anything if they hadn't. He was in any case more concerned with his own present situation, and much as he hated the thought of losing Marsh Farm, obtusely he felt a sense of gratification that the Byrne brothers would be deprived of their livelihood if the goods were destroyed. I'll tell Matthew in private that they were threatening Jim, he meditated, and that's why I agreed to go in with them, then he pursed his lips and regretted his admission that he, and not Jim, had been responsible for Carlos's death.

The sky over Marsh Farm was a blazing red and spumes of thick black smoke rolled and curled for miles in every direction, and he knew that the fire had a good hold. He put out his hand and felt a few drops of rain. 'Hold off a bit,' he murmured. 'Hold off.'

He went back inside the house and sat deliberating by the fire for a while, then he went upstairs and lay fully clothed on his bed. The fire in the grate burned low but the coal scuttle was empty, and he felt a brief sense of annoyance that Rosa or Delia hadn't filled it. The room became gradually darker as the lamp flickered for want of oil and he turned his eyes to the window and the glow in the sky.

He dropped off into a spasmodic dream-filled sleep and then woke with a sudden start. The room was dim, the lamp and fire having gone out, and the sky outside was dark and heavy. He could hear the rain driving against the windows and he gave a sudden shudder. A ghost walking over his grave. He sat up. He didn't like the darkness, never had, it seemed so like death, closing in on him.

I'd better get up. The others will be back once 'fire is out. I'll go outside, reckon to them that I was there all the time. That's it. He rose from the bed. I'll go across to Marsh Farm, see it for myself; or what's left of it. He stumbled downstairs and out into the yard and the drenching rain, and heard the murmur of Matthew's and Rosa's voices as they came down the track. He rushed across the yard and into the stable and hid, watching them through a crack in the door as they entered the house. Then stealthily he came out, bent his head low against the deluge and turned towards Marsh Farm.

Rosa was making a hot drink and Matthew and Jim were putting on their damp coats again when there came a hammering on the door. 'More trouble!' Jim muttered. 'I'll go.'

It was Fred, ridden over from Hedon to find out what was happening. 'I got your message from Delia and notified 'authorities. She did well, did lass, riding all that way on her own and in 'dark. But no sooner had I informed 'constable than we saw 'smoke in 'sky and guessed summat was up, so I came over. It's tekken me some time! Roads are awash. You'd never get a cart or waggon through. 'Hoss has had to pick its way here.'

He took a gulp of the tea that Rosa had handed to him. 'There's a right storm brewing up. Thunder's crashing over Hedon and 'town's lit up with lightning. And 'tide's high. I heard tell afore I left that Spurn peninsula'll likely be breached. Aye, I reckon there'll be some flooding along Humber bank afore 'day's out.'

They told him what had happened. That the barn was burnt out and that Byrne had perished in the fire. Rosa gave him a plate of cold ham and bread and he said that he would get straight back and call off the law.

'Where's your da?' he asked. 'Gone back to bed?'

'We don't know,' Jim said. 'We were just going out to look for him. We haven't seen him since last night.'

Fred pursed his lips and pondered. 'I'd better stop then and help you search. You don't want 'same bother as you had over Henry.'

Rosa drew in a breath and she saw Matthew and Jim glance at each other. None of them had thought that anything had happened to James Drew. They just assumed that he had taken it into his head to disappear for a few hours as he frequently did, and would turn up again and not say where he had been.

Rosa went upstairs after the men had gone out and looked out of her bedroom window towards the river. She could see the turbulent white crests dashing against each other and just one ship tossing and pitching, its white sails bellying as it dipped and plunged, fighting its way towards the nearest safe haven of Stone Creek. There were no ships going out towards Spurn and she guessed that there was a heavy sea running beyond the Point and that ships were sheltering within the port of Hull.

It was almost as black as night, the thunder cracking in the distance but constantly getting nearer, judging by the decreasing gaps between the shafts of lightning and the thunderclaps.

Though she felt shaky and exhausted and looked longingly at her bed, she went downstairs again and seared shin of beef in the iron pot over the fire, then chopped up some root vegetables. The men would need something hot to warm them when they came back in, for they would be soaked to the skin with the constant deluge of rain.

Harry put his head round the door. 'Any chance of a sup o' summat, Miss Rosa? I'm gasping.'

She poured him a small tankard of ale and asked him if he had seen Mr Drew.

'Nay, I reckon he'll be sheltering somewhere if he's any sense. He'll not be out in this downpour.' Harry was quite dry and she asked him where he had been. He gave a crooked gap-toothed grin and said he'd been grooming the horses and polishing the brasses in the stable. 'No sense in being outside in this weather,' he said. 'Maister'll turn up when he's ready.'

The back door crashed open and Matthew burst in. 'Harry! I've been looking for you. Come on! Embankment's broken near to Marsh Farm. River's flooding in. We've got to get livestock onto dry land!'

'Embankment's broken!' Harry put down his tankard. 'Never!'

Matthew nodded. His face was flushed with exertion. 'Can't get near enough to see, but it looks as if a whole section has gone and 'dyke is filling up.' He put his hand to his forehead and wiped the sweat away. 'And 'tide hasn't reached its maximum yet. We're going to be in real trouble!'

Rosa took off her apron and sat down to change into her outdoor boots again. 'I'd better come too,' she said. 'I can help to drive 'sheep.'

'Please, Rosa, if you will.' Matthew was grateful. 'We need all 'help we can get. If we can't contain it, then whole of farmland will be flooded.'

She looked round for something suitable to wear to keep out the rain. Her cloak would be useless, too heavy and cumbersome. Then she remembered something, and bending to a deep drawer in the kitchen brought out a rolled-up voluminous grey raincape that had belonged to Mrs Drew, which she used to wear when feeding the hens during wet weather.

She put it on. It came below her ankles, and had a hood which she fastened over her head.

'Good heavens, that was Ma's!' Matthew gave her a quick smile as she went outside. He was already mounted on a mare. 'That should keep you dry. Come on,' he held out his hand, 'up behind me, we've no time to lose.'

James Drew walked briskly towards Marsh Farm, taking the track and not cutting across the fields of stubble where he would have been easily seen. He bent below a low hedge as he saw Jim leave the farmyard and close the gate behind him.

Once Jim was well away from the area, Drew

went across the yard and stepped in through the doorway to the smouldering ruins of the barn. There was little left: the still smoking, blackened shafts of the waggon and box cart, a pile of iron bands which had encircled the brandy casks and the metal blades of scythes and sickles, their wooden handles burnt away, but nothing else.

'So what's happened to Byrne?' he muttered. 'Jim said that he was here with Matthew and Rosa.' His eyes narrowed. Had they caught him? Or had he escaped the law? Was he now on his way off the island? 'Good riddance anyway.' He heaved a sigh of relief that he might now be cleared of any misconduct. There was no evidence here to show that he had ever been involved with the Byrne brothers.

'Best get back, then,' he muttered and bent down and crumbled some of the still hot black-ened wood between his fingers and rubbed it around his face, across his forehead and his cheeks, then he did the same on his breeches, leaving sooty marks.

A brilliant fork of lightning made him blink and thunder crashed above him as he stepped back into the yard, and another downpour began. He made a dash for the granary and decided to wait a little longer before returning home.

He'd waited about half an hour and was wondering whether or not to leave, as the rain showed no sign of abating. His clothes were soaking wet and he was beginning to feel a chill. Then he became suddenly alert. He thought he heard a sound coming from outside, not in the yard, much too faint for that, but a definite noise, like a clunk of metal.

He tentatively put his head outside the granary door. There was no-one there, but, yes, there it was again. He looked towards the direction of the sound and in the gloom of the grey dawn saw two figures with their backs to him walking alongside the dyke. One was carrying something beneath his arm, something which clunked, something like wood and metal banging together. 'Spades,' he breathed. 'Why would anybody want to be carrying spades in this weather?' Guns perhaps? he thought, if they were poachers or duck hunters, but there surely wouldn't be any wildfowlers out in this rain, they wouldn't be able to see their target, nor would the wildfowl be flying.

He crept after them, curious to know who they were and what they were doing. 'On my land,' he muttered as the rain ran down his face. 'They've no right to be here.'

Then the two men stopped and had a short conversation. One shook his head, and the other, who he saw now was indeed carrying spades, briefly touched his companion on the shoulder, then turned away and strode off in the direction of the river. The remaining man turned his head. Drew recognized him and took in a short sharp breath. It was Byrne. John Byrne.

As if there was some kind of sixth-sense communication between them, Byrne turned around and a lightning flash lit up the sky. 'Drew!' he shouted and his voice was lost in a crash of thunder. 'We meet again.'

Drew stared. Byrne seemed demoniacal, his face was black and his red hair spiky and dishevelled. Drew's heart started to thud. He looked like a fiendish evil spirit depicting the horrors of hell. 'Byrne?' he faltered. 'Is it you?'

'It's me, all right,' and by his accent Drew knew that it was indeed him. 'You didn't think you'd seen the last of me, did you?' He gave a screeching sound somewhere between a raucous laugh and a cry of pain.

He stepped forward towards Drew, who took a step back. 'No, Mr Drew. You'll never be rid of me. We'll be in hell together, you and I.'

'No! No!' Drew's voice grew wild. 'Not me. I go to church. I've committed some sins, I grant you that, but I'll be forgiven when I die. I'll be given salvation!'

'What?' Byrne laughed again and came nearer and Drew moved backwards. 'After your sins? Fornication! Deceit! And who really killed Carlos? Not Jim.' He shook his head. 'He wouldn't have had the guts to do it.'

Drew looked over Byrne's shoulder. On the embankment a figure was waving his arms as if to catch their attention. He was also shouting something, but with the roar of the howling wind, the cracking of the thunder and the rain pelting down, he couldn't hear what he was saying. Then he saw him start to run. He raced down the embankment into the fields and along the track towards Stone Creek.

Drew pointed. 'Your brother,' he said hoarsely. 'He's calling you.'

Byrne smiled. 'Oh, yes! And do you know what he's saying? I know what he's saying.' He continued to stare at Drew and added before he could answer, 'He's telling me to hurry up before the land is flooded. Before the river breaks through and we're all drowned.'

Drew gasped. 'The spades! You've broken through 'embankment!'

'That's right. And the dyke, and the ditches and the drainage channels. The sluice gates are open and the dams are broken. It's amazing just how much digging two strong Irish labourers can do when they set their minds to it.'

Drew looked round. The dyke was full, as were the ditches along the sides of the fields, which he'd noticed as he'd walked here earlier. He lifted his eyes again towards the river and saw the fast tidal flow of water gushing through the embankment, down into the lower land and towards them.

'You devil,' he shouted. 'I'll lose my sheep and cattle. 'Land'll be waterlogged. I'll not be able to plough!'

'That's right.' Byrne nodded. 'That's what I'd planned. Well, I'll be off! I'm so glad we met again, Mr Drew. I said to Seamus that what I wanted more than anything in this world was to see your land flooded. Perhaps the river will take it back! That's where it came from, wasn't it? From the bottom of the Humber.' His eyes glittered. 'Perhaps that's where it really belongs, and you with it.'

He turned away and bent his head against the onslaught of wind and rain. There was a sudden flash and the sky was lit by sheet lightning, illuminating the whole of the land. Drew saw the widening flow of water as, spilling over the already overflowing dyke, it rushed in their direction. 'Look out!' he shouted and turned to run, but Byrne kept on walking, his head bent to the ground.

Drew turned again as he lumbered away and saw the rush of water knock Byrne into the flooded dyke. He made no attempt to save himself but simply threw up his arms as the waters of the dyke covered him.

'He's gone then,' Drew panted, as heavy-footed, he rushed away. 'He'll not get out of that dyke. It's too deep and too wide for anybody to save himself. I couldn't have helped him. No chance of me getting him out, no matter how I tried.' Already he was making up answers that he could give if he should be questioned.

He looked back again. The rush of water was heading fast towards him. The tide was exceptionally high and the embankment, once weakened, would break through in other places, flooding not only Marsh Farm land but Home Farm land too, which was divided from it only by ditches and sparse hedges.

He tried to run faster towards Home Farm house and safety, but his heart was beating rapidly and his breathing was laboured. Another burst of forked lightning and he blinked. Did he see someone in the distance? Was someone coming to rescue him? He shouted, but his voice came out weak and pitiful. Another flare, simultaneous with a clap of thunder, lit up the sky and yes, there was someone on horseback. Two people.

He stopped and held his chest. He had such an excruciating pain. He turned around and saw the sweep of water behind him and knew he must get out of its path. He looked up. The man was dismounting. Drew put his hand to his head. The rain was running down his face, he could hardly see. Was he hallucinating? The young man looked so familiar, and the woman he was helping down in the long raincape and hood – why! It was Ellen!

'Ellen!' he called. 'Ellen!' No, how could it be? But yes! Of course. The man he was looking at was himself. He remembered such a time when he had ridden with Ellen behind him. He had laughed at her old raincape and promised her another when he had grown rich. She had been so lovely then, he had told her she deserved something better. 'I'll get you another coat, Ellen,' he shouted. 'I promise, I will this time.' She ran towards him and put out her arms as if pleading with him. 'I've been wicked, Ellen. So very wicked. Forgive me!'

The water rushed behind him, knocking him off his feet and sweeping him along towards the dyke. His head went under as the waters claimed him for their own, and as he came up for the final time he called with his last gasping breath for absolution of his sins, not to God in heaven but to his long-suffering, compassionate wife. 'Ellen! Forgive me for I know not what I do.'

As the waters washed over him in a final baptism, and his lungs filled, he saw the women of the night smiling and beckoning to him. He saw his son Henry, drunk on smuggled brandy and dead from drowning, and remembered, with his last spasm of breath, that someone else shared his watery grave. Carlos! And he reached out to push the Spaniard away as his skeletal bones bumped against him.

A lone figure stood for a moment on the high embankment with the tidal waters raging below him, and saw his brother swept away into the dyke that they had damaged. He knew that his brother could have saved himself, but had chosen not to. His face was blackened and ravaged by the fire and his hands were so badly burned that he knew that he would never have been able to face anyone or work again. Only a life of pain and disfigurement lay in front of him. Seamus crossed himself and turning towards Stone Creek he put his head down and walked away.

CHAPTER THIRTY-SIX

Matthew helped Rosa down from the mare and saw that Fred was struggling to move a flock of sheep from a field of stubble but couldn't control them. In the distance there were groups of men running towards them, farmers who had been alerted by Jim and who were attempting to move all the livestock to safety.

Another flash of lightning and a crack of thunder, but not so loud and the sky seemed to be lighter, showing that the storm would soon be over. 'Get those strays, Rosa,' he urged, 'they're sheltering under yonder hedge. I'll give Fred a hand.'

Rosa set off to where the sheep were huddled together, her raincape billowing as the wind caught it. It was then that she saw Mr Drew. He was running as if the devil was after him, but it wasn't the devil, it was a swell of river water rushing across the land. 'Mr Drew!' she screamed. 'Watch out! Come this way! Away from the dyke.'

Instinctively she ran towards him, her arms stretched out. 'Mr Drew! This way!'

He seemed to hear her for he stopped and looked up, and it was as if he was smiling at her and calling something. 'Hurry,' she shouted. 'Hurry!'

But it was too late, and she screamed for Matthew to come as the rushing waters swept James Drew off his feet and carried him towards the swollen dyke. 'No,' she cried, and thought of Henry and how the waters of the dyke had claimed him. 'Not another Drew!'

She splashed towards him, the water almost up to her knees, but now there was no division between field and dyke or ditch as the river poured in, covering the fields and tracks and footpaths and making a lake over James Drew's land. The ground disappeared beneath her feet and she fell forward into deep water. 'Matthew!' she screamed. 'Matthew! Help me!'

Matthew heard her cries as he was halfway across the field and turned swiftly. He stood for barely a second as he watched her run towards a man, indistinguishable in the gloom and rain, and saw him swallowed up by a rushing torrent of water and disappear. As he sped towards them he saw her stumble and fall.

'She's in the dyke! Oh God! She's fallen into 'dyke. Jim! Fred! Hurry.' He was frantic with fear as he ran, his boots kicking up sprays of water from the flooded fields. 'Rosa! I'm coming. I'm coming.'

She was still struggling as he reached her, but then her head went under the water and he could only see the top of her rain hood. He tore off his coat and jumped into the dyke, reaching for her, pulling her up by the hood. He gathered her into his arms and trod water, hampered by his heavy boots, calling to her and crying, 'Rosa! Rosa. Don't leave me. Don't leave me!'

Jim plunged to the ground. 'Give her here,' he called, and the water lapped around him as he lay flat on his stomach reaching out his arms. 'Come on! She'll be all right Come on! Just tread water. That's it, this way.'

Matthew felt that he was dreaming as he did as he was bid, and it was as if he was reliving a former scene, when they had pulled Henry from the ditch. Only this time it was Rosa, his only love, who was being dragged from the deathly waters.

'She's all right. She's all right!' Jim had tears streaming down his face as he spoke, and Matthew knew that he too was thinking of Henry as they bent over Rosa, who was retching up river water.

The other men had rushed across when they heard the commotion and on seeing that Rosa was safe, turned to reach and recover the other person in the dyke. 'It's Mr Drew!' someone said. 'We can do nowt for him,' said another. 'He's a goner.' The men took off their caps and gazed down at James Drew. 'Was he trying to save her?' the question was asked.

'No.' Jim got up from Rosa's side and left Matthew holding her close. He looked down at his father. 'I saw what happened. She was trying to save him.'

*   *   *

The Drew family gathered once more when news of their father's death reached them. The twins, Lydia and Nellie, came, Flo came with her Tom, and Maggie and Fred came with the baby, bringing Delia and Mrs Jennings with them.

Rosa hugged her grandmother. 'I've missed you, Gran,' she whispered. 'I'm so sorry about the fire.'

'It's nowt,' her grandmother said. 'It'll soon mend. It's onny brick and timber. As long as you're all right. That's what matters.' She had heard the details from Fred on his return home to Hedon.

'Maggie and me have got summat to tell you,' Fred began.

'Not another babby already?' Flo said slyly.

Maggie blushed. 'No, silly! Not yet anyway. But we shall have another bairn.' She gazed down into the crib where the baby was sleeping. 'We're so happy with little Ellen that we want to give her a sister or brother.'

'Go on then,' Fred urged. 'Tell 'em 'news.'

'Give Rosa her papers first,' Maggie insisted. 'We're dying of curiosity.'

Fred handed Rosa a large thick packet. 'It's from 'lawyer,' he explained. 'He said would I apologize for 'delay but he had a lot of searches to do.'

Rosa took the packet and, glancing at Matthew and then at her grandmother, she broke the seal and opened it as Maggie started to speak.

'You'll never guess,' she began.

'No, we won't,' said Flo, 'so hurry up and tell us.'

'Fred and me,' Maggie had a big smile on her face, 'we're coming back to Sunk Island! Fred's got tenancy of that smallholding near to North Channel.'

'It's got sheds and barns where I can work and store all my tools. There's plenty of work on Sunk Island and we'll be near enough to Patrington for me to work there as well.' Fred too seemed pleased with himself. 'Maggie wanted to come back,' he said, and looked affectionately at her. 'Since we had 'babby, you know. She's wanted to come home.'

Jim and Matthew were pleased, and Delia already knew about it. 'We'll be like a proper Sunk Island family again,' Flo said with a catch in her voice. 'Even though Ma and Da won't be here. Don't you think so, Rosa? Somewhere we can allus come back to.'

Rosa looked up from the papers. Her head was in a whirl. The lawyer had apologized for the delay in his letter which was enclosed with the original documents. He explained that he had had the papers translated and that it was a last Will and Testament of her father Decimus Miguel Carlos, which left all his worldly goods, including his ship, the *Rosa Maria*, to his wife, Mary Carlos, formerly Jennings, or on her demise to any children which they might have. There was also a letter within the documents which gave details of his family in Spain, with the request that they should be told of his death if they did not already know.

'I have been informed by the Customs and Excise department,' the letter went on, 'that the ship was requisitioned and then sold, some years ago, and the balance of money raised from the sale is deposited in a bank account. Proof of identity is required in order to release this money, which I do not expect will be difficult in this instance.'

'Yes,' Rosa said vaguely and cleared her throat. 'I'm so pleased for you, Maggie, and for you too, Fred.'

They will be a whole family again, she thought, just as Flo says. Maggie and Fred will be the head of the family, even though it will be a different name. She looked at Mattthew, who was gazing at her. He hadn't wanted to let her out of his sight since the flood. Jim seemed to have had a weight lifted off his shoulders and was more sure of himself, making decisions and carrying them through, though he was quiet in her presence as if his conscience was still troubling him. Only Delia seemed to be pensive since her return home from Hedon and Rosa saw her now looking down at the baby Ellen, with a sort of longing on her face.

There was to be a triple funeral today, for there had been three inquests and three bodies were to be conveyed to the churchyard. Firstly Mr Drew, who had taken many secrets with him, those which were known to some members of his family never being spoken of. Secondly John Byrne, escapee from the law, with his face so blackened that he was hardly recognizable, who had drowned with no family to mourn him. His brother Seamus had gone, no-one knew where, but Rosa had guessed, when Harry had come in just after the flood and remarked that he had seen something he had only ever seen twice before, even though he had lived all of his life by the river.

'What's that then, Harry?' Jim had asked.

'I saw a ship with its sails scandalized!'

'What's that mean then?' young Bob had asked.

Harry had drawn himself up in self-importance at imparting knowledge. 'It's when a seaman drowns,' he said. 'They let all 'sails hang loose and fly 'flag at half mast. It's a form of respect. I saw a cutter doing that down at Stone Creek on day after 'flood. I reckon somebody was lost overboard during 'storm.'

Rosa had said nothing but gazed into the fire. She had been sitting by its glow for hours, contemplating in silence the past events. It must have been Seamus, she thought, mourning his dead brother.

They had found another body too when the waters had receded. At least, they had found skeletal remains. Those of someone who had died long ago. Too long ago to be identified. The discovery had been made near Marsh Farm, close to where the ditch had collapsed, and at the inquest it had been decided that it was the missing Spaniard, Carlos, whose body had lain undetected at the bottom of the ditch until it was washed up by the river water. Today he was to be buried again, in a Christian manner, next to his wife where he belonged.

'So what's 'news, Rosa?' Flo asked curiously.

Rosa took a deep breath. It was a big decision,

but one she was determined to make. One she had to make, otherwise she would never really know who she was.

'The news is,' she said, and dared not look at Matthew for she knew for sure that she would see only shock and dismay. 'The news is – that I'm going to Spain to meet my father's family.'

CHAPTER THIRTY-SEVEN

She left before winter began. Before the ghostly vapour of November mist hung over the fields and before the roads out of Sunk Island became an impassable morass through rain or snow. She also wanted to leave before she changed her mind, before the look of misery on Matthew's face persuaded her that she shouldn't go.

Jim had come up to her on the evening of the funeral and with his head bent had muttered, 'I'm sorry, Rosa. It's because of me that you're leaving. Because of what I did.'

But he had already told Matthew of what had happened all those years before, a great out-pouring of his grief and regret that he hadn't been man enough to speak out, and Matthew had told Rosa, and she in turn had remembered what their mother had said about trying to forgive should she discover something which caused her pain. She had put her arms around Jim's waist and hugged him. 'That isn't 'reason I'm going and I know now that it wasn't your fault. It's finished now, Jim. We must put the past behind us.'

At the burial service, as she watched her father's remains being placed with her mother's, she had felt a great sense of peace that they were finally together, her mother no longer searching and her father found at last.

Towards James Drew she felt a numbness and wondered how someone who had appeared so God-fearing and righteous could have been so hypocritical and callous, with total disregard for others, paying only lip service to his religious beliefs. For John Byrne she felt only sadness that he had lived a tormented embittered life, and had offered up a silent prayer for his repose.

When the family realized that she wouldn't change her mind about going away, they had insisted that it was too dangerous and improper that she should travel alone, and she had replied that she didn't intend to, that she would advertise in a national newspaper for an experienced travelling companion.

This she did and had three replies. One, which she accepted, was from a man and wife, Mr and Mrs Bennett, who were travelling to Spain to visit their son who was a teacher in Zaragoza, and who was to be married to a lady of that country. They would be glad, they wrote, if she would care to accompany them, though they explained that it would be a difficult and hazardous journey, especially at that time of year. 'Our son is to be married in May,' they wrote, 'and we would therefore wish to be across France and at the foot of the Pyrenees, where we will wait for the winter snows to melt, before continuing our journey.'

Matthew drove her down the long straight

Ottringham road, towards Hull, where she was to catch the London coach the next morning. He had wanted to stay overnight at the inn to see her set off safely to London where she was to meet her companions, but she insisted that he return home. 'This will be the least hazardous part of my journey,' she said, 'and I must become accustomed to being self-reliant.'

He remained silent until they reached the boundary of Sunk Island, then he drew the mare to a halt and staring straight ahead, said, 'I haven't tried to persuade you not to go, but I can't let you leave without saying that I shall feel as if I have lost my arms and legs and soul when you have gone. I shan't be whole again until you return.' He turned towards her. 'You will return, Rosa? You will come back to me? To Sunk Island?'

She gently touched his face. 'I'll miss you, Matthew. But I have to go. My gran once said that I had built a protective shell around me and I think that she was probably right. Half of me belongs here on Sunk Island, but I don't know where the other half belongs. I must go away to find out. I must break open that shell to find out who I really am.'

'I love you, Rosa,' he said, and her heart went out to him.

'And I love you,' she whispered. 'As I always have. You must hold that knowledge in your heart.' He kissed her then and she saw tears glisten in his eyes, but hope dawning too, even though she had made no promises of when she would return.

It was a bright sharp morning and the sun shone over the fields, giving the clear brilliant light which was so special to Sunk Island. There were no rain clouds and here and there where flood water was still held in pools and dew ponds, the sun caught it and cast a reflected scintillating dazzle across the land.

'Look,' Matthew said, with a break in his voice as he remembered her fondness for the long-legged wading bird. 'There's your heron. He's left his nest to see you off.'

A grey heron stood with its head hunched into its shoulders near to a dip in the land which was filled with water. Then, as if disturbed, it lifted its long neck and pointed its yellow bill towards them and in awkward flapping flight lifted off and flew across the meadow towards the marsh-land and the river.

One spring had passed and now there was an-other and she was on her way home. She had written to give an approximate date of return, but the journey had gone well, much better than the expedition out, when she had seen more snow than she had seen in her life before, and she arrived in England earlier than expected. She bade goodbye to her companions, who were returning at the same time, and travelled by coach from Dover to London then Hull, where she hired a horse and trap and set off alone to Sunk Island.

The weather was warm and the fields and meadows of Holderness were dry, the greening corn swaying and rippling like a gentle tide, and she decided that rather than take the road from Ottringham she would travel on towards Patrington, and cross the bridge over onto Sunk Island.

Her heart beat faster as the horse clip-clopped over the bridge and she could see before her Marsh Farm, her old home. The barn was rebuilt and there was smoke curling from the farmhouse chimney. She smiled, Jim must have turned over a new leaf, or maybe Gran has been in and made it like home again. She urged the horse on and stopped at the farm gate.

There were pigs in the pen and piglets squeaking, and around the yard hens were scratching and there was a dog lying by the door. It barked when it saw her and ran to the gate to greet her. The door opened and Matthew came out. He stood in amazement for a moment and then rushed towards her, sweeping her out of the trap and into his arms.

'Rosa – oh Rosa! Why didn't you say – I would have come to meet you.' His words tumbled over each other in his joy to see her.

'I wanted to come on my own,' she said. 'I wanted to savour the moment when I stepped onto Sunk Island again. To feel its peace and tranquillity.'

He held her away from him, 'Is it really you?' She seemed to have a warm glow about her, the effect of the Spanish sun he supposed, and she was wearing a red travelling outfit and not the dark one she had worn on her outward journey. Then he smoothed his hands over her glossy black hair which was knotted behind her head and held with red braid and a sparkling comb. 'Or am I dreaming as I have done so many times before?'

'It's me,' she smiled. 'Just 'same as before.'

He rushed back to the house to close the door and told the dog to stay and jumped into the trap with her, taking the reins to drive to Home Farm.

'So where's Jim?' she asked. 'I saw 'smoke coming from the chimney.'

'He's out in 'fields somewhere. We've been lighting fires every day.' He shrugged and shuffled in the seat as he spoke. 'Keeping it aired as Gran Jennings says we should. You'd notice 'barn has been rebuilt?'

She nodded. He seemed different, or was it that she was looking at him through different eyes? Through grown-up eyes which had seen so many other sights on her travels, and not the familiar eyes of a girl who had grown up with him. He was more mature, more handsome, more vital than the boy she had known. His face and arms were sun-browned and his back and shoulders seemed broader, and she felt a curious excitement just looking at him.

'You must tell me all that has been happening,' she said, and as she looked around saw that the fields had dried from the flood, although some had been left fallow and where there were some wet patches, clumps of yellow kingcups and pennywort were growing. She gazed across towards the embankment and saw that it had been rebuilt.

'Oh, we go on much the same,' he said softly,

turning towards her. 'Nothing much happens here on Sunk Island as you well know. We plough and sow and reap and go about our business, just as always, and the river keeps on flowing.'

She made no answer but gazed at the vast open landscape of fields and meadows, at the scattered farmhouses and cottages, and the infinite expanse of sky with pale clouds drifting across it. She heard the trilling cry of curlews as they swooped and glided towards the estuary, she saw a kestrel hovering high over the dykes and the flight of a sparrowhawk as it dipped low over the hedges, and knew that she was glad to be home.

The next morning she was well rested from her long journey and came down to breakfast which Delia had prepared, and ate with Jim and Matthew. Her grandmother was busy in the back kitchen, preparing the midday meal for the labourers who were laying new drains on the land. Delia kept glancing at her and said eventually, 'Weren't you scared, Rosa, travelling all that way to a foreign land?'

'Yes,' she replied honestly. 'I was, and on that first night in the inn in Hull, I almost changed my mind about going.'

She glanced at Matthew and remembered their poignant goodbye as he had left her there. 'There were so many strange noises in the inn, footsteps on 'stairs and people talking, that I was very nervous of being alone, and I locked my bedroom door and lodged a chair against the knob in case anyone should try to come in. I could hear such a clamour of people, dogs barking and clattering of carts and carriages outside my window, that I could hardly get to sleep, and I determined that 'following morning I would leave a message with the London coach that I was unable to travel, and get 'carrier back to Patrington.

'But the next morning was bright and sunny and 'coach was waiting, and the coachman so friendly and obliging, that I decided that at least I would travel to London as my seat was already booked.' Her eyes brightened. 'And I enjoyed the journey, even though the coach was very rocky; there were so many things to see and towns to pass through, and then Mr and Mrs Bennett were there to meet me at my destination, and I could tell immediately that they were very experienced travellers and so assured of what to do that it made it easier for me to decide to go on after all.

'If you like, tonight after supper, I'll tell you all about it. About crossing 'Pyrenees on a mule and who I met.'

Delia nodded but looked anxious and started to clear away the dishes.

'Your gran says that I must take you for a walk to 'river this morning, Rosa.' Matthew beamed at her – he seemed so elated. 'She's most insistent so we'd better humour her!'

'Aye,' Mrs Jennings called, having heard their chatter. 'Go now. Don't delay. 'Tide'll be turning.'

'That's what I want to do, more than anything,' Rosa said softly. 'To look at the Humber. I've missed it so much.'

Delia sat down at the table after Rosa and Matthew had gone out and pensively gazed into space. 'What's up, Delia?' Jim laced up his boots.

'I was just wondering what it'll be like now that Rosa's back.' She pressed her lips together. 'There'll be three women in 'house and it's not as if Gran Jennings is our ma or that Rosa is my sister! Not a proper sister. I don't know how it'll work out.' She put her hand over her mouth and her eyes were filled with anxiety.

'Listen,' Jim said softly and leant towards her. 'You know that we've been doing up Marsh Farm house and that Matthew's been spending a deal o' time there?'

She nodded and bit on her lip as he continued. 'Well, we've had tenancy changed over. I'm going to run Home Farm and Matthew's got Marsh. There were too many memories there for me ever to make a go of it, but we didn't want to lose it and Matthew said he'd like to have it. Now,' he lowered his voice. 'I reckon that Matthew will ask for her – Rosa, I mean – and if she'll have him, then they'll go to live at Marsh Farm and you and me'll stop here.'

'But I'm no housekeeper,' she moaned. 'You know I'm not!'

'I know that you're better now, under Gran Jennings's instructions, than you were twelve months ago.'

She conceded that that was true and he went on, 'So, if Rosa accepts our Matthew, then you and me and Gran Jennings'll stop here.' He patted her hand. 'And she'll mek you into a good cook and one day some young chap'll come along and see your bonny face, and when he finds out you can cook and bake and keep house as well, why, then he'll carry you off and I'll onny have Gran Jennings to look after me!'

She started to smile in spite of her misgivings. 'But what if somebody should tell about me – and my babby,' she sniffled. 'Nobody would want me then if they find out.'

'Find out?' he said firmly. 'No! We'll have none of that. We'll be honest and straightforward and say what happened. We'll have no more secrets. Everything will be above board from now on. You'll tell of how you made a mistake and if this fellow that you might meet has owt about him and loves you truly, then he'll still want you anyway – and if he doesn't, then he's not welcome here.'

Rosa peered into the ditches as they walked. The primroses were in bloom, as were the cowslips. Water speedwell and forget-me-not had opened their blue flowers and water mint was creeping along the sides of the ditch and bending rounded heads towards the water. There was a promise of summer in the sweet smell of blackthorn blossom and cow parsley, the sound of warblers in the hedges and the warm aroma of sheep and horses.

'Spain was so vivid, so colourful.' She bent to pick a buttercup and the single braid, which she had plaited as she used to, swung over her shoulder. 'But I missed the delicate colours of English flowers.' She put the yellow flower

439

beneath Matthew's chin and smiled at the golden reflection on his skin. She linked her arm through his as they walked. 'My father's family live in a small village in the mountains. It took three days to get there from Zaragoza, travelling by mule and donkey. We climbed to a high plateau and the village was surrounded by trees. My first feelings were that I was totally hemmed in. I had no feeling of space and of course there was no river, only mountain streams.

'All of the family had come to meet me, for Mr and Mrs Bennett's son had kindly sent a message to them from his home in Zaragoza. He and his new wife travelled with me and acted as interpreters. My father's brothers and sisters and their children – my cousins! – oh, so many of them, all came to my grandmother's—' She smiled. 'My *Spanish* grandmother's house to meet me.

'My father's younger brother, the eleventh child, was only eleven months younger than my father and apparently was the most like him, they were almost like twins seemingly. He was olive-skinned and always smiling; his hair was black, his teeth very white, his eyes dark and merry and he wore a gold earring. I have a picture now in my head of how my father might have looked.'

Matthew had stayed silent as she was speaking, for this was the first time she had talked of her new family and he wanted it to unfold as and when she was ready.

'My grandmother, who of course couldn't speak English and neither could I speak her language, on meeting me for the first time, beckoned me to sit beside her. She stroked my face and loosened my braid and brushed out my hair, smoothing it with her fingers and murmuring something, I knew not what, and then she pinned a flower in my hair. When I asked Mr Bennett what she was saying, he said that she called me her English princess who had come home to her.'

They were approaching the river and Matthew took her hand to help her up the embankment to stand on the top. She closed her eyes and drew in a deep breath to absorb the salty scents of the estuary and gave out a great sigh. Then she looked up- and downriver. The Dutch fluyt was moored just off Stone Creek. 'The ship is here again,' she said in surprise. 'I wonder why? Shall we walk down there?'

'I meant to tell you,' he said, as they turned in the direction of the creek. 'Your gran has had a visitor. Seamus Byrne came to see her.'

'Seamus?' she said. 'He came back? But why would he go to see Gran?'

'Everybody else was out, your gran was the only one at home. He wanted to find out where his brother was buried and he was so grateful when she told him that we had attended his funeral. That we had forgiven him. He broke down and cried, she said, and told her that his brother hadn't been wicked, but that his mind had turned when he was in prison. He also said that when John Byrne was a young man, he had admired your father above all others.'

'I'm so sorry,' she began. 'I would have liked to

have seen him. My last memories of Seamus were not good.'

'Well,' he said, 'Seamus told Gran Jennings that he'd bought shares in a ship and was working from Holland, but legitimately now. He's turned over a new leaf apparently.'

She laughed. 'I'm not sure if I can believe that!'

As they approached Stone Creek they could see the ship out in deep water. The light was good and they saw that the hull was freshly painted and the name too on the side of the old ship was newly outlined in red. The *Rosa Maria*.

Rosa gave a deep sigh. For it to be here now, just as she had returned, seemed incredible. There were men moving about on board and preparing to sail. Other seamen were up on the yardarms and jib booms. One man on deck seemed to be giving orders, and Rosa narrowed her eyes for she saw him raise an arm in their direction.

'His build looks rather like—' she began.

'It is!' Matthew answered.

'Seamus?' She was astonished. 'Has he bought shares in my father's old ship, the *Rosa Maria*?'

'Seemingly so. He wanted to know when you were coming back and although Gran Jennings couldn't tell him exactly, he said to her that he would wait as long as he could.'

'I wonder why?' she said curiously.

'We were all waiting for you, Rosa,' Matthew said softly. 'And me more than anybody. I was so full of black despair when you first went away. I didn't know how I would survive, I missed you so much.'

She turned her eyes away from the ship and looked at him. 'Whilst I was in Spain, my grandmother asked if I would stay with them in their village and make my home there. They had a lovely house, the largest in the village, though it wasn't a castle,' she added with a smile.

'But I said that I couldn't as someone was waiting for me at home. Someone whose love was as enduring and constant as the river which ran by our land was constant in its ebb and flow.' She touched his face with her fingers. 'That someone who, when he kissed me goodbye, had kissed my heart awake.'

He bent towards her and she lifted her lips to meet his. The sound of a faint cheer came from the *Rosa Maria* and they both turned and laughed as they saw the seamen on deck waving to them.

'I've brought you something back,' she said, and put her hand into her skirt pocket. 'It matches one that was my mother's.' She took out a small box and gave it to him.

Carefully he opened it and lifted the white silk which covered a plain gold ring.

'It's Spanish gold,' she said. 'It once belonged to my grandfather. He left it to be given to his son, Decimus Miguel, my father, if ever he should return to Spain, and my grandmother wanted me to have it in his stead.

'I said that I would love to accept it if I could give it to my special person, as I already have one which my father had given to my mother.'

They put their arms around each other and Matthew kissed the top of her head and she knew that she had never felt such happiness.

'*All hands on deck.*' The call carried on the wind. The seamen were running the rigging and adjusting the yards and sails. '*Cast off!*' They heard the rattle of the capstan and the anchor cables as the anchor was hauled aboard. Then a command rang out but they couldn't catch what it was. The red flag with the white circle was hauled down from the topgallant mast and another hoisted. It was white and ragged at the edges but it fluttered in the breeze which was always brisk and frolicsome by the river, and clearly showed the red rose in the centre.

'*Make sail!*' The sails unfurled and began to fill and the sun shone on them, turning them to pale gold. Rosa and Matthew watched in silence as the stately old ship's timbers creaked and groaned and its canvas thundered. '*Stand by!*'

The *Rosa Maria* began to gather way and commence its voyage towards the tip of Spurn and the Humber mouth and the open sea. Rosa held her breath for a brief moment and felt a poignant, wistful emotion. Matthew gazed down at her and she smiled, then together they lifted their arms and waved a final goodbye.

THE END

THE ROMANY GIRL
by Val Wood

Polly Anna could not remember her father, and after her mother died, in poverty, when Polly Anna was just three, the workhouse was the only place for her. Helped by Jonty, a young misfit who became her best friend, she ran away with the fairground folk and became a horserider and acrobat – travelling to Bartholomew Fair, Nottingham Goose Fair and Hull Fair. Her friends became the circus people and the gypsies, and her home the caravans and tents of the travellers.

Meanwhile, in a great house in the Yorkshire Wolds. old Mrs Winthrop had never given up hope of finding her daughter, who eloped with a handsome Romany and was never seen again. Her young neighbour Richard Crossley set out to find the missing daughter, and discovered the colourful world of the fairs and the gypsies. He also discovered Polly Anna – once the waif from the workhouse, and now a fully-fledged *Romani Chi* – the Romany Girl.

9780552146401

EMILY
by Val Wood

From shame and imprisonment to a new life

Emily was only five years old when she was sent away
from her Ma and Da and her brother Joe to go and live
with old Granny Edwards. Growing up to be a loving
and hard-working child, she goes into service at the age
of twelve at the house of Roger Francis, whose
connections with Emily's own family prove to be closer
than she could ever have imagined. Roger's daughter
Deborah takes a fancy to Emily, and when she moves
away to another household in Hull Emily finds that
her new employer's son, Hugo, is to marry Deborah.
But Hugo, too, has become obsessed with Emily he
dishonours her and betrays her, bringing her to the
very depths of ruin.

Imprisoned, tried and transported to Australia, her life
seems finished – until she is reunited with the one man
who can save her misery and bring her wealth and
happiness

9780552147408

GOING HOME
by Val Wood

For Amelia and her brothers and sisters, the grim past which their mother Emily has endured seems very far away. A striking and independent young woman, studying to be a teacher in York, Amelia is looking for a purpose in life, and hopes especially to become acquainted with the two young gentlemen who have travelled all the way from Australia to meet her family. Ralph Hawkins, bringing with him his friend Jack – a handsome half-aboriginal Australian – has come to Yorkshire to look for his roots. He finds Amelia, whose tangled family history is inextricably bound up with his.

Ralph Hawkins's whole world was turned upside down when he learned that he had been adopted by the couple he had always called his parents. In his quest to find his real mother, he uncovers some cruel and unpleasant truths, before at last realizing where his true destiny lies.

9780552148540

HOMECOMING GIRLS
by Val Wood

Hull, 1874.

Clara had always wondered about the beautiful, mysterious Jewel Newmarch, who was adopted as a baby and now turns heads wherever she goes – her exotic looks point to her origins far away from the streets of Hull. Even at her twin sister Elizabeth's wedding, Clara knows that Jewel is the belle of the ball. And as Jewel looks on at the happy, newly-married couple she feels a restlessness and intense longing to know her own roots.

And so the two girls decide to return to Jewel's birthplace in America. In discovering the mysteries of Jewel's past the girls realize that this is a life-changing voyage of discovery for both of them, as they learn important lessons about family, friendship and home. But most importantly, love. . .

9780552163989